Mythspring

From the Lyrics and Legends of Canada

Edited

by

Julie E. Czerneda

and

Genevieve Kierans

Red Deer PRESS

5 4 3 2 1

Published by: Red Deer Press
                        A Fitzhenry & Whiteside Company
                        1512, 1800–4 Street S.W., Calgary, Alberta, Canada T2S 2S5
                        www.reddeerpress.com

Acknowledgements: Financial support provided by the Canada Council, and the Government of Canada through the Book Publishing Industry Development Program (BPIDP). Also provided by the Alberta Foundation for the Arts, a beneficiary of the Lottery Fund of the Government of Alberta.

Canada Council   Conseil des Arts
for the Arts   du Canada

ONTARIO ARTS COUNCIL
CONSEIL DES ARTS DE L'ONTARIO

Library and Archives Canada Cataloguing in Publication
    Mythspring / edited by Julie E. Czerneda & Genevieve Kierans.
    (Realms of wonder)
    ISBN 0-88995-340-6
    1. Fantasy fiction, Canadian (English). 2. Short stories, Canadian (English).
    3. Canadian fiction (English)—21st century. I. Czerneda, Julie, 1955- II. Kierans,
    Genevieve III. Series.
    PS8323.F3M97 2006   jC813'.087660806   C2006-900328-9

U.S. Publisher Cataloging-in-Publication Data (Library of Congress Standards)
    Mythspring / edited by Julie E. Czerneda & Genevieve Kierans
    [350] p. : cm.
    Summary: Stories inspired by the lyrics and legends of Canada.
    ISBN 0-88995-340-6 (pbk.)
    1. Fantasy fiction, Canadian (English). 2. Short stories, Canadian (English). 3. Canadian fiction
    (English)—21st century. I. Czerneda, Julie, 1955- II. Kierans, Genevieve. III. Title.
    [Fic] dc22   PS8323.F3M974 2006

Credits: Edited for the Press by Julie E. Czerneda and Genevieve Kierans
                        Cover Art and Design by Kenn Brown and Chris Wren, Mondolithic Studios
                        Text Design by Karen Thomas Petherick, Intuitive Design International Ltd.
                        Printed and bound in Canada for Red Deer Press

Mythspring

Realms of Wonder

Contents

"Dedicated to my family, friends, and Clarion 01, with thanks
to Julie for taking a chance on an emerging writer. My special
thanks to management and the nurses at
Toronto East General Hospital."

— *Genevieve Kierans, Winter 2006.*

A Special Introduction
by Julie E. Czerneda

Probably the most common question asked of an author is "where do you get your ideas?" Occasionally, it seems as though the questioner suspects there's an address or website, kept a closely guarded secret by those in the trade.

The real answer looked at me through the bright eyes of my co-editor, Genevieve, that first time we met. It's deceptively simple. Ideas come from being engaged in life. There are potential stories bubbling up from every encounter, observation, and scrap of information that comes our way. The very songs we hear and stories we're told can inspire. The key is not to be a passive consumer, but to take the world into yourself, to think and imagine and dream, then to create something new.

This is what Genevieve has done. Make no mistake, this isn't my anthology. I'm along for the ride and enjoying every minute of it. Genevieve's fascination with Canada's abundant music and myth, her unquenchable creativity, are amply demonstrated by the two stories of hers you'll find here. Her enthusiasm for the work of other writers led her to propose this anthology, which I've happily helped produce.

We hope that you, our readers, come away from *Mythspring* with new ideas of your own. For that's what creativity's about. That's what life's about—being part of the world and giving yourself back to it.

Welcome to *Mythspring*.

Julie E. Czerneda

Lies

by Stan Rogers

At last the kids are gone now for the day,
She reaches for the coffee as the school bus pulls away,
Another day to tend the house and plan,
For Friday at the Legion when she's dancing with her man.

Sure was a bitter winter but Friday will be fine,
And maybe last year's Easter dress will serve her one more time,
She'd pass for twenty-nine but for her eyes,
But winter lines are telling wicked lies.

Is this the face that won for her the man?
Whose amazed and clumsy fingers put that ring upon her hand?
No need to search that mirror for the years,
The menace in their message shouts across the blur of tears.

So this is beauty's finish! Like Rodin's "Belle Heaulmie're,"
The pretty maiden trapped inside the ranch wife's toil and care.
Well, after seven kids, that's no surprise,
But why cannot her mirror tell her lies.

Then she shakes off the bitter web she wove,
And turns to set the mirror, gently, face down by the stove;
She gathers up her apron in her hand,
Pours a cup of coffee, drips Carnation from the can.

And thinks ahead to Friday, 'cause Friday will be fine!
She'll look up in that weathered face that loves hers, line for line,
To see that maiden shining in his eyes,
And laugh at how her mirror tells her lies.

"Lies" (1981)
by Stan Rogers, Northwest Passage,
Copyright © 1981 by Stan Rogers, Fogarty's Cove Music, SOCAN*

Mirror, Mirror

by
Genevieve Kierans

At last the kids are gone now for the day,
She reaches for the coffee as the school bus pulls away,
Another day to tend the house and plan,
For Friday at the Legion when she's dancing with her man. *

The week Marie-Hélène Carter acquired the magic mirror began, like every week and indeed most days, with chaos. This particular Monday morning, however, seemed worse than usual. The winds had veered southeasterly over the weekend, bringing with the warmer air the smell of mud across the fields and the first hint of spring. Encouraged by the strengthening sun, rivulets of water trickled from under the massive snow piles that lined the long drive to the highway, and the snow itself, thus dehydrated, acquired a translucent, crusty texture sharp as razorblades. Snow, Marie-Hélène knew, had many ways of harming a body, not the least of which was this milder guise of bubble glass threaded with black bits of gravel and dust thrown up by the plows. There would be scraped palms, torn jeans, and skinned knees this week, now that winter was wearing out.

Winter's wearing out, and snow's wore out, she often thought. Snow's just pure wore out, come spring.

Like me, whispered her heart.

At the best of times seven kids were a handful. On schooldays they somehow managed to multiply themselves into seven times seven. Today, infected by spring fever, their energy and voices ran high.

"*Maman*, where's my homework?"

"*M'man*, Jimmy won't wear his mittens!"

"I don't like peanut-butter 'n' jam…"

"Ow! Serge kicked me! Ma, Serge kicked me."

"Did not. Was Marco."

"You liar!"

"Ma! Jimmy didn't cover his nose when he sneezed!"

"Ma, can we make maple syrup this weekend?"

At this point Happy, the farm's beagle/terrier mutt decided there was a grand game afoot that she absolutely must participate in, and added her excited barking to the chorus. Sighing internally Marie-Hélène waded in and sorted the voices into seven kids again.

"Louise, your homework's by the breadbox where you left it. Jimmy, put your mittens on or no cookies after school. And use a Kleenex when you sneeze. Jane, peanut butter is what I made. I'm not a restaurant. Serge, don't kick. Mary, we haven't collected enough sap yet for syrup. Give it another week. Happy, QUIET! All of you, get crackin', or you'll miss the bus."

She bundled them out the door and stood watching on the porch as their brightly coloured heads covered in her warm hand-knitted *toques* trudged up the half-frozen drive and disappeared around the corner. She knew they'd take them off, along with mittens and scarves, as soon as they were out of sight. She couldn't help that, but at least she made sure they were sent off properly dressed.

Agreeing noisily, Happy raced madly after them as far as the bend, then rocketed back to the house and into the kitchen where, after circling her tail a few times, she curled up with a contented sigh on a braided rag mat beside the decorative but non-functional cast-iron oven, *her* work done till the kids came home.

Marie-Hélène looked across the patchwork of still-frozen fields. Here and there a dark furrow poked its shoulder through the snow mantle, giving it the appearance of a slightly moth-eaten blanket. To the right of the farmhouse, beyond the barns, the orchard climbed the gentle slopes of the Mount St. Bruno foothills. To her left, a few acres away, a thin line of poplars marked the boundary of the property and the road beyond. She could just make out the occasional car through their barren trunks. Come summer, brush would grow up between the trees and completely screen any sign of the outside world. Summer was her favourite time. Though the days were long and the farm demanding, Mark was home and the family whole. Late winter was the time she liked least. Every year she felt more lonely and tired and worn out.

As if to remind her that winter was not prepared to leave just yet, a stray gust from the north, damp and cold, slapped the side of her face. Wind was changing again. She looked towards it and marked the thick dark clouds gathering on the horizon. Weather coming up the river. Snow maybe. Or freezing rain. If she was going to do the shopping before it squalled, *she'd* best get crackin'.

She went back inside and poured herself a coffee to sip while she made up the shopping list. Someone—Mary, she suspected, she had the sweet tooth—had been into her tin of Carnation and put the empty back in the fridge. *Maudit*! The sweetened condensed milk was the one little luxury she allowed herself. There was no other milk left either, so she had to drink her thick, dark coffee black.

M-I-L-K she scrawled, with emphasis, at the top of a piece of foolscap as though, with enough vehemence, she could conjure the missing beverage. C-A-R-N-! The pencil point snapped. *Merde*!

Of course, the other pencils in the handle-less mug that served as pencil cup were in a similar non-functioning state and the one Bic was dry. Why didn't people ever throw dead pens away? Irritable now, she up-ended the mug over the trash and dumped the contents out. After a moment's reflection, the faded mug joined them. It had seen better days.

Like the pencils.

Like me.

Sure was a bitter winter but Friday will be fine,
And maybe last year's Easter dress will serve her one more time,
She'd pass for twenty-nine but for her eyes,
But winter lines are telling wicked lies. *

She finished her list with a bit of black crayon she found in the junk drawer. This week Mark would be home from the rigs out west. Home for the summer. Home to run the small farm they both loved. She didn't know when exactly. Could be tomorrow or maybe Wednesday. Depended, like all things in Canada, on the weather. And on what rides he could hitch. But it'd be nice to have a roast ready to go for whenever he got here. Maybe a nice pork and beans? Mark loved her pork and beans, sweetened with their own maple syrup and served up with sauce from their own apples. He'd promised he'd be home before Friday. Friday was the spring dance at the Legion up in St. Bruno, an event they'd not missed since they'd been married and before. It was at a Legion dance that they'd met, seemed like a lifetime ago. And at a Legion dance that Mark had proposed, shy and awkward. He'd spoken almost no French and she minimal English. Still, when they'd looked into each other's eyes, they'd understood each other well enough. She'd been the belle of the county then, bright-eyed and raven-haired, with half a dozen suitors including Jean Charbonne, whose family owned the biggest *cidrerie* of the region, and Bernard Tremblay, who had 100 acres. But when she'd looked into Mark's eyes, she'd known he was the one.

And now look at me, she thought, catching sight of her reflection in the old wood-framed mirror that hung by the kitchen door, just under the birch-twig crucifix Marco had made in kindergarten.

Look at me.

Seven kids and a lifetime running the family farm had taken the stuffing out of her. Her slender girlish figure was now hard, sharp angles; her dewy complexion was pale leather. And the lines… Like the kitchen doorpost where, every birthday, the height of the kids had been etched and recorded, her face was a network of lines chronicling the years and events of her life. Lines across her forehead. Lines around her eyes. Lines down her cheeks and lips. Why couldn't the damned mirror just lie! She couldn't really be that withered. But the mirror showed her only an old face; wrinkled and worn-out. Like the snow. Like the pencil cup…

Is this the face that won for her the man?
Whose amazed and clumsy fingers put that ring upon her hand?

No need to search that mirror for the years,
The menace in their message shouts across the blur of tears. *

She got up and plucked the handle-less mug from the trash. On it a faded Disney Snow-White danced in perpetuity with a nameless dwarf. Mark had bought her the cup when they'd been sparkin'.

"You're my Snow-White," he'd told her. "I'm just a big-nosed dwarf."

"You're *my* handsome prince," she'd replied. "And I love your nose."

Marie-Hélène Carter began to cry.

All lies, all those lines are telling wicked lies.
Lies, all lies. Too many lines there in that face,
Too many to erase or to disguise, they must be telling lies.

—•—

The storm hit as she pulled away from the small strip-mall that was the nearest shopping to the Carter farm. Preoccupied, Marie-Hélène did not pay as much attention to the weather conditions as she might normally have done or she might have avoided the shortcut along the back road.

She had bumped into Régine McQueen in Miracle Mart, the local mini department store. Régine had married an Englishman as well; a stockbroker from Montreal named Steve.

"Steve McQueen like the movie star," Régine had bragged, showing off her substantial engagement ring. "Once we're married, my name will mean Queen of Queens."

Marie-Hélène had not seen Régine since she'd been married fifteen years ago. She had always been a pretty thing with blond curls and a generous bosom. She hadn't changed at all.

"Marie-Hélène!" she trilled across the store. "Marie-Hélène Lachance. *Mon Dieu!* Is it really you? I hardly recognized you."

All lies, all those lines are telling wicked lies.
Lies, all lies.

Embarrassed, Marie-Hélène dropped the lipstick she'd been considering and turned to face her erstwhile schoolmate.

Régine wafted over from the lingerie section and enfolded her in a Chanel embrace.

"My dear Marie-Hélène, how are you?" Régine kissed the air on either side of her cheeks. "*Eh, ma belle!* How you've changed—Well kids *will* do it to you, *ç'est sûr. We* stopped after two. *Une fille; un gars.* One of each. Who needs more?"

Too many lines there in that face,
Too many to erase or to disguise, they must be telling lies.

Marie-Hélène shrugged and smiled a bit more broadly.

"And the cold air. Cold air sucks the life out of the skin. You really ought to use a good face cream. It would protect your skin. And a good foundation would go a long way towards minimizing those lines. I know. That's what I do now, you know, sell skincare. At Sears. How's your man—what was his name? Jim? Mark? Tell him to bring you into town. I'll fix you up, we can do lunch…"

Lies, all lies.

As Régine babbled on in her artless mix of English and French, Marie-Hélène's tight smile stiffened slowly and a vein began to throb behind her right eye. This was not a good day to be running into Régine. What was she doing in this corner of the world, anyhow?

So this is beauty's finish! Like Rodin's "Belle Heaulmie're,"
The pretty maiden trapped inside the ranch wife's toil and care.
Well, after seven kids, that's no surprise,
But why cannot her mirror tell her lies. *

"…And of course, Botox works wonders, if you're prepared to go that route… *ç'est pas* cheap, you know…"

Like a fracture slowly spreading across a mirror, the tension from Marie-Hélène's frozen smile was now creeping down the back of her neck. When it reached the vertebrae that had been whiplashed that time the old Ford truck had hit the deer, the old pain kindled again.

Soon, said a thought, it would reach her heart...This time her thought-voice sounded like Régine.

Firmly, as though talking to her kids, Marie-Hélène interrupted. "That sounds lovely, Régine. I'll call you. But now I really must go. Weather's coming."

She had beaten a hasty retreat to the parking lot, lipstick forgotten and eyes smarting. The sunshine of the morning had vanished behind a heavy cloud cover and it was beginning to spit. At that moment all she wanted was to be far away from the Régines of the world. On the farm, she was safe. On the farm, she was queen.

But why cannot her mirror tell her lies?

The rain turned to sleet that turned to sticky, sloppy snow. The windshield wipers slowed as snow clogged their hinges. The wind howled around her and whistled through the gap between window and frame where Marco had picked away the felt gasket. Despite new snow-tires, the Ford skidded from side to side across the single cleared lane. On either side, the hulking shapes of hardened snowplow tailings loomed like amorphous ashen giants, hemming her into a slippery, murky canyon. It had gotten quite dark, though it couldn't be much past three. She flicked on the high-beams, but the swirling snow only reflected the light back, dazzling her eyes and further diminishing visibility. She slowed further, not wanting to miss the turn-off.

When she'd been a kid, she'd loved snowstorms. Not because they often meant school was cancelled, but because, like a thick fog, they had seemed to her a magical gateway, a portal to another time or dimension. The real world dissolved, and for several hours was superceded by a white landscape in which she was the only inhabitant. In snowstorms, she had fancied, the laws of reality were suspended and anything might happen.

Without warning, a large black shape—dog? wolf?—leapt out of the shadows and froze directly in front of the truck. She veered and slammed on the brakes. The truck hit a patch of black ice beneath the snow, spun around three times and hurtled into a snowbank. Marie-Hélène hit the windshield and lost consciousness.

—•—

She was awakened with a jolt by a dreadful wailing, like that of some tortured soul from hell, ululating from the shifting shadows above her. A thick blue haze eddied around her in time to the howls. For a moment she was too terrified to breathe, and could only stare in panic at the steeply peaked roof above her as cold shivers crawled down her spine. Maybe this *was* hell?

Then she recollected the accident and her other senses returned. She found herself stretched out on a lumpy sofa and covered by a none-too-clean Hudson's Bay Point blanket, its white background and bright indigo, red, green, and yellow stripes but distant memories. A cold compress on her pounding forehead seemed to be melting and trickling water down her aching neck. Her hands and feet prickled with that uncomfortable, just-thawing-out, itch. Her nostrils were assailed by the pungent mixture of thrice-boiled coffee, burning pine, and stale tobacco. Beneath those aromas were older scents, familiar smells that her befuddled head couldn't quite name, though it knew it ought to.

Groaning, she pushed herself to a sitting position, dislodging a one-eared black cat that had settled itself on her legs. It hissed in a most unfriendly way, then proceeded to wash its face.

"*Doucement, ma vieille, doucement*," said a gruff voice. Gently, old lady, gently. It was unclear whether the voice was addressing her or the cat.

The voice disengaged itself from a chimneyless stove it had been stoking in the far corner of the hut, and turned to face her. It belonged to a giant of a man, tall of stature and broad of shoulder. *Un Indien.* Or as one must say nowadays, a Native Canadian or a Member of the First Nations. His broad weathered face was more lined than a dried apple, telling tales of seasons long gone. Yet his raven hair was untouched by frost; it was pulled away from his face into a single *queue* down his back. He wore Army Surplus khaki pants, mukluks, and a heavy plaid shirt.

Or did he?

As he moved across the crackling illumination thrown by the old stove, it seemed for a second that his clothing morphed to ghostly buskin, decorated with wampum and animal teeth. A wolf's pelt, complete with muzzle and fangs, draped head and shoulders. His eyes were as unfathomable as the night sky.

From the murky recesses of childhood shadowy memories stirred within her, so vague as to seem but dreams of memories. Storybook pictures and fragments of legends twisted in her jangling brain, as she tried to make sense of the stranger and his flickering appearance. *Le Beau Sauvage*, he was called in some tales. At first a fairytale savage who became a handsome prince, the term eventually evolved to mean any noble native who succored the helpless. Which in the early days of New France meant supporting the early settlers against the prior inhabitants. *Le grand Manitou*, he was called in the earliest tales of the land, the native spirit guardian of the woods, awesome and unknowable and beyond the laws of man.

Marie-Hélène blinked and the impression dissolved, but not before she caught a whiff of crisp balsam pine and cedar in her nostrils.

The *Indien* lit a Players Unfiltered and inhaled raspily. "You feel more good?" he asked through a plume of blue smoke. His voice was deep and gravelly.

"Fine. *Merci*."

She recognized her surroundings, now. An abandoned sugar shack not unlike her own, twice as long as it was wide, its timbers saturated with decades of evaporated maple sap, the nooks and crannies redolent with generations of field mice. The dreadful howling was nothing more fearsome than the wind being funneled through the open sides of the venting cupola on the peaked roof.

Marie-Hélène tried to get to her feet. "Thanks," she repeated. "But I have to go now, get home to my kids."

From the inky ceiling, something black and screeching dove for her face and she fell back to the sofa with a shriek.

The *Indien* loomed over her. "*Non*. Don' tink so. *Blanche-Neige*, she say no. Not yet."

"*Blanche-Neige*?" Despite efforts to the contrary, she knew her shaky voice reflected her growing unease. *Blanche-Neige*? Snow-White? Mark's nickname for her. What was he talking about?

The man lifted his arm and an enormous black crow settled on it with a smug caw.

"*Blanche-Neige,*" he introduced proudly. "She is beaut, *non?*"

Beginning to fear she was in the clutches of a madman, Marie-Hélène smiled nervously as her eyes slid to the door. Maybe, if she ran?

The crow cawed a warning, making her jump. Its master laughed.

"*Non.* No. *Blanche-Neige,* she say no. You heet head bad. Outside, bad storm. You wait." He paused as the crow screeched again, several times. The black cat ignored it. The *Indien* listened attentively.

"*Blanche-Neige,* she say keedz fine. You no worry. She say Louise take care leetle ones."

How did he know her eldest daughter's name?

Had he been following her? Stalking her? Spying on the farm?

Now seriously alarmed, Marie-Hélène wondered for the first time how the man had happened to have been so conveniently out there, in the storm, just in time to rescue her from freezing or bleeding to death.

She frantically made and discarded several escape plans. She had no idea where she was or in what direction to run—assuming her shaking legs could outrun him. Leaving shelter in a snowstorm was lunacy, unless one was on familiar terrain. Her best course was to rest, regain her strength, play along with him...

As though agreeing with her, *Blanche-Neige* cocked a bright black eye at her and bobbed its head.

"First you eat, then we feex bump on head. OK?" He shook his bird off his arm and it hopped onto the back of the sofa where it began to preen. Its talons and bearded beak looked very large and dangerous so close. Her saviour, or captor, or stalker, or whatever he was, went back to the stove where a battered kettle began to whistle.

Fix bump on head? What the hell did that mean? Stitches? Salve? Aspirin?

The *Indien* returned carefully carrying a steaming cardboard cup. Marie-Hélène bit back an hysterical bark of laughter. Instant soup? First Nations Brand Cup'o'noodles?

"*Des lentilles.* Good. You eat."

Instant food or not, it smelled good, and her stomach growled appreciatively. She needed all her strength. She accepted the hot cardboard gingerly.

As she wolfed down the lentils, her companion pulled an ancient wooden footlocker out from behind the sofa and rummaged around in it for a while, humming a tuneless song. The one-eared black cat began to purr.

"How to feex?" he asked suddenly. "*Blanche-Neige?*" The crow cawed an answer that seemed to displease him. "*Le mirroire? T'es pas fou, toi?*"

Blanche-Neige did not seem to take kindly to being called crazy. She cawed again, five times, angrily. Then flew into the rafters.

"Ok, Ok. Don't be so touchy. The mirror it is." He pulled out a battered hand-mirror, of the sort that had once been sold as a part of a Victorian dresser set, with matching brush and comb. It was made of some dark wood, ebony perhaps, and gilt with beaten silver, now tarnished as black as *Blanche-Neige*'s feathers.

"Dat bird," said the *Indien*. "Always she know better than me." Marie-Hélène recognized in his voice the same irritability she'd felt that morning, and offered no reply.

He thrust the mirror at her. "Here."

"Uhh. Thanks?" She wasn't sure what to say or do. She didn't need to see her reflection.

All lies, all those lines are telling wicked lies...

"You look. You feex. Feex big bump." The *Indien* tried to keep his impatience out of his voice. "Then you go."

The going part sounded good to her. Play along, said her heart.

But she didn't really want to look.

The pretty maiden trapped inside the ranch wife's toil and care...

She turned the mirror to her face, but avoided looking at it.

Too many lines there in that face...

"Look!" ordered her companion.

She looked.

Lies...

What a mess! Her thumping head ought to have prepared her. But it hadn't. An enormous purple-red goose egg obliterated the left side of her forehead and had swollen shut her eye. The swelling wrapped around her temple and into her grizzled hair. A jagged gash in its centre was crusted with congealed blood.

And through it all…

Lies, all lies…

Through it all ran wrinkles, seaming her skin like a desiccated prune.

Tears blurred her good eye.

"Non, non," said her companion. He blotted her tears with a Kleenex. "No cry. No blink. Or the *magique*, she no work. Look at bump. See it go. But no blink."

Sick at heart, she looked again.

And looked.

And *looked*.

And it began to seem to her that her face wasn't quite as bad as she had first thought. For one thing, the cut was really not the bloody gash she had first supposed. More of a shallow cut. No. That wasn't an apt description either. Just a scrape, really.

And the bump! How had she thought it covered her whole eye? Why, she could see both her eyes quite clearly in the mirror. There was hardly any swelling. Or pain, even, now that she thought about it.

Then she noticed something that took her breath away. The crows' feet at the corner of her left eye seemed rather finer than they had been. Surely they had been more deeply etched? Now they seemed to be getting thinner, finer… Why, they were actually *fading* as she looked.

The mirror was not only healing her. *It was making her younger.*

She gasped in amazement. And blinked. And the impression stopped as suddenly as it had come.

"Good. You fix," said her companion. He had come round behind her and peered at her reflection in the mirror. She could see him clearly over her shoulder. *Blanche-Neige* had returned to his arm and waddled up to his shoulder where she began to tweak his fur.

Fur?

In the mirror's reflection, the *Indien* was once again clad in buskin and wampum and a wolf skin headdress.

Now," he continued, "you go." He raised his arms like a conjuror and the beads rattled. Then *Blanche-Neige* spread her powerful wings and cawed.

And everything went black.

—•—

It was night when Marie-Hélène opened her eyes. The storm had subsided, and the fresh, young snow gleamed in the pearly light of a nearly full moon. Outside the comparatively snug cabin of the truck, it was nearly as bright as day. The dashboard clock proclaimed the hour a little past six.

There was a slight throbbing in her left temple, but a glance in the rear-view mirror assured her there was minimal damage. No bruise even.

She turned the ignition key, reversed, and hit the gas peddle. The powerful snow-tires gripped the road, gained momentary purchase, then slipped and spun in their tracks. She tried again. And again. In vain.

Sighing, she zipped up her parka. Nothing for it. She would have to dig herself out.

The new snow smelled clean and sweet as she stepped into the soft drift. The gusting wind of earlier had subsided into a playful breeze that tugged at her hair and tickled her cheeks. It was a picture-postcard-perfect night.

As she waded through the snow to the back of the truck where the shovel and rock salt was kept, the pristine evening was briefly bathed in blue radiance.

Marie-Hélène paused and looked down the road. A plow. It would dig her out.

Feeling lazy, she climbed back into the cab to wait for it. And think about her strange dream.

That was when she noticed the small hand mirror on the front seat.

—•—

Monday's storm had been furious but brief—the temper tantrum of a spoilt child used to an entire winter of having its own way. There would be several more such storms, Marie-Hélène knew, before winter was gone for good. But spring would not be denied for long. The sap was running, the buds were swelling and, under the kitchen window, the first snowdrops had hatched.

She hummed to herself as she hustled the kids out the door. Mark had called last night. He'd be home Thursday, in plenty of time for the dance. She would wear her blue dress from last Easter and dance the night away with her man. She felt like a kid again, as giddy as Régine used to be at school. For tucked away in the pantry behind the home-made preserves, carefully wrapped in her only silk scarf, was the battered black mirror she had found in the Ford.

She hadn't looked into it yet. She tried to tell herself that she had dreamed the entire thing. Magic mirror, indeed!

But then, how to account for its presence? And if it were present, then why couldn't the rest of the dream have been real?

Today, she decided, was the day she'd put it to the test.

The pretty maiden trapped inside the ranch wife's toil and care... *

She stood on the porch watching as her progeny's brightly coloured heads trudged up the half-frozen drive and disappeared around the corner. Happy raced madly after them as far as the bend, then rocketed back to the house and into the kitchen where, after circling her tail a few times, she curled up with a contented sigh on her mat.

Marie-Hélène looked across the patchwork of still-frozen fields. A good many dark furrows poked their shoulders through the thinning snow mantle. It no longer looked anything like a blanket, moth-eaten or otherwise. More like one of Mary's attempts at baking, the icing shoveled on in uneven patches.

Marie-Hélène went back inside, took the pork roast out of the freezer to thaw, and put the navy beans into brine to soak. Then she poured herself a mug of boiled coffee, dribbled Carnation into it, and retrieved the magic mirror from behind the apple preserves in the pantry.

"Now, Happy," she told the dog, "you will see a thing."

At the sound of her name, Happy thumped her tail a few times on the mat, but did not bother opening her eyes.

Marie-Hélène took a deep sip of coffee and picked up the mirror.

She knew what she would see. Lines, lines, and more lines. Furrows across her forehead. Crows' feet around her eyes. Deeply etched laugh lines around her mouth. So many lines, recording every year, every month, every day of the past twenty years. Like the newel post where the kids' birthdays were logged. Somewhere, underneath all those lines… the young girl she had been, all those years ago, when she had first met Mark.

The pretty maiden…

Today, she would bring that maiden back.

She had thought long and hard about how to proceed. About which lines to tackle first. And she had decided upon the crows' feet around her eyes, for it was her eyes that Mark had most admired, back when they'd been sparkin'. On Friday, when they were out dancing, he would look into her eyes, and they would be unmarred by any age lines. She even had a lie ready, in case anyone remarked on her rejuvenated appearance. One Régine had given her. Botox.

Lies, all lies.

She took a deep gulp of coffee to fortify herself. Then slowly lifted the mirror to her face. She remembered she must stare at one spot, and couldn't blink, if the magic were to work.

She looked, half afraid she'd imagined the whole episode, despite the proof of the mirror.

And she looked.

And *looked*.

Was it working? She wasn't sure.

She looked harder.

She saw her face, lined with years of care and toil. Lined with years of tears and laughter. Lined with the wind, and the sun; the summers and the winters; the days and the nights. Then a picture of Mark swam unbidden into her mind. And her heart swelled with love. She thought of all their years together. Of all the loving they'd done, all the kids they'd had. She thought of this Friday when, wearing last year's Easter dress, she'd be dancing in his arms, looking up into his weathered face, catching her reflection in his adoring eyes—Marie-Hélène set the mirror, gently, face down by the stove.

She didn't need its magic. She had Mark's eyes.

In Mark's eyes, she was forever the maiden he had married. That mirror did not tell lies. It was the only mirror she needed, the only reflection that mattered.

Then she shakes off the bitter web she wove,
And turns to set the mirror, gently, face down by the stove;
She gathers up her apron in her hand,
Pours a cup of coffee, drips Carnation from the can.*

Marie-Hélène sipped her coffee and smiled to herself. Tomorrow, she would take the mirror out near her sugar shack and bury it. Meanwhile, the day was young. Perhaps she'd bake a pie to have after the roast. Somewhere outside a crow cawed three times.

Her smile broadened.

Spring was coming and her man was coming home.

And thinks ahead to Friday, 'cause Friday will be fine!
She'll look up in that weathered face that loves hers, line for line,
To see that maiden shining in his eyes,
And laugh at how her mirror tells her lies.*

From Algonquin mythology come the many and varied legends of the Windigo. Its territory ranges from the Maritimes to the Northwest Territories to the Rockies. Thirty-seven variations of the name Windigo appear in published accounts, from "Wendigo" to "Onaouientagos." The Windigo takes almost as many forms as names: it can be a giant demon, an insubstantial spirit, or it can apply to a person possessed by the desire to eat human flesh. There are a few common elements: the Windigo is always a cannibal and always comes in the winter months.

Source:

Windigo: An Anthology of Fact and Fantastic Fiction (1982)
edited by John Robert Colombo, Copyright © 1982 by John Robert Columbo,
Western Producer Prairie Books, Saskatoon

Windigo

by
Mark Ladouceur

"You're lost, aren't you?"

"I'm not lost," Tom said to Iris.

George grabbed the armrest as his brother mashed the old Buick's accelerator to the floor. The car crested the hill and tried to follow the snowy road, down and around. The car fishtailed back and forth and Tom cursed, wrestling with the steering wheel.

Iris clung to the dashboard. "You're going too fast." Fear edged into her voice. In the headlights, snow rushed at them, creating a tunnel effect. Trees and rock faces loomed on both sides of the road.

"Shut up, Iris," Tom said. The Buick downshifted and pushed the V8 into a crescendo. Tom was going faster than he should, but George was too scared to say anything.

"The snow's too heavy," Iris said. "You can't possibly see where you're going." The wipers thunked back and forth. BTO was taking care of business on the Parry Sound radio station. The car dove down a hill through the blowing snow.

Tom looked over at Iris. "Babe, I—"

George saw something in the road ahead, just coming into view; man-shaped, but taller, indistinct and white. The headlights' white glare revealed pale yellow eyes within a swirling vortex of snow. Arms extended from the sides of it, ready to catch the oncoming car.

"Tom!" George yelled.

Tom's head snapped back around to face forward.

"What the—" Tom jerked the wheel too fast and the car slewed first left then right. They passed through the vortex, disrupting it. George heard a cry of hunger that no human could have produced, high and hateful, and felt a cold he had never felt before, a stabbing icicle through his heart. Terror struck George to the depth of his soul. Iris screamed. George craned around to look at what they'd just passed through, but there was nothing there. Tom lost his fight to bring the car under control. The Buick spun around and went off the road trunk first, still doing almost fifty. It dropped down into a stand of trees and stopped with a jarring crash. Everything was silent except for BTO, working overtime.

Tom was the first to speak. He always was. "Are you both okay?"

"Yeah," Iris said slowly. George saw she was shivering hard. So was Tom.

"George?"

"What? Yeah." He was shivering too. The heat in the car was gone. Frost now coated the inside of the windows and the vinyl seats creaked as George moved. He fumbled and finally undid the seatbelt. The rear door squealed opened on bent hinges, pushing snow out of the way. He sank knee-deep and fought his way forward. The snow ran over the top of his Kodiaks and down inside. He threw up twice, then sat back in the snow, ignoring the cold. The car's high beams pointed up at an angle into skeletal trees on the opposite side of the road.

Those eyes. He thought for a moment, had he imagined it? The arms reaching for them and the scream; it may all have just been a trick of his mind. The last few weeks had been stressful and he hadn't been sleeping much. Maybe he'd just imagined all of it.

"Hey, George, you feeling better now?" Tom slapped his hand down on George's shoulder.

"Bit."

"Come on. Let's see how bad this is."

George nodded and followed Tom up to the road. The snow came down in large fat flakes, drifting silently, obscuring his vision.

"No way we're getting the car out without a wrecker, that's for sure," Tom said. "Damn, damn, damn it!" His voice rose in frustration.

"Tom, what did you see, just before we spun out?"

"Snow, snow and more friggin' snow."

"You didn't see...something in the road?"

Tom looked at him and raised his eyebrows. "You rattle your head a little?" Tom trudged back down the slope. "There wasn't nothing there, George, just a gust of wind caught us."

Nothing there, George said to himself. *Nothing there. Just an overworked imagination*, he thought. Except that for just a moment, the snow appeared to form the shape of a large man moving across the road to the far side. George took two steps back and fell down the embankment, sliding to the bottom.

What a crappy night, George thought. *Why did I let Tom talk me into this?* It had been hard to give up two promising jobs, one right after another, and now be wondering what to do for money. Tom's new job, running smuggled cigarettes up to Bear Island for a friend, was illegal, and the fact that George was helping out gave him a constant guilty feeling.

"Tom?" Iris called, her voice sounded muffled and flattened by the heavy snow. She was standing by the car. "Can we get out?"

"No way, no how."

"I told you you were driving too fast, didn't I?" Iris nagged.

"Hey, it's not my fault. It's his fault." Tom pointed at George. "Scaring the crap out of me, yelling and all that." It was never Tom's fault.

George felt a wave of fresh guilt. It probably *was* his fault. He'd thought he'd seen something in the road and scared Tom into spinning them out.

"So what are we going to do, just stand around?" she asked.

"Walk," was Tom's answer.

"Walk where?" Iris asked.

"We passed some places a little bit back. We can spend the night there."

"Break and enter?"

"Hey, Iris, just let it go."

George kept quiet. He continued to work over what he'd seen, ignoring the back and forth between Tom and Iris. Something about it didn't jibe with his own imaginings. The feeling of dread and those eyes. A single word floated up in his mind: Windigo.

The wind picked up suddenly then, whipping the snow into a stinging blast and sounding to George like a scream. His hair stood up, hearing it.

"See? It's just the damn wind," Tom said. It subsided quickly, but George's fear remained.

The car was a write-off. The trunk had popped open on impact and snow was already starting to cover the cartons of cigarettes. Tom tried to close it, but it wouldn't stay.

"Cripes, they're going to be ruined. Ah, hell." Tom kicked the crumpled rear bumper.

"Hey, come on, we should get moving," George said.

"See, George agrees with me," Tom said. "We need to find someplace to spend the night."

He clapped George on the shoulder then moved towards Iris. She pulled away. Tom held his arms open for a moment and Iris relented. Tom pulled her close and winked at George. George turned away, embarrassed.

Tom knew George liked Iris. In fact, George had met her before Tom had, and had confided in his brother. Tom said that he'd talk to Iris for George. Tom, however, was the one who got her. He told George that Iris wasn't interested and only liked him as a friend. The feeling of betrayal still burned.

'It's not my fault,' Tom had said then, too.

George struggled up onto the road, trying to ignore them, but Tom and Iris followed.

"There were some cottages back a little ways on one of the side roads."

"Are you sure?" Iris asked.

"Course I am."

Tom got his way. They headed back.

—•—

None of them was dressed for the weather. Despite the forecasts, Tom had said they'd be able to keep ahead of the weather on the way home from Toronto. Tom hadn't wanted to wait. Tom had gotten what he wanted. But the weather overtook them around Burk's Falls as they were going north on Highway 11. They'd left 11 near Sundridge after hearing the highway ahead was closed with an accident.

George's feet were numb in his Kodiaks and his coat was too thin with age to be much good. There was no wind chill; good, since that would really be a killer. Around them the forest was quiet, muted by the snow. Occasionally a branch cracked, or snow fell with a whump from its perch in a tree. George noticed that all the sounds were coming from behind, as though something followed them.

He tried to tell himself it was nothing, just his imagination.

They followed the road hoping to come to a side road where there were cottages. The cottagers tended to put their names on signs at the intersections. Most would be vacant and closed up for the winter. It was too far to walk back to Sundridge now, even in good weather, from where they'd gone off the road; the middle of nowhere it seemed to George.

"Wish I had a cell phone," Tom said.

"Wouldn't help; there's no coverage out here," George said.

"What we should have done was go back to that gas station we passed," Iris said.

"No way." Tom pulled the collar on his leather jacket tighter. "It's too far."

"It's better than breaking in," Iris said with disapproval.

"Let it go, Iris. Hey, George, what the hell do you keep looking at?"

George hadn't realized that he'd stopped. *Why did I?* George asked himself and shivered. The eyes; a little way back he thought he'd seen two pale, yellow eyes. He couldn't see them now. Fear crept back into him.

"Something's following us," George said. *Windigo.*

Tom stood next to George and pointed the flashlight back the way they'd come.

"What was it?" Iris asked.

"Must be a bear," Tom said.

"I don't think so. Bears don't come out in the winter, they hibernate," George said. Tom knew it, but he must have been trying to keep Iris calm. George usually didn't contradict his brother, but he was scared now and he didn't want Tom blowing this off. Something was out there.

The wind picked up and they heard a howl not far off.

"Wolf then," Tom said. "Don't worry, I've got enough ammo for a whole pack. They get too close, I'll put some buckshot in them."

"I don't think it's a wolf either," George said. He was shivering again.

"What makes you the expert, Mister Nature Boy?"

"I saw yellow eyes behind us."

"Oh, now I know. This is one of Grandpa Joseph's old stories, isn't it?" Tom mocked him. "Which one?"

George treasured the times, sitting at Grandpa's knees, when the old man had told him the tales of their people—legends and myths—and he hated Tom's tone whenever he spoke of Grandpa Joseph. "The Windigo," George said, and could almost hear his grandpa's raspy voice: 'Windigo, comes down from the north during the five moons of winter to hunt. It can possess a man, make him eat his friends and family. Its hunger never stops. It flies on the wind, or takes the form of a giant, taller than the trees. Once you're in its gaze there's no escape.' This story had never failed to scare George.

"You know that's all crap. Grandpa Joseph was crazy. Dad said so."

Grandpa Joseph *had* gone downhill at the end. George remembered visiting him in the home, his mind taken by Alzheimer's. The last time they'd visited him, Grandpa had had a moment of lucidity. He'd looked at George. 'You have a true heart. Don't let anyone change that. Tom is too much like your father,' Grandpa Joseph had said. 'They don't believe in the old stories.'

George did believe, or always thought he did. Having said it now though, 'Windigo's out there,' it did sound ridiculous.

The wind picked up in an instant, roaring through the trees. George shielded himself from the blast of snow. Tom screamed as something that was only a shape in the snow carried him away through the trees and into the darkness. Iris screamed as Tom disappeared from view. She tripped trying to backpedal away, picked herself up and ran. Then the wind was gone.

Not the wind, the Windigo.

George picked up the shotgun that Tom had dropped. He had to go after Tom.

And do what?

But Iris needed him too. He didn't want to let her run through the woods alone. George nodded to himself; his decision made, and started to run in the direction Tom had disappeared.

"Iris!" he called over his shoulder. "I have to find Tom. Wait wherever you are. I'll come back for you."

In places the snow reached almost up to George's knees and it hid roots and stones that caught his feet, threatening to trip him. He used the shotgun, clenched in both hands, to push the brush out of the way, not that there was much of it. The path his brother's body made as the Windigo dragged Tom along was obvious.

George found Tom face down in the snow, motionless. Approaching carefully, George raised the shotgun and turned in a slow circle, expecting at any moment to see the Windigo's yellow eyes staring back. Seeing nothing, George knelt in the snow and rolled Tom onto his back.

"Tom." George shook his brother's shoulder. "Tom."

With a long, slow blink Tom came around and focused on George. "Cripes…"

"The Windigo took you."

"What?" Tom asked. "But it's not real." His voice sounded much less sure than before.

George helped Tom up. "Are you hurt? How do you feel?"

"Okay, I guess. Sore, but nothing feels broken. Not like that time I fell off the roof." Tom had broken a leg and an arm then, George remembered, playing on the roof of their family's home.

"We have to find Iris." George let go. Tom wobbled and then recovered.

"Yeah, let's go."

Her tracks were easy enough to follow and she had run only a short distance. They found Iris huddled and shivering under the scant shelter of a spruce tree. Iris saw them approach and ran into Tom's arms. Tom pressed his face to the base of her neck and inhaled deeply, like he was getting her scent. They held each other long enough to make George uncomfortable.

"Okay, get a room." George's tone wasn't as light as he'd hoped it would sound.

"You know where to find one?" Tom asked.

"No. But we better start looking."

With a half-moon now revealed by the retreating clouds, and the snow reflecting its light, they were able to pick out a line of cottages visible through the trees on the lakeshore. A short hike brought them there. The windows of the cottages were dark and empty. Tom led them to the closest one.

"So we're just going to break in?" Iris asked when Tom hefted a log from the woodpile.

Tom turned on her. "Freeze to death out here then."

"Iris." George took her wrist in his hand, hoping she'd get the message and not blurt out any more smart-ass remarks.

"Sorry," she said.

Using the log like a police battering ram, Tom smashed the door. Wood from the doorframe burst and splintered under the force of Tom's blow. There was no power and no water. Their breath came out in clouds in the cold, still air. It was a small place: one central room that was a kitchen and living room and two bedrooms directly off that. A woodstove sat along one wall. White sheets covered the furniture and tin plates with mouse poison sat in the corners.

"Iris, find some candles. George, bring in some more wood and make a fire. I'll check for food. I'm hungry."

George propped the shotgun by the door and went back outside to the woodpile. It surprised him that Tom hadn't asked to take back the gun. He stacked as much as he could carry and found himself checking over his shoulder to see if the shotgun was still there. It was.

Iris had lit half a dozen candles when George walked back in and set his load down by the woodstove. Tom sat tearing pages from a book and throwing the crumpled balls into the woodstove's open mouth. Tom lit the paper and stacked some kindling on top. George cringed at the abuse, but Tom didn't care for books much.

"So what is there for food?" George asked.

"Canned crap. That's all. Nothing good."

Iris came out of one of the two bedrooms with an armload of blankets. She passed one each to George and Tom and kept the third. Tom pulled away when she tried to snuggle in. George could see the hurt in her eyes.

"Tom, are you feeling okay?" Iris asked.

"Yeah, fine."

"What was it like?" George asked, hearing the fear in his own voice.

"Like falling," Tom sounded unconcerned. "It was just like that. Then I blacked out." He turned to George. The kindling hissed as it dried and burned. "You still think it was Grandpa Joseph's Windigo?"

"What else could have done that?"

Tom stared at the fire and a look of confusion clouded his eyes. "I don't know." Tom put two logs on the fire and closed the door. George watched him get up and lie down on the couch. Iris caught George's eye asking silently what was up with his brother. George shrugged. He knew what he feared, but couldn't say it out loud. The Windigo had possessed Tom.

Iris took a spot in the recliner and drifted off. Periodically, George stoked the fire and watched his brother sleep.

The sight of Tom being carried through the air flashed in his mind's eye. He'd always believed in the legends Grandpa Joseph had told him. But he'd never had an encounter with anything that could be called supernatural. Even now, everything tonight could be explained as natural. Almost everything. The Windigo had taken Tom, but it hadn't eaten him. So what had happened to him? George's eyes strayed to the shotgun. He picked it up and held it in his lap.

Every so often George put another log on the fire. The movement helped keep him awake. The cabin, or at least the area surrounding the woodstove, started to warm. Tom tossed and turned and mumbled before finally standing up.

"Too warm here." With no further explanation, Tom walked into the farther of the two bedrooms. George heard the bedsprings creak. Iris stirred, but drifted off again.

Sitting cross-legged by the stove, facing the bedroom door, George fought to stay awake. *If Tom is a Windigo now, how do I tell?* What had Grandpa Joseph said about them? George concentrated on remembering. Was the part about it having a heart of ice true?

George shook his head. "This is crazy," he said to himself. Grandpa Joseph's stories had put the belief in George that there were things out there beyond mundane reality, even though George's faith in them had never been tested. Not until now. George would have to wait. *If he tries to attack us, I'll know. I just have to wait until then.*

His head drooped forward and he felt himself falling into sleep. George pushed himself to sit up again and open his eyes. Tom watched him with pale yellow eyes from the couch.

"Hey, little brother."

George's hands clenched on empty air where the shotgun had rested a moment earlier.

Tom stood up and his head almost touched the ceiling now. "I'm hungry." In a single, long step Tom stood beside the recliner where Iris slept. The sleeves of Tom's coat barely reached his elbows. His legs had grown too. Worst, though, was his mouth, lined with sharp teeth and too broad even for his oversized head. Tom reached down, took Iris's arm and with a twist pulled it off. He chomped down and tore a hunk of meat away.

"Want some?" Tom asked and offered the remains of Iris's arm to George. Stumbling backwards, George found the open door behind him. Tom had grown again, so large now that sitting on his haunches; his head still touched the ceiling. The last of Iris, her foot, disappeared into Tom's mouth and he smacked his lips.

"Time for the second course."

George took off running only to find the thigh-deep snow holding him back. George knew Tom followed him without looking. He could hear the whistling intake of breath and the roaring exhalation behind and above him. Wood cracked and splintered as Tom shoved aside entire trees in his pursuit.

George knew this wasn't real. He forced himself toward

wakefulness, like surfacing from beneath a great depth of water. Tom's
hand closed around him, cold and frost-rimed. He lifted George up.

"Not real. Not real. Not real."

George jerked awake, hands closing on the shotgun in his lap. Fear
slowly retreated and the pounding of his heart slowed. The fire in the
stove still burned bright, telling him he hadn't been asleep for long.
Standing, George looked to the recliner; empty.

"Iris."

Then he heard the sound of wet tearing and chewing coming from
the bedroom where Tom had slept. George felt his hair stand up on the
back of his neck. His hands went cold and sweaty. He stood rooted in
place beside the woodstove. With a great effort he picked up the bat-
tery-powered lantern they'd found.

Run! His mind told him. *I know what's in there. Run!*

"He's still my brother."

George lifted his left foot and put it forward, advancing cautiously
toward the open bedroom door. The barrel of the shotgun wavered, as
did the lantern, in his shaking grasp. Light from the lantern cast shifting shadows around him. His grip on the trigger was taut, a hair's
breadth from setting the shotgun off.

In the bedroom, Iris lay on the bed. Tom sat hunched over her; not
the distorted Tom of George's nightmare, but just Tom, ordinary in his
appearance except for the blood on the sleeves and front of his shirt.
Their eyes met.

"It's not my fault," Tom said. "I was just so hungry. She came in
here and her smell, it drove me crazy. I couldn't think of anything, but
what she'd taste like."

Tom slid off the bed and advanced on George, baring his teeth and
holding his hands like talons at his side.

"You believe me?" Tom asked.

"I do believe," George said and heard his voice crack and his throat
constrict. "You're the Windigo."

Tom stood only a pace away when George tightened his grip on the
shotgun and it went off. The muzzle flash cast a huge distorted shadow
of Tom on the far wall and the sound drowned out both their screams.
George fell flat on his backside and Tom did the same. The lantern hit

the ground and broke. The room went black. The acrid smell of gunpowder filled the air, almost covering the smell of blood.

George couldn't hear anything over the ringing in his ears. His heart boomed in his chest. The gun was a dead weight in his hands. He threw it aside and fled into the cottage's main room.

He knew that he had to make sure the job was finished, but couldn't make himself go back into the bedroom. Instead, George threw open the woodstove and pulled out a half-burned log. It seared his hand, making him scream, but he kept his grip and sent it in a glowing arc through the bedroom door. He did it again and again, hearing Grandpa Joseph in his head.

'Fire's the only way to get rid of the Windigo once it's inside someone. You have to burn up the body. Burn it up until there's nothing left.'

George ran from the cottage as flames danced over the bed linens and the rug. He fell to his knees just over a dozen metres from the porch and plunged his hands into the snow. He stayed frozen there while the red and orange light of the fire lit the trees around him.

After a time ashes drifted down around him and he could feel the heat on his back. Wood popped and cracked and the fire roared. A rushing gust of wind swept over him.

George clenched his fists and repeated, "It's just the wind."

"Do ghosts exist? Are there UFOs? Is there any evidence for the existence of ESP or Psi? Does astrology work? Is it possible to predict the future? Is reincarnation a fact, a fiction, or a little of both? What is the evidence for life after death? Does the sasquatch roam the interior of British Columbia? Has any treasure ever been found on Oak Island?

"... Anyone who looks long and hard enough will no doubt find rational explanations for the mysteries in this book. There is no need to resort to a supernatural explanation to account for any one of them. At the same time I am aware of the fact that many of the mysteries are motifs of folklore which are widespread in distribution. They are so tangled in history and lore that it would be fruitless to do more than record their presence and suggest their nature and appeal. Yet there is always the possibility—the hope, the fear—that the genuinely inexplicable is operative."

From
Mysterious Canada (1988) by John Robert Colombo.
Copyright © 1988 by John Robert Colombo. Reprinted by permission of Knopf Canada/ Doubleday Canada/ Random House Canada.

All the Cool Monsters at Once

by
James Alan Gardner

Ogopogo was the beginning.

He rose from Lake Okanagan at dawn on the first of May. He was seen by pretty much everyone in Kelowna, B.C.—it's hard to miss a bright green water-snake who's half the length of a football field. The monster emerged from the lake in City Park, then squiggled onto Highway 97 North (otherwise known as Harvey Street) and slurped straight through the middle of town.

Relatively speaking, Ogopogo was well-behaved. He ate a few squirrels that got in the way, and a yappy Pomeranian who didn't know when to shut up. But the snake didn't touch any people. He didn't do much property damage either...considering. When you're the size of a railway train and move in snaky curves, it's hard not to sideswipe cars as you slither down a main street. But the monster didn't go out of his way to cause trouble. He was clearly on some schedule, and didn't waste time going all Godzilla on the local populace.

The people of Kelowna stayed well-behaved too. Ogopogo was a city mascot: a tourist attraction, even if most people hadn't believed in him. Besides, back in 1950 someone talked the B.C. government into protecting Ogopogo under the provincial Fisheries Act. Sure, that was only a publicity stunt, but it was still illegal to shoot or otherwise endanger the monster. Best to leave the giant snake alone. People stood back and took photos, then scooped up souvenir dollops of slime that fell off the creature as it passed.

Within minutes, the photos were on the web and the slime samples were on eBay.

— • —

The Kelowna office of the RCMP called Vancouver to ask for instructions. Mounties in Vancouver assumed their Kelowna colleagues were playing a joke; but after seeing the monster on somebody's webcam, and listening to feverish news reports from the Kelowna TV station, Vancouver RCMP did the sensible thing: they phoned Ottawa and said, "This is a federal matter."

Hours passed as bureaucrats fought over who did and didn't have to deal with the situation. By the time the smoke cleared, responsibility had been handed to a committee consisting of General Richard C. Briggs (Canadian Armed Forces), Paulette Leblanc (Deputy Minister of State), and a nondescript man from CSIS named Mr. Smith.

They were just getting together to discuss Ogopogo when a boatful of pirate ghosts appeared near Oak Island.

— • —

Oak Island lies off the southern coast of Nova Scotia...just a tiny piece of land, but it holds one of Canada's biggest mysteries. In the middle of the island, someone long ago dug a "money pit": a booby-trapped hole that may or may not contain buried treasure. Stories say that a famous pirate—maybe Blackbeard or Captain Kidd—buried tons of stolen loot in the pit. Nobody knows for sure, because no one has ever dug to the bottom. The sea always floods in first, mixing with the soil to form a quicksand that's killed a lot of treasure hunters. Other diggers have been killed in strange accidents, and even in fights over who'll get the gold once it's found. All these deaths have made some people think the treasure is guarded by a curse. Only a few trinkets have ever been recovered; but every few years, someone else tries an excavation. Who can resist pirate gold?

The island is private property, but sightseers sit in boats offshore and look at the pit with binoculars. Imagine their surprise when they saw a ghostly ship, flying the Jolly Roger, rise out of the hole like a submarine surfacing. The ship righted itself, then sailed across the meadow surrounding the pit—as easily as if the ship were on the sea. When the pirates reached the ocean, they headed west through Mahone Bay.

Dozens of boaters saw the ship. They took pictures of its tattered sails and the crew of skeletons walking its deck. Someone phoned the *Weekly World News* and said the ship was just like *Pirates of the Caribbean*. The editor of the *News* was giddy with excitement, till he found out the story was true. Sadly he said, "We can't publish the truth. It would set a bad precedent." Instead they published a piece on Bat-Boy marrying a 900-pound woman with Elvis as the best man.

—•—

The committee of Briggs, Leblanc, and Smith weren't amused by the sudden appearances of Ogopogo in the west and pirate skeletons in the east.

"Now Quebec will want monsters too," said Briggs.

Leblanc glared at him.

"I'm just saying," Briggs told her. "This sort of thing always gets out of hand. Alberta will want *three* monsters, Ontario will want *four*, Newfoundland will ask for subsidies because it doesn't have any..."

Mr. Smith cleared his throat. "Isn't the more serious problem what these monsters want? If it was just Ogopogo, we could probably keep him happy by airdropping a few tons of fish. But what do we do with phantom pirates?"

"Give them phantom pieces of eight?" Leblanc suggested.

"Hard to come by," Smith replied. "And who knows what phantom cannons might do to maritime shipping?"

"The military has *real* cannons," said General Briggs. "We can blast the pirates and bomb Ogopogo."

"You can't bomb Ogopogo," said Leblanc. "He's an endangered species. And he's popular. This committee isn't authorized to do anything that would hurt the government in opinion polls. Besides,

Tourism B.C. would scream blue murder. Do you know how much money they make off Ogopogo each year? Ogopogo dolls, Ogopogo postcards, Ogopogo bumper stickers..."

"Tourism B.C. shouldn't complain," said Smith. "Thousands of people are rushing to see Ogopogo even as we speak. Every hotel from Victoria to Trail will soon be full. If nothing else, every major news service in the world is bound to send reporters."

"We'll bomb the reporters too," said Briggs. "That's what I call a win-win scenario."

Leblanc glared at him again.

"Neither the snake nor the pirates are causing immediate trouble," said Smith, "apart from traffic jams of gawkers trying to get a peek. But I worry about the big picture."

"What big picture?" asked Leblanc.

"Why these supernatural creatures are coming out of hiding," said Smith. "And which monster's going to show up next."

—•—

Next was the Sleeping Giant near Thunder Bay. He woke.

If you thought Ogopogo was big, consider a man made of stone who can be seen from fifty kilometres away. When he got to his feet, a *lot* of people took notice. On the plus side, he soon waded into Lake Superior. On the minus side, he was big enough that his head stayed above water, even with his feet on the bottom of the lake.

The giant spent a few minutes washing off the moss he'd acquired since the last Ice Age, then he clambered out of the water and headed west along the Trans-Canada.

—•—

In Ottawa, General Briggs growled, "We can't take any chances. I say we blast the Wawa Goose before it gets up too."

"Finally," said Leblanc, "something I can agree with. All in favour?"

—•—

The first sasquatch was sighted north of Regina. Tourism B.C. cried foul: "Everyone knows the sasquatch is native to the Rockies. A sasquatch in Saskatchewan must be fake." Alberta supported B.C. until another sasquatch was sighted in Medicine Hat; then Travel Alberta told Tourism B.C. to go pound sand. The Medicine Hat sasquatch was immediately nominated to represent Alberta in the senate and invited to be Grand Marshall of the Calgary Stampede.

More Bigfoots showed up all over the west: one riding the ferry from Nanaimo to the mainland; one hitching a ride south from Fort McMurray; a male-female couple crossing University Bridge in Saskatoon; more in Moose Jaw, and Brandon, and Buffalo Jump.

Within a day, you couldn't drive the Trans-Canada anywhere in the prairies without seeing big hairy men, women, and children trudging eastward, either singly or in packs. Often, they had scruffy dogs trailing behind them, and behind the dogs, anthropology professors frantically taking notes.

In response to the west's outbreak of Bigfoots, Northern Ontario went wild with Windigos. Kenora (called by some "The Windigo Capital of the World") had a parade of the shaggy white beasts slouching along 2nd Street South: two dozen of them leaving frozen footprints in their wake. Buildings on either side of the street were quickly covered in ice. Parked cars got buried under snowdrifts two metres deep... which was uncommon for May, though not unprecedented.

More Windigos trekked through Sudbury; the intense chill of their bodies opened up cracks in the Big Nickel. Some emerged from the uranium mines outside Elliot Lake—they were just as cold as other Windigos, but had an awesome radioactive glow that made them easy to track by helicopter, even at night. Others were reported in Timmins, White River, and Kapuskasing: some flying on the wind, some swimming down streams, some surrounded by their own personal blizzards.

Considering that Windigos are famous for cannibalism, photographers switched to telephoto lenses, and anthropology departments sent grad students instead of professors. "But we have no reports of violence," Deputy Leblanc told Briggs and Smith. "Creatures that spread ice and snow aren't popular, but we're talking about Northern Ontario. Those people can handle low temperatures; they just lock themselves inside and listen to Shania Twain albums."

Briggs said, "We could still bomb the monsters, just to be sure."

Leblanc, as usual, glared at him. "Does our air force even *have* bombers? Or are you just going to toss sticks of dynamite out of a Hercules?"

"What bothers me," said Smith, "is why the Windigos *aren't* eating people. Cannibalism is a Windigo's standard M.O. All our profilers agree. So if legendary cannibals have suddenly changed their ways...why? What's going on?"

Leblanc said, "One of the sasquatches ate a cat in Portage la Prairie."

Briggs scoffed, "Everybody eats cats in Portage la Prairie. Cats are called 'Manitoba Chicken.'"

"Eating a cat is not the same as eating people," said Smith. "I'm grateful no human has been hurt, but it makes me worry when a leopard changes its spots."

"Leopards?" Leblanc asked. "We don't have leopards in Canada."

Smith said grimly, "Not yet."

—•—

Quebec's first monster was a loup-garou in Chicoutimi. At dusk on May 3, she was a middle-aged woman drinking coffee at the Tim Horton's in Place Saguenay; then the full moon rose, and the woman sprouted fur. Her nose grew, her ears turned pointy, and her fingers mutated into claws. Ten more seconds and she was three metres tall: a giant wolf-thing who threw back her head and howled before sprinting off into the night.

Shortly afterward, a bunch of Goth teenagers showed up and ordered the same kind of coffee.

—•—

"So this woman," said Briggs, "just turned into a werewolf..."

"A loup-garou," Leblanc corrected him.

"What's the difference?"

"Bill 101."

"Fair enough. So this woman turned into a loup-garou and just ran out of town without hurting anybody?"

"She mauled a few people," Leblanc said. "One man in particular—"

Mr. Smith interrupted. "CSIS files indicate the man was wearing a Maple Leafs cap."

"Oh," said Leblanc. "Then forget I mentioned it."

"But the point still stands," Smith said. "Why didn't she act like a normal werewolf—"

"Loup-garou," Leblanc said.

"Sorry. Why didn't she act like a normal loup-garou? Why didn't she go on a rampage? Why aren't the Windigos eating people? Why is Ogopogo simply slithering along the highway as fast as he can go?"

"He's still on the highway?" Leblanc asked.

"He took 97 north to the Trans-Canada. Now he's heading east. Look at the map."

Briggs, Leblanc, and Smith were sitting in a small command centre in the East Block of the Parliament buildings. Like any good command centre, it had a map on the wall with flag-pins stuck into it. Each pin marked the known position of a monster, colour-coded according to type: blue for big things (like Ogopogo and the Sleeping Giant), red for habitual killers (like the Windigos and the loup-garou), black for undead (like the pirate ghosts), and green for "weird but harmless" (like the sasquatches). The country was beginning to look like a rainbow pincushion.

"Have you noticed," said Briggs, "that everything out west is moving east, and everything in the east is moving west?"

"You think they're trading places?" Leblanc asked.

"Or meeting in the middle," said Mr. Smith. "Right around Winnipeg."

Leblanc said, "What would monsters do in Winnipeg?"

Smith replied, "What does *anybody* do in Winnipeg?"

"Uhhh...I'll get back to you."

—•—

Newfoundland finally got on the board with fifty headless fishermen. Apparently, decapitation is a major occupational hazard in the fisheries: in story after story, someone falls overboard and gets sliced through the propellers before anyone can do anything. Sometimes, the body floats and the head sinks. Sometimes, the body disappears but the head gets caught in the nets. One way or another, head and body get separated...which is why every village in the province has a story about some poor guy whose body was recovered but whose head was lost, or vice versa. *"And now on stormy nights, the headless fisherman wanders the shore, waiting for his head to float back to him."*

Hence the fifty headless fisherman who appeared in St. John's harbour and wandered into town. They stank of the sea, they were wet and bloody, and most had been nibbled by fish during their time underwater...but they were greeted with cheers and applause. "Finally!" said someone. "The Rock's got monsters of its own."

Taverns all over the city opened their doors in case the deceased wanted to wet their (truncated) throats after so long in the deep. But the fishermen just staggered zombie-like through the streets till they reached the Trans-Canada. There they turned west, and joined the great supernatural migration toward the centre of the country.

—•—

"Maybe it's a protest march," Leblanc suggested. "The monsters plan to put on a political demonstration."

"Why?" Smith asked.

"Why does anyone in Canada go on protest marches? To demand better health care." Leblanc nodded to herself. "Yes. It makes sense. Those headless fishermen obviously *need* good medical treatment. And the Windigos...they probably only eat human flesh because of some vitamin deficiency. Yes, that must be it. These monsters are coming out of the woodwork as a cry for help."

Smith looked at her. "You honestly think they're marching for better health care?"

Leblanc's face fell. "No. But I *understand* protest marches. I don't understand monsters."

"Maybe the monsters intend to fight each other," Briggs suggested. "They're gathering for a great big battle. Or a sports tournament. East versus west...English versus French...living versus dead. Maybe they won't choose sides till they actually meet. Ogopogo and the Sleeping Giant will be captains, and they'll take turns choosing players—"

Smith interrupted. "What kind of sport can you play with headless fishermen?"

"Luge. Having no brains is a plus in Luge. And bobsledding too. Maybe the monsters will hold a full Winter Olympics. The loup-garou could probably speed-skate on her claws. The sasquatches can play hockey, and those Windigos are probably tremendous skiers."

"Skiing?" Smith asked. "In Winnipeg? In May?"

"Windigos make their own snow," said Briggs.

"In Winnipeg, they'll have to make their own hills too."

"You never heard of cross-country?"

"Stop arguing," Leblanc told the two men. "If we're sure these monsters are heading for Winnipeg, we need a plan for what to do when they all come together."

"Bomb Winnipeg!" said Briggs. "Then blame it on the Winnipeg Blue Bombers!"

Leblanc buried her face in her hands.

—•—

In Toronto, hundreds of albino alligators poured up from the sewers. Nobody paid much attention, but you'll see the gators show up in a dozen American TV shows that were filming around the city.

—•—

Up in Whitehorse, a flaming Sam McGee was seen walking hand in hand with Hila, an Inuit ice spirit. (Gives new meaning to the phrase "polar opposites.") Other Inuit spirits were spotted across the Territories, along with half-human walruses, talking polar bears, and seals that never lost their legs.

Around Ungava Bay, a flock of thirty million ookpiks—the stuffed toys, not real arctic owls—flew over the region in a gigantic cloud that darkened the sky for hours and left the tundra littered with fluffy droppings. One observer said, "They were very very creepy. But cute."

—•—

Outside Moncton, people started a vigil at Magnetic Hill. It was, after all, New Brunswick's most famous oddity. No one was sure what kind of monster would show up there—maybe a giant horseshoe magnet would rise up out of the earth, or the entire hill would sprout legs and walk away—but whatever happened, Magnetic Hill was considered the province's best bet for joining Canada's supernatural shenanigans.

As it turned out, however, New Brunswick's first leap into the unexplained was the Coleman Frog: a giant frog on display in a Fredericton museum. Supposedly, the frog was real—grown to a meter and a half wide by daily drinks of buttermilk, but accidentally killed in 1885 and kept on display ever since. Visitors to the museum often remarked how much the frog looked like a not-very-good papier-mâché model...but sometimes life imitates art, doesn't it? On the evening of May 4, the frog gave a mighty croak, smashed out of its glass display case, and hopped away into the darkness.

New Brunswick's legislative assembly met in emergency session to discuss if they really wanted the province to be famous for a big fake frog. They decided no. In fact, the legislature embarked on a new tourism campaign announcing that New Brunswick was the one place in Canada that *didn't* have monsters: YOUR MARITIME HAVEN OF PEACE AND SANITY.

Then a giant horseshoe magnet rose out of the earth at Magnetic Hill. It waddled off westward, using the two bottom ends of its horseshoe as legs.

—•—

The people of PEI have always denied that Anne of Green Gables was a vampire. When others suggest that Anne strongly resembles an un-aging demon who's taken the form of a spunky young girl in order to lull victims into a false sense of security, experts from Charlottetown point out that Anne actually *did* age over the course of several books and not once was she depicted as lusting for human blood. The province has three dozen lawyers on call twenty-four hours a day, ready to fly anywhere in the world to sue anyone who even *speculates* that Anne might have been a loathsome creature of evil whose famous pigtails were actually tentacles that could hold strong men in an unbreakable grip while Anne tore out their throats.

So it is mere happenstance that the suspiciously sweet-faced Anne materialized from mist on the front step of Green Gables *precisely at midnight* on May 4. We should draw no conclusions from the fact that she immediately pounced on an after-hours tourist and dragged him into the shadows from which he emerged, much paler, a few minutes later. It's only coincidence that a giant red-haired bat with pigtails was seen taking wing from the Green Gables property immediately after-ward, flying (of course) westward.

Anne didn't appear because she was a *monster*. She's a *legend*. There's a difference.

—•—

On the morning of May 5, Briggs, Leblanc, and Smith were all late in getting to their command centre, thanks to an outbreak of urban fanta-sy all around Ottawa. The Wild Hunt was raging down 417, goblins ter-rorized motorists on Riverside Drive, and the Unseelie Court had held some kind of feast in the National Arts Centre before trashing the place and heading west.

"The prime minister is *very* displeased," said Leblanc. "Sussex Drive was invaded by Faerie Black Dogs and the PM's lawn is a mess." She paused. "On the bright side, Rideau Hall got visited by pixies. They did quite a nice job repairing the governor-general's shoes."

"Don't worry about the Faeries," Smith said. "Most of them are already moving fast toward Manitoba. The others will presumably leave once they've had their fun." He looked at the others. "Anything else to report?"

"The Sleeping Giant reached Winnipeg," Briggs replied. "Then he turned north to a place called Grand Beach Provincial Park. It's on the southeast shore of Lake Winnipeg. The giant has settled down there like he's waiting for something. Sasquatches are in the area too, and we expect Manipogo to join up with them by late afternoon."

"Manipogo?" asked Leblanc.

"Another snaky lake monster," Briggs said. "This one's from Lake Manitoba. Pretty much an exact copy of Ogopogo, though Travel Manitoba denies the rip-off."

"They would, wouldn't they," said Smith. "Although...what if Ogopogo is male and Manipogo is female? If they're getting together to breed..."

"Bomb 'em," said Briggs. "Bomb 'em *now*."

Ignoring the general, Leblanc said, "We have another problem. The prime minister's office has received an official complaint from the American embassy. They're annoyed that Canada has monsters but the U.S. doesn't. They say we've violated NAFTA."

"Are there monsters *anywhere* else in the world?" Smith asked.

Leblanc made a face. "There've been claims from Loch Ness, Transylvania, the Bermuda Triangle, and several other places that depend on superstitious idiots for tourist dollars. As far as we can tell though, they're all just hoaxes—people dressed up, or pictures faked with Photoshop. Canada is the only country with real verifiable monsters."

"So why does the weirdness stop at the Canadian border?" asked Smith. "Sasquatches, for example—they're supposed to live all over the Rockies, right? So why haven't any shown up in Washington state...or Oregon or California?"

Briggs muttered, "Maybe because the U.S. Air Force isn't so stingy with bombs."

Leblanc sighed. "I've spoken with the prime minister and he's prepared to authorize a single bomb: to be dropped on the monsters if and when they all assemble at Lake Winnipeg, if and when it seems they're doing something that threatens the country. But all three of us have to agree the bomb is necessary."

"Yes!" said Briggs, pumping his fist in victory. "I'll call Comox and tell them to pull our bomb out of mothballs."

— • —

All that day, ticket-takers at Grand Beach Provincial Park stayed busy with a steady stream of incoming "guests." Half were supernatural: the monsters we've already mentioned plus phantom hitchhikers, platoons of flying witches, numerous dinosaurs that avoided extinction, and a few obscure oddities like the Tobacco Monster—a leafy-green beast from Ontario tobacco country that spits stinging juice into the eyes of anyone working in the tobacco harvest. None of these eerie visitors were charged admission. How could a ticket-taker stand in front of Ogopogo (or even worse, Anne of Green Gables with a tiny drop of blood on her pinafore) and say, "That'll be five dollars please."

Besides, the park raked in oodles of money from *non*-supernatural guests: people who'd heard Grand Beach was Canada's Bizarreness Central and who wanted to see the freak show firsthand. They couldn't get close to the monsters—the Windigos sat on the edge of the gathering, blowing subzero gale-force winds at unwanted spectators— but people could still stand beside any park road and watch outlandish creatures arrive. Ghosts. Woolly mammoths. Shapeshifting animals. Walking corpses. Hundreds of beasts from aboriginal tales: some comical, some talkative, some fierce.

A few monsters even spent time with the onlookers. Coyote chatted up several good-looking women, and Crow tried to pick spectators' pockets. The Oak Island pirates let children walk the plank for ten bucks a head (provided the price was paid in loonies, which looked enough like gold doubloons to keep the pirates happy). Several witches opened fortune-telling booths, and the loup-garou agreed to bite a few Goths in exchange for raw meat.

Everyone had a pleasant day. None of the park-goers realized that the Canadian Armed Forces had transported their one and only bomb from Comox to Winnipeg in a rattletrap CC-130. By nightfall, an air crew was only awaiting orders before making a bombing run.

—•—

"Ready anytime you give the okay," said Briggs.

"There's a large civilian presence on the ground," said Mr. Smith. "You can't bomb them."

"The monsters have kept their camp separate from spectators. Drop the bomb in the middle of that camp, and we'll get all the beasties without touching anyone else."

"But not yet," said Leblanc. "The monsters haven't done anything to deserve being bombed."

"Those pirates were drinking rum in a provincial park," said Briggs, "and not in an authorized camping area."

"We need a better excuse than that," said Leblanc.

"The sasquatches don't have their dogs on a leash."

"Not good enough."

"The Faerie Lords are hunting without a license."

"What are they hunting?"

"Other Faerie Lords."

Leblanc scowled. "Faerie Lords aren't protected by Manitoba game laws." She stared at the command centre's map. All the flag-pins were crammed into a tiny region on the shores of Lake Winnipeg. "There's an obvious potential for trouble, but we aren't justified in bombing all those creatures unless something truly bad happens."

—•—

Something truly bad happened.

An anthropology grad student who'd been drinking rum with the pirates decided to sneak into the main part of the monsters' camp. His intention was to record any "folk music" the sasquatches might sing around their cook-fires. Twice the drunken grad student was driven off by Windigo blizzards. The third time, he got in his car and drove into the camp, pressing forward despite furious snowstorms sent by the

Windigos to force him back. The car got inside the Windigo defenses, where it was immediately seized by the pull of the giant horseshoe magnet. The grad student jumped from the car as soon as he realized he'd lost control...but the car continued faster and faster toward the magnet until it accidentally sideswiped the flaming Sam McGee. In accordance with urban legend, the car instantly exploded. Neither Sam nor anyone else was injured, but the thunderous burst of flames was seen by military helicopters spying in the night.

— • —

"An explosion in the camp!" Briggs cried. "The monsters are going on the attack!"

"We don't know that," Leblanc said.

"No," Smith agreed. "But can we afford to take a chance? Those monsters could kill thousands of innocents under cover of darkness."

"They could be eating people even as we speak," said Briggs. "Human meat is the new Manitoba Chicken."

"We have watchers in the area," Leblanc said. "Can't they see what's happening?"

"No. The Windigos have spread a blizzard over the entire park."

In fact, the Windigos had created the blizzard to put out flames from the explosion. Unfortunately, all of Grand Beach was hidden by the clouds of snow. Briggs, Leblanc, and Smith had no idea what was happening inside the clouds. As Briggs had suggested, the monsters might be eating all the people camped nearby. In fact, nothing sinister was going on, but the command centre in Ottawa didn't know that.

"We have no choice," said Smith. "Better safe than sorry."

He and Briggs turned to Leblanc. She looked unhappy, but she nodded. "All right. Drop the bomb."

— • —

The plane was already in the air. It had been circling the area, waiting for the go-ahead. Now it changed to a course that would pass over the monsters' camp in five minutes.

On the ground, sasquatches fought through the blizzard to see if the anthropology student was all right. Headless fishermen did the same for nearby campers caught in the sudden storm.

Four minutes...

The Sleeping Giant picked up the student's car and the giant magnet (which were now locked magnetically together). The giant yanked the two apart and gently placed the car back into the nearest parking lot.

Three minutes...

The pirates handed out rum to warm up anyone caught in the blizzard. For those who didn't want liquor, the witches brewed up tea.

Two minutes...

Ookpiks surrounded cold people with their fuzzy bodies, like blankets. Anne of Green Gables offered to hug people too, but no one took her up on the invitation.

One minute...

With the fires now out, the Windigos let their blizzard subside. The skies cleared. The loup-garou (who had superb night vision) pointed up at the approaching plane.

Thirty seconds...

Then suddenly, zoom! The UFOs arrived.

They came at light-speed from all over Canada: from Gander, Shag Harbour, Summerside, Miramichi; from Rimouski, Shawinigan, Deep River, Port Hope; from Falcon Lake, Swift Current, Camrose, and Suffield; from Duncan and Dawson, Yellowknife and Alert. Some had bits of winter wheat clinging to their bottoms after making crop circles. Some had gill nets slung over them, and lobster pots dangling below. Some were scraped from where they'd brushed against mountains in Jasper; others had dents from collisions with the Cape Breton highlands or bumpy landings on the Canadian Shield. Many were still wet from leaving their underwater lairs: Atlantic, Pacific, Hudson Bay, the Great Lakes. All were as bright as the Northern Lights...as glistening and perfect as an ice surface after the Zamboni.

The silver spaceships (now surrounded by a yellow haze like the sun) stopped directly over the assembled monsters. Ogopogo raised his massive head and said to the anthropology student, "They're taking us away. It's your world now."

"Don't go!" cried the student. "I still have so many questions..."

"I'm sure you do," said Ogopogo. "We're *made* of questions. But not answers. Good-bye."

The shores of the lake exploded with light. To this day, witnesses can't agree if the light was like a bomb going off or hundreds of alien transport beams dragging thousands of monsters up into spaceships. But when the light faded, nothing was left behind except people staring into the dark.

Epilogue: One year later, Briggs and Leblanc were married, with Smith as best man. The newlyweds spent their honeymoon in Grand Beach Provincial Park.

Two years later, something large and green was spotted briefly in Lake Okanagan. Stories sprang up that Ogopogo hadn't really left with the UFOs; at the last moment, he slipped into Lake Winnipeg instead. Cautiously traveling only at night, he'd made his way home.

Sasquatches have also been sighted from time to time. And ghosts. And decapitated fishermen waiting for their heads to float in.

Maybe those Goths who were bitten by the loup-garou now turn into wolves on full-moon nights.

Or maybe those are all just myths.

"Paris has its catacombs, while London has more than 40 abandoned Underground stations. New York City has its legends of Mole People. But what about Toronto? Most people don't think of Toronto harbouring hidden treasures in its subway system... or anywhere for that matter. But even Toronto's utilitarian subway network has secrets of its own ... The Toronto Subway had a Lost Station the moment the subway opened. When the Yonge Subway began operating from Eglinton Station to Union on March 30, 1954, a hollowed-out cavern beneath Queen Station waited for a subway that never came ..."

From:
"Toronto's Lost Subway Stations" (2005)
by James Bow, Copyright © 2005 by James Bow, Toronto Transit Website Archives.

Over Lunar White

by
Lorne Kates

Attention aspiring urban explorers! Do you want to discover the secrets Toronto's subway system holds? Do you want to experience what goes on in the tunnels firsthand? We're extending an open invitation for a guided tour. Meet time is in one week, 3am, at the construction yard at Yonge & Hayden. Bring a flashlight.

Chester folded the clipping from the underground 'zine, and slipped it back into his pocket. He crossed his arms, and leaned against the brick wall. He stood in the darkened alley, waiting for anyone else to show up. The flow of pedestrians along Yonge Street had steadily declined over the hours. Now, the street was all but abandoned, still in the mixture of moon-and-city light. He looked up and gazed at the full moon peeking out from the clouds.

Soft footsteps echoed from down the alley. He stood up, and squinted, peering into the shadows. Someone was walking towards him. He shuffled about and wrung his hands. If they were another neophyte explorer, he'd have some company. But what if they weren't? How could he explain loitering in a dark alley? He should just go home.

No. He shook his head. No. He wanted to see the tunnels.

The figure stepped out of the shadows. A young woman. She smiled at him. "Hey."

He smiled back, still nervous. "Hey."

"You here about the article in the paper?"

The wave of tension that had been building inside of Chester crested and faded. He relaxed. "Yeah," he said, "And you?"

"I'm your guide."

She was younger than he expected. She didn't look any older than twenty—probably the same age as him. Like him, she was dressed dark, from head to toe. A frizzy ponytail of a colour indistinguishable from black peeked out from beneath her toque.

"Hi," he said, keeping his voice low, "I'm Chester."

She shook his extended hand. "Victoria."

"Can I call you Vicky?"

"No. Ready to go exploring?"

He nodded.

She marched back down the alley, her strides long despite her shorter stature. Her backpack looked heavy, but hardly made a sound.

"What about the others?" he asked, falling in step behind her. "Aren't we going to wait?"

Victoria shrugged. "Everyone who's here is here."

"But—"

She turned to face him her arms crossed. "Okay, we better get things straight right away. Why are you here?"

Chester blinked. "What do you mean?"

"I want to know why you're here—why you want to explore. 'Cause I'll let you know right now, I don't go exploring with darkness-psychos, CHUD seekers, or role-players."

"I—" he hesitated.

She cocked on eyebrow. "Well?"

"I want to see what's down there," he replied, firmly. He met her gaze and grinned. "I guess I'm just nervous."

"About going somewhere you're not supposed to go?"

"About getting caught."

She nodded. "Yeah. Well, if anyone asks, you dropped your keys. Come on. The subway doesn't stay closed forever."

—•—

They followed the alley to a fence, and hopped over it into the construction yard. Chester took careful steps over the rough, uneven dirt floor. Asphalt that had once paved the ground now lay broken in piles. Equipment, machinery, and tools lay scattered about the site. The full moon cast deep, sharp pools of shadow.

They darted across the yard, hopping from shadow to shadow. She stopped once to point to a blinking light atop a portable office. "Camera," she whispered.

"Can they see us?" Chester returned, as quiet as she.

"They? Snort."

"Did you just say 'snort'?"

"There's no mice in this mousehouse. Cameras are meant to make people think they're being watched." She stood and strode swiftly towards the opposite fence, where the construction site encroached a sidewalk. Victoria knelt.

"Give me a hand." She reached down and curled her fingers around a steel grate in the ground.

Chester looked down. "Is this—"

"Yonge Street? Yes. The yard covers part of the sidewalk. Uhg." The grate creaked. "Hand. Give me. Now. Help me lift this grille."

Chester wiggled his fingers under the grate. Lifting in tandem, they swung it open. Victoria clicked on her flashlight, and pointed it down—into the hole.

An iron step ladder, bolted to the wall, ran down the entire length of the shaft. A layer of dirt stained everything—bricks, rungs, and even the air. The filth was so ubiquitous that Chester couldn't tell the difference between dirt and shadows.

Victoria laid her hand on Chester's shoulder, pushing him back a step. She knelt, and slipped into the shaft. "Test each rung before you use it, okay?"

"Sure. But why?"

She cocked an eyebrow. "They're reconstructing this place for a reason. Think rust." She paused. "Which reminds me—"

Victoria pulled something out of her pockets. "Here."

Chester took them. Gloves.

"Like I said, think rust."

"Yeah."

As Chester slipped on the gloves, she descended. "Good?" she called up, her voice echoing.

"Yeah. They fit like, well, gloves."

The top of her head vanished below the surface of the street. Chester waited a moment, then followed her down the ladder, wedging the swing gate shut behind him.

—•—

Chester descended slowly. Although the shaft itself was dark, he could see the bottom, six or seven metres below, illuminated by Victoria's flashlight. The rungs of the ladder were not evenly spaced. Some were warped beyond use. Others simply were not there. He hugged the wall for balance, pressing his face against the cool, dank brick. He could feel the soot and gunk rubbing onto his skin. Victoria's hand touched his leg. "Almost there. Three more rungs."

Chester nodded. He climbed down the final rungs, and at last put his feet on solid ground. He stood on a ledge, less than a metre wide. Chester shone his light into the pit. Metal reflected the light back.

"Rails."

"Welcome," Victoria announced, her voice hushed, "to the Yonge Street subway tunnels."

The tunnel walls, slabs of smooth concrete, rose straight up, meeting the flat ceiling at 90 degree angles. Only by a wild stretch of the imagination could Chester ever guess the concrete's original colour. Beyond the edge of the ledge was a metre-long drop to the tracks. The far side of the pit had a ledge, too, but no wall. Instead thick pillars rose at regular intervals, dividing the northbound and southbound tracks.

Chester marveled. The pit, the tracks—he had only ever seen them through dirty subway windows, blurred by speed. Now there they were, illuminated by his flashlight, two, brilliant strands of shining silver, scarred by long, thin wear lines. They stretched off in either direction, lost to sight as the tunnel curved. An ambient buzzing sang in Chester's ear. He strained to make out its source.

"The third rail?" he asked.

Victoria nodded. "In all its electric beauty." She played her light along the sides of the rail-pit. A thick, black casing ran parallel to the tracks. "It's under there."

Chester opened his mouth, but she spoke first. "Yes, it's on. No, don't touch it. If you have to step over them, use the safety steps." She indicated the metre-long neon yellow blocks of wood nailed to the casing at regular intervals. "Also, don't touch anything on the walls."

She pointed her flashlight to the rows of pipes, cables and wires on the opposite wall. "Not all those wires are insulated. That, and any of those pipes could be a steam pipe. Breach a 250 p.s.i. pipe and—well—instant lobster."

Chester shuddered. "So, where are we?"

Victoria squared her shoulders, and spoke like a tour guide. "Right now, we're on the Yonge Line, which runs north and south. That way," she pointed behind Chester, "is north. Just around the bend is Bloor Station. We're not going there."

"How come?"

"The Bloor/Yonge hub is a transfer point between the north/south and east/west lines. It's also the subway's busiest station; about 160,000 people a day, give or take a few thousand."

"Sure, but I thought the platforms were closed."

Victoria rolled her eyes. "That many people leave behind a lot of trash. Who do you think is in the station, right now, cleaning it up?"

"Hmm."

"We go south—back to where it all began."

—•—

Although the ledge was wide enough to walk comfortably in single file, obstacles cropped out from the wall: traffic signals, caged gas lines, and cement tunnel supports. They walked in the pit instead, alongside the rails.

"Since we're going south, we'll stick to the northbound tunnels."

"Why?" Chester grinned. "Are you worried a train will sneak up on you?"

"Yes."

He swallowed.

Chester stood chest deep in the pit. He could sense the enclosure of the ledge as a pair of encompassing, shoulder high walls. He tapped his foot against the track. Bolted to the ground, it felt heavy, solid.

He gazed at the tracks, and thought about them. These same tracks ran, for tens of kilometres, off in either direction; unbroken, immovable. Uncountable times in the past, he'd stood on a platform, mere metres from them. They may as well have been in a different universe.

"Toronto's subway was Canada's first," she orated, "A city referendum approved it in 1946. Construction began on these very tunnels in 1949. The subway opened five years later."

Chester nodded. He listened with interest, but also kept an eye-and-a-half out for tripping hazards. The subway lights, strung along the walls, cast pools of diffuse orange light barely bright enough to distinguish details. Odours hung in the still air: grease, mould, metal, ozone.

"Want to guess why these tunnels are square, while others are round?"

Chester shrugged. "Some they dig and some they bore?"

Victoria raised an eyebrow. "Yes, actually. These are of the 'cut-and-cover' variety. They dig them out, pour the cement, then cover them back up.

"Tonight, we'll walk south six stops to the original terminus of the line: Union Station. It's the southernmost part of the subway system. From there, it curves back north, and the newer University/Spadina line begins.

"You're going to get to see, up close and personal, the oldest tunnels in the entire subway."

They approached a bend in the tunnel. As Chester rounded it, a bright light burst into his view. His heart thumped, and he swallowed a surprised yelp. His grip on his flashlight tightened. His feet froze to the ground, even though they desperately wanted to run. He faced down the overwhelming light—

—and it faded. His eyes adjusted, and the splash of light took shape. An archway. The mouth of the tunnel. Two of them, in fact. Except for a couple widely spaced pillars, there was nothing separating the tracks. The tunnel felt wider, more open.

"Wellesley Station," Victoria whispered. "We're going to move to the last pillar, and from there see if the coast is clear."

She clicked off her flashlight, and slunk towards the pillar. Chester followed suit.

Victoria crouched by the pillar, poised in shadow, listening. She moved back two steps, and pressed her face to Chester's ear.

"Someone's on the Wellesley platform," she whispered.

His heart thumped. Wellesley Station had two platforms, and both sets of tracks ran between.

"I heard footsteps—but I can't tell which side they're on. If they're on our side, it's cool. There's a sneak-space under each platform. If someone falls onto the tracks—they can duck under the lip of the platform, to dodge the train. We can use it to sneak past them."

Chester nodded. "If they're on the other platform, they'll be able to see us. What then?"

She patted his shoulder. "Then we wait for them to leave. At this point, we can't very well say we dropped our keys, can we?"

—•—

They waited.

Victoria sat at the mouth of the tunnel, metres away from Wellesley Station. Chester crouched by her feet. Only cement pillars, spaced uncomfortably far apart, stood between the northbound and southbound tracks. The ambient sounds of the subway station, no longer dampened by thousands of bodies, filled the air. Halogen lights blanketed the tiled platform, but did not reach into the tunnel's maw.

"He's still there!" Chester whispered.

Halfway down the platform, poised on the yellow warning line, stood a sentry clad in red and grey. He was still, hands by his side, staring at the tracks.

"What is he looking for?" Chester asked.

Victoria shrugged. "The mice usually just take a look and stroll along." She stole a quick glance around the pillar, and shuddered. "I've seen that look once before."

"Where?"

Victoria took a breath. Her smile faded. "A while ago. My first expedition, actually. Lawrence Station. That place is amazing; there's playgrounds, hidden nooks, and machinery *everywhere*. I was giddy out of my mind by the time I left! I snuck out of the tunnels, and back onto the platform, to catch the train home."

Chester shuffled closer. "When the train came, I hopped onto the first empty car. At least, I thought the car was empty. It was—except for the security guard! I only saw him after the train was moving. I was at the front of the car, and he was at the back. He sat there, arms at his side, staring at me—" She locked eyes with Chester, and imitated the intense stare of the guard on the platform. "—just like that!

"I did my best to look nonchalant—but damn, I knew he knew where I'd been. Hell, how couldn't he? I was dressed in black. My face was smeared with subway-tunnel dirt. I even had a copy of an underground magazine in my hands. He knew I'd been exploring, and he wouldn't take his eyes off me."

She wrapped her arms around herself, and lowered her eyes to the ground. Chester leaned closer. His gloved fingers twitched. "One station passed. Two stations—three. He kept me under his gaze, but he didn't make a move. And neither did I. My butt was pinned to that seat. I didn't know what he'd do if I moved. He had me.

"The train passed Davisville, and still, he didn't move. That's when I got scared. If he wasn't going to take me to the security offices there—then what was he planning on doing?"

"What did he do?" Chester asked.

"He watched me." She blinked. "A couple more stations passed, and I started freaking out. I had to get off that train. I wasn't going to make it all the way to Queen. The train pulled into Wellesley station—" she leaned closer, and enunciated, "*this* station. The doors open, and *bam*, I bolted—out of my seat, out the door! No minding the gap, no watching my step. I ran up the escalator, out the turnstiles—and I didn't stop running until my lungs were ready to fall out."

Chester swallowed. "What happened?"

She took a breath and continued. "Turns out, I was running for nothing. He couldn't follow me. Do you know why?"

"Jurisdiction?"

She shook her head, slowly, side to side. "If only. You see, the next day, I'm reading the newspaper and right there, in the local news, there's this story about a TTC guard who died on duty. Sudden death, causes unknown."

Astonishment crept onto Chester's face. "He died before he could report you?"

Victoria's eyes narrowed. "Nope. They found his body sitting in the back of the train. He'd been dead since the start of his shift—four hours before I stepped foot on that train."

Chester swallowed. "You rode the train with a corpse? I can't blame you for running. That'd freak me out, too."

"I'm sure it would. But—"

"But?"

"But something else truly, and I mean *truly*, freaked me out about it—even to this day."

She leaned closer. "You see, when I ran up the escalator, I couldn't help but to look back. That 'dead' guard wasn't at the back of the train. He was standing on the platform, staring across the station at me," she stabbed her finger at the man on the platform, "just like that."

Chester felt eyes boring into the back of his head. His neck stiffened, and refused to move.

Victoria patted his leg, and craned her neck around the pillar. A swirl of itch formed on Chester's heel. He reached into his boot to scratch.

"He's gone," Victoria announced.

"Where?"

She shrugged, and bounced to her feet. "Let's go."

Victoria crept towards the mouth of the tunnel, staying low and in the shadows. Chester wiped sweat from his forehead, and followed. He whispered, "You made that story up."

"Did I?"

"Yeah. To scare me."

She shrugged. "What would be the fun of crawling around in the dark without a ghost story?"

"Then you did make it up." he stated. No answer. "Right?"

Victoria marched on.

—•—

Even though the guard was not in sight, they snuck through the station under the lip of the platform. It seemed a better option than tempting fate out in the open.

Hunched over and head down, Chester stayed close behind Victoria as they scrambled through the station. He crouched, trying to keep his body below the yellow trimmed lip of the platform. As long as he stayed low, he'd be all but invisible to anyone on the northbound platform. He kept his eyes focused on Victoria's crouched form. His flank was uncomfortably exposed.

Black clothes offered no protection against the glare of fluorescent lights.

He concentrated on nothing but taking steps forward, until he was through the station, safely back in the darkness.

Chester blew out a breath, and took in a slow, deep one to replace it. He looked behind him. The well-lit platforms, framed in the darkness of the tunnel, seemed distant and harmless. No one chased after them.

"How many more platforms do we need to go through?" he asked.

"We're going to Union so…" she mulled it over, "four more."

"Eep."

She rolled her eyes. "If you think being in the lights of a platform is scary, then be glad you aren't in the lights of a speeding train."

Chester swallowed, and scratched at the itch that formed in the back of his neck. "Good point."

"I know," she quipped. She clicked on her flashlight, and led on.

The tunnels curved. They rounded the bend, and the looming luminescence of Wellesley Station vanished.

Once more, they were surrounded by the confines of tracks and cement. Chester kept his eyes on the pool of light Victoria's flashlight cast. He wrung his gloved hands together. These tunnels seemed different than the last stretch. There were more tripping hazards in his path; ruts in the cement, rungs in the tracks, and uneven sewage grates. He noted each one as they came into his line of sight, and moved to avoid them.

He glanced about at the scenery as he walked. Machinery of all sorts reached out towards the tracks. Traffic signals hung on the walls, and bizarre creations of pipe and steel clogged the spaces between the pillars. Thick pipes and cables loomed overhead. The air was still, and heavy with odours unknown.

"There's a lot more stuff in these tunnels," Chester commented.

"There sure is," Victoria replied, "and all of it in the wrong places. The tiny stuff is along the walls. If a train passes, there's nothing to hide behind. And all the big stuff is between the pillars—so there's no escape."

Chester scratched his neck and turned his attention back to the scenery.

Cryptic signs dotted the walls. Chester squinted and tried to read the tiny, arcane writings of one of them. He could barely make the letters out. He tried to focus on the words, but his eyes kept slipping off the sign, into the shadows—the omnipresent, visceral shadows. He looked about, blinked twice, and looked about again. He waited for his eyes to adjust, and they didn't.

He couldn't make out details in the dark. He looked at the lights overhead. The tunnel only had a single, sparse string of dull, orange lights. The congested separating wall blocked the light from the south-bound tunnels. And the stations—he couldn't see either station. The tunnel curved sharply in both directions, completely cutting off any sight of the stations.

Only Victoria's flashlight lit the way. He turned to face it—and it flickered out.

Chester swallowed hard. His pupils ached. He tried to call out, but couldn't make his mouth move. He couldn't see her without her flashlight.

Flashlight!

His own flashlight!

He grabbed at his flashlight, pulling it out of his pocket. His fingers shook, and the tube slipped from his gloved hands. He fumbled for it, bouncing it once, twice—and down it went. The flashlight hit the ground and he heard it roll.

Chester dropped to his knees, and swept his hands about, feeling for the flashlight. He pushed aside pebbles, crumpled paper, and foil wrappings. His breath, quick and shallow, echoed off the cement floor. He flailed sharply—something under his fingertips. Cold, hard. He grabbed at it, and wrapped his fingers around something solid.

The rail.

Chester froze. He felt the rail beneath his fingers, but could barely make it out. It reflected the soft, diffuse orange light. He stared directly at the rail, but each time, his vision slid off, back into the unlit areas of the tunnel. Shapes suggested themselves, half visible, half reconstructed from what he remembered being there.

He relaxed his eyes, and let the darkness flow. He held out his other hand, his fingers dangling, slowly, until he touched steel. He ran his gloved hands along the cold, solid rail.

A soft sound wafted to his ears. Metal scraping against metal—like something being screwed into place.

"Victoria?"

"Hang on, I'm working on it."

"This—" he whispered, caressing the track, "This is—so neat. Every day, hundreds of thousands of people zip past this very spot, and roll right over this very section of rail. But how many of them have actually stopped and touched it?"

"So—you're not afraid of the dark?" she queried.

The darkness felt tangible around him, but he felt no malice. "No. At this point, with the way the tunnel curves, I think I'd be more afraid of a light."

Victoria clicked the flashlight back on, shining it on Chester. He could see his own hands now, resting on the shiny metal. The mystery slunk away. It was just a rail.

"Why? It's not far to College Station. If a train sneaks up behind you, I'm sure you could outrun it."

Chester scooped up his flashlight and stood. He clicked on the light. Victoria was already a few metres away, moving down the tunnel, towards a curve. A blind curve. "No," he said, "A train would come at us."

"Hmm?"

"We're walking against traffic. A train wouldn't sneak up behind us. It'd come at us."

Victoria stopped. She shrugged her shoulders, shifting the weight of her backpack. "Yeah, it would." She continued on.

Chester jogged, caught up with Victoria. He fell in step beside her.

"Next up," she said, "College Station."

—·—

Chester waited while Victoria scouted ahead. He peered around the mouth of the tunnel, watching her. She moved lithely around the pillars separating the tracks, until she had a good view of the entire station. She hopped back onto the tracks, and waved "all-clear" to Chester.

They strolled casually through the station. Chester took time to appreciate the art on the walls: a series of hockey players, clad in blue-and-white, rendered in tile-mosaic.

The art wasn't new to Chester. He'd seen it plenty of times when the Leafs used to play at Maple Leaf Gardens. Nothing about the artwork had changed—only the angle from which he viewed it.

Chester stopped at the mouth of the tunnel. He turned to take a final look at the sprawling art, taking in the whole scene. The station seemed so still, so silent.

A distorted voice echoed through the station.

"**priorrun**"

Chester's chest clenched. He dropped low and backed out of the station. When he felt the darkness around him, he hissed at Victoria.

"Security!"

Her light snapped off. She crouched beside him, and whispered, "Where?"

He scanned, straining to see anything moving, but the station remained empty and quiet.

Moments passed. He whispered back, "I don't know. I heard a voice—in the distance, I guess."

"What'd it say?"

"I don't know." He mulled, but could not make out what he'd heard. "It sounded all tinny and distorted—like over a radio, or an intercom." He pulled his eyes from the station and looked at her. "Didn't you hear it?"

Chester looked at her expectantly. She shook her head and turned back to the tunnel.

He grabbed her hand and spun her back around. "I *heard* something!"

She yanked her hand away from his, and shot back, "You *think* you heard something." She took a breath and rubbed her hand. "Look," she said, her words calmer, smoother, "Chester, look all around us. Cement and ceramic! This place is, like, one big echo chamber. Sometimes you—you hear things. Can you hear anything now?"

He closed his eyes, and tried again. He strained. He couldn't hear anything

"Exactly."

He listened a moment more, then acquiesced. He turned, and found himself standing alone in the tunnel's mouth. Victoria had already started down the tunnel.

He jogged, and caught up. His gut roiled and boiled a question past his lips.

"Do you always go off by yourself?" he threw at her, his words a half-second ahead of his brain. He heard his tone of voice echoed back to him and regretted it. "I'm sorry—"

"I'm only by myself," she interrupted, "if you don't come with me." Yeah.

Chester swept his arms out. "Lead on."

She nodded. "Leading on. Next stop, Dundas Station. From there, we'll be passing right under the Eaton's Centre. Need to do any shopping?"

"No thanks. One B&E per night is enough for me."

"Seriously, Chester, relax and enjoy the scenery while it's not zipping by at fifty klicks."

That, actually, was good advice.

Presently, nothing separated the north and south tracks. He took advantage of the wide open tunnel and the sufficient lighting to scope out the details.

Black boxes were mounted on the walls at regular intervals. They were a metre or so above Chester's head, but would be eye-level for a train conductor. Chester turned to face the first one they passed.

It had four circular lights, one on top of the other. At the moment, only the second from the bottom, a red light, was lit. The yellow and green lights above it, and the white light below it, remained dark. Chester cocked his head. The fourth light seemed out of place.

"Hey, Victoria," he called over his shoulder. "What's this one for? The bottom, colourless one."

"It's a change signal. Hrm." She pondered. "It lights up when the signals are on a timer. Basically, it means 'Heads up, this red signal is going to change soon.' Yellow means 'go slow.' Green means 'go.'"

"Haven't I seen a different type of signal—something like two signals on top of each other?"

She threw him a look over her shoulder. "Yeah, the divergent signals. They're two of these sets of lights on top of each other. You find them when the tracks split. The top set means 'go the normal way.' The bottom set means 'go the divergent path.' You won't see any of them on this stretch of track."

"Why not?"

"There's no place to diverge to. You're more likely to see a double-signal around places like Davisville, where the trainyards are, or Yonge and Bloor, where the two lines intersect. Sometimes the trains switch lines around there."

"Through Lower Bay?"

"Bay Lower," she corrected. Victoria's eyebrows scrunched. "What do you know about Bay Lower?"

He frowned slightly, unsure of what to make of Victoria's inquisitive tone. "It's the hidden station," he answered, his words coming out cautiously. "Bay Station is on the east/west route, right in between the two north/south lines. Bay Lower is beneath it. It connects the two lines, but it doesn't get used."

"That's the one. How do you know about it?"

He shrugged. "I guess I've heard about it. They film movies there, don't they?"

She nodded. "Yeah, sometimes." She turned her focus back to the tunnel. The partitions had begun again, segmenting the tunnel. Around the curve of the tunnel, Dundas Station came into view. "Though, it's not *the* lost station. It's *one of the* lost stations. Do you know about the other one?"

He chewed on his lip, and scratched the back of his neck. "No, I don't. Where is?"

"Lower Queen is about two stations that way," she pointed ahead, "And a good ten feet straight down."

"Straight down?"

"It *is* a hidden station."

"How do you—"

Chester's words were cut short by a muffled, distant voice.

Crackle. "*priorone*" Hiss.

It came from ahead, from the next station. The static echoed a moment before dissipating into the silence.

Chester's eyes found Victoria's, and silently questioned. She nodded. She'd heard it, too.

They scrambled for cover.

—•—

"You're right," Victoria whispered, crouched next to Chester. "It sounded like a radio. Or the P.A. system, but way quieter."

"Did you hear what it said?"

"Static, mumble, garble... I don't know!"

A breeze picked up and tossed some loose papers around. It whispered across Chester's ears. He scratched the back of his neck.

"I don't hear anything now," stated Victoria. "Right. Let's hustle through. Dundas is boring, anyways."

They crouch-ran through the empty station.

At least, Chester could only hope it was empty. Every centimetre of the station bore down on him as he ran. The lights, the posters, the tile—they all pointed at his hunched back. Faster, faster, not fast enough! He could feel everything focused on him like a headlight. Faster—

Through the mouth of the tunnel. He threw himself behind the separating pillar, and panted, trying to catch his breath.

No one followed. He leaned his head against the cool, solid pillar and calmed himself.

"Hurry up," Victoria called from further down the tunnel. The tracks curved upwards, in a hump, forming a horizon. She stood atop of the hill, a silhouette surrounded by orange. Chester could not see the next station past her.

"So is Queen also boring?" he asked, catching up to her.

"Mostly."

"What about the hidden part? Are we going there?"

"Nope."

"Why not?"

Victoria paused. "I don't exactly know how to get into it."

They crested the hump in the tracks. Up ahead, the fluorescent light of Queen Station came into view. They walked in silence. The lost station stuck in Chester's mind.

"But you know where it is?"

Victoria was silent for a moment. "More or less—yeah, I know where it is." They paused at the mouth of the tunnel. Queen Station's platforms were empty. They continued. "Heck, we're probably walking over it right now."

Chester's heels itched at the thought. "If you know where it is, then—"

Victoria cut him off. "Because. Look—when the TTC first built the north/south line, they knew they wanted an east/west route, too. They wanted it to run along a major, central east/west road. At the time, the heart of the city was Queen Street. So they figured they'd build a line along Queen, with a transfer point below the existing Queen Station."

They passed through the station. Chester let the sights pass him unheeded. Just another train station he'd seen hundreds of times. He paid even less attention to the tunnels between Queen and King.

He listened.

"By the time funding for the second line was approved, Toronto had grown. Its heart was further north, on Bloor street. So they gave up on the Queen line, and built the Bloor line we all know and love today.

"Except that they'd already started construction on the Lower Queen station. They'd roughed it out, laid some piping, and poured some cement. But then the kill orders came, and they abandoned the station. They never laid tracks, and never got round to connecting it to the existing subway system.

"So, unlike Bay Lower, there aren't any divergent tracks leading to it. There may be some doors into the cavern, but you can bet they're locked up tight. The station isn't on any maps. Heck, for a good chunk of the '80s, the TTC wouldn't even acknowledge it existed."

"Fair enough." They strolled along in silence for a moment. Chester barely noticed as they passed through King Station itself. "Would you go if you could?"

Victoria nodded. "Everyone knows where it is, but no one can get to it. I've always wanted to go. Haven't you?"

Did he? "A hidden station does sound neat. Too bad we won't get to see it."

They paused at the end of King Station. Ahead, past the mouth, the tunnel curved sharply to the right, vanishing into darkness. Victoria tossed a gaze over her shoulder, back north. "Yeah, too bad." Her eyes fell over his shoulders, looking past him.

He followed her gaze, down the straight, narrow tunnels. He could, just barely, see all the way to the Queen Station. "You aren't thinking of going back, are—"

He didn't finish. Victoria grasped his arm and hissed, "I see someone in Queen!"

Chester strained. A figure, barely more than a dot. Clad in grey and red. Motionless. Staring?

Behind them, down the northbound tunnels, a sound tore through the tunnels, muffled and faint, but unmistakable. It crackled, and hissed, and echoed. The same call.

"PrrirUn"

The sound echoed, reverberating off the walls. Victoria swore softly. "They're in our tunnel."

"We can't go back," Chester answered, his eyes fixed on the figure back at Queen Station. "Do we say we dropped our keys?"

"No," she answered, "Run!"

Victoria turned and ran to the third rail. She planted her foot on the nearest safety step, and catapulted over the partition, onto the southbound tracks.

"Right. Run."

The call, coming from the northbound tunnels, still echoed in Chester's ears. He ran from it, following Victoria. He leapt over the partition. He landed and crouched. He spun around and looked back down the tunnel.

On the distant platform stood a figure, staring back at him.

"Victoria, he knows we're here!" He reached behind, his hand grasping for hers. He felt only empty air. "Victoria?"

He turned about. He caught a fleeting glance of her, running down the southbound tunnel towards Union Station—and then lost sight of her in the shadows.

Footsteps echoed. Footsteps everywhere!

The tunnels exploded with sound once again. *"**PrrorUn**"* Distorted, crackling. The soft "n" sound lingered, bouncing off the walls, and faded into an echo. A rhythmic echo. Soft, hard, soft, hard.

The sound of the echo took on a shape of its own. A low, rumbling sound, full of bass and metal. It sounded like—

No.

Chester laid his hands on the track. They were vibrating. He stared back down the tunnel, following it passed Queen Station, until the tracks crested, several kilometres away.

He could see no train. But the sound was unmistakable—and undoubtedly coming right at him.

The figure on the Queen platform stared.

He forced words through his throat. "Victoria," he whispered hoarsely. He stood and took a step back. "Train!"

He turned and ran after her.

—•—

Chester bolted into the tunnel, shouting after Victoria. The tunnel banked sharply, creating a blind curve. He couldn't see any further than a few metres in either direction. The spot from his flashlight bobbed and weaved wildly, barely giving him a view of the narrow, cramped tunnel. The place felt tight, confined. There were no inlets, no hidey holes, and no space between the partition pillars. It felt like—

The horrid sound of metal wheels squealing on metal tracks shredded the air behind him.

—like a dark, winding death trap.

"VICTORIA!"

He pushed harder. Just around the bend, he saw her pumping legs. Wind blasted at the back of his neck—air forced through the tunnel by his pursuer.

He shouted. "Train!"

She couldn't hear. He knew that. She didn't need to. The monstrous, overpowering sound was unmistakable.

Wind whipped his face and slammed into his back. He closed the distance, and caught up to Victoria. The tunnel curved away, endless. Union Station was too far away. He couldn't even see the northbound tracks; machinery filled every gap in the cement separator.

He could feel the train on his heels.

The tunnel began to fill with bright, glaring light. On the periphery of his vision, something glinted—there! Up ahead, to the right, in the wall! A rusty metal grate, barely half a metre high.

The tunnel was as bright as day.

He seized Victoria's hand, and threw himself at the grate, ramming it with his shoulder. He crashed into it, and it gave way.

He fell through the gate and hit the ground.

Wood splintered beneath him and the ground, too, gave way. He fell. He felt air whipping past his face.

Impact!

Pain shot through him. He tensed and curled up. He shut his eyes tight, covered his ears, and cowered.

Far overhead, an unseen train screamed past.

—•—

The last, dying remnants of the train's screams faded away.

Silence.

Chester groaned and rolled on his side. Dust and splinters flaked from his clothing. He took stock of his body. His back and legs throbbed. He wiggled his toes and fingers. No sharp pains; nothing felt broken.

He unwrapped his arms and braced himself to stand. He blinked dust from his eyes. Where was the flashlight?

"Victoria?" he called out. "You okay?"

His hand connected with the metal shaft. He wrapped his fingers around the flashlight, feeling for the switch. He clicked on the light and looked around.

To his left and right rose dirty, wet brick walls, barely more than a metre apart, stretched up to a ceiling far overhead. The walls formed a long, narrow tunnel, lined with pipes. The tunnel started here and stretched out into darkness in the other direction. The ceiling was cracked, smashed inwards. Beyond the Chester-sized hole in the ceiling, he could see the swing gate.

"Hey, Victoria," he called out again. "Where'd you land? Are you okay?" He wiggled to his knees, shaking off the dizziness. He looked around. Aside from debris, the tunnel was empty. Frantically, he shone the light about.

"Victoria?" Where was she? She had to be here. He'd pulled her from the path of the train!

Was she a level above? He stood tall and gauged the distance. He couldn't jump it—but maybe he could shimmy his way up the narrow shaft. He braced his feet and looked up. A cloud of dust motes flowed down from the ceiling, into his face. He coughed and shut his eyes.

Noise, the sound of squeaking metal, filled the brick tunnel. Chester swung the light upwards, illuminating the hole.

Metal flashed. The gate swung shut, echoing its metallic clang through the tunnel. He shook the dust from his eyes.

A single, white circle of light shone from beyond the sealed gate. A tiny circle—a flashlight. "Victoria?"

The light clicked off, leaving darkness in its wake. Though dust in his eyes still blurred his vision, he saw, beyond the grate, an indistinct silhouette steal away.

"Victoria?"

He played his light across the grate, but she wasn't there. She wasn't anywhere to be seen. He looked about at the narrow brick walls, lined with overhead pipes covered in mildew and condensation. A steam tunnel!

The tunnel stretched away several metres into the distance, where it split at a T-junction. Condensation dripped from the pipes, littering the floor with puddles of dirty water. Water spattered gently, echoing off the dank brick walls.

Another sound, from behind and above, flowed into Chester's ears. His fingers seized up on the flashlight, gripping it tightly. A sound he could barely make out, but one he dreaded to hear.

Distorted and tinny—**"prruronbeelor"**

Chester held his breath and shrank a step backwards into the tunnel. He took a last, furtive glance. Victoria wasn't here. She must have gone down the tunnel. It was the only path—the only path away from who-ever owned that radio.

He turned on his heels and ran. His feet splashed through the puddles of water, spraying filthy droplets. Ahead, the tunnel split at a T-junction. Chain fences covered both ways—and both had gates.

—•—

Chester slowed his pace, and pondered both paths. He shone his light down the one to the left. The light reflected off a metal surface, in the distance. A ladder, leading up, to a grate. The delicate sound of car tires wafted down from it.

Chester spun on his heels, turning to the left, to the exit! He took one step—a blinding light clicked into existence, shining into his eyes. He threw his hands up, stopping dead in his tracks. Broken pixels of afterimage twinkled in his vision. He held out his hand, staggering, feeling his way towards the gate.

The sound of swinging metal—and a resounding clang. He shook the dazzle from his eyes and bolted for the gate. He threw himself against it, shook it, pounded on it. The gate, fastened shut, did not budge.

Beyond the gate, the flashlight silently bobbed. The light clicked and vanished. Soft footsteps padded away.

Chester's eyes adjusted to the darkness. He saw the owner of the footsteps, a receding silhouette. The size, the shape—that was no security guard.

"Victoria!" he called out to her, shaking the fence. "Let me out of here."

"You're a liar, Chester."

"What?" he shook the gate, but it didn't budge. "Why do you think I'm a liar?"

"I know you are a liar, Chester," she replied, softly. "This isn't your first time exploring, is it?"

Chester took a step back.

"What do you really know about Bay Lower?"

"Nothing," he replied, baffled. "I've never seen it."

"You know what it looks like. "

Chester opened his mouth to refute her—but found that he couldn't. He knew.

—•—

The first thing he'd noticed was that the lights were on. Traffic signals, exit signs, fluorescent lights—all of them. He'd always figured that they wouldn't bother lighting a station that they never used.

He'd clicked off his flashlight and marveled at the sight. Bay Lower. *The* Bay Lower.

Every step of the walk down the divergent path from Museum Station had been exhilarating, but nothing came close to the excitement he'd felt taking the first step into the station.

He'd wandered down the platform, following a path that few others had walked, taking in sights few others had seen.

Although the design and architecture was nigh identical to the publicly accessible Bay Upper, there were subtle differences. The empty trash bins. The lack of modern payphones. The faux New York style graffiti.

"This is neat," he'd said.

"It looks exactly like Upper Bay."

"Well, sure, the architecture is identical, but come on—" a wave of his hands had accentuated his words. "It's not just another station." He'd turned to face her. "This is *Bay Lower*."

Victoria, leaning against a pillar with her arms crossed, had rolled her eyes.

—•—

Chester staggered back, his mouth agape. He closed his eyes and shook his head, but her image lingered. The image of her—a memory, or an illusion?

"Who are you?"

He looked up and stared at the silhouette. The light hovered, glaring in his eyes. He took a step forward.

She said nothing.

Chester clenched his fists, and lunged forward. He crashed against the gate, pounding it, shaking it. The chain links rattled, filling the tunnel with a cacophony of jangles. "I've never met you before in my life!"

"Really?"

The flashlight clicked off.

She was gone.

He gave the gate a last, futile shake and let it go. Locked tight. He had no other choice. He turned and started down the long, dank steam tunnel.

He kept his shoulders hunched and his head low. The rough ground, uneven and warped from years of heat and dripping water, tripped him more than once. Rusty pipes randomly belched wisps of steam.

Chester staggered, following his flashlight when possible, and grabbed at the wall for support when steam, dust, and darkness conspired to blind him. Heat permeated the tunnel. A film of sweat coated his brow.

The tunnel, filled with curves and corners, wound and twisted. Chester turned the corner. Metres ahead, a sign hung from the ceiling. *Exit*. Beneath it, a red door stood ajar. He ran towards it.

The door slammed shut. He grabbed for the handle. The door clicked.

Locked.

He kicked the door and blew out a hot, frustrated breath. "Dammit!"

An itch crawled up the back of Chester's neck. He scratched at it, gloved fingers against skin. He turned around, back the way he came. A flicker of light, further down the tunnel, caught his attention. It bobbed, casting its glow about his face. He squinted and raised his hand, shielding his eyes.

The overhead lights brightened, filling the steam tunnel with diffuse orange illumination and sharp, short shadows, drowning out his flashlight. He clicked it off.

The single, white light shone brightest of all. And behind that light—the silhouette—

"Let me out of here," he called out to her. "I want to leave."

"So did I."

"What?"

A sharp hiss answered. Steam rose from a distant pipe, engulfing the light. The cloud glowed from the inside. Wavering shadows danced about inside the whirling mist. It rolled in, advancing on Chester.

"Leave me alone!" he shouted.

"Leave you alone, hmm?" her voice answered, flowing down the tunnel like the cloud of steam.

The overhead lights flickered and died.

Chester fumbled for his flashlight.

"Leave you all alone?"

—•—

"Let's get out of here," she'd said.

He'd stopped to look at a bench, crouching to see it from a specific angle. "I knew I recognized this one. From that movie. Y'know, that one with that girl."

"Let's go," she'd answered impatiently. "We've got a lot of ground to cover."

"What? Aw, come on." He'd turned to argue, but she'd already hopped off the platform, onto the tracks. "Victoria, we've barely seen anything."

"You can come back another time," she'd called, already at the mouth of the tunnel. "The trains start running in a couple hours, and I still want to see—"

"Stop rushing me," he'd back shot at her. "If you're so worried about time, go on ahead. I'll meet you there."

Her eyes had rolled. "Chester, you've never taken the Yonge divergent tracks before. They're tricky. I—"

"Just go," he'd growled, louder than he'd expected. His rough voice had echoed back. "I'll catch up."

She'd turned on her heels and stormed off. Chester, determinedly, had continued exploring on his own. It had taken only seconds for the tunnel to swallow up the sound of her receding footsteps.

He'd stopped and gazed at the wall. Some film crew had changed the tiling, renaming the station to "Charon." Weird.

At the edge of his peripheral vision, Chester had caught a glimpse of a single white light shinning at him from the tunnel Victoria had gone up. He'd gritted his teeth and turned to confront her. "Damn it, Vic—"

The light hadn't come from a flashlight. It had come from the traffic signal. An orb of lunar white shone beneath the red signal.

Subtle vibrations had shaken the ground. A wisp of wind had rolled through the station.

The red light on the traffic signal had flashed, on and off, its timer triggered by the approaching train—coming from Museum, heading for the Eastbound tunnel to Yonge.

The tunnel Victoria had taken!

There weren't supposed to be any trains. Not this late at night. He'd opened his mouth, and tried to choke a warning passed his tight, closed throat. It had come out hoarse, inaudible.

The sound of metal on metal had grown closer.

His feet had frozen to the floor. The tunnel had glowed, and the breeze picked up.

—•—

A blast of wind ripped through the roiling, glowing steam. It parted the fog and slammed into Chester, knocking him over. The naked light shone in his eyes, painfully bright in the darkened tunnel. He scuttled backwards, away from it.

"Leave me alone!" he shouted.

"Abandon you? In the tunnels?" The light clicked off. "In the dark?"

"No!" he screamed back, and got to his feet. He drew his flashlight and clicked it on. The steam was gone, dissipated. He spun around, shining his light about. Everywhere he looked, he could see only empty tunnel.

An itch raged across the back of his neck. He spun about, flashing his light back down the tunnel. The shadows seemed to leap away from him. Was that a silhouette?

He had to find a way out!

He turned and ran.

Footsteps followed him.

Chester pressed on, breathing hard, straining against the heat. The heat was everywhere, as omnipresent as the rust. Rust coated every metal surface so, despite the heat, Chester dared not take off his gloves.

The gloves that fit his hands perfectly. How had she known? How *did* she know his hands?

He threw a glance over his shoulder. He could make out her shape, further back than before. He could outrun her!

Chester's foot came down wrong. He snapped to attention and caught his stride. His foot dangled halfway over a hole in the ground— an open ventilation grate. He shifted his weight backwards, wobbling. He threw himself sideways, landing solidly against the wall, and grabbed a pipe.

The pipe, rusty and fatigued from years of corrosion, cracked in his gloved hand. It rattled and hissed, rising in pitch—and burst. A bath of white, solid heat spewed at Chester's face. He threw up his hands and staggered away from the blast. His heel dangled—dangled over emptiness. He teetered and threw out his arms, reaching to regain his balance, reaching—

Reaching for the silhouette in the steam. Her silhouette. He reached out his hand. He tried to reach her.

And missed.

He toppled through the wide hole, wind whipping past his face.

—•—

Chester had sprinted down the platform, wind whipping past him, towards the tunnel, the red light flashed at him, shouting at him to S*top! Stop! Stop!*

"Victoria! Train!"

Wind had whipped past his face as he'd run down the narrow, cramped, windy tunnel—a long, unbroken death trap.

Every signal he'd passed threatened him with their lunar white orbs.

"VICTORIA!"

The rails had vibrated and screamed metallic screams. Light had flooded the tunnel, and air blasted his back. Chester had screamed, his voice drowned out by the roar of the train.

He'd caught up to Victoria.

Everything had blurred.

The light from Yonge Station had shone beyond the next bend. He'd run past her, towards the station.

He'd thrown himself onto the platform—

—•—

The ground met him, hard. The flashlight shattered and all went dark.

Chester moaned. He clutched the dirty ground and staggered back to his feet. He didn't hurt. He had his breath.

A light split the darkness; a circle of brilliance shining in his eyes.

He blinked, and raised a hand to shield himself from the glare. He squinted.

Her silhouette stood behind the light, framed by the walls of the narrow tunnel.

He took a menacing step towards her. "I *didn't* abandon you," he growled at her, "I came into the tunnel for you!"

Silence.

He faced her, staring into her glare.

"What do you want from me, Victoria?"

"Run."

The light grew, flared, and swallowed her silhouette. It hurt his eyes, but he didn't look away. The flare receded, but did not fade. It shrank into the distance, wavered—and snapped into place.

Headlights!

The ground vibrated. Metal squealed against metal.

The train blew its horn.

Chester ran.

The wind picked up, air forced through the tunnel, whipping past him. It blew hard against his bare neck, making his skin itch.

The tunnel lit up bright—far too bright. He could see every detail; the walls were narrow, and solid; no ledge, no holes. Nowhere to hide.

Up ahead, not that far way, was the mouth of the tunnel, and beyond that—a station. *Escape!*

He pushed, his legs afire, his heart pounding. The tunnel filled with the deafening squeal of the train's futile brakes. *Too fast to stop—*

The mouth—just steps away! *Faster!*

The train was on his heels—he could feel it *right behind him!*

Blinding light filled his entire field of vision—

The station!

He closed his eyes and threw himself at the platform. He hit the ground, covered his head, and screamed.

—•—

The security guard, a looming sentry in grey and red—had stared from across the station. A blank stare. Eyes wide, cheeks ashen, arms at his side. The guard had stared—just stared.

The call had come over the P.A., echoing for all to hear.

"Priority One, Bay Lower Tunnel. Priority One."

—•—

The voice faded away. Chester lay on the ground, his arms over his head. Silence filled the air. The voices echoed no more; the train did not scream at his back.

He opened his eyes, and looked.

Her heels softly clicked against the cement floor. One booted leg, then the other, stepped into his line of sight, less than a metre away. She knelt down, sitting on her heels. Chester looked up, into Victoria's face. Her mouth was a thin, straight line. Her eyes were soft and inquisitive.

Chester's shivered, his whole body shaking. The awful sound of the train rang in his head. He could still feel the train touching his heels.

Victoria placed a gloved hand on his shoulder.

He threw it off, and scampered away from her, putting his back up against solid wall.

"Priority One," he whispered, his voice hoarse. "*Incident involving a person contacting a train.*"

She said nothing. Only nodded.

Chester's stomach clenched. "You didn't make it out of the tunnel."

She shook her head, side to side, her ponytail gently swishing.

"I passed you. I ran right past you. I wanted to get to the station. I left you—to die!"

"Chester—"

"I left you in the tunnels—so you wanted me to know how it felt?"

The sensation of the train on his heels sent a wave of shivers through his body. She moved closer, her gloved hand reaching out for him. He scurried further back, sliding up the wall, getting to his feet.

"You wanted me to know how your *death* felt?"

Victoria's eyes narrowed. "No." She lashed out, grabbed his hand— and yanked his arm.

Hard.

He shut his eyes tight as pain shot up his arm—

—•—

He'd screamed at the pain in his arm, the searing, shooting pain.

The station, just steps ahead! It's so close, almost there. He can't—
he can't push any harder—

He'd screamed to drown out the instincts echoing in his brain. *You
can run faster if—*

No! He couldn't—he couldn't let go of her hand!

He'd screamed, and had pulled her along as hard as he could—

—and had felt the train on his heels.

—•—

The pain in his arm subsided, fading to a dull ache.

"You see, Chester, that's the thing," she whispered, "You *didn't*
leave me alone in the tunnel." She ran a gentle thumb over his palm,
then squeezed his hand, tight. Affectionately. "That's what I wanted—"
she paused "—I needed you to realize."

"You never let go of my hand."

He opened his eyes, and looked down at her hand in his. A guilty
thought gnawed at him. "If I had, I could have run faster," he muttered,
"I could have made it to the station—"

Victoria shook her head, and shone her light over his shoulder. "No,
Chester," she said, "you wouldn't have. You proved that."

He turned his head, and looked back down the tunnel he'd just run.
Far off in the distance, the tunnel ended at a wooden retaining wall. The
distance felt disturbingly familiar.

"Priority One," he said, "Incident involving a person or *persons*
contacting a train."

"At least," she sighed wistfully, "it was only us."

Chester blinked and reached into his pocket. He took out the folded
piece of paper.

It wasn't a clipping.

It was a proof page.

—•—

In a tiny downtown apartment, made even tinier by a home printing press, Chester and Victoria had read over the proof for the ad. That night, they'd walk the route, to ensure its safety, and accuracy. Then, if everything was okay, they'd run the ad in the next edition of their urban exploration 'zine, *"You Are Hereby Authorized…"*

—•—

Chester smiled, ruefully, and tucked the proof back into his pocket.

Victoria smiled back. "We always said we'd make it here one day, didn't we?"

"Here?"

"I thought that—well—if nothing else, then we should at least get to see it."

Chester fixed her with a puzzled look. She squeezed his hand, "This is Lower Queen."

"No way," he said. She nodded.

"It is."

"Then the route we planned—" his voice trailed off.

"—would have worked," she finished.

Hand in hand, they wandered the roughed out station. Layers of old, solid dirt littered the floor. The walls were rough and unfinished. There were no tiles on the floor or wall. Ahead, the tunnel opened up—into a subway station. At least, a rough mimicry of a subway station. There were no rails, but the path the track would run was clearly defined. Poured, roughed-down cement formed a mound running parallel to the tracks—the platform, narrower than regular subway platforms. Lights hung at seemingly random intervals, but none of them were on. They saw everything by Victoria's flashlight.

Wide-eyed, they took in the sights. The unfinished walls, the tens of metres of exposed ductwork, the holes in the floor that dropped away into darkness. Pipes, tools, wooden planks, and spools of thick wire dotted the landscape of the unborn station.

"The famous lost Queen station. Dark, dusty, dingy, and full of junk." Victoria grinned widely. "Très cool, huh?"

"Damn straight," Chester agreed.

They hopped onto the roughed-out tracks, and walked the station to its far end.

Chester paused, and took a last look around. He turned to her and smiled.

"Wanna go explore?"

Victoria nodded. "Yes. Yes, I do."

They left, hand in hand, to do just that.

—•—

A piece of paper flutters to the ground, breaking the heavy silence in the abandoned station. It lands, and becomes just another bit of garbage, left to waste away, its text never to be read by living eyes.

Attention aspiring urban explorers! Do you want to discover the secrets Toronto's subway system holds? Do you want to experience what goes on in the tunnels firsthand? We're extending an open invitation for a guided tour. Meet time is in one week, 3am, at the construction yard at Yonge & Hayden. Bring a flashlight.

"Buried Treasure

"In 1760, two French ships ran into heavy seas near Main Duck Island and foundered. One of the ships attempted to sail into the harbour at Main Duck's, but the ship broke apart on the point. There were a few survivors, who salvaged some supplies and a chest of gold from their broken vessel. The gold was buried somewhere on the island. One by one, the marooned sailors died of cold and starvation and were buried, until there was but one left. This poor sailor's skeleton was found many years later, far from the graves of his fellow crew members, and the point where the ship foundered has been known as Graveyard Point ever since. The chest of gold still waits on Main Duck Island."

From:
The Legendary Guide to Prince Edward County (1994)
by Janet Kellough, Copyright © 1994 by Janet Kellough,
Kellough Productions, Picton, Ontario.

Under Summons

by
Tanya Huff

Eyes squinted against the early morning sun, Diana Hansen walked down the lane toward the Waupoos Marina listening to the string of complaints coming from the cat in her backpack.

"The boat is leaving at seven-thirty," she said when he finally paused for breath. "If we'd gotten up any later we'd have missed it."

The head and front paws of a marmalade tabby emerged through the open zipper and peered over Diana's shoulder toward the marina. "I thought need provided for Keepers during a Summoning?"

"Need has provided, Sam. There's a boat leaving for Main Duck Island this morning."

He snorted. "Why can't need provide a boat at a reasonable hour?"

"It doesn't work that way. Besides, cats do that hunt at dust and dawn thing—you should be happy to be up."

"First of all, I'm not hunting. And second," he added ducking down into the backpack as a car passed them, "I'd rather have sausages for breakfast than a damp mouse."

"Who wouldn't."

Another car passed, bouncing from pothole to pothole.

"You'd better stay down," Diana told him, hooking her thumbs under the padded shoulder straps. "It's starting to get busy."

"Oh yeah," the cat muttered as a pickup truck followed the two cars. "It's a real rush hour. I'll be napping if you need me."

The Ministry of Natural Resources trawler was tied up at the nearer of the big piers out behind the marina. Pausing at the southwest corner of the big grey building, Diana scoped out the crowd. Most of the twenty-four other travellers were older couples, sensibly dressed in long pants wearing both hiking boots and hats. Half a dozen women were obviously together and just as obviously part of a club—unless they'd all accidentally worn the same lime green t-shirt. There was a sprinkling of younger adults and three teenagers. Two girls, probably sisters, and a boy. They were the only ones in shorts. The boy caught her gaze and smirked. He was a good-looking kid—and he knew it.

"Okay, everyone, listen up!" A forty-ish man wearing Ministry khaki climbed up on wooden crate and waved a clipboard. "Some you already know me but, for the rest, I'm Gary Straum and I'll be your guide this trip. The young man driving the boat, is Jamie Wierster. He knows almost as much as I do about the island so if I'm not available he'll do his best to tell you anything you need to know."

A ruddy-cheeked young giant leaned out of the tiny cabin and waved.

"I just want to remind you of a few things before we get started," Gary continued as the two girls giggled. "Main Duck Island is part of the St. Lawrence Islands National Parks system and is a nature sanctuary. You may not take samples of the plant life away with you—this means no picking, no digging, no collecting seeds. The wildlife is to be left strictly alone. If there's a disagreement of any kind between you and any creature living on that island, I will rule in favour of the creature. Anything you carry in must be carried out. If you can't live with that, I suggest you leave now." Gary smiled as an older man grabbed the back of the teenage boy's skater shirt and hauled him back by his side. "All right then. When I read your name, come and pick up your life jacket…" He gestured at the open steel locker beside him. "…put it on, and board. The sooner we get going, the more time we'll have to spend on the island."

Diana's name was the last on the list. She hadn't put it there and she felt a little sorry for the actual twenty-fifth person who'd been bumped to make room for her but there was a hole in the fabric of reality out on Main Duck Island and it was her job as a Keeper to close it.

Feeling awkward and faintly ridiculous in the life jacket, Diana sat down on a wooden bench and set her backpack carefully at her feet.

"I saw the cat. When we passed you in the lane."

She answered the teenage boy's smile with one of her own as he dropped onto the bench beside her. According to the boarding list, his name was Ryan. Ryan, like everyone else on the boat, was a Bystander and, given the relative numbers, Keepers were used to working around them. "Of course you did, Ryan. *Please* forget about it."

It really was a magic word.

He frowned. Looked around like he was wondering why he was sitting there, and, after mumbling something inarticulate, moved across the boat to sit back down in his original seat. The girls, Mackenzie and Erin, sitting on the bench in front of him, giggled.

"I get the impression you're not the giggling type."

It was one of the older women, her husband busy taking pictures of Gary casting off and jumping aboard.

"Not really, no."

"Carol Diamond. That's my husband Richard. We're here as part of an Elder Hostel program." Her wave took in the rest of the hats and hiking boots crowd. "All of us."

"Great."

"Are you traveling on your own, dear?"

"Yes, I am."

Carol smiled the even, white smile of the fully dentured and nodded toward the teenagers. "Well, how nice you have some people of your own age to spend time with."

Diana blinked. Two months shy of twenty, she did not appreciate being lumped in with the children. Fortunately, between the motor and the wind it was difficult to carry on a casual conversation and Carol didn't try, content to sit quietly while her husband took pictures of Waupoos Island, Prince Edward Point, waves, sky, gulls, the other people in the boat, and once, while he was fiddling with the focus, his lap.

The three pictures with Diana in them would be mysteriously overexposed.

So would at least one of the shots south across Lake Ontario but Diana had nothing to do with that.

"Hey!" Ryan managed to make himself heard over the ambient noise. "What's that?"

Everyone squinted in the direction he was pointing. A series of small dark dots rose above a sharp-edged horizon.

"That's our first sight of the island; we're about five miles out." Gary moved closer to the teenager. "Well done."

Ryan turned just far enough to scowl at him. "Not that. Closer to us."

Also a series of small dark dots rising and falling with the slight chop. Then, suddenly, they were gone. The last of the dots rose up into a triangular point just before it disappeared.

"That looked like a tail!"

"Might be a loon," Gary offered.

"Fucking big loon!"

"Ryan!"

Ryan rolled his eyes at his father but muttered an apology.

"It's probably just some floating junk." A half-turn included the rest of the group in the discussion. "You'd be amazed at the stuff we find out here." His list had almost everyone laughing.

Lake monster wasn't on it, Diana noted.

—•—

As Main Duck Island coalesced into a low solid line of treetops joined by land with a lighthouse rising off the westernmost point, Gary explained that it had been acquired by the park service in 1998 having been previously owned by John Foster Dulles, a prominent lawyer who became American Secretary of State in the Eisenhower administration. The island was 209 hectares in size and except for the ruins of some old fishing cabins—which were posted—none of it was off-limits.

"The lighthouse?" one of the lime-green t-shirt group asked.

"Is unmanned and closed to the public but you can go right up to it and poke around."

Mention of the lighthouse started the shipwreck stories. There were a lot of them since the area around the island was known as the grave-yard of Lake Ontario and contained the wrecks of a number of two and three-masted schooners, brigantines, barges, and steamers dating back to the sinking of a small French warship enroute to Fort Niagara with supplies and a pay chest of gold for the troops that went down in late fall around 1750.

Diana was beginning to get a bad feeling about the location of the hole she had to close.

As Jamie steered the trawler into School House Bay, Gary told the story of the *John Randall*. She'd anchored in the bay for shelter back in 1920 only to have the wind shift into the north and drive her ashore. Her stern hit a rock and her engine lifted up and she broke in two.

"The crew of four scrambled up onto the bow and remained there for ten hours washed by heavy seas and lashed by a November north-easter. They finally made it ashore on a hatch cover and stayed with the lighthouse keeper nine days before they were picked up. You can still see the wooden ribs and planks of the ship in the bay."

"So no one died?" Ryan asked.

"Not that time." With the dock only metres away, Gary moved over the port side of the boat and picked up the rear mooring line. "But a year and eight days later, the Captain of the *Randall* went down while in command of the *City of New York*. His wife and his ten month old daughter went with him."

"So sad," Carol sighed as Gary leapt out onto the dock. "But at least they were together." She twisted on the bench to look back the way they'd come. "I bet those waves hide a hundred stories."

"I bet they hide a hundred and one," Diana sighed, hoisting her backpack. She was not going to enjoy explaining this to Sam.

—•—

"In the water?'

"Essentially."

Sam's ears saddled. "How *essentially*?" The echoed word dripped with feline sarcasm.

"Under the water."

"Have a nice time."

Down on one knee beside him, Diana stroked along his back and out his tail. "There's a lake monster out there too. Looked like a sea serpent. Probably came through the hole."

"And that's supposed to make me change my mind?" the cat snorted. He peered off the end of the dock into the weedy bay. "Frogs pee in that water you know."

"That's not..." She probed at the Summons, trying to narrow it down a little. "...exactly the water we're going into."

He sat back and looked up at her, amber eyes narrowed. "What water are we going into, exactly? If *we* were going, that is?"

"Southwest." She straightened. "Toward the lighthouse."

"I'll wait here."

"Come on. The nature hike went through the woods. We'll take the beach and avoid an audience." About to lift the backpack, she paused. "You want to walk or ride?"

Tail tip twitching, he shoved past her muttering, "What part of I'll wait here did you not understand."

The beach consisted of two to three metres of smooth gravel trimmed with a ridge of polished zebra mussel shells at the edge of the water. As Diana and Sam rounded a clump of sumac, they saw Ryan, a garter snake wrapped around one hand, moving quietly toward the two girls crouched at the ridge of shells.

"You think we should get involved?" Sam wondered.

Before Diana could answer, Ryan placed his foot wrong, the gravel rattled and both girls turned. Although he no longer had surprise on his side, he waved the snake in their general direction.

"Look what I have!"

Braced for shrieking and running, Diana was surprised to see both girls advance toward Ryan.

"How dare you!" Mackenzie snapped, fists on her hips. "How would you like it if someone picked you up by the throat and flailed you at people?"

"The poor snake!" Erin added.

"I'm not hurting it," Ryan began but Mackenzie ran right over his protest with her opinion of the kind of people who abused animals for fun while Erin gently took the snake from him and released it.

"In answer to your question," Diana snickered as they started walking again, "I don't think we're needed."

A little further down the beach, two even larger snakes lay tangled together in the sun on a huge slab of flat rock. The female hissed as they went by. Sam hissed back.

"Don't be rude, Sam, it's their beach."

"She started it," Sam muttered.

About half way to the lighthouse, with the teenagers out of sight behind them, Diana headed for the water.

"Is it here?"

"No, it's farther west but these shoals go out over half a mile in places and I'd rather not be visible from shore for that long. I don't want to have to maintain a misdirection when we're wading waist deep."

"When *we're* wading?" Sam sniffed disdainfully at the mussel shells. "Lift me over this, would you."

"Actually," she bent and picked him up, settling his weight against her chest, "why don't I just carry you until we're in the water."

"Yeah, yeah." He sighed and adjusted his position slightly. "It's going to be cold."

"It's Lake Ontario, I don't think it ever gets warm. But don't worry, you won't feel it." As the water lapped against the beach gravel a centimetre from the toes of her shoes, Diana reached into the Possibilities and wrapped power around them. Then she stepped forward. "There's a nice wide channel here," she said, moving carefully over the flat rock. Sam would be completely unbearable if she missed her footing and a wave knocked them down. "We can follow the rift out to deep water and…"

The bottom dropped out from under her feet.

She stopped their descent before the channel grew uncomfortably narrow. The last thing she wanted was to get her foot stuck between two rocks while under three metres of Lake Ontario with a cranky cat. Well, maybe not the *last* thing she wanted—being forced to sit through a marathon viewing of Question Period ranked higher on the list but not by much.

Thanks to the zebra mussels, the water was remarkably clear—the one benefit of an invasive species that blocked intake pipes up and down the Great Lakes. Enough light made it down from the surface that they could easily see their way.

"Of course I could see anyway," Sam reminded her as she let him go. He swam slowly around her, hair puffing out from his body. "Cats see much better than humans in low light levels." A little experimentation proved he could use his tail as a rudder. "You know, when you don't have to get wet, swimming is kind of fun. Hey! Is that a fish!"

Since the fish was moving in the right direction and Sam didn't have a hope of catching it, Diana merely followed along behind, half her attention on the Summons and the other half on the cat.

"Sam, come on! This way! We've got to go deeper."

"How deep?" he demanded, scattering a small school of herring.

"Right to the bottom." She slipped one arm out of her backpack and swung it around so she could pull out her flashlight. "Now come on and stop bothering the fish."

"Something has them freaked."

"They probably don't get a lot of cats down here."

"I don't think it's me. Mostly, I seem to be confusing them."

"Welcome to the club."

"What?"

"Never mind." The water was definitely getting darker. Jade green now and, finally, a little murky. "If not you, what?"

"Something big."

"The sea serpent?"

He was back at her side so quickly that the impact sent her spinning slowly counter-clockwise. "Maybe."

Diana stopped the spin before her third revolution. A Keeper spinning three times counter-clockwise near an open accident site could have unpleasant—or at the very least unlikely—consequences.

"How can you have a sea serpent in a lake?" Sam snorted in a tone that said very clearly, *I wasn't scared so don't think for a moment I was.*

Diana shrugged. "I don't know. I guess because lake serpent sounds dumb."

"What's that?"

She turned the beam of the flashlight. A small piece of metal glinted on a narrow shelf of rock. "We should check it out."

"Is it part of the Summons?"

"Yes… No…" She started to swim. "Maybe." Feeling the faint tug of a current nearer the rocks, she half turned. "Stay close. I don't want you swept away."

He paddled a little faster and tucked up against her side. "Good. I don't want to *be* swept away."

"We're lucky it's so calm today. On a rough day with high waves, there's probably a powerful undertow through here."

"Don't want to be eaten by an under-toad," Sam muttered.

"Not under-toad. Undertow."

"You sure of that?"

Glancing down into the dark depths of the lake, Diana wasn't so, just to be on the safe side, she stopped thinking about it. The older Keepers got unnecessarily shirty about the accidental creation of creatures from folklore. As a general rule, the creatures weren't too happy about it either.

"It's the clasp off a chain purse." The leather purse itself had long rotted away. "Hang on…" Slipping two fingers down into a crack in the rock, she pulled out a copper coin, too corroded to be identified further.

"You should put that back."

A second coin. She tucked them both into the front pocket of her jeans.

"Okay, fine. Don't listen to the cat."

"I need them."

"What for?"

Good question. "I don't know yet. Come on."

"Come on?" Sam repeated, paddling with all four feet to keep up. "You say that like I was the one who paused to do a little grave robbing."

"First of all that wasn't a grave, and second," she continued before Sam could argue, "I haven't actually robbed anything since the coins are still here. In the water."

"In your pocket."

"That only counts if I take them away with me."

"So you've borrowed them?"

"More or less."

"Less," the cat snorted.

Diana let him have the last word. It was pretty much the only way to shut him up.

By the time they reached the bottom, the only illumination came from the flashlight. The water was a greenish-yellow, small particulates drifting through the path of the beam.

"Are we there yet?"

"A little further west."

The bottom was still mostly rock but there were patches of dirt supporting a few small weeds in spite of the depth. They followed a low ridge for close to half a kilometre, stopping when it rose suddenly to within a few metres of the surface.

"This is the place," Diana said, sweeping the light over the rock. "Somewhere close and... Sam, what are you doing?"

He was floating motionless, nose to nose with a good-sized herring. "Staring contest."

"You can't win."

"Cats always win."

"I don't think fish have eyelids."

Sam's tail started to lash, propelling him forward. "You cheater!"

Diana couldn't be sure but she thought the fish looked slightly sheepish as it turned and darted away. "Never mind that!" she yelled as Sam took off in pursuit. "We're right on top of the Summons so I'm thinking—given where we are—that we've got to find a wreck."

"In a minute!" Sam disappeared around the edge of the shoal. "I'm just gonna teach that cheating fish a..."

"Sam?"

"Found it."

"Found what?" Diana demanded as she swam after the cat. "Oh."

Much like Main Duck Island itself, the shoal rose almost into a nearly vertical underwater cliff on the north side but fell off in layers to the south. On one layer, about a metre and a half up from the bottom, the skeletal prow of an old wooden ship jutted out from the ridge, huge timbers held in place in the narrow angle between two slabs of canted rock and preserved by the cold of the water.

"Well this is..."

"Obvious," snorted Sam. "Big hunk of rock rising toward the surface.

Exposed wreck. Probably been a hundred divers down here every summer."

"Probably," Diana agreed swimming closer. "But this is where the hole is, I'm sure of it. Somebody did something sometime recently."

"Oh that's definitive," Sam sighed, following her in.

The hole she'd been Summoned to close was not part of the wreck but in the rock beside it where a narrow crevice cut down into the lake bed.

"Isn't the word hole usually more of a metaphorical description," Sam wondered as Diana floated head down and feet up, peering into the crevice.

"Usually. Still is mostly." The actual opening between this world and the nastier end of the Possibilities stretched out on both sides of the crevice but it was centered over the dark, triangular crack in the rock. "There's something down here."

"I'm guessing fish poo."

"And you'd be right."

"Eww."

"But something else too." Tucking the flashlight under her chin, Diana grabbed onto a rock with her left hand and snaked her right down into the crack. "Almost…"

"If you lose that hand, are you still going to be able to use a can opener?"

"I'm not going to lose the hand!"

"I'm just asking."

Sharp edges of rock dug into her arm as she forced her hand deeper, her jacket riding up away from her wrist. One finger tip touched… something. Even such a gentle pressure moved whatever it was away. A little further. Another touch. She managed to finally hook it between her first two fingers.

"Uh, Diana, about that sea serpent…"

"What about it?" She'd have to move her arm slowly and carefully out of the crack or she'd lose whatever she was holding.

"It's either heading this way from the other side of the wreck or the Navy's running a submarine in the Great Lakes."

"I pick option B."

"And you'd be wrong."

Time to yank; she could always pick the thing up again. Unfortunately, a sharp tug didn't free her arm. Upside, she managed to hang onto the thing. Downside, approaching sea serpent.

Wait! If her arm was stuck then she didn't need to hold the rock and if she didn't need to hold the rock…

She grabbed the flashlight and aimed the beam toward the wreck, hoping it would be enough. Pulling power from the Possibilities over a hole would not be smart, not considering where that hole lead. There were worse things than lake monsters out beyond the edges of reality.

Framed between two rotting timbers, green eyes flashed gold in the light. Mouth gaping, the sea serpent folded back on itself, and fled, the final flick of its triangular tail knocking a bit of board off the wreck.

"Looks bigger up close," Diana noted, trying to remember how to breathe.

"Ya think!" Sam snarled, paws and tail thrashing as he bobbed about in currents stirred up by the creature's passage.

"Maybe it was just curious."

"Sure it was. Because you get that big eating plankton!"

"Whales do."

"*Some* whales do and that was not a whale! That was a predator. I know a predator when I see one!"

Diana tucked the flashlight back under her chin and reached out to stroke the line of raised hair along Sam's spine—the Possibility that allowed them to move and breathe underwater granting the touch. "You're shouting."

He speared her with an amber gaze. "I don't want to be eaten by a sea serpent."

"Who does?"

"Who cares?" he snapped. "The point is, I don't. Let's get that hole closed and get back on dry land before I'm a canapé."

Diana had to admit he had a point, although she admitted it silently rather than give him more ammunition for complaints. The serpent was better than ten metres long and almost a metre in diameter. A five kilo cat would be barely a mouthful. The sooner she got the hole closed, the better.

Carefully, but as quickly as she could, she worked her right hand out of the crack and when it was finally free, dropped a fragment of bone into the palm of her left.

"The graveyard of Lake Ontario," Sam noted solemnly, his cinnamon nose nearly touching her hand. "There's more than just ships at rest down here."

"Not every body washed ashore," Diana agreed with a sigh. "I'm betting there's more of this body down in that crevice."

"You think it got smashed and that's what made the hole?"

"I think someone—probably someone diving around the wreck—smashed it, deliberately, and *that's* what made the hole."

"You need to get the rest of the bone out."

It wasn't a question but she answered it anyway. "I do."

"Great. Considering how long the first piece took, we're going to be down here forever and that serpent's going to come back and it's going to be kitties and bits. You're the bits," he added.

"Thanks, I got that. You're not usually this fatalistic."

"Hello? Lake monster. Cat at the bottom of Lake Ontario."

"You worry too much. Now that I've got one piece out I can call the rest to it. It'll be fast." She held the hand holding the bone out over the crack and Called. Other fragments floated up, danced in the water, and after a moment or two, formed most of a human jaw.

Suddenly conscious of being watched, Diana whirled around to see a herring hanging in the water. "What?"

Silver sides flashing, it swam about two metres away then stopped, turned and continued staring.

"Is that your friend from before?"

"We're not friends," Sam snorted. "Get on with it."

Diana studied the jaw. "There's a tooth missing."

Sam looked from the curved bone to the Keeper. "*A* tooth?"

"Okay, a bunch of teeth and the rest of the skeleton but right here… see where the reformed jaw is a different shade?" She touched it lightly with the tip of one finger. "There was a tooth in there until recently. Who ever did this, cracked the jaw and took the tooth."

"Why?"

"People'll notice if you come up from a dive with most of a jaw but you can hide a tooth."

Sam licked his shoulder thoughtfully, frowned when his tongue made no impression on his fur thanks to the Possibilities keeping him dry, and finally said, "Cats don't care about the things we leave behind."

"People do. Disturbing a body—even one this old—in order to get a souvenir is illegal, immoral, and kind of gross. So, now we have a problem."

"The lake monster."

"No."

Before she could continue, Sam shifted so he was almost vertical in the water and pointed upwards with one front paw. "Yes!"

A long line of undulating darkness passed between them and the surface, turned and passed again a little closer.

"Okay, problems. I need the tooth to close the hole."

"Great." Sam kept his eyes on the serpent, one pass closer still. "So call it."

Diana reached out and grabbed him as the lashing of his tail propelled him upwards. "Two problems with that. One, it might be locked away and not able to move freely and two we don't know how far away it is and staying down here indefinitely's really not an option. We need to go to it."

"And?"

"And that's not a problem given that we've got the rest of the jaw, we'll just follow it. The problem is, I can't pull from the Possibilities this close to the hole."

"So we leave and come back another day. And when I say we come back," Sam amended as he wriggled free and started swimming toward shore, "I mean you."

Diana grabbed him again. "Did I mention that the serpent has to go back through the hole before I close it? If we leave and come back, the serpent could be anywhere, not to mention that another serpent—or worse—could come through."

"You're just full of good news."

"But I have a plan."

"Oh joy."

"You won't like it."

He sighed. "Why am I not surprised?"

"I'm going to use the Possibilities that are keeping us dry and breathing."

"There's a problem with that." He squirmed around until he was looking her in the face. "They're keeping us dry and breathing."

"We take a deep breath and the next instant we'll be standing by the missing tooth."

"That doesn't sound so bad."

"We'll just be a little wet."

"When you say a little, you mean…"

"Completely."

He locked his claws in her jacket. "No."

"Would you rather be eaten by the lake monster?"

A glance toward the surface. The serpent was close enough that the broad band of lighter brown around its neck was visible. It seemed to be picking up speed with each pass, confidence growing as nothing opposed it.

"Sam?"

"I'm thinking."

There were teeth visible just inside the broad mouth. Rather too many teeth in Diana's opinion. Rather too many teeth suddenly facing them. And closing fast. Really, really fast. "Take a deep breath, Sam."

"I don't…"

"Now!"

And they were standing, dripping, in a basement workshop, the room barely lit by two low windows.

"I'm wet!" Claws breaking through denim to skin, Sam leapt out of Diana's arms and raced around the room spraying water from his sodden fur. "Wet! Wet! Ahhhhh! Wet!" Tail clamped tight to his body, he disappeared under the lower shelf of the workbench.

"Oh for…" Far enough from the hole that all Possibilities were open to her, Diana reached. "There. Now you're dry."

"I'm still sitting in a puddle," came a disgruntled voice from under the bench.

"So move." Taking her own advice, Diana stepped out of a puddle of her own and held out the jaw. "Can you hear that?"

"I have water in my ears."

"Sam!"

"Fine." He crawled out from under the bench, shook, and sat, head cocked. "I hear tapping."

"Can you find it?"

The look he shot her promised dire consequences.

"I'm sorry. *Would* you find it? Please." Not a compulsion, just a polite request. Compelling cats had much the same success rate as Senate reform, which was to say, none at all.

The tooth was in a small plastic box, tucked inside a red metal tool box, shoved to the back of an upper shelf.

"What's the point of having a souvenir no one can see?" Sam wondered as the tooth settled back into the jaw with an audible click.

"I guess the point's having it. Let's go."

"In a minute." He walked over to where a full wet suit hung on the wall, neoprene booties lined up neatly under it. Tail held high, he turned around.

"What are you doing?"

He looked up at her like she was an idiot and she supposed it was a pretty stupid question.

"Good aim," she acknowledged as he finished. "I just hope they don't have a cat that can be blamed when he puts that boot on next."

"They don't."

"You really got upset about him taking that tooth," she murmured bending and scooping him up.

"Please," he snorted settling into the crock of her arm. "I got *wet!*"

"Who are you?"

They stared at each other for a moment, and then Diana turned toward the piping voice.

A little girl, no more than five, stood in the open doorway, half hanging off the door knob. Behind her, a rec room empty but for a scattering of brightly coloured toys.

Diana glanced down at the jaw and smiled. "I'm the tooth fairy," she said, reached into the Possibilities and allowed the bone to pull them back to the wreck.

The serpent was nowhere in sight but since they hadn't been gone long, she figured it hadn't gone far. The trick would be getting it to come back.

"Sam! Now what are you doing?"

He paused, up on his hind legs, front claws embedded in a squared piece of timber. "Is that a trick question?"

"Just stop it."

"Fine." Sighing, he swam back over beside her. "Now what?"

"We need to lure the serpent back through the hole before I can close it."

"I refuse to be bait."

"I wasn't going to ask."

"Good."

She nodded at the lone herring watching from the shelter of the wreck. "I need you to talk to your friend."

"It's a fish."

"So?"

"It's not a friend, it's food."

"So you can't talk to it."

Whiskers bristled indignantly. "I didn't say that!"

"I need you to ask it to get a school together, get the serpent's attention, lure it back here, and peel away at the last minute so that the serpent goes through the hole rather than hitting the rock."

Sam stared at her. "You want me to convince fish to be bait? Why don't I just convince them to roll in breadcrumbs and lie down under a broiler?" The darker markings on his forehead formed a 'w' as he frowned. "Actually, that's not a bad idea."

"If they do this, the serpent will be gone and they'll be a lot safer."

"Provided he doesn't catch them and eat them."

"I'm not saying there isn't a risk. Just try."

As Sam swam over to the herring, Diana slid her back pack around onto her lap and undid the zipper. She needed something that would write under water on slippery, algae-covered rock. Pens, pencils, markers, bag of biodegradable kitty litter, litter box, six cans of cat food, two cat dishes, box of crackers, peanut butter, pajamas, clean jeans, socks, underwear, laptop; nothing that would work. The outside pockets held her cellphone, a bottle of slightly redundant water, and... a nail file. Possibly...

"She wants you to sweeten the deal."

"She does?" Diana glanced over at the herring. "How?"

"She wants you to get rid of the fish that suck the life out of other fish."

"There's vampire fish in this lake?" All at once, the dark corners under the rocks looked a little darker.

"Get real. They're called sea lampreys and they came into the lake after World War II and decimated the native populations. TVO special on the Great Lakes," he added when Diana blinked at him.

"Decimated?"

"It means ate most of."

"I *know* what it means."

"Hey, you asked," he snorted. "What do you say? They're not supposed to be here, no one would miss them, and you can't lure the serpent without herring cooperation. She just wants her fry to be safe." He paused and licked his lips.

"You're thinking about fried fish, aren't you?"

"Yeah."

"Well, stop." If she gave the herring what she wanted, Diana knew there'd be consequences. More healthy native species of fish in the lake for one thing. Actually, more healthy native species of fish in the lake was about the only thing. She couldn't see a downside—which was always vaguely unsettling.

"You can't do it, can you?"

"Of course I can do it." It was disconcerting that her cat was using the same argument on her that she'd used on him. "Technically, as a Keeper, if I'm asked for help to right a wrong, I can't refuse and sea lampreys in the lake seem to be definitely a wrong."

"So what's the problem?"

"I'm not sure fish were included under that rule."

"Very anti-ichthyoid of you."

"Anti-what? Never mind." She waved off his explanation. "You're watching way too much television. Okay, tell her I'll do it but it has to be after the hole is closed. I can't access the Possibilities until then."

"She wants to know why she should trust you."

Diana glanced over at the herring. "Because I'm one of the good guys."

"She only has your word for that."

"Sam!"

"Okay, okay, she didn't say that. You get to work; I'll convince her you're trustworthy."

"Thank you." Setting the jawbone carefully aside, Diana began to scratch the definitions of the accident site onto the rocks around the hole with the point of her nailfile, the algae just thick enough for it to leave a legible impression.

"Incoming!"

"I'm almost done."

"Maybe you don't quite understand what incoming means," Sam shouted as the first herring whacked into her shoulder.

Diana scrambled to get the last definition drawn in the midst of a silver swirl of fish and dove out of the way in the instant of clear water that followed.

Given a choice between diving face first into rock or returning back where it had come from, the serpent chose the second, less painful, option.

The instant the tip of its wedge shaped tail disappeared, Diana grabbed the definitions and slammed the hole closed. When she looked up, three dozen silver faces stared back at her, all wearing the same expectant expression. Well, probably expectant; it was surprisingly hard to judge expression on a fish.

"Okay, okay, give me a minute to catch my breath." She tested the seal on the hole and reached into the Possibilities. Turned out there were a lot of sea lamprey in the lake and over half of them had to be removed from living prey.

"Where'd you put them?" Sam spun around in a slow circle, lazily sculling with his tail.

"I dropped them in the Mid-Atlantic."

"There are sharks in the Mid-Atlantic."

"So?"

"Sharks eat lampreys."

"Sharks eat Volkswagens. What's your point?"

"We've been down here for hours, we missed lunch, and I'm hungry. Can we go now?"

"In a minute, I have one more thing to do."

It was only a part of a jawbone but once it had been a part of a man who'd sailed the lake.

Diana set the bone down beside the wreck and waited.

He hadn't been very old. Under his knit cap, his hair was brown, long enough to wisp out over his ears and there was a glint of red in his bad teenage moustache. He was wearing blue pants with a patch on one knee. His heavy sweater looked a little too big for him but that may have been because he was wearing it over at least one other sweater, maybe two. At some point, not long before he'd died, he'd whacked the index finger on his left hand, leaving the nail black and blue.

Pulling the two copper coins from her pocket, Diana bent and laid one on each closed eye. "To pay the ferryman," she said feeling Sam's unasked question. "He's been in the water long enough, I think he'd like to be back on it."

A heartbeat later, there was only the wreck and the rocks.

The coins and the jawbone were gone.

"Now can we go?"

Diana slung her backpack over one shoulder and picked up the cat with her other hand. "Yes. Now we can go."

—•—

Carol Diamond was standing on the shore when she came out of the water. Her eyes were wide and her mouth worked for a moment before any sound emerged. "You went... you were... in the..."

"I went wading."

"Wading?"

"Yes. You saw me wading. Then I came out of the water..." Diana stepped over the ridge of zebra mussel shells and set Sam down on the gravel. "...and I rolled down my jeans and put my shoes and socks back on."

White curls bounced as she shook her head. "You were under the water!"

"Couldn't have been. I'm completely dry."

"But you…"

"But I what?" Diana held the older woman's gaze.

"You went wading?"

"Yes, I did."

"But that water must be freezing!"

"I hardly felt it."

"Well," Carol laughed a little uncertainly, "it must be nice to be young. Doesn't that rock look just like an orange cat?"

"You think? I don't see it."

Sam sighed and headed for the dock.

Ryan sat between the two girls on the way back to the mainland. There was a fair bit of giggling from all concerned.

The lake was calm, the silvered blue broken only by the wake of the boat and a small school of herring rising to feed on the water bugs dimpling the surface.

Sam had eaten then curled up and gone to sleep in her backpack. Dangling a bottle of water from one hand, Diana leaned back against the gunnels and listened to Gary Spraum list just some of the more than fifty ships that had gone down between Point Petre and Main Duck Island. She didn't know which ship her sailor had been from, but it didn't really matter.

He was home now.

"The *Metcalfe*, the *Maggie Hunter*, the *Gazelle*, the *Norway*, the *Atlas*, the *Annie Falconer*, the *Olive Branch*, the *Sheboygan*, the *Ida Walker*, the *Maple Glenn*, the *Lady Washington*…"

"*The loup-garou is the Canadian counterpart of the European werewolf (literally man-wolf)—a human being transformed into a wolf or able to assume wolf form. The superstition came to New France with the first settlers: the voyageurs believed in it, and it came to be confused with the Wendigo of the Algonkian Indians.*"

From:
Folktales of French Canada (1979)
edited by Edith Fowke, Copyright © 1979 by Edith Fowke,
NC Press Ltd., Toronto.

Walking with Wolves

by
Alison Baird

Madeleine stood very still, her eyes on the wolf. He was not a stone's throw away from her, watching her as intently as she was watching him. The seconds dragged on: Madeleine couldn't run, or utter a sound. She stood paralyzed, her heart thudding against her ribs. Oh, she had been warned before not to wander in the forest alone, especially when the sun was going down. She'd been cautioned a dozen times at least, and now—now that it was too late—she wished she'd paid heed to her parents' warnings.

She could not shout for help. Around her lay nothing but trees, a primal immensity of virgin forest. Her settlement could not even be seen from here; it might not exist, nor the entire colony of New France for that matter. Coming to this remote glade had always given Madeleine a peculiar thrill, half fear and half pleasure, as though she had stepped back in time to that earlier age of unsettled wildness, and stood in it all alone…

Oh, how could she have been such a fool!

The wolf still had not moved. He was huge, nearly as big as a donkey, with fur so dark as to be almost black. There was about him an arrogant majesty that took her breath away, even in the midst of her fear. He studied her with his great golden eyes, his sharp ears angled forward, his black nose quivering as he drew in her scent. And now, slowly, he advanced upon her. Still she could not stir, but stood transfixed as he walked all around her, staring and snuffing. She waited for the snarl and flurry of his attack.

But the great beast merely nudged her arm with his muzzle, sniffed, then withdrew again. Madeleine stared at him in amazement. He wasn't going to hurt her, after all. Why—he was just like a dog—a big dog! She expelled a long breath, her fear suddenly evaporating, and spoke to him softly, watching the way his ears pricked and swivelled to hold the sound of her voice.

"Madeleine! *Madeleine!*" The voices of her father and her brother Baptiste rang out suddenly through the trees behind her.

The wolf turned and made off—not in fearful haste, but rather in a leisurely manner that suggested he did not care for the company of those approaching. In a moment he was gone, his black fur blending into the twilight under the trees.

"Where have you been, girl?" demanded her father, crashing through the underbrush. "You know we don't like you wandering so far in the woods after sundown."

"I didn't mean to go far, Papa—honestly I didn't. And then I saw a wolf, and I didn't like to run from him, in case he chased me."

"A *wolf!*" Baptiste exclaimed, stopping short. "You saw a wolf?"

"Yes—a big black one. But he didn't hurt me. He was quite friendly, like a dog."

"You're a terrible liar, Madeleine," said her younger brother frowning. "You never saw any wolf. Wolves are *fierce*—if you'd come across one he'd have eaten you up in an instant."

"I'm not a liar!" Madeleine protested, indignant.

"Well then, maybe you saw a fox or something, and thought it was a wolf."

"You think I'd not know a wolf from a fox!"

"That's enough now," said their father, coming between them. "This is the last time I'm warning you, Madeleine. Never go into the woods after dark!"

Madeleine looked down at the ground. "I promise."

They walked on to the settlement together in silence. Madeleine knew that she was in disgrace. But she loved the forest so, found its allure impossible to resist. She went to it whenever she could, wandering off the well-trodden tracks into the green inner groves, watching with interest the cautious comings and goings of the animals that lived there. She loved it in spring and in summer and even in the winter, when the boughs were bent under the weight and strange enchantment of the snow. But it was never more beautiful than now, with the autumn painting it in brilliant colours—red, copper, orange, and all the wondrous hues of the sugar maples. The air was clear and cool in her nostrils, with a faint tang of woodsmoke. She had finally yielded to its enticements this evening, walking further and further into the trees and paying no attention to the gathering dusk.

At night the forest was another place altogether, a mass of shifting shadows and mysterious sounds. Her parents had told her eerie stories of it, tales spun from those shadows on winter evenings by the fire. There were savage beasts in it, they said, and natives with bows and arrows, and other things that did not belong to the daylight world at all: the imp-like *lutins* who would mischief you if they caught you alone, and the *feux-follets* which glimmered like ghostly lanterns through the night, luring unwary travelers off safe paths toward pits and precipices. And there was the werewolf, the *loup-garou*, who was more fearsome still: for though he prowled the forest of nights in his wolf-shape, howling with his ancient hunger, by day he wore a human form—might even be your own neighbour…

There were dark and nameless terrors, too, that only the natives knew about. This was an alien forest, not altogether reconciled to its newer inhabitants: at sundown it seemed to grow larger, becoming dark and immense as the night itself, full of rustlings like conspiratorial whispers. Now as Madeleine and her father and brother picked their way slowly through the dusky wood, its shadows and murmurs made them draw a little closer to one another. When a voice hailed them suddenly from its depths, they all three jumped violently.

"Ah, mes amis! Good evening to you!"

Madeleine and her brother turned to stare at the group of tall, rugged-looking men strolling easily through the underbrush. They looked like, surely they must be—

"Coureurs de bois!" said Baptiste excitedly. Madeleine too gazed

for all she was worth: the *coureurs*, after all, were famous throughout New France. Paddling the rivers of the wilderness in their birch bark canoes, the fearless fur-traders braved all the dangers of the wild to obtain beaver-pelts for the big markets in Montréal, purchasing them from the natives in exchange for ornaments of silver. They were incomparable woodsmen too, rivalling even the natives in woodcraft, living a glamorous life of risk and adventure. But most of the *habitants* in the settlements now frowned upon the *coureurs de bois*, and said they were irresponsible rovers who lured young men away from farming. Many traded without a license, and they were wild and often drunk when they visited the villages, singing their rollicking ballads all night long and brawling playfully with each other and with the natives who often accompanied them. When sober they carried themselves like princes, looking at the *habitants* with pitying disdain.

Madeleine felt her heartbeat accelerate at the sight of the leader, a man she had often seen before, watching him surreptitiously when he was not looking her way. He was in his early thirties, tall but not heavy of build, with a dark bushy beard and bold brown eyes. That beard, it looked so soft, and the face above it was so comely! He wore a red shirt, open at the neck, and brown trousers and boots of caribou-hide. She knew his name, though she had never exchanged a word with him: this was Alain Dulac, whose exploits were legendary even among the *coureurs*.

"Well met, friend," he greeted her father amiably. "And you would be—?"

"Jean-Paul Cadieux," replied her father guardedly.

"Cadieux!" Dulac raised one dark brow. "Then this lovely young *demoiselle* would be your daughter. The little Wild Girl I've heard so much about." The brown eyes twinkled at Madeleine. "You like the forest, *hein*?"

"Oh yes," she exclaimed, forgetting her shyness. "I go to it whenever I can."

"So do I. I'm more often in the woods than within doors. The forest is my home, you might say. Have you ever lain out all night, Madeleine, with the stars for a ceiling? I have."

"Aren't you afraid of the Indians?" asked Baptiste, wanting to be noticed too. "There are so many hereabouts, and not all of them are friendly."

"The Indians?" Alain threw back his head and laughed. "No, the Indians and I understand one another. I don't meddle with them, and they don't meddle with me."

He was magnificent, thought Madeleine. He wasn't at all afraid. To be able to speak with him, after watching him so often from a distance, filled her with delight.

"And you, Madeleine?" Dulac pressed. "Is it true what they say— that you're not really your father's daughter?" He looked inquiringly at Jean-Paul, who relinquished the tale with reluctance. Madeleine listened only absently as they all marched onward through the wood: it was a tale that she had heard often before, and she preferred to give her attention to Alain.

"...It is sixteen years ago, now, that I went out with my brother and some other men of the settlement to hunt in the forest. There were two wolves with a litter of cubs that we had to kill, before they went after our livestock. It did not take us long to find them, the grown wolves lying with their cubs before their den: we shot them all, one by one.

"Then I heard a rustling noise in the den. Another cub, or so I thought: and I drew nearer, my gun at the ready. The rustling sounds came closer, but I did not shoot yet—and it is a mercy I did not. For out of the den came not a wolf-cub but a human child! It was a little girl, barely old enough to stand, and all naked. My friends and I congratulated one another on having saved the poor babe from being devoured by the beasts, which must have carried her to their lair. But when we took her away with us she began to wail, like an infant taken from its mother, and suddenly I realized the truth: this child must have been raised by the wolves in their den!

"I could scarcely believe it myself at first, but old Père Joseph agreed with me, and told me that such things had been known to happen before. He believed that Madeleine's good angel intervened for her, instructing the wild wolves to care for the child until such time as members of her own race should deliver her."

"And nothing was ever discovered of her own family," said Dulac. It was a statement rather than a question.

"Nothing. I think they must have been travellers, passing through the woods, and been set upon by Indians or wild animals and killed. No one ever came here to the settlement inquiring after a lost child, and though we asked far and wide, sending messages to other settlements, no one in the region knew of one. So Père Joseph asked if we could take in little Madeleine, as we came to call her, and we did."

"What an extraordinary tale!" Dulac looked at Madeleine. "And so that is why you aren't afraid of the beasts in the forest—you came from there, yourself!"

"Yes—and I saw a wolf this very evening, farther back in the woods, and he really was friendly—" Madeleine began eagerly, but her father now turned to her and Baptiste with a curt, "Come, now—home!"

Madeleine had to obey. But she was very aware of Alain Dulac's eyes upon her as she unwillingly walked away.

—•—

Ville Ste. Marie was perhaps the smallest and humblest settlement in all New France. It had a single dirt road where pigs and chickens roamed and gossips gathered, and a little wooden church that stood in the centre of the few houses almost protectively, like a fowl in the midst of her brood. The dwellings were all of wood, any chinks in their walls crudely stopped with clay, their roofs slanting steeply so that the snow would slide off in winter. The farming fields that ran down to the river's edge were long, narrow strips of land, the original fields granted by the *Seigneur* having been divided up many times among the heirs of each family. Madeleine's home was no different from any of the others. There were only three rooms in the house, a stove in each one for heating. All the furnishings were of wood and very plain.

As she sat beside the window now, looking at her reflection in the panes, Madeleine told herself over and over not to be foolish. Of course Alain did not really find her attractive. She was not at all pretty, Madeleine: her eyes were dark and her hair black and tangled and her skin was browned with sun. Some of the visitors to the settlement had actually taken her for a native. No one had made her an offer of marriage, though she was all of seventeen; men's eyes did not linger on Madeleine, and the woman looked askance at her: Cadieux's wild daughter from the woods.

It was just as well, she told herself defiantly. Her heart had always grown heavy at the thought of being married—of having to spend more time within doors, and not being able to go off to the woods all by herself. The forest was calling to her now as she sat here, staring into the night beyond the reflection of the hearth-fire. The shadows of her parents and siblings passed to and fro in the window, insubstantial as ghosts next to the reality of sky and trees and distant hills. She liked this window best, because from it one could see no houses at all.

Presently a bell rang clearly through the dusk, and her parents and little siblings—Baptiste and Marie-Claire—all set down what they were doing in answer to its summons. It was the bell of L'Eglise de Notre Dame, calling them to vespers. Her mother, Céleste, gathered them all together, and the family set off through the evening for the little wooden church.

As they drew near they noticed Alain Dulac and his companions perching at their ease on a fence and singing snatches of woodland songs.

"You should be in church," Céleste rebuked them.

"What? Go indoors, on a night like this?" Dulac retorted. He pointed toward the northern sky, where the auroras glimmered like many-coloured curtains waving in a wind. "See! The heavens themselves dance to our music!" His companions burst into song again.

"Come along," ordered Jean-Paul roughly, noticing that Baptiste too was gazing at the men in open admiration. "You *coureurs*, if you really wanted to make yourselves useful you could join us in the hunt tomorrow, and help us kill that wolf."

"Why, what terrible crime has this wolf committed?" asked Alain, amused.

"It is not what he has done, but what he will do to our livestock if we do not stop him," retorted Jean-Paul.

Alain roared with laughter. "So! He is to be executed without trial, for something he hasn't yet done? Poor fellow!" Jean-Paul turned from him in disgust.

They reached the church door and joined the other villagers inside. As she knelt in the pew Madeleine lifted her eyes to the carved figure of the Virgin, robed in blue with the infant Christ in the crook of her arm. They gazed down at her wisely, the mother who was a virgin and the child who was not a child, and for an instant she felt there might be some hope for her, a power she might appeal to. *Please don't let me have to marry, don't take my freedom away...* she prayed. But then the wooden figures were eclipsed by the tall frame of the priest, as he took his place in the sanctuary. Kindly old Père Joseph had died last winter, and this new priest, Père Antoine, had a stern face and a voice that was harsh and resonant with authority. When the time for the sermon came he glared out upon the congregation from the pulpit.

"My children, evil times are upon us, with the coming of these wolves that would invade our settlement and fill us all with fear." Heads in the congregation nodded gravely. "But beware, good people," Antoine continued, "of that worse evil that lurks within, not without! Beware the wolf who comes to raven the flock of the Lord! For from the fangs of that foe there can be no deliverance, when once your hearts have been corrupted and placed under his sway! Cast out evil, therefore, and beware the wolf that seeks, not your life, but your soul; the wolf whose name is Satan!"

A silence fell over the villagers. Shadows seemed to lurk all around them inside the dim church, lit only by stove and candles: furtive shades moved beyond the reach of the light. And when they rose at the service's end, the shadows arose with them and followed them out into the night, making them walk closer together than before, and speak only in whispers.

And suddenly, without warning, those shadows of fear seemed to come to malevolent life: slinking shapes appeared all around them, moving just beyond the light of their lamps. Everywhere they turned there were pale eyes gleaming in the dark, star-like clusters of watchful luminous orbs. An entire pack of wolves stood all about them on the road!

Women and children screamed; men cursed and wished for the weapons they had left behind in their houses. The *coureurs* were long since gone from their fence: there was no one to help them.

Only Madeleine felt no fear. As if in a dream or a trance, she found herself walking forward—found she was not at all afraid. Her empty hands were held out before her. People were shouting behind her, but she paid them no heed. Her eyes were on the wolves… in particular, on an immense black one who sat on his haunches at the head of the pack, with the calm assurance of a leader. As she approached he rose to all fours, coming forward to meet her.

"Please," she found herself saying. "Please go away—you must go away." The shadow-shapes milled to and fro. The big black wolf gazed at her thoughtfully, his massive head thrust forward, his eyes intent. She looked past the lamplight reflected in those eyes, to the depths where a more than lupine intelligence seemed to gleam. "Go," she said again. "They'll hunt you, kill you all. Please, you must leave this place!"

The wolf looked long at her; then he turned, as he had done in the wood, and made off unhurriedly into the dark. The other wolves followed him.

A strange forbidding silence had descended. Madeleine turned to see the villagers all staring at her; and when she walked toward them they retreated, as if in fear.

"Come, Madeleine," said Céleste at last in a low uncertain voice, taking her daughter by the hand. "Let us go home."

Madeleine could feel all those eyes at her back as she turned to obey. They chilled her as the eyes of the wolves had not.

—•—

Next morning Madeleine noticed the sidelong glances, the conversations that ceased abruptly whenever she approached. She saw the way the matrons snatched their children out of her path with quick, hissed warnings. And she was aware of something beyond all these things; an atmosphere of steadily increasing tension, like that before the onset of a storm. Whispers followed her, everywhere she went.

"… and the big wolf in front, did you see? He was black—as black as coal! The Devil always appears as a black animal, so my mother told me…"

"No, he was a *loup-garou*! The men went into the forest today, along with the *coureurs,* to hunt for the wolves—but they found nothing there! And why do you think that was?"

"What are you saying?"

"This Dulac man and his followers: they *are* the wolves! They were nowhere to be seen last night when the wolf-pack attacked; today they reappear, and suddenly there are no wolves! Can it be coincidence? They are werewolves, all of them; and now they have Jean-Paul's girl under their spell..."

Madeleine stayed indoors for the rest of the day, her head bent over a pile of mending, half-afraid to meet the eyes of her own family members lest they, too, should be filled with fear and suspicion. When at last the evening came she slipped quietly out the back door and leaned against the wall of the house, shutting her eyes and breathing in the cool leaf-scented air.

"Madeleine?" said a voice.

She opened her eyes. "Alain!" He was there, leaning over the wooden fence.

"I've heard all about your exploit last night, *ma petite.* The girl who walks and talks with wolves!"

"I—I don't know what came over me. And now everyone thinks I'm a witch, and you're a werewolf!"

He grinned. "You don't say!"

She suddenly noticed that he was carrying all his gear. "Alain— you're not going away?"

He raised a bushy brow. "You sound as though you were sorry."

A sudden shadow of doubt touched her mind, driving all her other worries away. "You *have* got a license to trade, haven't you?" she asked anxiously.

"A license, what's that?" he asked with a look of exaggerated innocence.

"*Alain*! You know how the King feels about controlling the fur trade—the authorities have been told to *execute* anyone who goes off into the woods now without a license!"

"Indeed! And who are these gentlemen that I should do all they say? The King's only a man, after all—a man who lives in another land, far away across the sea. What has he to do with me, or I with him? You and I, Madeleine, we're free spirits—we don't live by other people's rules."

Madeleine, despite herself, felt a fierce longing come over her at those words. "I wish I could be a *coureur de bois*," she said wistfully. "I'm sure I could hunt and paddle a canoe as well as anyone, and learn the ways of the woods. Instead I have to stop here at home and do the washing and mending and baking like—like an old woman."

His eyes were fixed on hers, curiously intent. "Then come with me."

Madeleine felt she had not heard aright. "Come—with you!"

"Come with me—to the forest. See the wilderness, Madeleine—with me."

"Oh, don't tease—I can't bear it!" She turned angrily away.

He vaulted the fence lightly, took her by the shoulders. "I mean it."

She whirled, staring up at him. "But I couldn't just—go off with you—it would make a scandal, people would say we ought to be wed—" she said feebly. "I'm in enough trouble as it is—"

"Why, then we'll wed," said Alain carelessly. "But not in *this* place. Come with me and we'll find a missionary in the woods somewhere who'll marry us."

"But—I must have Papa's consent—"

"Consent! Yours is the only consent that matters." The brown eyes laughed and she looked away. Was he only jesting after all? She pulled free of his hands and fled back into the house.

"Madeleine!" she heard Alain call after her. "My friends and I, we're going upriver. If you come after us, you'll find us in the woods further up, around the bend."

"And what was all that shouting about?" demanded Céleste as Madeleine rushed indoors.

She stood there in the centre of the room, her chest heaving. "Maman—Alain Dulac—he says he wants me to marry him!"

"Are you mad?" cried Céleste, throwing down the shirt she was mending. "He's thoroughly unsuitable, that one! He'll never give any wife of his a roof for her head and a home for her children. Most likely he means to abandon you in the woods once he's tired of you. Oh, he's handsome enough, but he's no good, no good at all."

Jean-Paul arose from where he had been sitting by the fire. "Madeleine will not be marrying anyone. I have been talking to Père Antoine, and we have both agreed that the best thing for Madeleine now is to send her upriver, to a convent in Montréal."

Madeleine stood dumbstruck for the space of a second, her mouth wide open. Then in three long strides she crossed the room to stand before her father. "I'll never go to a convent, Papa! Never!" she cried passionately.

"Madeleine!" exclaimed Céleste, scandalized. "How dare you talk to your father that way? He knows what's best for you. And if no one in the settlement will have you for a wife, that's your own fault for behaving the way you do. Always running off to the woods—after dark, too! There've been rumours that you have an Indian lover, an Indian who teaches you witchcraft—"

"What!"

"How can you blame the gossips for making up such tales? If you'd only behaved like a respectable young woman..." She looked pointedly at the girl's long dishevelled hair, in which a fallen leaf hung tangled.

"I won't go to a convent! I would die in a place like that—surrounded by walls!" She knew, deep down, that she was going too far, but her emotions had hold of her and they swept her along in their reckless flow.

Jean-Paul turned to her, really angry now. "You'll do as I tell you, or I'll take a birch rod to you as I did when you were six. It would do you good to be in a place where you *must* obey the rules."

Madeleine's face worked, but she made no reply: wilful though she might be, there yet was something in her that was always quelled by authority. Dropping her eyes, she went silently to her corner by the window. Her inner resolve, however, had only hardened at her father's words. She could no longer stay here. What had Alain said? Something about the men going further upriver, if she wanted to follow them. She suppressed the little whisper of unease that arose in her at the thought. *I'll go there when it gets dark—I'll find my way through the woods to their camp. Alain may love me and he may not, but it's better than going to a convent...*

A low murmur came from the opposite end of the house: her

mother was telling Marie-Claire a story. "…All the guests were assembled when there came a knock at the door; and in walked a handsome, bearded stranger with a fine beaver cloak and caribou moccasins…"

She knew this tale; it was an old one, that she'd heard many times. There were some in the settlement who would swear that it had actually happened: to a cousin of theirs, or a friend in another settlement, up the river…

"…The fiddler played merrily as they danced the jig. Young Blanche was flattered that the handome stranger wished only to dance with her. But when he offered her a jewelled locket in exchange for the simple cross she wore at her neck, she guessed the truth at last. It was the Devil himself! Quickly, she ran to her room for the holy water she kept there…"

Céleste had raised her voice, and Madeleine sensed that this particular story was aimed at her. Did Maman suspect the plan that was forming in her mind?

"…and *le Diable*, he drove away in a rage, in his sleigh with the big black horse whose hooves left a trail of fire. So all young ladies must beware: one never knows if a handsome swain might not be Satan himself!"

Madeleine turned her gaze toward the window, watching the trees grow black against the sky, and closed her ears to her mother's voice.

—•—

She left when she was sure the others were sleeping, stealing out like a thief and closing the door very softly behind her. Once outside she was seized with misgivings. To leave her family, the security of home—was she mad? Wandering off into the woods was all very well, but she had always been comfortably aware that she could return to the settlement when she wished. To set off alone, into the wild world—!

With an effort she thrust her fears aside. She would have been sent away in any case: the choice, she reminded herself, was not between Alain and home, but between freedom and the confines of the cloister. She blinked back angry tears, and set off through the night with a swift determined stride. A full moon hung above the trees, lighting her way.

It was adventure that awaited her now, and the freedom she had always yearned for. But once she had got deeper into the forest she began to be afraid. It was so very dark, with the moonlight muted by the branches; so full of furtive sounds, of shadows that seemed to be stalking her ...

Madeleine froze. No, it wasn't her imagination. There *were* shadows moving alongside her—following her through the trees. She could hear the sound of their breathing, the sound of stealthy feet.

"Alain?" she called softly.

There was no reply.

"Alain—is that you? Don't play games with me, please!"

And then she came into a glade, where the moon shone down upon her, and she saw her companions clearly.

Wolves! A dozen of them at least, walking silently behind and before and all about her. Their musky smell filled the air, their moonlit eyes glimmered through the screens of leaves. She halted, watching them tensely. Would they let her be, as they had done before? Or were they preparing to attack her?

And now some dream or fever seemed to seize her brain, for looking ahead of her she saw the familiar figure of Alain Dulac, coming toward her from the depths of the forest. Walking right through the midst of the wolves without fear. Her mouth moved, shaping his name.

"Yes, Madeleine," he said simply. "It is I."

She gave a choking cry compounded of relief and bewilderment. "Oh, Alain—I've run away—I've come to be with you—but Alain, the wolves: how is it they don't attack us?"

"These are my friends." He smiled. "I too was raised among wolves—these very wolves, in fact. This is my pack: we go everywhere together."

"You *too*!" Madeleine gasped. "But—how incredible! You never told me—"

"Little Madeleine! I think you do not understand, even now." He stood beneath the shadow of a tree, where the moonlight did not touch him; she could not see his face. "I walk freely among them because I am one of them, because they know their kin." And then he was gone, like a shadow when the moon is covered in cloud; and in his place there stood the great black wolf.

She cried out, and the wolf in its turn melted back into the man. He came toward her again, and she retreated in voiceless terror.

"I have sought you for years," he told her softly. "I know well the wolf-den from which you were taken." He drew nearer still. As before, when she had encountered him as a wolf in the wood, she was seized with a strange paralysis. He smiled again; white teeth flashed in the moonlight. "I am a werewolf, Madeleine. A *loup-garou*. I and my friends, we have come for you."

"No—no!" she screamed.

And then she was running—but wildly, hopelessly. The forest was so very dark, she could not see where she was going. Where were the lights of the settlement? Branches clawed her and caught at her clothes: she beat them back in panic, knowing all the while that she could never hope to outrun her pursuers.

Madeleine stumbled, fell her length upon the ground. She lay there unmoving, like a deer run to earth, hearing the running paws and panting breaths of the wolves. She must go with them, or be torn to pieces if she refused... Ah, why hadn't she listened to the warnings of Céleste and the priest—?

Then there were footsteps approaching, the footsteps of a man; and a hand was on her hair, stroking it. She lay silent and unresisting.

"I will tell you a story, Madeleine," Alain's voice said in her ear. "A story of a group of men who came upon a den of wolves many years ago. Little did they know that these were no ordinary wolves: they could take on human forms when they wished to. How, I cannot tell you: for the time when wolves and men came together lies far back, at the beginning of the world... In any case, this wolf-family's powers were of no use to them, for the attack was swift and sudden and they died before they had a chance to change their shapes. The only one to survive was a little she-wolf cub, who had not yet left the den.

"She cowered there in terror, not knowing what to do. She had never yet tried to put on a human form. Then the men came closer, and in desperation she made her attempt, in haste and without skill; reasoning that the human creatures would not harm one of their own kind, she became a human child. But a human infant is not so wide-awake and aware as is a wolf-cub. The little she-wolf lost her memory when the transformation was made: when she was taken away by the men she soon forgot that she had ever had another life.

"My friends and I meant the villagers no harm—it was not their lives or their animals we sought, but you. Our pack has searched for you for years, up and down the river, in man-form and wolf-form, ever since we first heard of your family's death, and that one of their cubs was missing. You were never meant to live a human life, Madeleine: you were made to be free, like us."

It was strange, but the forest no longer seemed dark to her; a pale light filled it now, each leaf and blade of grass standing distinct before its own sharp shadow. A thousand scents, a myriad of sounds she had not noticed before overwhelmed Madeleine's nostrils, sang in her ears. She rose, clumsily, saw beneath her in the moonlight two grey furred forelegs, two wolf's paws. The big black wolf now stood where Alain had been, and as she watched he turned around and loped off through the trees.

She stood on her strong, new legs, staring about her: she could see, now, where the lamps of the settlement glimmered yellow through the trees. A cry burst from her at the sight, long and forlorn; but the howl tapered into silence, and was not repeated.

Turning, she bounded away through the trees: awkwardly at first, then with a growing grace, while around her in the forest rose the moon-music of the wolves.

My first exposure to music from Martha and the Muffins'
This Is the Ice Age was on the radio when I was fifteen or
sixteen. The track "Women around the World at Work" was
on heavy rotation on CHOM-FM here in Montreal, and it's
one of the songs that first got me interested in post-punk
New Wave. When I finally bought the album, it rapidly
became one of my favourites.

I played the album obsessively. It haunted me. Its
sinuous rhythms, its surreal atmosphere, and its gorgeously
imaginative and playful lyrics utterly seduced me.

My story "This Is the Ice Age" is not the first time I've
been inspired by the music from _This Is the Ice Age_. In
college, for a free-form dance class, I created a one-man
choreography based on "You Sold the Cottage" for my final
exam. The teacher was so moved by my passion and
enthusiasm that she gave me a perfect mark. Or maybe she
just liked the song. It's great music.

Although most of this story was inspired (obviously) by
the album's title song, other tracks contributed to the mix.
The aural mood of the entire album is reflected by the
struggle between warmth and cold at the heart of my story.

— Claude Lalumière
Montreal, winter 2006

Source:
This Is the Ice Age (1981) by Martha and the Muffins,
Copyright © 1981 by Martha and the Muffins,
rereleased 2005 by EMI Music Canada.

This Is the Ice Age

by
Claude Lalumière

Distorted cars litter the bridge, quantum ice fractalling outwards from their engines, from the circuits of their dashboards. The ice has burst from their chassis, creating random new configurations of ice, technology, and anatomy.

There was no warning. In one moment the world changed: this is the ice age.

On our bicycles, Mark and I zigzag through the permanently stalled traffic. I try not to stare at the damaged bodies. But Mark is too engrossed to notice my queasiness. Too giddy. Goofy, even. For so many reasons, we were right to leave. Already, his face is brighter.

"Hey, Martha … Did you see that couple in the blue SUV?"

I wish I hadn't: ice snaked around their heads, crushing them together.

"Did you see—"

No, I didn't see. I don't look. At least I try not to. Mark copes in his own way; I can't fault him for doing it differently. He never told me how he lost his parents, and I never told him how I lost mine. I should be numb to such sights by now. In the city, they'd become part of the landscape; we'd ignored them. We'd been too cold to notice. Too cold to care. Barely out of the city, and already we're both thawing—at least a little.

I can't bring myself to tell him to stop. So I just pedal faster. I race off the Jacques Cartier Bridge onto the highway, where the number of cars on the road decreases with distance, leaving Montreal behind, heading for …

… For a new world? Maybe. A different world, at least. I just want us to belong somewhere.

People say the whole planet is like this now. But how can they be sure? Nothing works anymore. No television, no telephones, no computers, no radios. There's no way to communicate.

But they must be right. If the rest of the world were still intact, someone would have rescued us by now. The Army. The United States. Someone. Anyone.

"Martha!"

I look back, and Mark is pedalling hard to catch up to me.

I love how the wind lifts his long, dark hair. His smile is like a little boy's. Already, I've forgiven him for being so morbid, for being so wrapped up in his grotesque passion that he couldn't notice my distress.

Since I've known him, Mark has always protected me. Now he's relaxing about that. I like him even more this way.

He catches up to me, and we stop. We gaze at the transmuted cityscape we are leaving behind.

The sunlight's reflection almost blinds me; ice blankets the Island of Montreal. The skyscrapers of the financial district have been transformed into macabre, twisted spires. The tall downtown hotels bulge with ice—the tumorous limbs of a tentacled leviathan. Like a bed of gems, the city catches the sunlight and glows. Even the heat generated by all this light cannot dispel the cold. The air carries an autumn chill, even though it's mid-July. The ice radiates cold. It never melts; it's so hard it can't even break.

The Quantum Cross, the icon of the city's new order, rests atop Mount Royal.

I close my eyes, not yet ready to cry. Eager to forget. But the memories come anyway.

—•—

All I did was shut my eyes, and the world took on a new shape.

Sunday afternoon: my sister in the upstairs bathroom, obsessing over her looks; my parents driving out to the airport to meet Grandma.

Me: by the living room window, reading a book, curled up in the coziest armchair. I can't remember which book.

Here's what I remember: the sky was radiantly blue, and the sunlight hit the window with a harsh brightness. I had a slight headache. From reading, from the light.

Music: a trance/jungle mix spun in the CD player.

I closed my eyes. The music stopped abruptly. I heard a weird crunching sound. A cool wave washed over me. My eyes snapped open. The television looked like a cubist mobile of the Milky Way. In place of the stereo, a crystal statue of a lizard demon crowned with looping horns. The lamps were now surrealist bouquets. Pearly spikes punched through the walls, especially near electrical outlets and lightswitches.

In the distance, screams rose against the background of cold silence.

I shivered.

—•—

My sister, Jocelyne, would never meet her boyfriend again. In the upstairs bathroom I found her skull, neck, and chest skewered by the ice sprouting from her hairdryer.

I hurried outside, onto streets lined with transformed buildings, arrayed with wrecked, deformed vehicles. Wires barbed with ice dangled from poles and walls, lay splattered all over. An instant alien landscape transposed onto a familiar urban grid.

I ran. It was all I could do. I ran, trying to escape the affected zone. I ran. And ran.

Until I stumbled on my parents' car. They were smeared on the seat leather, pulverized by the ice.

I looked around. I'd reached the expressway. As far as I could see, there was evidence of the transformation. For the first time I noticed the new shape of the giant electric cross atop Mount Royal: a violent explosion frozen midblast. Towering over the city, the metamorphosed cross kept a vigil over this new world, claiming dominion.

—•—

Since that first day, I hadn't ventured outside. How long ago had that been? I was almost out of food. I awoke sporadically. Sometimes I snacked on stale crackers. I'd exhausted the canned goods. Days ago? Weeks?

In this new ice age, the ceaseless hum of automobile traffic had finally been quieted. The sound of airplanes no longer wafted down from above.

The city was silent. Cold and silent. I felt that silence in the hollow of my bones. The cold had seeped into me, had hardened my insides, had slowed the beat of my heart.

I stared out the window at the unchanging landscape and fell asleep again, to dreams of silent jets falling from the sky.

—•—

Even in my dreams, I heard him. Yet, I stayed asleep. The sounds of him taking and releasing his breath replaced the silenced engines.

Eventually, I woke, his presence gradually imprinting itself on me. And then I saw him: sitting on the edge of my bed.

He said, "Hi," neither smiling nor frowning. Waiting.

He had long black hair, and he was maybe a year or two older— almost a man. But he had the face of a little boy, and dark eyes so big that I saw deep into him, saw how he'd been hurt by the coldness of the world. Although I had never met him before, I knew him. In that moment I knew him.

"My name is Mark," he said; louder than a whisper, but without inflection.

I rested my head on his thigh. The touch of his callused fingertips against my scalp shot sparks of warmth through my body, began thawing the cold that had settled within me. I filled my lungs with air. The smell of his sweat eased the flow of my blood. I let go of my breath and moaned drowsily. I fell asleep again. No more falling jets. Finally, I rested.

—•—

"Quantum ice. Call it *quantum ice*." Daniel coined the term. The expression stuck. We heard it whispered everywhere by Montrealers who roamed their transfigured city like zombies.

Daniel was Mark's brother, but they were so different. Mark was tall and calm. Handsome. Daniel was short and nervous. Funny looking, in a bad way. And loud. Always chattering, listening to himself rhapsodize. His eyes were wild, always darting here and there, unable to focus on anything, or on anyone.

We saw Daniel infrequently. Usually when he wanted to bum food off his brother. Mark wanted him to stay with us, but, to my relief, Daniel resisted the idea. He'd disappear for days, waiting for Mark to fall asleep before he wandered off.

Daniel had his theory about the ice age. A bomb, he thought. A quantum bomb. The project of the rogue R&D department of some corporate weapons manufacturer. He claimed his blogging community used to keep track of things like that. He said reality—physics—had been changed at a fundamental level. Old technologies no longer worked. We needed a new scientific paradigm. Other things might have changed. Our bodies might not work quite the same way anymore. Nature might have changed. The food chain. The air. Gravity.

Daniel was a bit younger than I was; he certainly couldn't have been more than fifteen. He looked like the type who, before the ice age, got beat up on his way home from school. But the ice age had changed him; it had changed everyone. Daniel spoke with the intensity of the insane. A prophet desperate to convert his audience.

He was full of shit. Daniel was as ignorant as the rest of us. Nobody could know the truth. Maybe the ice had really been caused by aliens, or by magic, or … Maybe God had sneezed, or something. Probably, yes, it had been a bomb. Did it really matter? We couldn't bring back the dead. Besides, there was no proof anything beyond electrical technology had been affected. Fractals of quantum ice had erupted from the cores of our machines, from the wires that carried electricity, from the circuits and engines that fed on electric power. It had taken at most a few seconds between when everything stopped working and when the quantum ice appeared and expanded.

The state of the world: this strange new ice age.

—•—

Society had broken down. No social workers swooping down on orphaned kids. We had to take care of ourselves now. No more school. I didn't miss it. I didn't miss the jerks staring at my suddenly developed breasts. I didn't miss the other girls thinking I was too bookish and nerdy to be friends with.

Some fears make you flee, others make you stay. Mark said hundreds of thousands of people had already left the city. Many more must have had died. At least a million people, we estimated. In hospitals. In cars. In elevators. On escalators. In front of computers. Using appliances. Snapping photos. Shooting videos. Taking food out of the fridge. Carrying a cellphone in your pocket meant ice bored into your pelvis. The technology that triggered the ice was everywhere.

The corpses, too, were everywhere. The city should have reeked of rot and decay, but the ice preserved what it touched. I ignored the dead. Every day, no matter where we went, Mark and I saw the bodies claimed by the ice, but we never mentioned them.

There were still thousands of survivors who had stayed behind. They wandered the streets, lost, alone, barely aware of each other. The cold seeped into everyone.

Mark kept me warm, but I still hadn't thawed completely. I hadn't even cried yet. The placid coolness of the ice age, that utter absence of emotion, was almost comforting.

Together, Mark and I fought off the encroaching cold.

We played hide-and-seek in deserted malls. The electronics shops were frozen supernovas.

We explored the metro tunnels. The flames of hand-held torches, reflected on blooms of quantum ice, lit our way.

We walked on rooftops, holding hands, the ice-encrusted city spread below us.

—•—

At night, Mark spooned me. We went to bed with our clothes on. I took his hand and slipped it under my shirt, holding it tight against my stomach. He nuzzled my hair.

He always woke before me. Always came back with scavenged food. One day, maybe we'd kiss.

—•—

Daniel acquired followers. He changed his name to Danny Quantum and started believing his own hype. It was creepy, the way these lost people gravitated towards him—obeyed him, even. Orphaned kids. Businessmen in suits that had known better days. Middle-aged women with hungry, desperate looks. Cybergeeks bereft of their only lifeline.

Daniel and his followers gathered in the heart of the city, on Mount Royal, below that monstrous thing that had once been a cross. Daniel turned it into the symbol of his new religion. He didn't use the word *religion*, but that's what it was.

Mark brought me to Daniel's sermons. Daniel didn't use the word *sermon*, but that's what they were.

Feel-good catchphrases tinted with Nietzsche. New Age gobbledygook rationalized with scientific jargon. Cyberpunk animism. Catholic pomp sprinkled with evangelical alarmism. Eroticized psychobabble. Robert Bly mixed with Timothy Leary.

We'd climbed up some trees on the outer edge of the area where Danny Quantum's rapt disciples sat and listened to the sermon. We could hear every word. Daniel knew how to pitch his voice. He was good at this. Too good.

I said, "Don't tell me you believe any of this nonsense." For the first time, it occurred to me that maybe I couldn't trust Mark. The cold seized my heart.

He said, "Of course not. But somebody has to keep an eye on Daniel. Who else is going to look out for him? Especially now." Mark looked away as he spoke.

As far as Mark was aware, his brother was the only person he knew from before who'd survived the ice age—or who hadn't left without a word in the initial panic. That Daniel was scary, that he was dangerous, Mark wasn't ready to acknowledge.

—•—

A fractallized airplane blocked the intersection of St-Laurent and Ste-Catherine, its tail propped up by the ice-encrusted building on the corner, the tip of its nose run through the storefront window of a store the ice had altered beyond recognition. Even the force of a plane crash couldn't shatter the quantum ice. Briefly, I wondered if it might have been Grandma's plane.

Someone had painted a likeness of the transmogrified cross on the hull, with the words *The Quantum Cross of the Ice Age* below it. That day, everywhere we went, we noticed fresh graffiti of the Quantum Cross, on the asphalt of the streets, on store windows, on sidewalks, on brick walls, on concrete blocks.

The next day, Mark and I bicycled out to the airport and stared at the planes: massive dinosaurs with limbs of ice, gore, metal, and plastic.

Before going home—neither my old home nor Mark's, but an abandoned townhouse near McGill University whose windows faced away from Mount Royal—Mark wanted to check in on his little brother. These days, Daniel never left the mountain. His acolytes brought food to him. Brought themselves to him.

I complained. "I'm too tired to bicycle all the way up there." More truthfully, I was increasingly queasy around Daniel and his sycophants, and I was eager to collapse in Mark's arms, even though the sun hadn't set.

He insisted.

So we wound our way up the sinuous gravel path, occasionally encountering Daniel's followers. Despite the cold, they wore white T-shirts —no coats, no jackets, no sweaters. On the shirts, in red, were crude drawings in thick dripping lines: bloody effigies of the Quantum Cross.

When we reached the cross itself, where Daniel's congregation assembled, I noticed that they were all dressed this way, no longer individuals but a hive functioning with a single mind. Danny Quantum's.

—•—

First I heard the singing. Mark had just beaten me at croquet for the third game in a row. I looked around, and then I spotted them: to the south of the croquet park, twenty or so people walking down the Jacques Cartier Bridge into Montreal.

One of them pointed at us, and the group headed our way. They waved and kept on singing. I thought I recognized the song. Something from the 1960s. The kind of stuff my parents listened to.

Mark waved back. He said, "Hold on to your mallet. If things get rough, swing for the head and knee them in the crotch."

They seemed harmless. Approximately as many men as women. Long hair. Handmade clothes. Artsy-crafty jewellery. A bunch of latter-day hippies. The song wound down when they reached the edge of the park. I noticed a few of them looked more like bikers. I tightened my grip.

Only one of them came up to us. The one who looked more *Saturday Night Fever* than *Hair*.

He said, "Peace."

Mark said, "Hi. Where are you folks from?"

"I'm from New York City. But we're from all over. Vermont. Ottawa. Maine. Sherbrooke."

Mark asked, "So, it's like this everywhere?"

"It's like this everywhere we've been. The whole world has changed. So many tragic deaths." But he made it sound almost cheerful, like a TV ad.

Mark grunted. Something about Saturday Night Fever—his calculating eyes, his used-car salesman voice—made me distrust him immediately.

"Are you two youngsters alone? It's safer to stay in a large group. We're gathering people to form a commune. To survive in this new age. To repopulate. We need children. Strong healthy children."

His eyes appraised me, lingering on my hips. I tensed my arms, ready to swing. Mark shifted, his body shielding me from Saturday Night Fever's gaze.

"Well, I wish you folks the best. It sounds like a great project."

"You and your friend should join us. We'd be happy to welcome you." He addressed Mark, but his eyes kept straying to my body.

"Thanks, but we're good here. This is home."

Three of the men in the group were big. Wrestler big. No way Mark and I could stop them if they decided to add me to their baby factory by force.

"Are you sure?"

"Yeah. Anyway, we should be on our way. Good luck." Mark took my hand, and we walked away. We held on to our mallets.

—•—

Mark slept. He didn't know, but I'd stayed awake through the previous two nights.

His mouth was slightly open, and he was almost snoring. I loved all of his sounds, even the silly ones. I traced his lips with my index finger; it didn't rouse him, but he moaned. It was a delicious noise.

I stared at him all night, scrutinizing every detail of him.

Dawn broke. As Mark stirred, I pretended to sleep.

—•—

The night Danny Quantum and his followers started sacrificing cats and dogs, I told Mark, "We have to leave."

I was bundled under three layers of sweaters, but the cold still bit. Even the heat from the fires around the Quantum Cross couldn't keep me warm. I was tempted to lean into Mark, for warmth, for comfort, but I needed to talk to him, and for that I had to stay focused.

"You tired?"

"No. I mean, go away. Off the island. Leave all this behind. Find somewhere else to live. Somewhere far. Somewhere safer."

I wanted him to say, *Yes, I'll go anywhere with you.*

He said, "Who'll protect Daniel? If I go, he'll just get worse. He'll be lost forever."

"Then talk to him. Make him stop this before …"

"It's not that easy. Not that simple. He doesn't hear what he doesn't want to. This is his way of coping. We've all lost too much."

"You know where this is heading. Soon, it'll be people being shishkebabed to satisfy Danny Quantum's megalomania. To feed the hungry bellies of his flock."

I didn't look at Mark. I didn't want his dark eyes to sway me. I stared at the fires burning at the foot of the Quantum Cross. I looked at Daniel, prancing and shouting. Like the maniac that he was.

"I'm leaving tomorrow morning. Getting away from Daniel. Far away. Find somewhere to grow food. Somewhere with fresh water. Head south, maybe."

Could I leave without Mark? I wanted kiss him. Would I ever? Even after all we'd shared, the cold still held our hearts in its grip.

"Don't, Martha. Don't make me choose." He turned his face away from mine and stared at his brother in the distance. When he continued, his voice was firm—firm enough to sting. "Besides, we've always lived in the city. What do you know about farming, or even about gathering food in the wild?"

"We can learn how to survive." Despite myself, doubt had crept into my voice.

Was I willing to stay and let this drama play out, despite its inevitable horrors? Wherever I would end up away from here, there might be other Saturday Night Fevers or Danny Quantums. Or maybe even worse.

One of Danny's people handed Mark a wooden stick. There was a roasted, skewered cat on it.

I said, "Are you going to eat that?"

He said, "I'll go with you. Anywhere."

—•—

Feeling the wind on my face, the smell of grass and trees tickling my nose, I race down the deserted road.

Mark is with me. Laughing. I laugh, too.

In the fields there are cows. Horses. Dogs. Sometimes people.

Some of them wave at us, smiling. Some of them shoot at us, warning us away.

We're not ready to stop yet.

≈•≈

"The Marysburgh Vortex

"So many ships have gone down in the stretch of water around Main Duck Island and Point Traverse the area as become known as "The Graveyard of Lake Ontario." In these waters compass readings are unreliable, shoals and sandbars lie treacherously waiting, and fierce storms blow up with no warning. The number of tragedies that have occurred rivals the infamous "Bermuda Triangle." Local lore refers to the area as "The Marysburgh Vortex" and any strange events are automatically attributed to its effect."

From:
The Legendary Guide to Prince Edward County (1994)
by Janet Kellough, Copyright © 1994 by Janet Kellough,
Kellough Productions, Picton, Ontario

Family Trees

by
Fiona Patton

AUTHOR'S NOTE: *Family Trees is the fifth in a series of short stories featuring four "County" families with extraordinary abilities inspired by tales of "The Marysburgh Vortex." Although the people in these stories are fictional, many of their experiences are real. They may not all be attributed to "the strange magnetic anomaly buried in the mud of Lake Ontario," but they might be. Regardless, this legend has given me the opportunity to explore the unique qualities of a unique and beautiful region of rural Canada. And you never know, "The Graveyard of Lake Ontario" might hold more wrecks than just those of schooners and sloops.*

The County in high summer was a lush jungle of green trees and high, waving grasses, the sounds of tractors, four wheelers, and balers vying with those of birds, dogs, and cattle. Seated in the dining room of his century farm house, George Prescott struggled to concentrate on the few words he'd managed to input into his laptop that morning before turning to the tiny brown dog, standing with paws pressed indignantly against the bay window, barking furiously—for the past hour—at George's twelve-year-old cousin, Jesse Frawst, out mowing the lawns. Pushing back from the scarred and battered harvest table he used for a desk, George fixed the animal with what he hoped was a stern expression.

"Lucky Charm Mynaker-Prescott, will you please be quiet?" He admonished. "I can't hear myself think, and Jesse can't hear you at all."

The Chihuahua gave a sneeze at the sound of his name, then trotted across the dining room to scratch imperiously at George's leg. With a fond, but exasperated expression, the man lifted him up with one hand and deposited him into the small, round dog bed beside the laptop.

"There now, settle down for half a moment, can't you?" he added. "The Gazette needs this article on wild turkeys by tomorrow. And you've just been..." He paused. Lucky knew both the words out and walk and allowed no change of plans once they were uttered. "So you don't have to..." Lucky also knew the word go. "Well, you just don't."

The dog gave another sneeze then, after digging furiously in the bed, curled up to rest his chin on the edge where he could keep both man and window in sight. Very, very slowly, his eyes began to close and George returned his attention to trying to decide whether poultry rooting in cow manure was funny or just factual.

Originally a tabloid journalist from Toronto, George had come to the County the previous spring to discover his family roots, and had stayed once that very eccentric four-clan family made up of Geoffries, Frawsts, Akormans, and Mynakers, had discovered him. Lucky had been *rescued* on a return trip to the city and had settled into the job of running George's life at once. Now, George penned what he called "slice-of-life" articles for the local paper and tried to untangle the family's complicated genealogy for a private book he was writing. Lucky ensured that George got enough sleep and exercise by making his demands known as clearly as only a four pound dog with a high-pitched voice could do. While keeping up a running commentary on it all, the younger members of the family had made it their job to ensure that their *townie* cousin's lawn didn't overwhelm his house and his house didn't fall down around his ears.

The sound of Jesse running over what sounded like a dozen logs with George's brand new lawn tractor made him wince, but since Lucky seemed disinclined to comment, he did his best to ignore it as well.

"After all," he observed. "You could be out there doing it yourself, old man, so count yourself lu…" A glance towards the—finally—quietly sleeping dog made him pause. "So get to work," he finished instead.

———•———

Half an hour later, just as he was beginning to get into the swing of the article, Lucky's wide, expressive ears lifted as the growl of the lawn tractor cut off. George barely got him onto the floor in time before the sound of the screen door banging sent him skittering across the hall. A moment later he returned at a run as Jesse ambled into the dining room.

"Heya, rat-dog," the boy drawled, scooping Lucky up under one arm. "S'all done, Uncle George."

"Excellent." George fished a twenty dollar bill from a chipped Chihuahua mug on the table and passed it over.

Jesse grinned. "Dad say's you pay me too much," he said, stuffing it into his pocket regardless.

George sniffed. "I'll be the judge of that," he replied haughtily.

"Yep; that's what I told him."

"Is he coming to pick you up?"

"Well." Jesse tipped his red Mill Valley Co-op cap up to reveal a shock of brightly dyed yellow hair. "Grampa Art say's he'll come by, unlessssss… you wanna bring me out to the Island."

He gave his elder cousin a sly smile as George's eyes brightened.

Originally the four families' ancestral home, Blind Duck Island lay just off the south-easternmost point of the County. A strange magnetic object buried half a mile out in the mud of Lake Ontario had wrecked havoc with local shipping for over two hundred years, creating what was commonly known as "the Graveyard," and interfering with all forms of power equipment, so when "the 'lectricity" had finally come to the southern townships after the war, the families had reluctantly moved across to the mainland. But the "anomaly" as it was known, retained a powerful influence on more than just compass readings and motor boats. It had endowed the descendants of Blind Duck's original settlers—a mysterious couple named Essen—with a host of metaphysical abilities to this day: the Geoffries could cast illusions so realistic that even they couldn't see through them; the Akormans could bend any piece of machinery to their will no matter how rusted or broken; the Frawsts could levitate objects—usually people—and had an uncanny rapport with animals; and the Mynakers had the Sight.

But only if they were born on the island itself *within sight of the anomaly*, so every year one or two couples moved out to the island to birth their children—risking any number of accompanying birth defects—so that they might share in the Essen legacy.

Born three hours away in Toronto, the Mynaker Sight George had inherited from his grandmother Dorothy remained stubbornly dormant no matter how many times he visited the Island, but he kept going, drawn by the mystery everyone else in the family took for granted.

Still, he thought glumly, he had promised to get that article in to Liz by tomorrow at the very latest. He really ought to finish that first.

Jesse followed his resentful gaze to the screen with a grin, the blue of his eyes suddenly several shades darker.

"Ya know," he said in a deliberately wheedling tone, "there's a flock of wild turkeys out to the north shore. It'd be kinda like research."

"You know my laptop won't work on the island," George retorted.

"Neither will my Game Boy, but I have to go."

"Don't say g… Oh, now you've done it."

George shot the boy a pained expression as Lucky, hearing the word go, began to bark excitedly.

"See," Jesse pointed out, chucking the Chihuahua under the chin. "The rat-dog wants to come. Don'tcha boy?"

"Regardless," George continued stubbornly. "The snakes are very active in July. I'd worry about His Nibs getting eaten."

"Caitlin'll be there; she'll make 'em mind. You know that animals obey the Frawsts."

"I know that animals have an affinity for the Frawsts. It's not the same thing."

"It is for Caitlin. 'Sides, it's tree plantin' day too," Jesse continued, waving George's car keys which had suddenly appeared in his hand. "You wouldn't wanna miss that, would you? It's a family tradition; only happens once every few years. Granny Gracie's gonna be runnin' it, an' you know how those old people like to talk. You'd learn an awful lot about our history."

The keys bounced up and down in mid-air with an almost hypnotic motion and George gave his young cousin the same stern gaze he'd fixed on the dog earlier. "Stop that," he ordered.

The keys froze three inches from the boy's grinning face. "I just figured you might like some help with your book, is all," he explained with perfectly crafted élan. "Since so many of us'll be there and all. An' Grampa Art did ask for you 'specially," he said, playing his trump card. "Said he needed your help with the barbecue."

"Where are your Uncle Fred and Uncle Brandon?"

"Gone fishin' with their dad."

George gave a deep sigh. "Fine," he agreed, knowing when he was beaten. "I'll get my notes. You find Lucky's collar and leash and put some dog food in a baggie for him; I don't want him stuffing himself sick on hot dogs and macaroni salad."

"And give me my keys back."

With the keys safely tucked back in his pocket, George went in search of some kind of pen and paper while Jesse ambled into the kitchen, the Chihuahua propped happily in the crook of his arm, one tiny paw pressed against his neck for support.

—•—

They found Daryl and Joe Mynaker helping their grandfather, Art Akorman, load half a dozen scrawny cherry and apple trees into a rowboat when George carefully pulled his SUV up beside the old, wooden wharf on Rocky Point. Across the water, Blind Duck Island shimmered invitingly in the summer sun.

"Like Bali Hai," he muttered as he set the parking brake.

"Like what?" Jesse asked.

"Nothing, it's before your time. Mind the dog!" he added as Jesse leaped out, Lucky right behind him. Once his paws touched the ground, the Chihuahua spun about and lifted his leg as high as he could to mark the front tire.

"And I just had that car washed too, you little brat," George muttered, coming around to snap a bright green leash to Lucky's collar as the dog yipped impudently back at him.

—•—

Art straightened as they made their way to the rowboat. Of an age, the two men generally sought out each other's company at family gatherings. Now, he threw one blunt hand out to catch his city-bred cousin as he slid over the last few inches of weed-covered rocks, Lucky under one arm, his briefcase under the other.

"Hey, George," he said amiably.

"Hello, Art. Jesse tells me that it's tree planting day," George replied once he'd regained his balance.

"Yep."

"I see. Um…" Loathe to demonstrate his ignorance of country matters more than he had too, George frowned uncertainly. "Isn't it a bit late in the year?" he asked finally. "I mean, I always thought it was best to plant trees in the spring."

"It is that." Pulling an old, faded, blue handkerchief from his back pocket, Art mopped at his face and neck before giving an eloquent shrug. "But Gracie got these up to Canadian Tire yesterday. Leftovers from the garden centre," he explained. "See she's what you might call…" He paused as the three boys snickered.

"Frugal?" George suggested tactfully.

"Tighter'n bark on a tree," Art finished. He jerked a thumb at the boat. "This'll be the last load, I'm hopin'."

"Not likely with two more passengers, Grampa," Daryl noted.

"Bull-pucky. Jesse can get his own self across, can't you, boy?"

Hovering a few inches off the ground already, Jesse turned eyes as dark as the night sky on his grandfather's face.

"Yep."

"I meant Uncle George an' his Rottweiler-wannabe," Daryl expanded with a grin.

George just sniffed at him as Art snuffed his handkerchief back in his pocket.

"We'll squeeze tight," he said. "I'm done in; 'an I want a beer and a sit before we get started. That rocky piece of crap ground Granny Gracie's chosen for young Janet is gonna be a pain in the butt to get a shovel into."

"Not too much. Auntie Pam an' Uncle Rick came out and softened it up this spring," Jo answered over his shoulder as he passed the last of the trees to Daryl. "An' Uncle Lloyd dug nearly a ton of shells, fish, an' green lake goo into it last week. It should be nice and marshy by now."

George glanced down at his new running shoes with a gloomy expression. "Just how many trees are we talking about, Art?" he asked plaintively.

"Welll... we got most of the kids out there, today," the older man estimated. "An' I'd reckon we've moved a couple dozen trees over already. That's the point of tree plantin' day. Gracie figures every generation outta plant somethin' that'll outlast 'em."

"We can do *most* of the diggin', Uncle George," Daryl offered chivalrously. "You an' Grampa just need to help with the *little* kids."

"There ya go," Art said with an evil chuckle. "All you gotta do is help me babysit. Can't be that hard, eh?"

George cast the other man a deeply suspicious glance. "So that's why you had Jesse lure me up here?" he accused. "To try and ride roughshod over a host of levitating, mind-reading, little hellions."

Art nodded laconically. "Yep."

"Oh, thank you so much."

—•—

A dozen children were waiting to help them unload when they docked at the only serviceable wharf on the Island, a narrow length of weathered wooden boards stretching out from the south shore. The trees passed from hand to hand until they were safely set on dry ground with a degree of cooperation that George found encouraging, until one misstep sent a pink-sneakered foot plunging into the water. Art ignored the furious argument that ensured until a flurry of signing snapped his head around.

"Here now!" he scolded. "I don't wanna see that kinda language!"

A chorus of barely contrite "Sorry, Grampas," mollified him enough to turn back to George. "Brianna an' Shane go to the deaf school," he explained. "So a course they gotta teach all their cousins every last cuss words they think of."

"Of course, I… yes, Lucky, in a moment. It's a pity *you* don't go to the deaf school."

Tucked too tightly into George's jacket, Lucky had begun to squirm and squeak as soon as they'd reached the dock. Now, he gave a sharp, commanding bark and Jesse's sister, Caitlin, reached out and deftly lifted the Chihuahua free.

"Just be careful with him," George said worriedly as half a dozen girls clustered about the tiny dog; a smug expression already plastered across his tiny face.

"We will!"

The cluster moved off at once.

"Because the snakes are bigger than he is!" George shouted after them.

"We know!"

Shaking his head, he carefully clambered onto the dock while behind him, Daryl and Jo leaped nimbly from the boat, a large cooler held between them.

—•—

"So, that's the famous family tree, is it?"

After lunch—which Lucky had managed to wheedle a lion's share of despite George's vigilance—Art lit his pipe, peering through the smoke as the other man lifted a rubber band-wrapped package from his brief case. The children crowded around excitedly as he unfolded a huge piece of paper which was in actual fact many pieces of paper taped and retaped together and covered in scribbles and smudges in both pen and pencil. Some attempt had been made early on to colour-code the four families in magic marker: orange for Mynakers, green for Frawsts, blue for Geoffries, and red for Akormans, but it was clear that George had either abandoned the idea halfway through or gotten too confused to keep it up.

Art tipped his green golf cap up to scratch his head. "Seems a bit..." he paused.

"Grubby?" Caitlin offered, Lucky cradled in her arms like a baby.

"I was gonna say muddled. Course, I didn't bring my readin' glasses," Art answered tactfully.

"Wouldn't a helped," Daryl observed, peering over Caitlin's shoulder.

The girl giggled as George gave an embarrassed shrug. "Well, it's just the first draft," he said in a defensive tone.

Art glanced over at him. "Thought you did a first draft a year ago."

"Yes, well, it turned out to be a little inaccurate," George admitted. "It's harder than I thought it would be. I found most of the family's birth records in the Greenville archives but that didn't really help. The generations overlap and criss-cross, never mind the names. There must be a dozen Lisas, Donnas, Jerrolds, and Ikes..."

"Not to mention Arthurs."

"Exactly. I did a Prescott family tree when my daughter Elizabeth was born. That went quite easily, so I suppose I thought this would be easy too."

"Well, likely that's 'cause you was just doin' one family 'insteada four. Here, settle down," Art added sternly as most of the children burst out laughing.

Scratching Lucky under the chin, Caitlin fixed her Uncle George with a dark glance. "*One* family?" she asked, her voice dripping with the kind of cutting disdain only an eight-year-old girl could perfect. "You only did your *dad's* family?"

George wilted under her disproving scrutiny. "Um.. yes, but now I'm making up for it," he offered. "I'm doing the Mynakers. My *grandmother's* family."

"What about your *mother's* family?" she demanded.

"Well, um... that will be next?"

Caitlin gave a haughty, unimpressed sniff, but returned her attention to the family tree as Joe pushed between them.

"I don't think here's right, Uncle George," he said, pointing past his sister's shoulder to one of the orange scribbles.

"I don't think this is right," George corrected absently.

"Yeah, uh-huh, this here. Great Auntie Janet married Howard Mynaker, not Harvey Mynaker. It was his sister Janet what married Harvey."

"Whose sister?"

"Howard's sister."

"Their mother's name was Janet too," Art added. "That'd be her there, I expect," he said, pointing with his pipe stem. "It was a popular name back then."

"Now too," his six-year-old great-granddaughter Janet Akorman piped up.

"Yep, now too."

"So, Howard and Harvey both married women named Janet?" George asked.

"Yep."

"Were they Mynakers too?"

"Yep."

"How did they manage to know who was who in conversation?"

"Oh, that was easy enough: Howard's Janet had a anchor tattoo on her forearm."

"Really?"

"No. Good Lord, George, you are gullible. It was a rose tattoo, a course. Ladies of that generation never wore anchors."

George sank into a sagging lawn chair. "I think I need a drink of water," he muttered as the children began to laugh again. Lucky leaned out of Caitlin's arms to lick his face as she nodded sagely.

"And an eraser," she said. "But don't worry, Uncle George. *We'll* help you."

—•—

An hour of loud, excited and rather *unhelpful* advice later, Art finally shooed the children away. "Did you lot come here to plant trees or confuse your Uncle George?" he demanded.

"Both," Caitlin retorted at once.

"Fine, you've done the one, now get to the other. That rain won't hold off forever. Carley, you go fetch Granny Gracie. She should be just about finished her nap by now." Pulling a bag of bags from an old bait bucket, he began to pass them around.

"The rest of you head off to the beach and collect a bag of lake weed each, wet or dry; don't matter. Then meet down to the old Essen place in half an hour." He turned to George, one hand cupped over his mouth. "That'll just about give Gracie enough time to pee an' find her teeth," he whispered. "Now remember," he said, turning back to the children, "any bits of metal you find, be sure to keep separate. The older kids'll show you what I mean. Now, get!"

The children scattered and George accepted a sleepy, unprotesting Lucky from Caitlin before turning an inquiring expression on Art. "Lake weed and... metal?" he asked.

Art tapped his pipe on the edge of the bait bucket with a shrug. "Gracie'll explain it," he said simply.

—•—

It was closer to an hour later when the host of children finally came together on the scruffy piece of pasture field that served as a lawn in front of the Essen farm house. An old woman of close to ninety years old sat in a huge Adirondack chair, wrapped in shawls and blankets despite the temperature. When the children threw themselves down around her, she fixed them all with a dark, almost luminescent gaze.

"So, who here knows the story of the Essens?" she demanded.

A dozen voices broke out at once until she stabbed an arthritic finger towards Janet Akorman.

The girl jumped up eagerly. "Samuel an' Mary Essen came here a long, long time ago..." she said at once.

"From a galaxy, far, far away," Daryl added dryly. Seated beside him, Jesse passed a mouthful of pop out his nose.

"Quiet down," Grace snapped.

"They were like the first Grandma an' Grampa," Janet continued, dismissing her older cousins with a toss of her head. "An' they had four girls an' they married four boys an' they had lots an' lot's of kid's who had us."

"In a nutshell," Grace agreed. "They arrived in seventeen-ninety

four, 'though where they came from remains a mystery to this day…"
Her eyes glowed brightly, and as one, the entire group—George included—turned towards the distant anomaly. "An' they settled right here on
this very spot."

She leaned back in her chair. "Now in them days there weren't too
many folk as would chose to farm on as barren a pile a rock as Blind
Duck Island was then," she continued. "The climate was hard, the
winds harsh, an' the winters cold an' long. So the Essens started out by
plantin' windbreaks, trees." She swept her hand towards a huge, gnarled
oak tree growing in the very center of the yard. "Like that one there, put
in the ground as an acorn by Samuel his very self."

A chorus of ooohhhs, greeted her, and she nodded sagely. "Now, as
Janet said, their four girls: that'd be Edith, Doris, Ruth an' Agnes, married four local fishermen, Garret Geoffries, John Frawst, Joseph
Mynaker, an' Roy Akorman, an' they carried on the tradition on their
own plots of land all around the island. Their families, that's us, have
done the same ever since, plantin' at least one tree for every member of
the family to this very day. I planted that there spruce when I was only
six-years-old," she said, jerking her head towards a tall tree just west of
the overgrown kitchen garden. "My boy, Kevin, planted that maple next
to it an' his boy, your Uncle Brandon, planted the cedar beside it."

Tucking herself more deeply into her shawls, she waved her hand.
"So, now you know the story of tree plantin' day. Go pick yer trees an
get on off to one of the four plots as you like. After that, we'll fire up
the barbecue again and have some supper before your folks come to get
you." She turned. "Arthur?"

"Yeah, Granny."

"Fetch me a beer."

—•—

"The lake weed works like compost, obviously. This ain't exactly the
Garden of Eden, soil-wise."

"And the metal?"

"Ah, the metal…" Grace gave George a cryptic smile.

The children had fanned out at once, the older helping the younger chose their trees and dig their holes, but it was nearly five o'clock before they were done. Art had already begun the task of cooking up another four dozen hot dogs and Lucky had long since fallen asleep in Grace's lap before they straggled back. As the smell of meat drifted across the island, George helped the old woman hobble down to the picnic tables, the dog tucked safely in the crook of his other arm.

"Mostly it's just bits offa this an' that washed up like the stones, but every now and then," she waved a finger at him, "you get a bit that just might be somethin' special, somethin' that just mighta come offa one of them ships busted up an' sank by the anomaly itself. Now that metal's real special. Trees growin' over that seem to have just a bit more strength in 'em. An' that's important. Most things in this world need a bit of extra strength to keep 'em goin'. Especially if it comes from a very special wreck."

Before George could ask her what she meant, she waved her hand at the sturdiest picnic table. "Help me over there."

She seated herself beside Art, who glanced over at George before handing her an empty grocery bag with a wordless smile.

"Now," she said sternly, passing it over. "You, go get yourself some lake weed, George."

He blinked. "Excuse me?"

"It's tree plantin' day." Her eyes narrowed dangerously. "Weren't you listenin' to my story?"

"Well, yes, of course I was," George stammered. "But..." he glanced from her to Art, then back again. "I thought, well, that it was for the children."

Grace raised a sarcastic eyebrow at him. "Already got a tree planted on the Island do you?"

"Well, no..."

"Then get goin'."

"But..." George sighed. "I'll never fill this bag before dark," he pointed out.

"The kid'll help you."

Tucking her fingers into her mouth, Grace gave a surprisingly loud whistle. The ensuing stampede caused Lucky to begin barking hysterically but, once Caitlin took charge of him again, he calmed, allowing her to begin combing out his belly fur with a Barbie brush, as the rest of the children headed for the beach at a dead run.

Jesse fell into step beside George as he followed them, a dubious expression on his face.

"This is silly," the older man confided once they were well out of Grace's hearing. "I haven't even got a tree."

Jesse laughed. "Sure you do, Uncle George. We picked it out for you first thing this morning while Daryl and Joe dug the hole."

George cast him a suspicious glance. "We?" he demanded "How many of you were in on this?"

"All of us."

"I see. Well, I must say, you're all very good at keeping secrets."

"We've had lots of practice."

"Yes, that is true. But I shan't trust any of you in the future."

Jesse just laughed at him.

—•—

They spent a few moments half-heartedly stripping bits of dried weed from the nearby rocks, before George glanced over at the boy again.

"You know, when I first came to the Island, your Uncle Brandon told me that we were descended from aliens."

He chuckled somewhat self-consciously, but Jesse just shrugged.

"Could be, I guess," he allowed.

"You're not serious?"

The boy shrugged again. "I dunno. Might be kinda cool to be like a Klingon or a Wookie or somethin'."

"Instead of like what?" George asked with a smile.

"Well, like mutants or superheroes, maybe. We sure aren't like other folk." Tipping his hat back in imitation of his grandfather, Jesse scratched at his head for a minute. "Course it'd be kinda cool to be a mutant," he added thoughtfully. "They've got some pretty wicked clothes. What would that tabloid you used to work for call us?"

George shuddered. "I'd hate to even speculate."

"Good thing it's a secret then, eh?"

"Good thing." Straightening with a groan, George frowned. "So, do you think those pieces of metal might actually be…?" he paused in embarrassment.

"Extraterrestrial?" Jesse finished for him in a dramatic voice. "Why not? The *little* kids all think they're gonna find a piece of Samuel and Mary's space ship, that's why they always search right about here, just in line with the anomaly." He raised his arm to draw a line out towards the lake.

"Did you, when you planted your tree?"

"Sure. Got into a big fight with Daryl 'cause he said my piece was nothing but a bottle cap."

"Was it?"

Jesse shrugged. "Probably."

"How old were you?"

"Around Janet's age, I guess." The smell of hot dogs made him turn. "So, *you* find any metal yet?" he demanded.

George shook his head. "No. I imagine the beach has been scoured clean by any number of searching children over the years."

"Yeah, but the lake always throws up more. You just gotta know where to look." Jesse rubbed at his stomach. "You should use the Sight. It'd go faster."

"You know it doesn't work that way for me."

"Why not? We're so close to the anomaly here you can practically taste it."

George glanced out across the water. In the bright, afternoon sun it almost seemed as if the waves were darker about a quarter mile out; darker, calmer, with maybe a hint of green shimmering up from the bottom.

He glanced about swiftly to make sure there was no Geoffries hiding behind the rocks casting an illusion to trick him, but they were alone on this part of the beach.

"I really don't think…" he began, then paused.

Jesse cocked his head to one side. "What…?" he prodded.

"It's silly, but maybe…"

"Maybe…?"

"Well, I thought I might have seen a glint of metal by the water just over there."

"So, go get it."

"It's probably just a bottle cap."

Jesse began to laugh.

—•—

"Lucky? Lucky Charm Mynaker-Prescott, get out of there at once!"

Back feet locked in the grass, the Chihuahua was shoulder-deep in the hole Daryl and Joe had dug for George at the entrance to the old Mynaker plot, digging furiously, dirt and grass roots flying everywhere. As George plucked him out, the huge white... something he had unearthed disappeared into his mouth drawing an impressed "Ewwww," from the surrounding children.

"Get that out... drop it!"

Prying the tiny dog's jaws open with two fingers, George removed the beetle grub from between his teeth and flung it into the long grass with a disgusted expression. Lucky gave him a matching one before squirming out of his arms and slinking off to hunker reproachfully at Caitlin's feet. George just shook his head.

"Honestly, you!"

—•—

"That's part's too ragged, Uncle George; it'll make your tree all scraggly."

"Break it off and just use the smooth part."

"Tuck it so'se it stands straight up in the dirt. No, like this."

"Yeah, that way when you set your tree on top it stays that way."

"An' your tree'll grow straight up into the air."

"An' not go all bent like Dylan's."

"You go all bent!"

"You make me!"

"Enough! Let the man work!" Grace shooed the gaggle of children away as Daryl and Joe helped George plant the crab-apple tree they'd chosen for him. Once the hole was filled in, tamped down, and watered, they stood back, leaning on their shovels as he'd seen their elders do a hundred times while he mopped at his face with Art's handkerchief.

"That'll flower all pink in the spring," Jesse told him proudly, passing him a bottle of water. "You'll be able to see it for miles."

"Yes, I will." George glanced around at the host of smiling faces, and nodded, suddenly embarrassingly overcome. "I... well, thank you."

The chorus of "your welcomes," made him blush.

—•—

Later that evening, as the sun set behind the trees, George sat staring out at the dark waters of Lake Ontario. After a large meal of burnt hot dog, Lucky had finally forgiven him for the grub incident and was now tucked safely inside his jacket, snoring in contentment. George chuckled.

"Do you think your tree will do well?" he asked Jesse who was standing by the water skipping rocks without taking his hands out of his pockets.

"I 'spect so," the boy answered, his voice sounding eerily like his grandfather's. "It's been in the ground a while now an' it got a good start." He glanced over, his eyes dark and luminous. "Figure yours will?" he asked.

George gave a sigh slightly tinged with sadness. "I don't know," he answered truthfully. "It's not so easy to be sure of things when you're my age."

"Sure it is," the boy answered, unimpressed. "You're a Mynaker, you can know things if you want to."

"I wasn't born here," George reminded him.

"So, use your bit of metal."

"For what, a telephone into the future?"

"Kinda, yeah."

Shaking his head, George pulled the piece of metal he had been instructed to break off from his pocket and studied it carefully. A green-tinged grey in colour, it was about half an inch long and rubbed smooth by its time in the water everywhere but at the broken end. He put it to his ear with an elaborate flourish. "No answer," he declared. "The anomaly must be affecting its transmission."

Jesse just rolled his eyes at him.

"Yes, well, I doubt that it's a piece of Samuel and Mary Essen's space ship, anyway," George said, rubbing it between two fingers. It felt warm and slightly tingly against his skin and he almost dropped it in surprise.

Jesse snickered at him as another rock sailed across the water. "Whatever it is, it's been down there a long time," he retorted, "so either way, it's got power. So whenever you need to use the Sight or you just wanna feel the Island, you just gotta rub it. That's what I do."

George's eyes widened. "You keep a piece as well?"

"Sure, we all do. That way wherever we go, the Island comes with us." He gave George a serious look. "We're different, Uncle George, all of us. That's scary sometimes, so we keep a bit of the Island with us for an extra bit of strength like Granny Gracie says. That way we can feel the Island and it can feel us, an' so can the trees we planted. The trees an' the metal, they're like family heirlooms, ya know?"

"Hm."

Two more rock skipped across the rippling waves. "So, now do you think your tree's gonna make it?" Jesse asked.

Squeezing the piece of metal in his fist, George nodded, his eyes darkening ever so slightly. "Yes, he said, with a smile in his voice. "I do."

"Good." Hefting a rock in his hand, Jesse flung it at the waves in the old fashioned way. "Figure that other family tree of yours will too?"

The older man sighed. Tucking the bit of metal back into his pocket he stood, one hand supporting the sleeping Chihuahua. "That seems highly unlikely," he answered. "Even the Mynaker Sight couldn't make that tree grow straight." Glancing out at the water he sent a silent salute towards the anomaly turning the water ever so slightly green in the setting sun. "But maybe I'll start again in the morning, anyway," he said, almost to himself. "*After* I finish that article on wild turkeys."

AUTHOR'S NOTE: The Tom Thomson Memorial Art Gallery has an excellent overview online of Thomson's life, death and art. From it, I learned of his wounds after his accident. I also had the good fortune to learn that "Dr. James McCallum... [was] a Toronto occultist," and was Thomson's friend and patron. As far as the artwork I describe in the story, it is not a real Thomson piece, but rather a conflation of two or more works, including "Canoe Lake, Mowat Lodge" and "Northland Sunset," both of which can be viewed on the site.

I chose to go to "The Canadian Encyclopedia" for confirmation on what I already knew about William Lyon Mackenzie King, that he "was a spiritualist, in frequent 'contact' with his mother and other dead relatives and friends." His dog Pat was often his conduit for these conversations. Nowhere does it say that he was a psychic detective instead of Prime Minister, but we know better, don't we?

Windigo: An Anthology of Fact and Fantastic Fiction (1982)
by John Robert Columbo, Western Producer Prairie Books, Saskatoon;
Additional Information from conversation with Vicky Barsaleau, Curator/CAO,
Sucker Creek First Nation Cultural Museum, Alberta; *The Canadian Encyclopedia*
(2000) McClellan & Stewart, Toronto; and *Joe's Cryptozoology Pages* (2000)
by Joseph Gagné.

Over the Darkened Landscape

by
Derryl Murphy

The train whistle blew three times, a harsh sound that sat me up and made me perk up my ears. Mac turned over in the rolling darkness, the only sound now the steady clickety-clack of wheels on the steel tracks.

He put his hand on my back and let it rest there for a moment. "Anything wrong?" His voice was groggy and his lips smacked loudly as he searched for spit for a too-dry mouth.

I shook my head and then nosed at his arm. Mac lifted it away and I licked his palm twice, then rolled up against him and fell asleep to the easy, pleasant sensation of Mac's fingers scratching me behind the ears and underneath my collar.

—•—

Next morning there was a quiet rap on the door and then it opened. Simon, our car's attendant, stepped in carrying a pot of coffee. "Good morning, Mr. King," he sang, cheerful as ever. "I trust your sleep went well." He opened the blinds to a pale blue sky and a never-ending march of trees as we wended our way through the northern woods.

He poured a cup for Mac, who was now up and blinking away the gumminess of sleep. After Mac took the cup Simon leaned down and scratched me under the chin. "And how's Pat this bright and cheery morning?" he asked in his best baby talk voice. I could put up with that, though, because he produced a napkin from his pocket and slowly unfolded it, revealing a scrumptious piece of bacon staining its pristine white surface.

I stood on the bed and shook myself in excitement, the smell almost a feast in and of itself. Simon dangled the strip of bacon above my nose, and after a couple more moments of olfactory ecstasy, I wolfed it down.

"You spoil that dog, Simon," said Mac. His eyes shone with mischief as he said this, and in response I sat on his pillow and noisily licked my rear.

"Oh, no, Mr. King," protested Simon as he folded the napkin and tucked it back into his pocket. "Pat is a wonderful dog, and besides, any pet of the greatest detective of our age deserves a little spoiling."

With these last words he gestured at the large tag that hung from the handle of Mac's largest suitcase. I can't read, of course, but the words on the tag were as well known to me—better, even—as to anyone else on this train, and well beyond: *Mackenzie King, Psychic Detective.*

Greatest detective of our age, my fragrant rear. Not without a little help, at least.

—•—

We reached the South River station late that afternoon. As usual, I allowed Mac to put a leash on me, and we waited on the platform while Simon sent out a porter with our bags. Of Mac's client, there was no sign. By the time the train pulled away fifteen minutes later we were the only two, aside from the ticket agent, who remained at the station.

"He's late," I said, scratching behind my right ear. "I don't like it when people are late."

"Be patient," said Mac. "He's probably had to fight off vicious bears and nasty black flies to get here."

"Nothing quite so civilized," came a voice from behind us.

We turned to greet a man wearing a grey wool suit (well, really, almost everything is grey to my eyes, but later Mac assured me that it was indeed grey) and carrying a handsome walking stick. "Dr. James McCallum at your service, sir," he said, and held out his hand.

Mac shook it. "Mackenzie King, Dr. McCallum. I'm pleased to make your acquaintance."

McCallum gestured for Mac's bags and a manservant stepped out from a nearby doorway and took them in hand. "Please follow me, Mr. King. We'll have you at the house in no time."

"Is this your house, Dr. McCallum?"

He shook his head. "I live in Toronto," said McCallum. "And I have a cottage at Go Home Bay on Georgian Bay. But we're here because this work recently came to my attention, and I wish to buy it."

"Which work is that?" asked Mac.

"More after we get there," answered McCallum.

We rode in a horse-drawn carriage instead of a motor car, following a dirt road for the better part of an hour until we reached the house—really a mansion—where McCallum was visiting, and where we would stay for the night. South River was a pleasant little town, primarily there for the lumber industry it seemed, and that industry was the source of the homeowner's wealth.

"Our host has been called away on business," said McCallum as we made our way to the house. "You and I will have dinner alone tonight, Mr. King. I shall see you at seven."

"I suppose that means I'm not invited to the table," I said, after the manservant had deposited our bags in our well-appointed room.

Mac shrugged. "We saw three dogs coming in, so it's not like the owner hates them."

"Hunting dogs," I replied. "Big hulking brutes that live outside all year round, I suspect. None of them ever come to the dinner table."

"Yes, well, you'll just have to take your meals in here, then, or perhaps in the kitchen. But whatever he needs me to solve, you're a part of the equation, so don't feel too left out."

I turned and nibbled at a sudden itch in my left thigh, and after Mac retired to the toilet to freshen up I jumped onto the bed for a nap.

—•—

Supper, Mac later told me, went well. A veritable feast, as a matter of fact, with only McCallum and a strange prickling sensation on the back of Mac's neck, coming, he was sure, from the next room over. After they were served the manservant brought me a silver bowl filled with various meats and cheeses, placed on an old rug so I wouldn't make a mess all over the floor. Apparently they had bad luck with dogs in this house.

After the meal, McCallum asked Mac to join him in the sitting room. The prickling sensation came from that same room, and as Mac entered, the feeling practically jumped onto his scalp. He promptly asked for my company, and McCallum sent word that I was to be brought down immediately.

I could feel it too, and I sniffed worriedly at the entrance to the room for several seconds before following McCallum. Mac hesitated another moment, and then came in as well. "What is it?" he asked our host.

McCallum shook his head. "All I know is that it comes from the item I wish to buy. Here, let me show you." He took us over to a wall that held several paintings, a variety of sizes and styles and, I imagine, of colours as well. All were of trees and lakes and clouds and other things that reminded the viewer of the northern woods, although each one exercised the artist's own particular vision. "Quite beautiful art," said Mac. "I think I've seen some work like this before, in Toronto and Ottawa."

McCallum nodded. "Still a new and mostly unknown thing, this Group of Seven, but I foresee big things for them. This is the one here, though," he pointed at a squiggly-looking painting of dead trees beside a lake, with a horizon that seemed to stretch on forever. "The artist's name was Tom Thomson, and I was his patron and friend."

"Was?"

"He died not long ago, at Canoe Lake, not far from here. The owner of this house came into possession of this, probably his last painting, and knew I would be interested in buying it. But…" he let his voice trail off.

Mac stepped forward, as did I. This painting was the source of whatever strange feelings came from this room. But I was too short to see if there was anything on the painting to tell us why, and so had to wait for Mac's opinion.

"Canoe Lake," he read, and then was silent for a minute or two. Finally, he pointed to one corner of the painting. "What is that, Dr. McCallum?"

McCallum took a swallow of his drink and nodded. "That's the problem, Mr. King. I have some sensitivity to occult matters, but obviously nothing like what gives you such renown. I don't know what it is, but I can feel, I *know*, that somehow Tom is in trouble."

Mac looked down at me. "Tom. You mean Tom Thomson, the artist who is dead."

McCallum nodded. "It sounds crazy, but I'm sure I'm right. Tom needs help."

"Dr. McCallum," announced Mac after a moment or two of thought. "I'll need this painting down off its hook and leaning against the wall. And then Pat and I will have to have this room to ourselves."

McCallum nodded and lifted the painting down. "How long will you need?" he asked.

Mac shook his head. "Hopefully not long. Close both doors, and don't come in until I call you."

McCallum nodded and left.

"Well, Pat, shall we see what this picture has in store for us?"

I padded over to the painting. The blot was small, in the bottom right corner, greyish-white to my eyes, and vaguely in the shape of a man. The energy it gave off was too negative, too disturbing, for me to look at it for more than a few seconds, and it certainly ruled out any direct contact with that portion of the painting.

"I sense something else over here," said Mac, kneeling now and pointing at another part of the artwork, some quiet shoreline along the far left. "Something much more positive."

I stepped beside him, relieved to be away from the awful sensation emanating from the other corner of the painting. "Shall we try to speak to whatever or whoever is involved in this side of things, then?"

Mac nodded, and took me up in his arm. "Can't hurt, can it?" And with that, he reached out and touched that artistic piece of shoreline with his other hand.

— • —

A slight breeze blew, and the tall grasses near the lakeside calmly hissed and scratched as they waved about. The smell was odd, to say the least, part great outdoors, part oil paint. Everything around us was slightly smeared, closer to reality than the actual painting had been, but still showing signs of brush strokes. Mac set me down. He also looked a little less than real, but not so off as the surrounding scenery.

We were successfully in the painting.

"Now what?" I asked. My voice was muted, hollow.

"I was thinking about asking Mother for help," said Mac, looking at me.

I looked inside, then shook my head. "She's not with me, Mac. Maybe she's off doing something else right now."

Mac shrugged. "Or maybe spirits of the dead can't exist inside an oil painting."

There came a sound from behind us, the scritch and pop of a match being lit, followed closely by the smell of tobacco and paint, both burning. "Spirits of the dead do just fine in oil paintings, fellows."

We turned. Sitting in a canoe on the lake was a man smoking a corncob pipe. I hadn't looked too closely at the scenery before, but now that I saw this man I could see that the perspective was a bit off, a result of the nature of being in a painting, I would guess. Was he ten feet away? Twenty? Was he really straight across from us, or was he a little higher and smaller?

He stuck his paddle in the water and pushed, whorls of paint and water slowly spinning off as he drifted to shore, where he climbed out to stand beside us. "Tom Thomson," he said, hand extended.

Mac shook it and introduced himself. Then Thomson leaned over and patted me on the head, thump thump thump, which I hate, and said, "And what's your name, pup?"

"Pat." My fur felt sticky and oily where he'd touched me, and I could see Mac trying to wipe his hand on his trousers.

"You lads here to help me, then?" He gazed off towards the far side of the lake, eyes squinting against the very setting sun he'd painted on that side.

Thomson was tall and thin, with a sharp nose and short dark hair. Suspenders held up his dark pants, and he wore a watch cap atop his head. There was a large bruise poking out from beneath the cap on the right side of his head, and dried blood trailed down from his right ear.

"Dr. McCallum sent us," said Mac. "He wants to buy this painting, and he's worried about you."

Thomson smiled. "Jim always did claim he was sensitive to things from the other side. My talent was always a little more personal." He took a puff from his pipe and then waved it at the perpetual sunset. "Beast that did me in is coming to finish the job."

The wind shifted, and a smell drifted across the lake and over my nose, rotting flesh and, strangely, cold breath overwhelming the sticky sweet odour of the paint. My fur danced and crawled in response, and then the beast howled: high, drifting, angry, not like a wolf, not like anything I'd ever heard before.

"Beast? What sort of beast?" asked Mac, his voice high and panicked.

Thomson hefted his paddle. "Windigo. Someone who took to eating human flesh years ago here in the north woods, pretty soon the bad magic worked its way over him and changed his body. Now he knows no thought but hunger, lust for a cannibal's meal."

"This Windigo killed you?" I asked.

Thomson nodded, pipe back in his mouth. The creature howled again, closer, and I saw that the dried blood was flowing from his ear again, slowly, like a thick stream of paint.

"Then how did it end up in this painting with you?" asked Mac. "For that matter, how did *you* end up in here?"

"Blood and paint tied us together," said the artist. "I knew he'd been stalking me for months before I died, so I took to stalking him as well. Found a thorny branch he'd scraped against, left a speck of blood, mixed it into my palette along with some of my own blood, then I finished this last painting, sprinkled in a bit of my own magic." He shook his head. "Didn't work the way I'd hoped, though. It tied us together, made it impossible for him to eat me, yes, but he could still bash me on the head and send me into the lake to drown. When I died, so did he."

"And now he's in this painting with you, and coming to, what, kill you again?" Mac's voice was incredulous.

"That's about the size of it," said Thomson. "Maybe he figures he'll get out when he does it. Or maybe he figures he's earned himself one last taste of raw humanity, not that the paints would make anywhere near a decent marinade." He smacked his lips together and grinned.

Across a meadow, trees parted, and from the darkness stepped a creature, immense, impossibly tall, dark grey body made of an artist's sensation of stone. Its eyes were black holes, empty and yet staring straight at us. Human bones decorated its body, necklace and bracelets and anklets. The painted air around it stirred and realigned itself as it fought to get out of the Windigo's way, and slowly it made its way towards us.

Against such a beast stood a dead man with a canoe paddle, another man with no visible means of defense, and a dog with a good set of teeth but not a lot of size.

"How can we stop such a thing?" asked Mac. "Pat, come here; we're leaving."

"And leave Mr. Thomson to certain death again?" I shook my head. "Uh uh. You can figure something out, Mac, I know you can."

"You talked about your mother when you first arrived," said Thomson. "I assume she's dead as well?"

Mac nodded. "She's usually good for advice and insights, but not at a time like this."

The Windigo howled again, now no more than ten paces away, the trail behind it nothing but a slurry of mixed up shades and lines, in the air and on the ground. When Thomson moved through the painting it changed as well, but always peacefully, and then it fell back into place. The Windigo did the opposite, disturbed the essence of the painting and left it that way, and it had to fight for every step. It wasn't natural to this piece of art, even though the paint held a taint of its blood.

"Can you find someone else and bring him here?" asked Thomson. "Does it work that way?"

Mac stared at the oncoming monster for a few seconds. Then he turned to Thomson. "I can try. Who am I looking for?"

"Big Goose."

"A *what?*"

"Not a what, a who. I don't know his Ojibway name, but he was a shaman, a medicine man, a long time ago." Thomson spun the paddle in his hand and hefted it, ready to swing at the giant monster when it came into range.

"What can this Big Goose do for us?" I asked.

"When he faced the Windigo he was turned into Missahba the giant, and defeated the beast." The Windigo was no more than a half-dozen steps away from us now.

"Great," muttered Mac. He mopped at the sweat rising on his forehead with a handkerchief from his pocket, his skin smearing into a new series of patterns. "So I get to go digging for a medicine man who may not speak any English so that he can come and turn into a giant and defeat the monster, all before this Windigo gets to us." His voice rose as he spoke, near hysteria by the end.

"Mac!" I barked. "Just try to find the Big Goose!" I jumped forward and bit the Windigo's foot, and at the same time Thomson swung his paddle through the air, connected with a solid thunk on the creature's forearm. It roared in response and slowly kicked at me, but I easily jumped out of the way.

Thomson hit the Windigo again, and this time it struck out and hit him in return. He stumbled back, his feet splashing through the shallows of the lake. "Hurry up, Mac!" I shouted.

"I'm trying, Pat, I'm trying, but nobody's answer…" Mac's voice trailed off, and the Windigo raised an arm, now close enough to strike him.

I bared my teeth and prepared to jump again, but a powerful new voice stopped me dead in my tracks. "Wetikoh! The Great Manitou helped me strike you down once before. Today he will help me do so again!"

I turned and looked, up and up and up. Mac was still there, but he was huge now, a giant every bit as big as the Windigo. The voice wasn't his, but it came from his mouth. He reached across and grabbed the creature by the throat; it let out a strangled cry and fought back, scoring lines in Mac's body, but it seemed to my colourless eyes that he didn't bleed, that instead the paint just furrowed and ran. He cried out and let go of its throat and it immediately leaned its head forward, striving to bite Mac, to eat his flesh.

"Tom!" I yelled. "We need to help!"

"I'm on it, pup!" Thomson called back. He ran from the water and pulled a book of matches and something that looked like a cross between a spatula and knife from his pocket. He knelt on the beach and, using the spatula, pulled portions of painted shore and plant together and built an enormous bonfire, which lit up with one spark of a match.

"Missahba!" he called. "Big Goose! Into the fire now!"

Mac—Missahba, Big Goose, whatever he was called right then— looked down and grinned, slapped the Windigo's head away just before it had reached his throat, then pushed it down towards the fire. "Your heart of ice will melt, Wetikoh, and the stone of your body will be destroyed."

The Windigo howled one more time, and then its body made contact with the fire, flames roaring higher and higher. The stone of its body cracked and popped, and within seconds steam hissed from the cracks as its heart of ice disappeared into the air. It made one more attempt to lash out, this time swinging at Tom, but he stepped back and took the spatula—something that Mac later told me was a palette knife—and worked away at what remained of the creature, scraped at it and rubbed its stone colours in until the paint of its body was a part of our surroundings.

"Thanks," said Thomson, looking up at the still-giant Mac. "Without you and Missahba the giant, shaman, I don't know if we could have stopped the Windigo."

"You did much of this, fire builder," said Big Goose. As he spoke, Mac shrank back to regular size, the excess paint spilling off and mixing with the background. "Medicine man," he said, now speaking to Mac from Mac's own body, "you may return me to the lands of my fathers."

Mac blinked in surprise. "Medicine man? Me?" He smiled, and then closed his eyes. I could sense the change as Big Goose returned to his own afterlife, and once more it was Tom Thomson's painting alone, with Mac and me as guests.

Thomson took his palette knife and put out the fire, painted it and the remains of the Windigo away, mixed them in with the shore and the woods. Then he took the palette knife to Mac's body and repaired the scratches and cuts that the beast had made. After he was done that he shook Mac's hand again and then reached over and scratched me behind the ears. "You both have my thanks," he said. "I don't know how you managed to make your way into here, but you saved me. Uncommon bravery, Pat, attacking the Windigo like that." He patted me on the head again, and I winced. "And without you, Mac, Big Goose would never have known to come."

Mac lifted me into his arms, prepared to leave. "What about you, Tom? Where do you go from here?"

Thomson reached down to a patch of gravel on the shore and picked up his corncob pipe. It had been stepped on, but instead of breaking it had spread into the paint of the shore, but with a few deft moves of his fingers he once again had a working pipe. He lit it, and after sending up some slow, twisting puffs of smoke, he smiled. "Why would I want to go anywhere? Canoe Lake was always my idea of heaven, and everything around you," here he waved at the surrounding landscape, "was my idea." He next picked up the paddle, pushed off the canoe and floated out onto the lake. Before he was too far away, he turned and shouted, "Be sure you tell Jim to take good care of this painting! I'd hate to have to leave!" And after one last wave he paddled off towards a horizon that had suddenly leapt forward.

We both took one last look at Thomson's rendition of creation, watched as it transferred itself from part of our world to a flat painting in front of our eyes. Mac set me down on the floor, and with a smile and a wink he pointed down to one corner, on the sand by the lake.

I stared closely for a second before I saw them: dog tracks, leading off into the bush.

"Toronto's most enduring ghost story (and my favourite) is that of Ivan Reznikoff and Paul Diablos, two stone masons working both on the construction of University College and the affections of the same young Toronto woman. Learning of his lady's infidelity, Reznikoff confronted Diablos and began to chase him with an ax. He took a swing at Diablos, missing him but leaving a gouge in the wooden door of the west entrance by the Croft Chapter House. Reznikoff chased Diablos through the unfinished building to the main tower. During their struggle, Reznikoff fell to his death. Diablos walled Reznikoff into the bottom of the tower, and he and the young woman ran off out west. After the Valentines Day fire in 1890, the remains of an unidentified man were unearthed at the college. Most of the bones and the stone mason's belt were buried beneath a tree on campus; the skull was kept by the University president as a paperweight. Unable to rest in peace, the spirit of Reznikoff appears to students and staff of University College particularly in the early weeks of November. To this day, you will find tucked in the corner between the Croft Chapter House and the colonnade two gargoyles carved by Diablos; one is Reznikoff, the other is Diablos laughing at him. You will also find the ax mark in the door by Croft Chapter House; during exams, some students will touch the mark to claim some of Diablos' luck, while others will refuse to go through the door to avoid the luck of Ivan."

From:
"University College & the Soldier's Memorial Tower" (1997-2003)
Website Content Copyright © 2003 by Toronto Ghosts and Hauntings
Research Society.

After November

by
Roben Goodfellow

The November wind had found a welcome place to pool and whirl amongst the University of Toronto's low stone buildings. It wandered across the faces of gargoyles and through the last tenaciously clinging leaves with a strange and throatless howl. It sped across the grass and vaulted the windows and walls, biting through the flesh of a lone standing student. A wet chill had weighted his clothes, bled through his skin, and settled in his bones until he ceased even to tremble. For all of that, the coldest and heaviest thing about Fergus was the gun in his pocket.

He had been here for what felt like forever but logically it had only been an hour that he'd been standing in place, looking from time to time at the step some ways off. It had been four hours since he'd seen *them* there together. The loop of that vision played over and over mercilessly in his suddenly small and helpless mind. Twisted and garbled quotations bubbled up through the image as it repeated itself again. *Three things remain; betrayal, alcohol, and rage. And the greatest of these...*

In his passable pit of a basement apartment he kept a book of lists. What to wear, what to eat. One hundred and one reasons why he loved Penny, twelve reasons to trust Nathan, eight reasons why he was studying modern social anthropology and not architecture as he'd planned, four secret reasons why he was actually not very good at modern social anthropology—after tonight, he was sure he could bump that one up to at least five or six reasons. And cross out the twelve, wonder after the hundred and one. He'd struggled with the slow sinking reality of the situation that patiently settled around him: it was a surprise, this information, it had to be. There was no way he could have seen it coming.

He'd got the off campus apartment to impress Penny, changed his major to please her and give them something else in common. Or maybe at least one thing in common, nothing was certain tonight. She had seemed impressed, appeared pleased. She'd smiled her shy and haunted smile for him and his knees had literally gone weak. He'd thought he knew what she looked like when she was happy. But that knowledge had changed with radiant and brittle image of her and Nathan and their sick little Judas kiss.

Well...if he was honest it was less of a 'little kiss' and ... what had that English chick in pop culture studies call it? *Full frontal snogging.* Kissage of an entirely different order than Fergus himself had ever been privilege to. Penny had sat decoratively perched on the steps with her overnight bag leaning against her shapely calf. Nathan had walked toward her with his hands in his pockets. He'd made a show of looking around *(without actually seeing,* thought Fergus, *I'd been standing right here)* and Penny had laughed. Nathan laughed with her and Penny had tilted her head in anticipation of a kiss. The kiss lingered, acting on Fergus like a paralytic drug, forcing him to look at the display of careless ease and familiarity. He'd introduced them several times, his best friend and his girl friend and they'd played at not remembering each other. *(They'd played me,* he thought*).* They knew each other, all right, intimate and fierce. Nathan had pulled back to admire Penny and her eyes had rolled under their shimmering lids. She grinned, all teeth and joy. Sad and haunted smiles for Fergus but really and truly, this is what the girl looked like when she was happy. They had stood and walked in the direction of Nathan's condo. When Nathan's hand had slid down her back to settle possessively on one hip, Fergus's eyes had snapped shut.

—•—

And so dutifully the jilted lover had played his part and devoted the last four hours in attempting to drink his body weight in various forms of alcohol. Beer, in an almost patriotic nod, followed by uncountable shots of that wretched liqueur the local university pub had had the indecency to have a special on, followed by whatever fell into his hand. He started at the campus local then rolled through several parties that had loud inviting music and unlocked doors. At one he'd given his jacket away, at another offered a spontaneous sermon on the evils of women and drink that had managed to clear a kitchen, and at yet another he'd acquired the gun. His mind swam to think of which party, but all he remembered was a jagged smile and a brief lesson on how to fire it and what a safety was. He'd staggered along Harbour to Spadina, and turned to stare down the street. Were it not for the compass point of the CN Tower, Spadina looked like another country. Red and gold signs flickered and blazed bright in a broad and welcome path. The sharp smell of spice and food had drawn his feet a few feet south and then tried to coax the contents of his stomach all the way north. Cars honked as he'd held on to the "no loitering" sign for support and he'd breathed deep, steadying himself. *Proud moments,* Fergus had thought, *modern social anthropology in action. Bloody change in the current cultural paradigm...*He'd stood and the cold night air formed a fist in his hair, pulling him back toward campus, toward the offending steps.

—•—

And so here he stood, staring, wandering hand fingering the gun in his pocket with curious and tingling fingers. Why he'd brought it ....maybe to scare them. He thought about that, the cold settling in as the minutes stretched. Might be good to scare them...they'd be at Nathan's now. Fergus had housesat for him a month previous...he still had a key.

Fergus's ears popped and a shiver went through him. He glanced back up the steps. Directly before him stood an absolute monster of a man.

Shorter than himself but somehow wider, the man had black hair, a beard and ice blue eyes that...glowed. *Impossible, trick of the light.* Fergus's mind raced back to recall footsteps and remembered none. The man had no trace of movement around him. He seemed to have been born where he stood. He looked at the younger man as though he were food.

Terrified, Fergus reached into his pocket for the gun at the same

time the older man's fists shot out to grab his shirt and a little skin, jerking him off his feet and forward. A broad forehead connected sharply
with Fergus' cheekbone. White pain sang through him, bringing with it
a shocking wave of undeniable nausea. He turned and fell to his knees,
retching on the pavement. When it was over, his stupor had fled and his
mind was utterly clear. He looked up at the stranger, who now wore an
expression of bemusement.

"You are sober now, yes?" the stranger's voice was rich and deep,
textured by a thick Russian accent, and Fergus nodded a hesitant reply.
The Russian leaned forward, hands on knees and said with purpose
"You punch sober!" and howled in laughter.

Fergus easily found thirty-six immediate reasons to feel unnerved
and frightened but no reasons to join in the other man's obvious mirth.
Gradually the laughter died down as the Russian realized there was no
sharing this joke, and he rolled his eyes and sighed, standing straight
and shifting position. He was dressed almost entirely in varying shades
of brown, from frayed leather shoes to the shapeless jacket pulled over
a deeply distressed sweater. He might have looked like a homeless
person had he not seemed so at ease, like a man standing in his living
room. And then there was the lack of smell…not just lack of the ammo-
nia-and-alcohol street person smell that Urban Sensitivities class had
said it was politically wrong to identify. There was no aftershave, no
soap, no BO, no…anything. Fergus's mind added number thirty-seven
to his list of reasons to be anxious. What kind of person had no smell?
He became aware that his dark and scentless companion was trying a
different tactic. He was speaking in the slow and careful manner that
was used for the mentally feeble.

"Is good trick. Yes?" the stranger grinned, and Fergus again nodded
mutely. A head butt that induced sobriety was definitely a good trick.
"Little boy, you have something that you are going to hand to me all
careful. You will not make me say what it is." *He knows,* Fergus
thought, *he knows what I was reaching for.* The younger man stood and
placed the small gun into the wide and calloused outstretched hand,
which rolled like a magician's hand to pocket the weapon. "Good done,
boy. Call me Ivan."

Wary of the stranger on more levels than he could comfortably register, Fergus once again nodded. His reeling and abruptly sober mind tried to categorize and list facts as he became aware of them. One, the campus was quiet, not even traffic sounds reached where the two men stood. Two, he was very cold. Three, he was unarmed and standing opposite a large and scary man who was talking again.

"I like November." Ivan tilted his head to the side and waited. After a minute during which neither man blinked, he sighed and asked slowly, as though talking to a small child, "Do you know why I like November?"

It seemed genuinely safer to continue to engage Ivan than to attempt escape. No noise meant no people around which meant no help should the evening redefine how it was going wrong. Fergus shook his head and tried to come across as more interested than terrified.

"Because is no sense of the passage of time." Ivan gestured outward with open palms and bowed slightly, welcoming Fergus to a new version of reality, "We have clocks to look at, calendar too, and since the first everybody war even a holiday to punctuate it. But in mind and body—no time passes in November. There is no harvest, no planting. Bad weather to work outdoors and so people sit, do little works. No celebration to prepare for or dread. Even, in some moments, you forget time exists." Ivan closed his eyes and rocked back on his heels. Like a deer freed from the headlights of a car, Fergus relaxed. He could have run, but now he wanted to stay and hear the rest. "No future to wander, no past to regret. Just now, and the choices are not tied to anything. Nothing ahead or behind—but this is delusion. Do you know delusion?" Ivan opened his eyes again and looked back at the younger man.

"I know what the word means, yes," replied Fergus, surprised by the levelness of his own voice.

"Do you know when you are deluded?" Ivan asked.

"I suppose I wouldn't be delusional if I was aware of being deluded." He thought of the last few months—he'd been delusional in thinking everything was all right between himself and Penny, that everything had been friendly with Nathan.

Ivan had turned, beckoning, and started walking leisurely toward the steps. Fergus' feet followed, the movement breathing warmth into his body. He dug his hands into his pockets while his mind did that math. There were faults, things he'd ignored or glossed over. Penny was attractive in a polished way, but she could be brutal to anyone she saw as less than herself. Going out to restaurants was occasionally embarrassing because she was short with the wait staff and made belittling comments about the flawed populous around them. If Fergus didn't indulge these moments of what he saw as shallow cruelty, her serpentine eyes would fog and the comments turned his way. Nathan was always leading the gang in some expensive and moderately fun activity, but there was a knife edge to his humour. Someone had to be the butt of his jokes, always, and Penny had been training Fergus in the fine art of pointing out targets. He was unsure, from time to time, if he loved Penny or loved that she was there to dote on; if he trusted Nathan or if he trusted an ideal of friendship. He wondered if there was any real affection there for the person, the individual rather than a model of something real. The loop of the kiss heaved up in his mind again, and he thought *oh yeah, there's some real affection there all right. Just doesn't involve me.*

"Sometimes is good to live in the moment," Ivan continued, "when you are doing good things. Things which make you feel full with satisfaction of self, like meaningful work or some kind of play you like. Good things in life—just go and do and enjoy. But sometimes is good to live beyond the moment, consider results before you act. When restless thought or anger drive action, is better to stop and think. If not…you may act unwisely and you can no more undo what you do than unsee what you've seen. You saw something tonight, boy. What?" They'd stopped before the steps and Fergus swallowed hard and began.

"I have a friend, and a girlfriend. I saw them here, kissing. I think….no, I know they're fooling around." It sounded pitiably small when given voice, but out of the corner of his eye he saw the older man nodding compassionately. "I…I think I wanted to talk to them." Out loud that part tasted like a lie. When he turned his head to Ivan he saw that the Russian didn't believe him either.

"Fergus." (One word and *starkterrorreturning* he'd never said his name.) "No one thinks good when drunk. No one talks with weapons. Especially after midnight." Ivan sat on the steps.

Fergus felt his shoulders stiffen. He really hadn't said his name, and he sure as hell would have remembered Ivan if they'd met. He thought back to the jagged smile that his drunken memory connected to the gun and Ivan shook his head. It wasn't Ivan who gave him a weapon; Ivan was sitting here responding to Fergus'…thoughts? Fergus took a step back and looked away, eyes settling on a rolling patch of fog…that wasn't rolling anywhere. His eyes widen and then he began to look around wildly at everything he hadn't been focusing on for the last twenty minutes—lights in windows, fog, distant headlights—all frozen and immobile. That's why everything was so quiet—everything had stopped. He considered the possibilities: he could be insane and hallucinating the exchange, dead and walking into limbo, or sane and live but conversing with someone who was neither. As the thought unfurled Ivan grinned and nodded, stretching his hands out again in a welcoming gesture. He leaned forward slightly.

"Listen, Fergus, little boy. One day you'll be dead. There is time beyond November, beyond now. It is before and ahead—even if you can't grasp it, is still there. When you are dead, if you've done a good job of minding future—not just tomorrow but all the years from now— and a good job of learning from your past people will remember you for how you lived. If not, people will remember you for how you died."

"Who *are* you?" Fergus clawed at some shred of normalcy. "Do you … um… do you teach here?"

"Sure," Ivan sighed "I am professor. I teach and sometimes kids learn. Mostly no, but you are all so young. So not all learning, but all my students."

"What do you teach?"

"Life. Which is …irony? Ironic. Earlier, you were cursing all women as vile and men as treacherous. Years from now you'll learn most women—most men, for that matter—are decent." Ivan grinned, tapping his fingertips together. "You just have very bad taste. I had bad taste too, and now no one remembers how I lived. All they remember is—" Ivan's fingers interlaced as he leaned back and Fergus felt his blood slow "—how I died." A moment passed while this thought sunk in and then Ivan shrugged himself up and stood on the stone steps. He folded his arms before him, and regarded the younger man with something between pity and regret. "Now, where were you going tonight?"

"To...scare them, I guess..." Fergus's voice drifted off. It was pointless to lie to someone who could see his thoughts.

"Just scare? Nothing more?"

"I don't know."

"And *that* didn't scare *you*?"

Fergus stared at his feet, breathless. He shook his head, once again mute and terrified. It wasn't the phantom before him that had him frightened though, nor the fact that the world seemed still. *What might he have done?*

"You weren't scared because you were stupid," Ivan's voice was kind as he continued, placing an arctic hand on his student's shoulder, "You know what happens to stupid people? When we don't think?"

Fergus looked up to meet Ivan's vividly hollow eyes. Years ago he'd rejected the story as a frosh week fable but now he believed. Ivan Reznikoff and Paul Diablo had worked side by side in 1856 and loved the same woman, who'd chosen Paul. Enraged, Reznikoff had chased Diablo with an axe through the grounds, the buildings, the tower...and had been killed himself in a fall. Diablo had walled the body into a tower, and within years the first sightings of Ivan began to be reported, always before a tragedy...

"Sometimes I am good teacher, with good students. Then no one thinks 'tragedy' and no one says later they talk to me." Ivan's voice seemed to echo off the fog that crept in around them. It was a solid fog, granite-grey yet vital in its ripple and flow. It hummed as it encircled them.

"What do you want from me?"

"I want you to be a good student." Ivan stepped away and down from the steps, turning so Fergus had his back to the building. "You know forever is not how it feels, yes? You know this when you are sober. The fire of revenge fades, it dies. Trust me. I've far more reason than you to be angry and I'm tired of being angry. Regret—this is what never ends."

How could they, Fergus thought as the loop played again in his mind, and Ivan raised a hand.

"They did. That's all. Their choice, you can't control. You control only you; how you see them, how you see you. Maybe you ... have respect for self, maybe you think you're worth better, move on. Maybe if you didn't see them tonight you'd marry girl, go into business with this 'friend.' Ten years later you see one of your kids has his nose. How much worse would that feel? Much worse. Be grateful for tonight."

Fergus thought about that. He couldn't imagine feeling worse about the whole stupid mess than he did, and didn't want to try. Penny wore a promise ring that was worth a year's textbook fees and hadn't showed any signs of returning it. She likely would have married him, for her own strange and circuitous reasons. It would have been a total fraud and who knows how long it would have lasted, how many years he would have lost to it.

"Now this." Ivan took the gun from his pocket and turned it over in his hand. "Bad souvenir. You'll be mad again tomorrow, off and on for some time. Maybe you want a souvenir of tonight—but not this, I give you something else. Agreed?"

Fergus nodded. Ivan pocketed the gun again and reached into the lining of his jacket. The humming in the fog around them grew to a cacophony as Ivan produced a small mason's trowel with a worn wooden handle. He turned it in his massive fingers as though showing off a precious gem.

"See? Better reminder of tonight, better lesson. Better to build your life than tear it down, yes?" Ivan smiled.

Fergus nodded again and reached for the tool. As his hand closed around the handle, his ears popped for the second time in an hour, and the discordant racket in the fog separated to distinct sounds: traffic, laughter, a distant party. Both Ivan and the fog were gone. He turned in the direction of Nathan's apartment, staring and thinking. No, he didn't want to see them tonight. Maybe he'd avoid them for a bit but eventually he'd be honest and tell them what he'd seen and didn't care to see again. Maybe they'd try to rewrite the history he'd seen between them, explain; maybe Penny would blame him. It didn't matter; he could only control himself. Fergus turned the trowel toward a streetlight and saw an inscription burned in a careful script. "Think not, because no man sees, such things remain unseen." He vaguely remembered the poem it was from but not if it was published before or after Ivan's death in the 1850's. That didn't matter either, he decided, carefully tucking the trowel into the back pocket of his jeans. Maybe the dead could learn from the living.

Fergus began to walk in the direction of his apartment, to prove the living could learn from the dead.

"Wherefore, the wolf-pack having gorged
upon the lamb, their prey,
With siren smile and serpent guile
I make the wolf-pack pay—"

The Harpy

by
Lynda Williams

Bean Creek might have been any place north of civilization with more men than women and one general store. Located on a river, it could be reached only by boat or a logging road.

Bean Creek was the sort of town that men collected in, once a year, to cash in and stock up: hard men, for the most part; lost men, who came north looking for something, didn't find it, but stayed anyhow.

Bean Creek was Candy Songful's kind of town.

Knowing when to arrive was important. It was no good coming when the tide of men was at its lowest ebb, with nothing but permanent residents in occupation, hunkered down waiting for money to flow. It was no good coming when the money was all spent and the flood of men had seeped away, again, into the bush. Knowing when to arrive was an instinct she'd developed when she took up the trade she had long since stopped working at and simply become. When she sensed Bean Creek was ripe for harvest, she roused herself from where she had been resting between jobs, and packed her trunk.

She needed very little, but she always brought her trunk.

Candy reached Bean Creek in a motorboat, sitting as far forward as she could, her impractical hat secured with a lemon-coloured scarf that was tied in a big floppy bow. She wore a yellow dance hall dress with creamy-green and pastel-purple flounces, set off by cheap jewellery that glittered, and lace-up boots of lemon-coloured leather.

The boat was captained by an old man with the stony taste of work about him, who sat in the back and said nothing, as the buzzing of the motor and the smell of gasoline grated upon Candy's nerves.

Along the way, they passed a strip of naked ground, denuded like a man's chin after shaving, with only the stubble of dead stumps left over from the harvesting of timber. She drew back her lips, like a wince, at the sight of it, showing teeth that were just a bit irregular, with one missing in the middle of her lower jaw. Whenever Candy was upset, she poked her tongue into that blank space in her mouth, where a dentist had extracted her tooth with pliers many years before, and turned the cold engagement ring upon her finger around and around. She did both, now, until the boat was past the bare patch and the river bank was dressed in trees, once more.

Candy Songful liked the quiet of the North. She liked the timeless majesty of the forest that cloaked the small, bitter traces of her prey, in the same way that mice were hidden by long grass until they moved, and gave themselves away. This was where she belonged.

Only the motor disturbed her peace with its droning, incessant reminder that change encroached upon her from all sides. She would have preferred a canoe or a paddle wheeler, but there were only motorboats to hire, these days. There were no horses in the cities, either, only motorized rail cars and carriages that choked the air with smells too different to define, and filled cities with too much of everything, too densely packed. She preferred to ply her trade here, in the North, where the towns called to her when they were ripe, the way they always had.

As they neared the landing at Bean Creek, she wondered if she had visited the town before, but the reception antennae bristling skyward in a half a dozen spots were alien and nothing else stood out for her to recognize. Perhaps Bean Creek had not been here the last time she came up this river, or perhaps it was called something else at the time. Every town she visited had long since merged in her mind.

Not the men, though. In a half a hundred years of plying her trade, up and down waterways by riverboat, ferry, or barge; and overland by carriage, rail, or car, to wherever she was drawn, she had never forgotten a single man. Each and every one who had nourished her remained an individual in her mind: a source of strength, making it possible to go on.

A new prospect stood, transfixed, on the muddy staging ground beyond the little wharf, as Candy stepped out of the motorboat, flashing her shapely calves. He was a young man, with a rough hewed sort of handsomeness, wearing work clothes and a baked-on tan. He pulled the stub of a cigarette from his mouth and put a foot on it, stifling it in the damp earth of the riverbank.

"Hello, " Candy said, brightly, and smiled.

The young man answered her with a stiff, wary nod.

She could get no immediate reading from him on as little as that, so added, "Is there a place in town where I might take a room?"

"There's the hotel," he said, and broke off to watch the old boatman heave Candy's trunk onto the wharf, with a grunt, and then straighten up, flexing his arms.

"Perfect." Candy smiled, her lips shiny with pale, pink gloss. "Would you be so kind as to show me the way, and perhaps even carry my trunk up?"

"Are you a whore?" he asked suddenly, point-blank.

Candy giggled. "Why, yes," she said, charmed by such directness. "Of course! There is work for me, in town, I hope?"

"Hotel is that way," he said, gruffly, pointing up the main street, which ran up an incline from the wharf for the length of about fifteen buildings before terminating in a wall of raw forest. "You can carry your own trunk," he added, and walked off.

Well! Candy thought, in a huff, and cast about for the old boatman, only to discover he had taken advantage of the interlude to cast off. She frowned, and reminded herself—again—not to pay such people in advance. She was good at making herself such mental notes, although less apt to make use of them later.

With a great sigh, Candy seized one end of her trunk in one well-manicured hand, gave a heave, and strode two steps before she realized she would need help, after all. She was simply not at her most vigorous right now. She made another mental note never to put off getting back to work for so long, but cheered herself with the thought that she had always got by before. Things would be no different this time, even if the world had changed—again—while she had been gone. The last time she had come out of hibernation for a feed, it was gramophone players and radios everywhere, closely followed by some idiocy about a far-away war. Things felt much calmer now, by comparison, the rhythms of northern life undisturbed by distant quarrels.

All the same, the cool reception of her first prospective customer and the prominent sprinkling of receiving dishes, looking like bowls set out for giants on the roofs of half a dozen buildings in so small a town, gave Candy pause. She sat down on her trunk, reassured by the comfort it offered, and made an effort to think it all through once more.

It was true that she was getting out of touch. She had noticed she returned to the world less and less often as it changed more and more. What if her prey changed, too? What if men stopped being selfish and cruel? What would happen to her if she starved? The very fact that she was frightened, at all, was proof that this return to the world was long overdue.

Candy stroked the weathered top of her heavy, wooden trunk as she looked around, cataloging what was familiar to her and what was not. In the end, she decided the familiar far outweighed the things she did not recognize, and she took heart.

Leaving her trunk where it was, with a parting pat, Candy marched up the slope in the direction of the rustic hotel, her lemon-coloured, lace-up boots acquiring a slick layer of light brown clay where they came into contact with the wet road. She slipped once or twice, but never badly enough to soil more than her footwear. Men emerged from buildings, one by one, to watch her pass, and her spirits rose with every stare she collected.

Her hips swung and her bosom giggled as she walked, casting smiles in the direction of the men who had come out to watch, and probing for more through the thin, wooden walls of the buildings that lined Bean Creek's main street, enroute to the hotel that the upsetting young man had pointed out.

By the time she reached her destination, she had attracted a small cloud of men, drawn forth by her presence. Those watching TVs had turned them off. A pair who had been listlessly gambling gave up, although one of them carried a couple of cards, forgotten, in one hand.

Two men waited on the hotel's front porch. A TV chattered point-lessly inside, behind them, just visible through the open door.

So that is all the big bowls on the roof tops are about, Candy thought, contemptuously. *Nothing but radio with pictures.* Between that insight, and the proof of her impact on the locals, she felt confident once more.

"Can I help you?" the older of the two hotel men asked. He was balding and fifty, with a dirty apron spread over a big paunch, but he had the air of being the one in charge.

"I want a room," Candy told him, brightly. "I will expect to be fed, as well. And waited upon. I need my trunk collected, to start. I'll give you one third of my take, in compensation. Believe me, you will make more than you have in six months."

The hotel owner looked surprised, then calculating. "I don't know," he said. "We've already got a girl working here, by the name of Roxy. I think one whore in a town this size is enough. And I don't like the look of you very much." He frowned at a dawning suspicion. "You from some kooky reality TV show, up here to make fools of us?"

Candy frowned. "A what?" She shook her head before anyone answered her, feeling impatient. "Let me explain in private," she suggested, and relaxed her jaw as she tightened her throat for a warm-up performance.

Her song had no words and no tune. Or none, at least, that human ears could make out. It focused like a beacon on the evil in the hotel owner who stood confronting her, suspiciously, on the porch. She sang him the guilt he owed his mother; the pain of an abandoned wife and child; and the truth of a wrong he'd done a partner twenty years ago. She sang to him in tiny, piercing needles, that reminded him of loved ones he had wronged; working, acid-like, on his defenses, and eroding his own bitter, selfishness.

It was only a sampler, only a hint—at this distance—of what she could do, but the hotel owner shuffled back, and shook his head, as if stung.

"I guess you can stay, sure," he said, a moment later, looking confused. Then he rallied, and turned his ill-humour on the lanky boy at his side. "Don't stand there gaping, Cam, go get the lady's trunk!"

The boy addressed as Cam all but fell off the porch in his hurry to do as he was told. He went galloping down the slippery street to where the trunk sat waiting by Bean Creek's little wharf, slipping on the damp earth every dozen steps in his headlong rush.

That's more like it, Candy thought, took inventory of the men around her with a smile, and marched up the steps to the porch.

The TV Candy had dismissed as picture-radio occupied pride of place in the main room of the hotel, which served as both restaurant and bar. Candy glared at it with a sharp, ill-defined feeling of offense at its newness, and felt with her tongue for the spot where the missing tooth was in her jaw. Then she lost patience, tensed, and emitted a silent assault that shorted the hated thing out.

The hotel owner did not seem to mind, or even notice.

"So happy we can do business," she told him, as he bobbed along in front of her, showing the way with hesitant hand gestures, as if she was a celebrity he feared to frighten off.

"Not at all!" he said, tears standing in his befuddled eyes. "It is my pleasure."

"Pleasure is my job," she assured him, and stopped. He stopped as well, face-to-face with her, eyes wide and mouth slightly open. She coiled a slim hand about his cauliflower ear with a touch like oiled silk. "What's your name?" Candy purred.

"Ben," he croaked.

She leaned forward, breathing on his upper lip, and sipping the shivers of pleasure rising off him in response. "Would you like to become my first customer, Ben?" she asked. "No charge. Consider it payment in advance, on our bargain."

Ben the hotel owner nodded, nearly breathless with excitement. He managed a single, wolfish look over his shoulder at the men on the street, outside, through the open door. Then he surrendered to Candy as she collected his big, tobacco-stained hand.

She let him show her which room was to be hers, on the second floor.

Once inside, she put her purse down on a homely dresser, took her hat off, and turned around, driven by a growing sense of urgency inspired by the tantalizing appetizer she had sampled so far.

"Lie down," she said, and gestured to the simple bed covered with a rough grey blanket.

He did it without even taking off his shoes.

Candy contained herself long enough to close the door. She crossed swiftly back to the bed, and sat down, her smile fixed on her face like makeup.

She glided her hand over the hill-shaped mound of his torso, not quite close enough to touch. "Now," she whispered, in a throaty voice, "Give me your selfishness!"

Her mouth darted to his like a striking snake. The dumbstruck look on men's faces in that critical moment always struck her as rather off putting, so she closed her eyes.

Inside, he was gritty and hot: a furnace of self-centred pity and hard, grumbling complaints about his lot. She probed his resistance to his mother's devotion; the way he had justified leaving his wife to pursue a younger woman; and the business acumen that quashed all considerations of friendship in the face of profits to be had. She lapped up his greed like a gravy sauce as she crunched on the meal of his mean-spirited self-interest, coated in the meat of his succulent, petty excuses. Here was a glorious meal of a man! No less delectable for being small in his achievements, because his potential was as great as that of any monster history had thrown up on its cluttered shores. He could have been a fine monster, given the chance.

Gleefully, she finished what she had begun on the porch, not merely stirring dormant guilt, but leeching his selfishness out of him like calcium sucked from bone; taking it into herself, to cure her of the need to care for anyone, and make her strong.

Candy disconnected from the kiss with a faint pop and sat up, feeling much better. Life glittered with renewed faith in her own brand of self-indulgence. Down at the wharf she had suffered doubts. Now just being Candy Songful was better than a million dollars, once more!

She looked at Ben, on the bed, and gave a giggle at the thought of how he would be diminished when he woke up, drained of his greed and ambition, forever separated from the insulation offered by his callous disregard for others. He would be doomed to failure, without the necessary cruelty to claw his way to the top of even so modest a hill as the one on the main street of Bean Creek, where his hotel stood.

Candy fixed her dress, retied the ribbon of her yellow hat, and fixed her bright eyes on the drying smears of clay on her high leather boots. She would get the boy who went to fetch her precious trunk to clean them, when he brought it back. Then she would order a meal and revel in her newly restored invulnerability, recounting all the nasty details of the hotel owner's life to the secret, silent audience of her heart of hearts, to fix it in her memory and keep it fresh forever. She could sometimes even get an extra squeeze of meanness out of old conquests when she recounted them, aloud, in the privacy of her room. She had always liked to hear herself talk.

On the bed, the hotel owner came around with a groan.

"Hello, Ben," Candy said, gloating at her triumph with the potency of the very smugness she had sucked from him moments before.

He stared at her, his big hands limp on the bed that lay so miraculously undisturbed beneath him, when he knew he had just enjoyed the most astonishing tryst of his life. Then his eyes filled with tears and he said, "Room's free. Food too. Stay as long as you want."

"That's remarkably generous," Candy told him, with a simpering bow in his direction. "But I would like some time to myself now, if you don't mind. Except for that boy of yours. Cam, you called him? Do send Cam up, with the trunk."

"Of course," he said, and floundered to his feet. "Of course." He made a patting gesture as if to reassure her of something, and scrambled for the door like a big, ungainly walrus out of water, grinning like a fool. "And thank you, thank you so much!" he said in parting, staring at her out of eyes that brimmed with tears.

Candy laughed the moment that he closed the door, drunk on her own power, and anticipating a particularly splendid evening of reminiscences.

"How did you do that?" a voice said, making Candy catch her breath with a gasp and spin around.

Emerging from the closet, where she must have hidden earlier, was a slip of a girl in tight blue jeans and a very revealing blouse. Her sandy brown hair was cut short in a style that left it longer in the front than the back, and she wore things in her ears that were attached by wires to a little box, the width of two fingers, that dangled around her neck on a black cord. Motorboats and radios were old annoyances, and TVs had already been dismissed as nothing really new, but Candy had never seen anything like this girl's wired necklace before, nor encountered such arrogance in a woman!

"Who are you!" Candy snarled.

Unperturbed, the girl answered, "Roxy. I work here. I'm headed south and working my way down. Same line of work as you, I'm guessing." Her tone changed to one of acute interest. "How did you get Ben to give you free room and board? With a kiss?" Roxy laughed. "You must use something wicked in your lip gloss."

Candy hissed. "What would you know, stupid child! But by all means," she added, with dignity. "Think what you want. So long as you go away. Now."

Someone knocked and then opened the door without waiting for a response.

The gangly boy named Cam struggled in backwards carrying Candy's trunk. The young man Candy had met, upon arrival, carried the other end of the trunk through the door.

At the sight of the second man, Roxy rolled her eyes and folded her thin arms. "I told you to go away, Bo," she said, with disgust.

"Not before you have listened to me, properly, just once," said the young man, straightening and stepping around the trunk.

Without help, Cam let his end of the trunk drop.

"Be careful with that!" Candy yelped as it settled with a clunk.

"I've already heard everything you've got to offer me, Bo," said the girl with the plugs in her ears and the little box-thing hanging around her neck with the wires attached. "Respectable boredom and drudgery just aren't in my plans. "

"And you still feel like that after seeing the alternative, in the flesh?" The young man asked, gesturing at Candy with an open palm. "Is that what you want to be, Roxanne? Is that what you want to become?"

"What, her?" exclaimed the girl, with a snort. "She's a caricature! She looks like some college girl hired to put on a show for the tourists at some dumb historic park!"

"What I meant," Bo insisted, "is that she is alone. With no one. No family. No friend to trust or man to love."

Roxy gave Candy a second once-over, showing more respect for the quality of her attire, this time, if not its antequated style. "Looks to me like she is doing all right by herself, if you put it like that," she remarked.

"I am not alone," Candy told them both, haughtily, offended by their ignorance. Then decided to enjoy the absurdity of the situation before she dealt with the problem of being observed by the girl, earlier.

"I had a man like him, once," she told Roxy, indicating Bo. She held up the hand with the engagement ring on it. "A man who made hollow promises to get what he wanted without paying for it, and then broke them all because men are simply like that. They can't help it. They make promises the way that women change their clothes. Inside them is nothing but self-interest and glory-lust. That is why they make fools of women who put their faith in love. Men know how to win. I learned that from them, and now I steal their power. I take it for myself, and leave them as vulnerable as I was, troubled by the pain that they cause others, and in need of people's goodwill. Cripples, dependent on a kind word from a loved one. Do I do well, in the material sense that you doubtless meant to imply? Oh yes, indeed, I have! I have enjoyed the best that any man can buy me, in my time, but that is nothing compared to the joy of being what I am—as satisfied as any eagle while it tears the belly of the thrashing fish upon the riverbank!" She shrilled in a high-pitched, joyful cry, soaring into song that stretched beyond any ordinary sound. "I am the harpy! I-am-I-am-I-eyyyy!"

Bo winced, and staggered. Roxy clapped her hands over her ears, and the boy called Cam collapsed upon the floor. Candy's shrilling broke into a manic laugh and died away except for the bright glitter in her blue eyes.

Roxy lowered her hands. Bo swayed, holding onto the frame of the bed's headboard to stay up. Cam remained on the floor, near the trunk, where he had collapsed.

Roxy said, in a quiet voice, "Far out."

Candy grew tired of all of this playing around. She crossed to where Bo was struggling to stay on his feet and chucked him onto the bed. While he was still disoriented, she shoved him down and covered him with her body, enjoying the more pleasing proportions of his own than she had her last victim's corpulent form. She drew back her head as he began to shake off the effects of her cry. She was impatient, but she remembered to smile.

"Kiss me," she said to him.

Bo looked alarmed.

"Hey!" the girl called Roxy rapped out. "What are you going to do?"

Candy rarely bothered to woo the men she fed on. It was normally enough to let them line up at her door, once she had made them maudlin with her siren song. And she took the kind of men who sought her out. Bo's reluctance confused her, but her hunger was aroused.

Even as she felt Roxy's hands grip her shoulders, she struck.

The kiss did not work properly from the start.

Bo had not invited her. He did not even want her. He wanted Roxanne, but there was little in that disappointed desire for Candy to sink her teeth into. Bo half realized that his childhood sweetheart was not who he thought she was. He still cared about Roxanne for the sake of their better childhood memories, and both their families, who could not grasp the depth of Roxanne's stubborn, selfish desires. In fact, there was very little of anything in Bo that was appetizing at all. He was a clean-living youth barely nineteen years old. He had never had a woman except Roxanne, and would have preferred to marry her. Giving each other a "test drive," as she'd called it, had been her idea. He was the one who had been used. The whole thing meant a lot more to him than it did to her. All she wanted to do was to go south, to enjoy the money, booze, and lifestyle of fame as a night club singer, whore or drug dealer, if necessary, that she had soaked up from TV shows. He wanted to stay up north, to take over his dad's fleet of logging trucks, and raise a family that would take over from him, one day, like a link in a sturdy, unremarkable chain. He would have gone south to save her, and had followed her this far before he realized that she didn't see it like that.

Roxanne wanted to be the sort of person that other people needed saving from.

In fact, it was Roxanne, not Bo, who felt more like Candy's usual meal. Except she was a woman! It was all wrong!

Candy realized with a nasty shock that her insights into Roxanne were much, much too vivid to be second hand! She opened her eyes to discover it was Roxy, not Bo, that she grappled with, Roxy who had her on her back, holding her down. The girl's thin arms had more strength in them than Candy thought they should. Fierce ambition burned in Roxanne's brown eyes.

"Make me like you! " Roxanne ordered. "Do it! Give me the power!"

Stupid girl, Candy thought, *it does not work like that!* She wasn't sure how it did work. She never had been sure. One day, with a particular client, months after she had been deserted and ruined, in the days when gold was making men like her beloved William turn evil with heartless ambition, it had simply happened. The first thing she had done was find William and take all his selfishness from him, until he wept for what he had done by deserting her and took his own life, in guilty repentance, unable to live with the knowledge. Everything had seemed obvious and natural after that.

Now there was this wretched, anomalous girl, confusing her with senseless demands. A girl, but a girl whose green spires of power lust called to Candy every bit as powerfully as Ben's more familiar, grizzled crimes.

Even so, Candy hesitated, never having fed upon a woman in all the long, seamless hours of her harpy life, and oddly disconcerted by the whole thing in the same way that she was put off by motors. But the very novelty of the situation destabilized her, and that she could not bear. No matter what the source, she needed a new meal of selfish arrogance.

Candy struck, mouth-to-mouth with the girl in tight blue jeans, and pumped out her wordless song.

There was a white explosion, like dying and being reborn. She was twenty-three, and in love with a dashing young man. She believed in that love when she ran away with him to seek their fortune; loved him enough to sell herself to raise the stake he needed; and died inside when he abandoned her to cope, alone.

The next thing she knew, she was weeping, curled up on the floor in a ball.

Strong hands took her by the shoulders and raised her to rest in a man's arms.

She stirred, groping blindly for a moment. "William?" she asked, confused.

"No," said the young man named Bo.

She blinked, and for an instant remembered what she'd come to Bean Creek for. She reached for all the hard, sustaining coals of pride and selfishness that had kept her safe for so long. She reached for the hard brilliance of her power, and found it gone. And in that moment, all her harpy memories were gone.

"What happened?" she bleated, in panic, and struggled to sit up, clutching his arms.

"Roxanne," Bo said, roughly, and paused to clear his throat. "Something happened between you. Now she's gone."

A long-legged youth shuffled over closer to her, on the floor, and added with apology, "She took your trunk."

"Are you engaged?" Bo asked her, raising the hand she wore William's ring on.

She tugged at the ring, the knife of grief in her chest driving her on. It came off. She threw it far away from her, across the floor.

"William left me," she remembered aloud, brimful with the pain of a betrayal that was decades old.

"You are different," Bo said. "So was Roxanne." He touched her hair gingerly. "My name's Bo Wallace," he said. "Who are you?"

"Candice," she said. "Candice—but I can't remember much more."

Even the pain in her chest over William was fading fast, as if someone had laid a thick, white curtain of gauze over her past.

"It is all right," said Bo. "I'll look after you."

—•—

Weeks later, in a much larger city to the south, the woman who went by the stage name of Roxy Bird when she performed to mesmerized customers at the seedy bar—where she had settled because the feeding there was truly fine—got around to engaging a locksmith to open her sturdy old trunk.

She waited until the locksmith had left, before she knelt to lift the latch. She smiled. She pushed it open with both hands. The smell of lavender wafted out.

Inside she found the body of a man with a fatal knife wound through the heart, preserved in pickling salt, and packed about with a fortune in gold nuggets and little, rotting bags of gold dust that filled up his empty eyes and gaping mouth.

"The first year of operation [of Long Island Flowering Mills, now Watson's Mill] was a great success and the partners decided to have a party on March 11th, 1861, to celebrate. Mr. And Mrs. Currier had arrived from Ottawa in the early afternoon to tour the premises. Some reports indicate it was Joseph who was showing his wife and a few other guests through the building, while other records seem to indicate that a Mr. Merrill was the guide. ... Mrs. Currier and the other guests were dodging the moving machinery when Ann's long crinoline dress became caught in the fast-turning shaft; she was flung against a pillar, hitting her head and perishing instantly.

"Even though Ann's life was short and her death was tragic, her existence in the mill seems to be continuing and be of a contented nature. She doesn't require a key to enter or leave the mill; she just seems to breeze in and out, as the spirit moves her.

"The second-storey corner window at the front of the mill nearest to the dam has been said to be "Ann's Window." It is the one where the sightings of her have most often occurred."

From
"The Mistress of Watson's Mill" in *Looking Back* (2004)
by Larry Ellis, Copyright © 2004 by Larry Ellis, Manitock, Ontario.

The Ghost of Watson's Mill Is Online

by
Daniel Archambault

L ifting up my crinolines and skirts, I stepped off the shore of Manotick's Long Island and up onto the dam. The river was nearly frozen. The trees were bare of leaves and the boughs of evergreens were weighed down by mounds of snow. A few ducks swam in small patches of open water below me and by the bridge downstream. My legs were freezing, and it was obvious that my jacket was far too thin for the weather as well. When had such a harsh a winter come? It did not matter. The weather was uncomfortable, and I needed to get inside.

I hurried across the dam, brushing by two children along the way. I rushed up the steps and briskly walked through the front doors of a stone flouring mill on the other side of the river. To my right was a staircase. I climbed up the stairs to the second floor. In this room, where belts and gears once whirred overhead, powered by the turbine and the Rideau River below, hardly anything moved. The shaft at the other end of the room spun freely.

The room, as it always did, reminded me of a story.

— • —

"What are you doing?"

Melanie turned to see that her brother had walked all the way back onto the dam and was almost to where she was standing. His fists were resting on his hips, and he wore that "hurry up and let's get going" look, which was ever so annoying.

"Didn't you feel that strange, cold wind?"

Luke rolled his eyes. "Yeah. It's called winter, you idiot. In case you hadn't noticed, it's freezing out here! Mom and Dad are already inside. They sent me out to get you. Hurry up!"

"I'll be there in a minute, okay? Let me watch some of the sunset."

"Whatever." He shoved his hands inside the pockets of his ski jacket, turned his back to her, and stomped up the stairs to the front entrance of the mill.

Melanie sighed. Her brother could make her so angry sometimes. She watched the ducks on the water to calm herself down. She didn't care what Luke or anyone else thought. No matter how cheesy the "strange, cold wind" sounded, it was not winter. It was something else, or, someone else.

Her eyes wandered up to a second floor window. It was Ann's window: the window through which many people had seen the ghost of Ann Currier. The young woman of twenty, just six weeks into marriage, had died violently there. Melanie hoped, as she did almost every day, that she would see Ann, but tonight as usual, Ann's window was empty.

She turned away from the window, hurried up the steps, and entered the mill.

—•—

I watched Melanie disappear through the front doors. Stepping farther away from the window, I began to pace soundlessly. A Christmas event was starting downstairs. People were singing carols.

I remembered the story again, as I always did in this room. There once had been a lot of machinery here. Belts had zipped along the ceiling. Thick gears had turned at my feet. I almost recalled how it felt to have the wake of quickly rotating metal blow past me. The metallic sounds of the machinery had nearly drowned out Mr. Merrill's voice as he had tried to explain the workings of the grain elevator and how it stored grain in the garner bin for grinding. I had been walking around the room, surveying the many gadgets.

I had felt a sharp tug. The world had blurred.

"Ann!"

There had been a pillar. I remembered feeling pain as I hit it and seeing my own blood running down over my eyes.

I held my head in my hands and cried. I felt like I was dying again. The more time I spent here, the more the pain of that day would run through my mind. I needed to put my spirit at ease.

It was then, for the first time, I decided I would contact Melanie.

—•—

After the fifth or sixth carol, Melanie left her mom and dad to go find some hot chocolate. People were selling cups of it on one of those fold-out tables at the end of the mill near the staircase to the second floor. She bought some and found a place to stand nearby.

She held the cup in both her hands and sipped at it. It was below minus twenty outside. Although the mill was heated, it was still a little bit chilly. The warmth of hot chocolate on a cold, winter's night made it taste all that much better.

There was a break in the singing. Some Ottawa Valley boys at the other end of the room started playing their fiddles. People were stomping and clapping and Melanie felt the stamping through the floor. The floor creaked and the musty smell of old wood became more prominent. The crowd moved back and cleared a patch for dancers. Five or six couples were soon stepping in time to the music.

Melanie watched her mom and dad out there: the lanky fellow with the curly red hair and beard with the tallish Japanese woman in his arms. She liked to watch them dance. She didn't get to see them dance very often: sometimes here, sometimes on New Year's Eve, but when she had the opportunity, she could gaze at them for hours.

With all the music and the dancing, Melanie didn't notice exactly when it became much colder. Underneath her winter jacket, she felt goose bumps. Cold air brushed her cheek like someone had opened the front door, but Melanie saw the door was closed. Besides, the wind came from the wrong direction. It came from the stairway to the second floor, or so she thought.

She then heard something move upstairs, like a person getting out of a chair at school. She couldn't believe no one else had heard it. She couldn't believe that no one stopped dancing or clapping and looked up. The fiddlers launched themselves into another tune as she stared upstairs into the blackness.

There was another short burst of dragging. Melanie decided to investigate. This could be her only chance ever to see Ann's ghost! Gulping down the little bit of hot chocolate she had left, she quickly stepped over the barrier that was supposed to keep people from the second floor and scooted up before anyone saw.

At first, she couldn't see anything. As her eyes began to adjust to the light, odd shapes began to jut out into the darkness. Some of the forms were softened, covered by blankets, others were jagged and strange: mill equipment.

Melanie knew one of the machines here might have taken Ann's life. The thought of Ann's death made her hesitant to wade into the darkness. The pillar that killed her was up here, still containing the impression of Ann's bloody fingernails as legend had it. She wandered around in the small patch of light that shone up the stairs to see if she could see her ghost, or the source of the noise.

Skritch!

She turned around quickly, seeing an old work desk and a chair to the side. *Skritch! Skritch!* The chair was sliding on the floor.

Skriiiiiittch! Bang!

Melanie dropped to the floor. Under its own volition, the chair slid a quarter of the way across the room and slammed into the wall. It fell over and rocked on its back to rest. The only sounds she heard were her own breathing and the distant fiddle music that wafted up the stairs, seemingly so very far away.

There was nowhere to hide. She would have to try and crawl back into the stairwell. But, before she could....

"BOO!"

She jumped, but quickly realized that her brother had sprung out from behind the desk. He was now sitting on top of it, holding his belly with laugher, and rocking back and forth.

"That was so awesome!" he said. He was laughing so hard he was crying. "I got you so good!"

"No, you didn't!"

"Oh yes, I did! I saw you! You were going to piss yourself!"

"I was not!"

"Was so!" Luke opened his eyes really wide and flickered his fingers at her. "OooooOOOooooo! Ghost of Ann Currier, Melanie! Better watch out! She's coming to get you!"

Melanie rose to her feet to leave, but stopped when she saw a dimly glowing woman in white behind her brother. The woman was wearing an old-fashioned dress that made her look like she was going to a party. Her long, blonde hair flowed down before disappearing behind her shoulders. She held the finger of her left hand over her lips and Melanie tried desperately to comply.

Her brother stopped smiling and giggling and began to smirk.

"Very funny, Melanie! What are you going to do next? Oh, look Luke! There's a ghost behind you!"

"No, actually," the woman said. "I was going to say that." Luke slowly turned his head to meet the gaze of her very black eyes. She smiled thinly at him. "Because, there is."

Melanie didn't recall seeing Luke get off the desk, but she believed it was a requirement for all his running and falling down the stairs that ensued afterward.

"I am so very sorry," the woman said. "I do not consider that proper behaviour, but your brother was being very mean. Unfortunately, I do not have that much time. Luke will certainly cause a stir downstairs shortly. Melanie, I need your help. Would you offer it?"

Melanie nodded.

"Good. Meet me near the front doors of the mill tomorrow at noon. I will explain everything you need to know then."

The woman vanished. A cold wind lifted the hair off Melanie's shoulders, leaving her in the dark room with only the sound of party guests running upstairs.

—•—

For the rest of the night and the next morning, Melanie felt her mom
was mothering Luke too much. It seemed that she spent a lot of time
going upstairs to check on him. The ghost certainly had frightened him
badly, but she couldn't understand why he needed all the attention.
Besides, Ann wasn't frightening; she was fascinating. Melanie had every
intention of crossing the river in an hour to see what Ann had to say.

After finishing up some of her homework, she looked at her watch.
It was a quarter to noon. She packed some books in her knapsack, just
in case Ann was late for their meeting, and headed out to the front porch
to put on her shoes.

"Hey, Melanie. Where are you off to?"

She turned to see her mother. She must have just come downstairs
after checking on Luke.

"I'm just going out for a walk, Mom."

"Can I come with you?"

"No. I'll be fine."

"Oh, all right," she said. "But be home for lunch at one."

"All right. Thanks, Mom."

Melanie stepped out into the afternoon, shutting the door behind
her quietly. It was very cold today; so cold, in fact, the hairs on the
inside of her nose seemed to freeze together when she inhaled. She
buried her face inside the collar of her jacket and ran to Watson's Mill.

When she got there, it felt like any other day. The old limestone mill
was silent. All five windows on the three floors were dark and it seemed
as though no one was there. However, she knew there was a ghost inside
the mill, waiting for her, and, for the first time, Ann's spirit was making
her nervous. Standing on the step for a few moments, she wondered if
she should knock.

—•—

I was pondering the strange flags just outside my window when I heard
a knock at the door. I noticed that Melanie was on the doorstep. I waved
to her and went downstairs to meet her.

"Good afternoon, Melanie. I am glad you decided to return. Would you like to walk outside? It is a lovely day even though it is a little cold."

"You can walk outside?"

"Yes, certainly. However, it is difficult to see me as it is not foggy today, and I do not wish to be seen by too many other people as I may scare them. Scaring people is the worst thing about being a ghost."

"If I can't see you, how will I know where you are?"

"You will feel my presence. I will be that 'strange, cold wind' you aptly described me as on the night of our first meeting. If we have trouble, we can always go back inside."

Melanie nodded and I stepped outside, closing the door behind us. Reaching my hand through the door, I concentrated on my fingertips to make them solid, and locked the door shut. This act was so habitual that I thought nothing of it, but unfortunately it made Melanie jump.

"Oh, I am very sorry," I said. "I do not have a key."

"It's okay. I'll try to get used to it."

"May I suggest we sit near the bank of the river? There is a bench over there, which ought to be clear of snow. The view of the river is beautiful from there."

Melanie agreed and we walked to the bench. We sat side by side, looking out onto the ice. The day was perfectly clear. The sky appeared sharp blue against the whiteness of the snow. Melanie seemed to be slightly more comfortable, but it was difficult to tell.

"Are you having difficulty seeing me, Melanie?" I asked.

She shook her head. "No. You look like a sketch made in white against the air. It's kind of cool but a bit scary too."

I smiled. "Do not be frightened. I mean you no harm. I only need your assistance."

She nodded. I could tell that she was still very apprehensive.

"Are you still willing to offer it?"

"I guess so. It sorta depends on what I have to do."

"I see. Please, allow me to explain. As you may or may not know, I am confined to areas only around the mill and the dam, and I would like to find out what happened to my husband Joseph. I died well before him. I think if we can find out what happened to him, it would put my spirit at ease. Would you do that for me?"

"Sure," she said. I was so relieved. Melanie continued: "I could help you check out the Internet first, since I can probably log onto our wireless ISP from down here. I'll bring a laptop over after lunch."

I had absolutely no idea what she had just said, but I had eavesdropped on enough conversations through the years to know it had something to do with technology. My solitary life around the mill had not offered me the opportunity to learn about such things. I was certain I would find out what she would do with this "Internet," "laptop," and "wireless ISP" later.

"Yes," I said. "If you feel we ought to search such things first, we will."

It seemed to me she was becoming apprehensive again. "I have to be back at one," she said, "I still have fifteen minutes before then. Can we walk out onto the dam? I wouldn't mind getting to know you."

"Yes, of course. It would please me very much."

We walked out to where I had brushed by her and her brother only a night before. She leaned on the black metal railing and I stood just behind her shoulder. It seemed like she wanted to ask me something, but it took her a long time before she did.

"Is it rude to ask you when you died?" she asked.

"No, not at all. I died on March 11th, 1861. Would it be rude of me to ask you when you were born?" My question seemed to get a smile out of her.

"May 29th, 1993."

"Oh, my. Do you realize we share the same birthday? I was born the very same day in 1841. That makes me only… one hundred and fifty-two years your senior."

"I never had a friend *that* much older than me before."

I chuckled. "Well, I suppose there is a first time for everything."

It took Melanie awhile before she had enough courage to ask me another question.

"Did it hurt when you died?"

"A little. To be honest, I really cannot remember how it felt very well. However, it still frightens me when I think about it. Do you mind if I ask you a question, Melanie?"

"No."

I pointed out across the river to the pair of perplexing flags that were just visible through the bare trees. "I am sorry, but I have been quite reclusive over the past hundred and fifty years, and I have spoken to no one in that time. Would you please explain what those two flags represent?"

"Well, the red and white one is the Canadian flag."

"The Canadian flag?"

"Yeah. Canada became a country in 1867. Oh, but you died before then."

"The colonies did decide to confederate," I said. "I can remember hearing some discussion of it. Which ones decided to join?"

"In 1867? Ontario, Québec, New Brunswick, and Nova Scotia."

"What is this 'Ontario?'"

"That's the province we're in right now."

"I see. The province of Ontario ought to be similar to the Canada West from my time, and I assume that Quebec is roughly similar to Canada East. I have heard of New Brunswick and Nova Scotia previously, however I have visited neither of them. What about Prince Edward Island and Newfoundland?"

"I don't know, but I think P.E.I. joined a few years later, and I'm pretty sure Newfoundland didn't join until 1949."

"I see. And the other flag? Is that the flag of Ontario?"

"Yes."

"How many provinces are there now?"

"Ten and three territories."

"Ten! And three territories! Canada now must be very big!"

"Yeah. It sure is. Songs have been written about it."

—•—

A few minutes later, Melanie said goodbye to Ann and ran back home for lunch. She was fifteen minutes late and hoped that her mother didn't mind too much.

"Hi, Mom. I'm home. Sorry I'm late."

"It's all right dear. There's some soup and sandwiches on the table."

"Thanks."

She sat down beside her brother and took a tuna fish sandwich from the plate in front of her. Her dad walked in and gave her mom a quick kiss.

"Hey, guys. Wanna go skating on the canal tomorrow? The N.C.C.'s decided to give it the green flag with all the cold weather we've been having lately."

"Oh, that'd be awesome!" Luke said. "Can we get hot chocolate and beavertails and all that stuff?"

"If the shops are open, I don't see why not."

"Cool," Luke said as he chomped down a few more bites of sandwich.

"Melanie? How about you? You want to go skating?"

"Well, I don't know...."

"Come on, dear," her mom said. "It'll be fun."

"Oh, all right. I guess so."

"That's the spirit," her dad said and gave her a big grin. She couldn't help but smile. "Now I'm going to the arena to get everyone's skates sharpened. Anyone want to come with me?"

"No, I'm okay," Melanie said.

"Luke? How 'bout you, sport?"

"I'll be ready in five minutes. Thanks, Dad."

Her dad left the kitchen and Luke immediately began tapping Melanie on the shoulder. "Did you hear that, Melanie? We're going skating and getting beavertails. This is going to be so cool."

"I think we've already covered how cool it's going to be, Luke."

He didn't answer her. He wolfed down the rest of his lunch, then ran to catch up with Dad. Melanie heard the front door clicking shut a few moments afterward.

"You were at the mill today, weren't you?"

Melanie almost choked on her soup, but stopped herself at the last moment. It wasn't a question; it was an accusation.

"Yes, Mom. I walked by the mill."

Her mom sighed. "I wish you would stop obsessing about the mill ghost, Melanie," she said. "It's not healthy. Learning about history is one thing, but when you start making up stories about ghosts that scare your little brother...."

"But, *I* didn't scare him!"

"Who did then? This ghost you saw?"

"Can I go for walk now, please?"

She started to sweat. She was being rude, and it looked like she was making her mom mad.

"I'm sorry, Mom."

"It's all right. You can continue to visit the mill, but promise me one thing. Don't scare you little brother anymore. On purpose or by accident. Do I make myself clear?"

"Yes, Mom."

"Good. You're excused."

—•—

With her laptop in her backpack, Melanie made her way across the dam and to the front steps of the mill, careful not to slip on the sheets of ice covering the concrete. Ann was waiting for her outside. For the first time, she wasn't too scared or weirded-out. Ann was becoming as normal to her as any of her other friends at school. She took the laptop out of her bag and Ann looked at it funny.

"Is this your 'laptop?'"

"Yeah, but it doesn't look like we'll get good reception here. We should probably try to login from somewhere on the dam or on the other side of the river."

"And what if we cannot?"

"Then I'll go home and do the search for you there."

Melanie first brought her laptop halfway out onto the dam and had trouble getting a signal there. She tried several times at many places along the dam before getting a login screen near the shore of Long Island. Looking over her shoulder, she saw Ann was still standing by the mill.

"Could you please come over here, Ann? I need your help. I just got the login screen and I don't think I can move without losing the signal."

Even though Melanie had trouble seeing Ann cross the dam, she soon felt Ann's coolness over her shoulder. She looked back to see a very faint, bewildered expression.

"Where do you get all of these interesting machines?"

"Oh, our family's very up-to-date. My mom's a real tech head. She works in Kanata."

"How remarkable," Ann said. "You can use this machine to retrieve information about Joseph?"

Melanie smiled. "Yeah. We've just got to type it into this search engine and we can get information from all over the world!"

She googled "Joseph Currier, last residence" in her browser and had several hits. Scrolling down, she found a result that seemed relevant. She clicked on its link, and it took her to a webpage which was a bit of a surprise.

"Did your husband ever have an interest in politics?"

Ann shook her head. "I do not know. He may have. Why?"

"Because his last residence was at 24 Sussex Drive, and that's the official residence of the Prime Minister. Wow, he could have been Prime Minister. I think that's a real possibility, because it says here that 'after Confederation, Joseph Currier was the Member of Parliament for the riding of Ottawa for four terms.' I can't remember there ever being a Prime Minister Joseph Currier, but I could be wrong. Let's see."

Melanie continued scrolling down the page, skimming the text until she found an explanation. "Ah, ha. I see. Joseph Currier built the residence at 24 Sussex drive. After your death, he married a Miss Hannah Wright. They lived there until their respective deaths in 1884 and 1901. The residence was later acquired by the Government of Canada in 1943 and renovated. The first Prime Minster to live at 24 Sussex Drive was Louis St. Laurent."

"Does it say where Joseph is buried?"

Melanie scrolled a little bit more and then went back to Google and checked out a few more pages. A few more clicks and she finally found it.

" 'After his death in 1884, he was subsequently buried in Beechwood Cemetery.' There's a link down here to a Mapquest search and it looks like that's downtown, near Rockcliffe."

"Is Rockcliffe far from here?"

"Not that far, only about thirty kilometres or so. It'll take about a half hour or so by car. Hey, wait. We're going skating on the canal tomorrow. It isn't far from there! Wanna come?"

"I cannot leave the grounds of the mill." Ann sighed. "I am sorry, Melanie. It is the main reason I decided to contact you for help. Thank you very much for finding all this information about Joseph. However, I do not think I will be able to visit his resting place."

A smile slowly crept to Melanie's face. "Wait a second! You might be able to see his grave after all!"

"What do you mean?"

"It's a little complicated, Ann. Can you meet me around seven tonight?"

"Yes. I will see you then, Melanie."

—•—

The sun had already set by the time I saw Melanie returning to the mill to meet me. There was no moon, so I could barely make out her form in what little light there was. When she reached the dam, she handed a dark case to me.

"Here, Ann. We should probably teach you how to use some software."

"Software? Is it similar to what we used to connect to the Internet today?"

She nodded. "Please, open the case."

I unzipped the case and took out the machine. The laptop was very thin and a silvery colour. When I pushed the button and flipped open its lid, it made a delightful chime and made some noises indicating the machine was working. Or at least, I thought the noises meant the machine was working. I really could not tell, since everything was still black. However, the wondrous panel in front of me then took on various shades of grey and the machine reassured me that it was setting itself up. Finally, I saw a picture of the mill and a little, black arrow in the middle of the coloured panel. I was beside myself with the wonders I was seeing in front of me. Thankfully, Melanie was far less bewildered than I.

"Ann. Can you see that small square on the base of the laptop? Drag your finger on it."

I looked down and saw it immediately. I dragged my finger on the square, and to my surprise, the arrow started to move!

"Great, Ann! Now see this thing over here?" Melanie pointed at a picture with some text that appeared in the magical panel. "All you need to do is move the arrow over top of it and press the button below the square twice. Do you see the button?"

"Yes. I do. I am moving the arrow on top of the picture and pressing the button twice. I do believe the machine is working."

"Yeah, it worked. Now, you see that spot down there that says 'connect?'"

"Yes."

"All you need to do is click it and you'll be connected. Turn the laptop back on and do that sometime around five in the afternoon so the battery doesn't run out; it should have four hours. Leave the computer like that and when I start up mine, you'll be able to see me in Ottawa when I am at the graveyard."

"Oh. This is so exciting. By any chance, do you have a pencil and paper? I would like to write these instructions down before I forget them."

She handed to me what I requested and I started to write quickly, concerned that I might forget her instructions and what she had just showed me. When I had almost finished writing them down, I heard a rustling in the bushes and I saw some snow fall off one of the branches.

"Melanie? Did you hear that noise?"

"What noise?"

"It sounds like an animal."

I heard the noise again and decided to investigate. When started to walk across the snow to the bushes, a frightened child started screaming and ran up the hill towards Melanie's house.

"Luke! Get over here!"

I saw Melanie chase him, but she stopped after a few steps, turned around, and started walking back.

"This sucks," Melanie said. "He's probably going to tell Mom, and I'm not going to be able to do this for you, Ann."

"Anything you accomplish for me now Melanie is far beyond what I had hoped. If you cannot go to the final resting place of my husband, do not worry. I do not wish to cause you any more trouble, so, please, return home."

I watched her leave, and I hoped that she would not risk anything too great for me.

—•—

The next morning, Melanie woke up with the rest of her family at nine thirty to dress for skating. It was going to be a cold day again at minus fifteen. After putting on long underwear and several layers of clothing, she walked downstairs to find her family had already started loading the car. She grabbed her skates and a few bags from the front hall and helped them finish packing.

Driving to the canal was uneventful. No one said that much on the way down. They just sat there and listened to the radio. Melanie wondered pretty much all the way there if Luke had said anything to her parents about her talking to the ghost last night.

They parked near the Rideau Centre, descended the stairs to the canal from Colonel By Drive, and walked down to one of the wooden benches at ice-level to do up their skates. *Bienvennu à la Patinoire du Canal Rideau/Welcome to the Rideau Canal Skateway* the sign next to her said. A full crowd was already out skating that Sunday. Over the murmur of many conversations, she sometimes heard the cries of playing children.

Melanie and her family skated slowly with the crowd of people until the Pretoria Bridge. It was a drawbridge made of metal and stone, and looked like something you'd expect to find in an English village. After passing under its black girders, the canal became wider and there was more room for people to move. They skated up to the Ritz where they had hot chocolate and picked up a beavertail at one of the stands near there. Melanie had one with lemon, cinnamon, and brown sugar on it. She loved how the sourness of lemon made the pastry not too sweet.

When it was close to suppertime, they all skated back and changed.

"How would you guys like to find someplace to eat downtown?" her mom asked as they were heading back to the car.

"That sounds great," her dad answered.

"I'd like to," Melanie said.

"Well then, it's settled," her mom said. "But first, I think I should go do some Christmas shopping. There are a few surprises that I have to pick up for you guys."

"I wouldn't mind going to the bookstore. I'll meet you guys here in an hour," Melanie said.

"You aren't going to that graveyard Luke told me about. Are you?"

So Luke had told her mom. Melanie felt like kicking Luke right then and there, but she had a feeling that it would make matters much worse. She sort of avoided the question instead of outright lying which she didn't want to do.

"I'm not going to do anything stupid, Mom. Trust me."

Her mom looked at her skeptically. "All right."

Melanie left the Rideau Centre, but she didn't cross at the intersection to go to the bookstore. Instead, she turned right and walked down along the street to where the bus bays were, looking for the number seven.

She promised her mom she wouldn't do anything stupid. She hadn't lied. It was too bad her mom didn't understand.

She found her bus, and without looking back, she boarded it.

—•—

The number seven dropped her off a half block from the gates of the cemetery. Stars were just beginning to shine through the twilight. With her laptop in her backpack and a map of the plots in her hand, she stepped through the front gates and set out to find the final resting place of Joseph Currier.

Throughout the cemetery, patches of bare hardwoods spread between the many plots. The trees' shadows were around her as she walked from plot to plot, trying to orient herself with her map and flashlight. As she tried to find her way, she stumbled past the headstones of Sir Robert Borden, Sir Sandford Fleming, Tommy Douglas, as well as many war veterans. The graveyard made Melanie uneasy. With encroaching dusk, the weather was growing colder by the minute. The trees creaked. Every breeze felt like it was another spirit on her shoulder. She felt like she was being watched.

After walking in the dark for a while, she found Joseph Currier's headstone in the third or fourth clearing she checked. It was old, grey limestone with his name etched onto it. Melanie felt kind of strange setting up the camera and the laptop here in a graveyard. However, this was the only way Ann would be able to see this place.

As she turned the power on and the hard drive clicked to life, another strange, cold wind gave her a shiver. She looked over her shoulder.

—•—

At first, I found the queer beeping sound confusing, but I soon realized the source of the noise was Melanie's laptop. I pulled the colourful panel open once again and noticed that it had changed: there was something that resembled a window in the centre of it, and in this window was a moving image of Melanie. It was astounding! She was on the other side of Ottawa right now, and we could see each other through this machine.

"Ann? You there?"

"Yes, Melanie. I am here. Can you hear and see me?"

"Yeah, I can, Ann. I can see you really well. Where are you?"

She looked very cold and quite nervous. I was becoming concerned. Even though the moving pictures were choppy, I could tell that she was shivering. I hoped that she was all right.

"I am out on the dam," I answered. "It is a new moon tonight. We are lucky."

"Look, I've found it."

The camera lurched over at a strange angle and I realized I was looking at the snow. Heaven have mercy. If she has been hurt, I will never forgive myself.

"Melanie!"

Someone picked the camera out of the snow, and it seemed to rise up and rotate until it was level with a man's eyes.

I knew those eyes, and my tears started to sting my own. Even through this machine, I could tell that it was my Joseph.

—•—

"I think I'm going to piss myself."

"I would rather it if you would not, young lady. Joseph Merrill Currier," the ghost said, extending his right hand, but Melanie was too shocked to take it. He withdrew it and returned his attention to the webcam and at the laptop. "Although you may be at a loss for words at this moment, I would greatly appreciate any help you could provide in learning how to use either of these machines. It appears that Ann is stuck inside one of them."

Melanie pushed herself out of the snow and hesitantly walked over. She became brave enough to start explaining how to use the laptop and the webcam. Talking with ghosts seemed easier with her second. She soon got the instant messaging service going, and Joseph rather liked the various emoticons he could use.

Melanie found herself just sitting back in the snow and watching Ann and Joseph talk. It was almost as good as watching her parents dance. No. It was better, but in a different way. Not only could she see they were happy, but she had brought happiness to them. She had brought them together.

Before she knew it, it was getting dark and she had to pack up her laptop and leave.

—•—

When the doors on the bus opened in front of the bookstore, Melanie's mom was standing right in front of them.

"Let me explain," Melanie started, but her mom cut her off.

"You promised me that you were only going to the bookstore."

"But...."

"No, buts. You promised me you were only going to the bookstore. You promised me that you were not going to do anything foolish like trespassing through a graveyard in the dark. You promised me that you'd give up on these foolish ideas about this ghost in the mill and tracing Ann's history down. You lied to me."

Her mom turned her back to Melanie and walked up the sidewalk and waited for the lights to change. Melanie ran to catch up, dodging pedestrians that were walking away from the intersection. She knew there was nothing she could say to her mom when she caught up to her, but she ran after her anyway.

They crossed the street and entered the Rideau Centre again. Luke and her dad were waiting just inside the doors. Her dad looked upset. He didn't talk, which meant he was really mad. Melanie didn't say anything; she just looked at her boots. Only her mother spoke.

"I'm tired. Let's go home."

They did, and no one said anything else to her until the next morning.

—•—

I was quite surprised that Melanie had not retrieved her laptop, but perhaps, her family and she had returned very late that evening. However, the next day, I was delighted to see her walking down Bridge Street and turning onto Mill Street when returning home from school. I waved to her. She did not notice me as she was looking at her feet and seemed to be quite glum. It then occurred to me to do something rash. I pushed open one of the windows and called down to her as she was rounding the corner to cross the dam.

"Melanie. Thank you for what you did last night. It was wonderful. However, you failed to get your laptop."

She stopped and waited for me. I shut the window, hurried downstairs, and stepped outside. As I handed the laptop to her by the front steps of the mill, I noticed she was crying.

"What's wrong, dear?"

"My parents are mad at me! They didn't want me scaring Luke anymore and they didn't like me chasing foolish things like ghosts, Ann! Mom made me feel like I've done something wrong, but I haven't!"

I sighed. I could understand how her parents felt and how she felt. Everyone had a right to feel the way they did, but it was not fair for anyone either.

"Melanie. In your heart, do you feel that you have done something wrong?"

"No."

"Then, the situation in which your family has found itself will pass with time."

"Yeah. It'll pass real slow when I'm grounded for a month."

I let her have a moment before I put my hand on her shoulder.

"Promise me one thing. Try to be kind to them."

She nodded and turned to walk away.

"Oh, and Melanie, would you do me another favour?"

"What?"

"When you come home from school, visit me sometimes. I love Manotick and the mill, but my solitary life here craves company on occasion."

That drew a smile. I waved to her as she crossed the dam and climbed the snowy hill to her house. I was already eagerly anticipating her next visit.

"Tattooed Inuit Woman" (2006) by Mondolithic Studios.

This Ink Feels Like Sorrow

by
Karin Lowachee

I inked the sky into my skin. There is no blue in it, it's the sort of sky you get when a storm is on the horizon. Look up and the colours are a swirl of dark greys and muddy whites, and maybe an angry red poking through, like Mars. This sky is the colour of my brother's eyes, with the same sword-anger in pinpricks of bronze. Other people called them hazel or grey, but I saw storms. Beneath my raw skin, this ink feels like sorrow.

You have to be careful what emotion the needles pick up. Colour set in clear glass jars on a disinfected shelf, the artist runs his finger over the labels, searching. Bruised indigo. Dissatisfied mauve. Predatory hunter green. But even those descriptions aren't wholly accurate, any more than colour looks the same to every person. We're all a little colour-blind. We're all a little empty of emotion, and that's where I come in. Or you come in, into my shop below street level with the gallery of designs and feelings on the wall. What do you want to feel today? I'll tattoo you with dragon rage or butterfly affection. Hollow skull apathy. Yes, I can even ink an absence. They say tattoos are addictive. I know that for a fact.

You stitch human skin, cover it with emotion, and pain and power become your drug.

—•—

Old beliefs in the Arctic say that the body is made up of a multitude of souls, and when you fall sick, it's because the small soul that resided in that part of your body, in the joints they say, that soul has departed. Is this why I am out of joint? Is this why I am the walking dead? My brother was my soul, in my legs and my arms and my eyes and my hands. He animated me, and then he left. Piece by piece he ripped himself away from the bits of me that make me move and breathe and feel. I have memories of gravel lots in Winnipeg strewn with dandelion heads—is that the right weed? I don't even know—those things that when you blow on them they float away like minute shredded clouds. Grey and white, gone in the breeze. I used to think them flowers until my mother told us they choked the roots and weren't like roses at all. I don't even know if that's true, but we, Shan and I, we believed it because our mother said so. Because our mother birthed us in Winnipeg by fault of a white man, and we grew for ten years as explorers among steel and cement. Maybe if I looked it up on the Internet I'll find that she lied about the flowers.

It doesn't matter. It's only a lie if you don't believe it. I can't remember when I stopped believing Shan. I can't remember when he became a lie. Maybe, because he's my soul, there's no difference between his lie and my life. Maybe, because he departed and I am a zombie as black-eyed as the face now inked on my back, I am the lie and he was the life. What do you call your twin brother when he picks up a needle but not for the ink? Are we so different? he asked. You ink emotion below the skin, where it fades. I inject emotion into the blood, where it sings.

I told him that his song faded too, or else why did he keep doing it?

Because, he said. I'm addicted.

—•—

We were blood. But as he transfused himself with poison, how much of the womb did we then share? What does memory matter now, but as spirits walking the path of another life? Our eyes are both the sky, but mine are blue and his were storms. These hurricane eyes ... one on each of my palms so when I raise my hands to a mirror there is more than myself looking back ... is this really Shan with his gaze traversed by my lifeline? He left me disjointed and so I tattoo him on my body, emotions I remember, to remember him. Or keep his evil spirit away. Or hold his good one close. Even if the emotions fade, the colour still grips. The images still look back. I raise my hands to the mirror in surrender and he doesn't even blink.

—•—

We both returned south for a better life. It sounds so simple and so earnest. Everyone wants a better life. *Better*, not best. It implies that the life you come from isn't that bad either. It's *good*. But you want better. Is that the only option? If you're not satisfied with the status quo, is it a requirement to look for better? On whose definition do we hang the word? What damage does it do when we don't get better? The Elders in our small cold community, who have lived there for decades, and their fathers before them, for decades still going back to millennia on the land—do they want "better?" Is better a dental plan that replaces the black gaps in their mouths? Is better an attention from the government in support of "tradition?" Is better the right to control your own resources, promote your arts and crafts, continue your language, educate your bored children, build a new ice rink, invite foreigners to bolster the scaffolding of your disparate communities? What we saw on TV didn't look much better, yet we left what we knew and bruised our foot-bottoms on the concrete of a southern city.

Mom was an addict too. She didn't blink when we got on the plane and propped our way to tall trees and taller buildings that could never withstand a Northern blizzard. Her eyes were as wide as the tundra.

—•—

Toronto is a Native word but I don't know what it means. Inuit means "the people" and I suppose they are my people. But then there was our father, and nobody knows what sort of person he was, other than he departed too. With less tearing of the physical kind, less of a scar on the body unless you looked deep into my mother's eyes. He left in a dart instead of a slow decline. Is this what our father gave us, Shan and I, this habit of disappearing? If our mother tattooed with knives, building scars like highways across her arms (off-ramps to the joints) and ingested herself with poison to escape the pain, or the confusion, or the fact of her life, then we must be the true children of our parents, each with a habit that takes more than twelve steps to break. Twelve steps from the tundra to the city? That would get you as far as the white land between towns, where any direction, if you don't know which way you're going or what you're doing, leads to death.

We went further south than our mother ever did, right to the border of another country. So many cars, Shan said. More cars than people, or so it seemed. More machine than flesh, and I wondered what I would do. My art deals in skin, not steel. My art that I carved in gravel as a child and, once among my mother's people, carved in snow that shone like diamonds when the sky was unfettered blue. No chains of clouds cast across its bright stare, you had to squint or go blind. Tattooing is an ancient art and traditionally done by women. Stitching the skin like they would their *amautiq*. Lampblack on sinew, pulled beneath the epidermis. Tell me these old women didn't infuse their marks with emotion?

The difference is I am a man. The difference is I don't ink in metaphor.

—•—

The first tattoo I did was on my brother. Fifteen years old with a ballpoint pen, a lighter, and a safety pin. I dotted the inside of his forearm in the points of the Big Dipper. *Ursa major*. Big Bear. The *Arctic*, deep blue. He said he felt loved. Of course you did, I said. It wasn't out of hate that I drew beneath his skin. No, he said. I *felt* loved.

And I had thought, bent over his arm, pulling the skin taut as I pricked him little by little, that here was something I could do that would never disappear. I would be embedded in his skin, twin beyond words and genetics, walking with him wherever he went. He was older by twenty minutes. This was permanent affection in case he ever forgot. In case he ever disappeared on me. I never will, he said.

Never is a strong word, but only in façade. It is as easy to puncture as skin.

When I mix my own inks, I infuse them with emotion. These are the colours you see. But while the pigment remains, the emotions do not. My clients know this on an unconscious level if not in conscious belief, and they come for the second degree thrill. My art is the horror movie of the tattoo world. Be safe in your manipulated emotions because the lights come up at the end. When you walk home you have nothing to fear, the shadows are just your imagination.

But in the absence of emotion, I want permanence. But it comes on broken feet and it never stays. It calls itself Grief, black ink, and even with its swallowing depths it is better than feeling nothing. But it never stays and there is only the absence.

When my brother left, he took my art.

—•—

You learn tattoo like a magician. Apprentice from a master artist, which I did in a fifty-year-old shop on Queen and Bathurst called Tribe. Appropriate, maybe, though the only tribe I felt a true affinity to was my brother. He was my shaman and my hunter and my matriarch. He knew my heartbeat because we shared one, thud thud thud in a tandem drum dance. Kids around us huffed gasoline in plastic bags, smoked joints, got drunk at two in the afternoon, playing hooky in their parents' cabins out beyond the town. We weren't that reality, but we weren't studious either. Shan played hockey on the lake ice with rough blades and rougher boys, and I sat on a mound of snow with my cracked hands making black charcoal marks in my notebook. I studied movement in the way he moved, both loose and aggressive, and listened to the wind. When older boys picked on me because I was skinnier and quieter, he beat them on the backs of their calves with his stick and sent them home in splinters.

The first tattoo I inked on myself was the shape of his smile on my right wrist. People thought it was a crescent moon. There is an origin myth among the Fort-Chimo Inuit about the sun and the moon. The male moon kissed the nipples of his sister sun, which she had darkened with oil and lampblack to reveal who had been mischievously visiting her during the night. The next morning she saw her brother's blackened mouth and fled from her family, who scolded her, in shame. They chase each other across the sky, the sun and the moon. I read that and wondered why is she ashamed? It wasn't her fault. I watched my brother's mouth blacken the longer he walked the streets of this city, jonesing, craving for a hit, prowling like a starved sled dog, and why should I feel ashamed? His habit is not my own.

These mild, inaccurate words. It's not a hit, it's a beat down with jackboots and baseball bats. It's not a habit, it's a prison. A maximum security prison with murderers and Mafia and white supremicists that you don't want to drop your soap around.

I look down at my wrist on clear nights and touch the shape of his smile. It feels dishonest now. It feels like an eclipse and he is hiding in wait for me, to ambush me with his disease and kiss me in the night when he knows it's wrong.

— • —

Shan had dreams of playing in the National Hockey League. He didn't particularly like the Leafs, the Canadiens were his team, but the longer we lived there in subway distance from the Air Canada Centre, the easier it became to love the blue and white jerseys. So much became easier. I acclimated to the milder weather so that even a pinch of a winter chill had me complaining at bus stops along with the rest of the Bay St. population. Suits plugged into cell phones and me in my tattered faux-wool and multicoloured scarf, going to meet Shan where he tried to hold down one coffee shop job after another. He had second-hand skates that he tied up and darted around on in Nathan Phillips Square. The reflecting pool became ice in the winter, sheer and smooth and dotted with children in puffed up pink and blue ski coats. I sat on the edges with my black notebook and sketched his slow glides. He never stayed on the ice for long. Too many kids, he said. We were nineteen.

He got fed up of smelling coffee and pinned a cash job at a replay music shop on Yonge. Next to hockey, he loved music. Our one-room, cockroach residence had a record player we'd stolen from someone else's trash, and Shan brought home vinyls of airbrushed old guys who all sounded like wannabe Sinatras. It wasn't our music but we liked it anyway for its absurdity. Shan also brought home weed he got from coworkers and laid out on the threadbare couch getting high in the damp months. There was no such thing as being on the land in Toronto. Any kind of weather didn't feel open or ever free, but hemmed in by the skyscrapers and capped by a ceiling of pollution. Too dank, too humid, too dark or too bright. Some days you could do nothing but stay indoors and hallucinate.

Don't be a cliché, I warned him.

He held out his arm to me for another tattoo. No fancy pigment or needles, he wanted it done like the first. Sterilized safety pin and the dark colour of a ballpoint pen. He wanted me to ink him on the vein. Did I give him the idea that it would be good to puncture that line? He never flinched, just smoked, looking at the ceiling as I bent over him with attention. In odd worship.

Now I think he just wanted to feel. He never commented on the design—I tattooed a knife in that spot. Remembrance of our mother? He just said, It felt like frailty.

Was that even an emotion?

It didn't matter, he said. How accurate are emotions anyway?

True, they aren't bullseyes. They are scattershot bullets. They rip you apart in a million directions until you dissipate into the void like an exploded star.

—•—

What if, Shan asked, you tattoo rage and the person goes out and murders somebody?

This was when I left Tribe and got in with an underground artist who worked out of a home shop in the Distillery District. He'd heard from my mentor that my clients kept coming back and sat in one time when I inked this girl with optimism. You know emotions aren't neatly labelled because along with robin's egg-blue optimism she got coloured by pink joy and desert yellow serenity. Three roses on the small of her back that began in flinching pain and ended with an embrace and a bounce in her step. She talked about her ambition to act and her application to RADA in London. She had a good voice that you knew could carry in a theatre and the kind of symmetry to the face that cameras and audiences love. She left the shop and we all were infected by her belief that she was going to receive an Oscar before her twenty-fifth birthday. I didn't tell her the tattoo wouldn't fade but her optimism would. Junkies don't need to know the drug they're taking. Do they care? It's about the fix.

I have to be careful with the ink I select, but this kind of art isn't foolproof. Who would want rage? Am I an ethical, moralistic fortune teller who never delivers bad news?

Don't we all have the right to feel something? Don't I grant a gift of emotion in a world of disconnected digital people? It's so easy to think the things you do impact more people than you actually do. Concern for that stranger makes you a better person. Impatience with your own family comes just as readily.

Maybe I'm just as bad as my brother's dealer. Maybe that's where the shame of the sun comes in. I've blackened my own mouth by telling the truth to the wrong people. Even when the people are family. It's easy to be truthful to strangers, they are less likely to judge. But family know your insecurities and they can use it like weapons. Especially when they want something from you. Patience, time … cash.

The Franklin Expedition, they say, would not have starved if they knew how to read inuksuks. Little stone men, piled knee-high, marking caches of food and pointing to caribou herds. There were signs of cannibalism. Desperate men driven to eat their own. What happens to the soul? The Inuit have a saying: *The great peril of our existence lies in the fact that our diet consists entirely of souls.* If animals give pause, propel thought and respect, how much worse if it's your twin?

I saw the signs and I did nothing. I starved him, and myself.

There is the tragic irony of history. We are never blind in retrospect.

—•—

I found him overdosed in a puddle of rainwater he'd let in from the open window. Miserable rain in a southern spring, suffocating moisture that clung to your clothes and the surface of your skin. Gangrene dampness that didn't cleanse a thing, only sheathed the city in a wet-cloth stink. We didn't have air conditioning and he must've opened the window for the circulation while he lay on our fake Moroccan rug and shot up. His arm was bound, his eyes were shut, and through the sore red pricks of needle marks his tattoos were darker scars. My tattoos. Graceful lines that had, over time, infused him with my emotion. Affection, joy, tenderness, compassion. Love.

But I am a magician and it's all trickery. This gift doesn't last except in its repetition of finite feeling. So when he couldn't have it, he turned to the drugs. Did he lack even still, with me beside him for twenty-five years, on this wild expedition to find an elusive passage through an unforgiving landscape? Why were we looking, did we have things to trade, two searching souls, a restlessness of feet? Was it just for the adventure that he bothered to be my brother? What did it mean to be each other's protectors and then relinquish your sword to a mercurial master?

I sit on a flight bearing north and wonder if I began his addiction. If you ink someone and they return, again and again, isn't that addiction? Did I feed his propensity just as much as my mother had while we were both still in the womb? We must've kicked against her poison. It must've made me scream so loudly that every movement of my hand and eyes, as an adult, as I passed a needle beneath some skin, shed my intent and emotions onto the other person until enough washes sloughed it all off. How much do we pass on without realizing it? If the dead linger in spirit and we require tattoos to keep the living safe, then what else remains of ourselves when we think it's only our hands moving? Our eyes? Our mouths? How much of ourselves lies waiting on a dirty rug, limp from life, quiet in time for a discovery.

He was my Northwest Passage. I was his. And we disappeared midstride, ignorant and ill-planned.

—•—

My mother didn't make it south for the funeral, not enough money out of a thousand to get that far, so I went North so she could ask me why. Why did this happen? Why did he do this? Why did you let him? In her silent house with her two adopted children, Aunt Alice's boy and girl that moved in when Aunt Alice moved to Churchill. They are ten and eight and look up at me and my tattooed neck and hands, all that's visible from beneath my clothes. I am something mythical, maybe. I have blue eyes and my hands have grey.

She sits outside smoking, without a coat. Late October weather, the first snow has fallen already, the bite of winter at this Inlet has already sank its teeth, but she is Inuit and I am acclimatized to a warmer sun. I'm bundled, held in. Tearless because it's too cold. She is just withdrawn. All of her emotions and her cheeks, sucked in without blood or life, like shrinking ice. The lines on her face are directionless and dry. We are technically a desert. Rain doesn't fall here. The sky is tearless too.

I watch the crust of snow break beneath my boots and she says, after an hour of silence: *You boys never should've left.*

"And then what?" I have to look at her though she's made a point not to look at me. "We should've stayed here, got jobs at the Northern packing groceries?"

"Don't you talk down to me." Don't you talk down to your home.

But it wasn't our home we left. As I sit there watching the crème brulé crust of the snow crack beneath my heel. How many hours had I spent here studying the way the light hits this white? The wind whips the fur on my parka against my cheek. It's like the nuzzle of a dog. The North is my family. You can love it and still want to leave. You can love it and still want to return. We lead inbetween lives. Some of us exist more solidly than others. And others prefer to fade away.

"Then I guess you'll be going soon," she says.

Then I guess I'll have to go. If I am inbetween then so is this Grief that visits me in the night. So is the scolding of my parent. So is my flight. Here on this parallel not even the ice is permanent.

She rises, flicking the butt of her cigarette away, and walks back into the house. The floorboards on the steps creak. I know this will be her last words on it and she will never speak of him again, like she never speaks of our father. Tragedy becomes too real if it's always talked about. Better to lose it in the bottom of a bottle or the black tar of blame.

I sit outside in the cold and watch the world become dark again. Not a city dark, with the skyscrapers and their evening eyes that become the stars that their light obscures. Walk far enough out of the town and there are no lights but the moon. But it's not a peaceful night. Somewhere close I hear the buzzsaw amplification of a machine—snowmobile—eating up the air. If I breathed in hard enough I'd smell the engine fumes. Faster than a dog team, but noisier and dirtier. Polar bears can still outrun them in the first few strides. What is our need to get better? Maybe it's only a matter of faster, easier, and a deception of convenience. My cigarette doesn't warm me. The Southern half of my blood now feels the chill even through a parka. This is the sort of ice wind that sinks bone deep and will come to haunt you in older years. This is a cold that lies in wait.

Some of us don't want to get better. Fear of disappointment, maybe. Fear of what you'll have to do when you're in a different place. Acclimate to new weather, walk a new route, look up at a different sky. We are creatures of habit, they say. Creatures of prison and the jack-boot. I can tattoo vermilion pain into my skin and feel it spider along my veins. Russet regret. Iron memory. The origins of my ink are the sun and the moon, black-mouthed siblings that forever chase each other across the sky. This is where emotion lies.

But this is where emotion *lies*. Once the feeling fades, I'm left with the lines and shapes on my body, telling the story of my brother. These are his eyes, his moon, his knife. This is his permanence.

"Like ships we were made to dance o'er our graves
One false move and we could be thrown
Buried alive before our due time
To rest at sixty below."

Safe Passage

by
Karina Sumner-Smith

I

Lia Weatherell sat on the edge of the north pier, feet dangling above the waves, and listened to her cell phone ring. It played a song, a catchy jangling tune that she'd loved just a few weeks ago and now could barely stand.

It was her aunt, she knew. Her aunt with no news and no comfort, no reason to hope, nothing but more worry and a quiet plea for Lia to come home before it got too dark. Home, Lia always wanted to ask. Home? Her home was in Toronto, a city where she'd ridden the street-cars at midnight in January; a city where she'd bought prescription medicine for her crazy mother at two AM as the patrons of the local bars flooded out; a city where the rush of traffic and the clatter of the nearby subway was as familiar as the sound of her own breath. She was not afraid of twilight in a little town like this.

And this was not her home.

The phone kept ringing, starting its song again, and Lia wondered what it would feel like to throw it into the lake. She imagined a tiny plop and splash, her little silver flip phone having no more impact than a tossed pebble. Then it would be just another bit of junk to wash ashore one spring with the old tires and driftwood, the beer bottles and tangles of seaweed-wrapped fishing line. Maybe it could catch a current and get all the way across the lake to Michigan; let them pay the roaming charges.

The ringing abruptly stopped, halting mid-tune. Lia sighed. From what she knew of Kincardine, the town wouldn't let anything go, not even a discarded cell phone.

Staring across the water, its surface just beginning to glitter with red and gold as the sun slid down the sky towards the horizon, Lia felt the hairs on her sunburned arms rise. She shivered. There was a cool wind coming in off the lake now, and it was only this, she told herself, pulling her arms in to her chest, that made her tremble.

Not stress. Not fear. Not the relentless weight of waiting.

Ring, she thought to her phone, not daring to look at it again. Ring. A second call would mean that her Aunt Jan had something more to say than tense words about a dinner going cold. It would be a sign that there had been news, any news. Lia's hand crept towards the shape of her phone on the concrete of the pier beside her. A second call might mean that the police had sent word—

—that they'd found her—

—that they'd found her body—

Curling her hand into a fist, Lia pulled it back into her lap. Stop it, she told herself, firmly, desperately. She would not think of that. But her phone did not ring and Lia had never before known that a beautiful August evening could feel so silent or so cold.

In the space of open water to her left, past the jutting shape of the south pier that mirrored in concrete the one on which she sat, the ghost of the ship *Ann Maria* materialized. It appeared as all ghosts of the past did: suddenly and without surprise, in the space of a breath. Slowly, Lia turned to look at the wreck. The once-proud ship was as it had appeared in its later days, long after a storm had tossed it ashore, causing the deaths of sailors and would-be rescuers alike; it looked as it had after the people of the town had taken its cargo and whatever else they could ashore and then let time and the weather take care of the rest.

Coming as she had been to this same pier nearly every night for the better part of two weeks, Lia had seen the *Ann Maria* before, as she had seen the living memories of so many other things. She had even gone down to the beach and waded in the water at the exact place where a sign on the shore pointed out the ship's final resting place and had found the keel, a great wooden backbone half-buried in sand and softened by lake water—all that remained of the wreck. Yet it was this vision, with broken masts stripped of sails and its wooden planking weathered, that Lia knew best. It leaned at a steep angle, masts bowed towards the lake, and Lia could almost imagine that even in its years of disintegration the ship was still straining for the safe harbour it had never reached.

The ghost ship reminded her of her ill mother, lost and probably dead. It reminded her of herself.

Yes, she thought, staring at the ghostly wreck of the *Ann Maria*, that was how she felt: lost and broken, caught upon a ground of sand. Falling to pieces in the slow rush of waves, and each of those pieces adrift.

She watched a child throw a Frisbee for his dog straight through the hull of the ship that only Lia could see. He laughed, and as the spray from the dog's frenzied leaping passed through the space where the ruined ship's sails had fallen, its rigging lost and tangled, Lia thought: yes. Yes. Exactly like that.

Ghosts aplenty haunted Kincardine's waters and the length of its shore, memories of proud vessels sailing again and again in time's eye to their ruin and destruction, and staring out across the water Lia wondered if she should count herself among their number. Day after day she had returned to this spot, letting grief and the past crash over her like storm waves. And for what? She still sat alone, around her nothing but concrete and open water and ghosts.

From behind her, as slow and mournful as the trail of Lia's thoughts, came a song. The notes played softly at first, then the volume increased with the tempo as the familiar sound of "Highland Cathedral" echoed across the water. More familiar to her than even the *Ann Maria* was the evening bagpipe player who piped the sun to its rest. It was a tradition, her aunt told her, built around a local story over a hundred years old. Each night in the summertime, a member of the Kincardine Scottish Pipe Band stood atop the squat white lighthouse in full kilt and regalia, raised his bagpipes high, and played until the last sliver of sun vanished beneath the horizon.

Lia had never particularly liked the bagpipes before, but now, with their songs her only company night after night, she'd come to welcome the sound. It was haunting and fearful, and yes, she thought, staring out across the water, even beautiful.

She turned to see the bagpipe player atop the lighthouse—and froze at the sight of the ghost behind her. It was a teenaged girl, clearly not much older than Lia herself—sixteen, seventeen at the most. She wore loose jeans with a red patch over one knee and an oversized t-shirt that advertised a local hardware store. Her hair was permed into a dark blonde halo that flew about her face in a strong wind that Lia could not feel. As Lia watched, the girl's left hand rose to protectively cover her stomach, while her right hand flew up to cover her opened mouth. The girl stared as if transfixed by something terrible at the end of the pier.

But it was not the girl's fear that immediately grabbed Lia's attention, nor the sudden realization that the stomach the ghost protected with that single hand was swollen with pregnancy, but her face itself. The ghost was only there for a moment, the space of a breath, perhaps two, and then gone. But it was enough. She looked different with her falsely curly hair and her familiar features made strange with youth, but one glance was all Lia needed. Recognition felt like a physical impact deep in her stomach.

It was the ghost of her mother.

Lia was still for a long, slow moment, staring at the empty space behind her. She could still hear the little boy on the beach playing with his dog, and the sound of his mother calling for him to come get dried off. A flock of gulls whirled overhead, circling and heading inland, while on the lighthouse the bagpipe player began to pipe out the slow opening notes of "Amazing Grace."

"Mom," Lia tried to whisper, but the word wouldn't come out. She wanted to bury her face in her hands and sob, but her features felt frozen, her lips numb and her eyes unable to do more than blink, her hands stiff and motionless in the cradle of her lap. There was only the slow wail of the bagpipe, its beautiful mourning, and the sun burning down to its nightly rest. Half the song had passed before she had the courage to turn again to look out across the water.

How many days had she searched for even a fleeting glimpse of this ghost? Eight days? Nine? Every day since coming to Kincardine, Lia had wandered the town, searching the places her aunt had said that Lia's mother had liked to hang out when they were growing up, peering at reflections, jumping at the sight of every teenaged ghost. And every day she had ended up at the pier and sat there roasting in the August sun until it vanished beneath the horizon, sweating, her skin burning even through her protective layer of sunscreen. Watching. Waiting. She didn't know where else to go.

Without closing her eyes, Lia could still see that fleeting image of her mother's teenaged ghost. Sixteen years old and pregnant, Linda Weatherell had curled one hand protectively around the swell of her stomach that would grow to become her only daughter, Amelia Jessica Weatherell. Was it shock that had transformed her young mother's face? Fear? Apprehension? What had she seen sixteen years past, right there on the end of the pier? Lia didn't know—there was no way for her to ever know. It was just a moment, a single instant of the past played back before her eyes.

And moments like this, instants of the past so briefly seen and so desperately searched for, might be all that Lia had left. Because Linda Weatherell, sixteen years older now than the ghost Lia had seen, was missing. She was crazy and off her medication and had vanished without a trace. No note, no phone calls, no clues, no leads.

Lia had come home one afternoon to find their downtown apartment empty, the doors unlocked, all the windows wide open as the air conditioner blew full blast. Her mother had been doing so well, Lia had thought. The new medication had stabilized her; she had held down her new job as a receptionist for almost four months, had cooked dinner every night and never once woken screaming. But Lia had found the bottle of pills spread out across the bedspread as if they had been thrown, and a mirror smashed on the bathroom floor, and she had *known* that something was terribly wrong. She had phoned her Aunt Jan, and the police.

Three weeks, Lia thought. What had happened? Where had she gone?

Lia took a long, shuddering breath and wiped tears from her face that she didn't remember crying. Behind her, the bagpipe player finished his last song, the final note of his instrument fading slowly. The Phantom Piper, he was called, and thinking of his name Lia smiled a sad and weary smile, for this phantom was the only ghost to haunt her still made of flesh and blood.

For a while she simply stared out across the water until the brilliant sunset began to fade, red and orange slipping from the sky as the stars began to come out.

"Enough," she said to herself at last, and rose to go. She brushed the dust from her shorts and grabbed her cell phone from the ground. Its message light blinked rhythmically.

"Don't worry, Aunt Jan," she said. "I'm coming."

—•—

Downtown Kincardine—such as it was—seemed more alive to Lia on that Friday night than it ever had before. Though the sky was dark, the street was lit to an electric cheerfulness and even the stars above shone brightly. She'd expected the centre of town to be all but empty, tired townspeople returning to their backyard lounge chairs, barbeques, and beds after the long summer day, but she was far from alone on Queen Street. The local pubs, bars, and coffee shops all had their front doors open wide, welcoming both the cool breeze and new patrons inside, while the patio tables and chairs were full almost to overflowing. As she walked, the sound of her sneakers against the sidewalk was lost beneath laughter, the murmur of conversation, and the clink of forks and glasses.

Nor were these the only people populating the main street of the town, but its other inhabitants only Lia could see—and she tried her best to ignore the ghosts. They were not so much the ghosts of a person or a thing, Lia knew, so much as the ghost of a moment. Not just important moments—births, deaths, shocks, destruction—but small moments too, tiny moments likely lived and then forgotten. An old man opening a newspaper; a mother straightening her daughter's bonnet and brushing a hair from her lace collar; children riding bikes through rain puddles. Other moments, too; moments with no people or human things of any kind. Just that morning Lia had left her aunt's house and seen the ghost of a great forest spread all about her, dense green undergrowth and trees, maple and hemlock, rising in a thick canopy to cover the sky.

And yet those moments, for whatever reason, seemed to imprint themselves on a place and play back in the present like bits of living video. From years of watching, Lia believed that these playbacks were not random but rather connected to the lives and moments occurring in the present. She wondered who had conjured up the physical memory of the *Ann Maria*—or the ghost of her mother. Perhaps Lia herself, her regret and her mourning. Or maybe it had only been the weather, the cool evening breeze and the darkening sky as sunset faded to night.

When she reached the Aztec, a small movie theatre whose display boards proudly announced the arrival of films that she'd seen in Toronto months before, Lia turned and began walking up Durham Street. It was quieter off the main road, the bustle of Kincardine's night life fading behind her as she walked. Shops gave way to subdivisions, the chatter of patio conversation replaced by the flicker of blue television light from behind open windows. A car passed slowly, heading downhill towards the river. But for a white cat, skulking around bushes at the edge of a driveway, Lia was alone.

It was almost a relief.

She wasn't sure what she wanted to avoid more—the living, breathing people and their happy lives or the ghosts of the town, the oblivious haunting past. Though all her life Lia had seen ghosts, never before had she been in a place where their presence was so felt as in Kincardine.

Wandering down the quiet street, subdivisions stretching to either side, Lia had to wonder why. In Toronto, there were streets and buildings far older than anything they had in this little southern Ontario town. Toronto had been a busy, bustling city while Kincardine—or Penetangore, as it used to be called, named after the river than ran through it—wasn't even a point on a map. The Walker House, the oldest building in Kincardine and neighbour to the squat white lighthouse and lighthouse keeper's museum, had been built—when? Lia thought back to the plaques and pamphlets that she'd read countless times in her weeks of wandering the town. 1850, she thought. The lighthouse itself was at least thirty years younger.

Yet both were still there, not untouched but as close to the original as the townspeople could keep them. Or, in the case of the Walker House, as close as they could get it again. In her wandering of the town, Lia had seen much of the Walker House, the old building that had been transformed from house to hotel to home—before burning. That was a ghost that reoccurred over and over again: the bright flames, the roiling smoke, and the lingering scent of ash.

Peering inside the building, Lia had seen blackened wood, thick curtains of plastic hanging where walls had once been. Lumber was stacked high in places. Yet from the outside, the place looked as it had for so many years before, all trace of soot and smoke gone, the new cream siding and the roofing shingles looking so close to the original that Lia had squinted a time or two to be sure that she was seeing the present rather than the past.

Maybe that was the difference, Lia thought. Kincardine wrapped itself in its history, building layer upon layer of life over the past, saving what had come before, while in Toronto progress plowed over the had-beens, the city inventing and reinventing and renovating itself by the year. The Royal York hotel, once the tallest building in the Commonwealth, had been topped with neon. Even the beautiful stonework of the Royal Ontario Museum was being buried beneath a structure of iron and glass.

It should have seemed beautiful, Kincardine's connection with its past, and maybe if she hadn't felt so foreign, so strange and lost wandering the streets she had already memorized, Lia would have loved the town and its ghosts. As it was, she couldn't help but feel like she was trapped in the tiny place and its past, and suffocating, as if the very air she breathed was thick with dust and ancient perfume.

Lia shook her head to clear it from such thoughts. The night air was cool and clean—far cleaner than anything she could breathe on a humid, smoggy night in the city. Listen, she told herself; if she paused, she could hear the sound of the river passing slowly beneath the bridge over which she'd crossed without noticing in her daze, and only very distantly could she hear the rush of cars.

It was quiet here, she thought. Peaceful. She could come to love this place, couldn't she? If she had to move—

If her mother never—

If her mother was—

She hated even thinking of the possibilities. Yet they lingered in her mind like the image of that teenaged ghost with her mass of falsely curled hair, baggy clothes to hide her pregnancy, and that look of fear crossing her face.

"Why?" Lia whispered as she walked, not knowing who she was addressing. Her mother? The town? The past? Why was she seeing this image of her mother now, and what was she supposed to do with the vision?

She'd seen the ghosts of people that she knew before, even while they were still alive, as she so desperately hoped was the case with her mother. Yet rarely had she come across the living memory of someone that she knew so closely or so well. For a time, years before, she'd thought it strange that she'd almost never seen the ghosts of her past selves haunting her small downtown apartment; that only once has she turned the corner to see the ghost of her mother cooking dinner on the stove, and it had been but recently that she'd seen her infant self playing with blocks on the carpeted floor. She'd come to assume that this was simply because she and her mother were already there, living and breathing in those spaces, so that their past was tied to their present. Lia couldn't see those ghosts the way she'd never seen her own back without aid of a mirror; it was part of her, too close to be seen.

But what did that mean for her mother—or her ghost? The vision scared her, for more reasons that Lia wanted to admit. That girl from the past had seemed so still, so frightened, so … sane.

Lia said her mother was crazy. She said it to herself, had even shouted it at her mother in moments of frustration or anger. Yet she had trouble saying that her mother was mentally ill. It sounded so final, as if her mother's mind had caught a disease for which there was no cure. But there was no escaping the facts: Linda Weatherell heard voices when no one spoke, she saw things that weren't there, she smelled smoke when there was no fire and felt rain in the middle of a parched summer day.

For a time Lia had believed that her mother must see ghosts of the past, as she did, and had clung to this belief in hope and fear—hope that it meant her mother really wasn't crazy, and fear that it meant that Lia herself was crazy too. But as Lia grew and watched her mother's behaviour, even had a few tentative conversations about what her mother was seeing, hearing and feeling, it became clear that that wasn't the case. Lia would watch ghosts come and go, even ghosts of strange things, amazing things, and her mother wouldn't so much as glance at them. And when Lia's mother had one of her fits, absorbed in sights or sounds that were not there, the room was invariably free of ghosts.

Lia sighed, her head down as she walked. She'd known that her mother was getting worse over the years—that her fits and visions affected her life far more than they had when Lia was a little girl. But it had been an easy thing to forget, thinking that everything could be solved by a new prescription or a bit more time, the steady progress of her mother's illness overlooked in the day-to-day routine of their lives. And now, suddenly, horribly, she was gone, and Lia was left looking back with a sense of guilt, wondering what she could have done to make things turn out differently.

Too late, she thought to herself. The past was past, done, gone. She could never change what had come before, only watch history play out before her eyes, and wonder.

II

Her aunt's house, when she reached it, was dark. Lia walked up the driveway slowly, staring at the black windows, the open curtains. In the daylight it was a cheerful house, white siding and hunter green shutters, with a wide maple on the front lawn and two wooden deck chairs sitting on a raised concrete patio. In the streetlight's pale glow it was just a house, silent and still.

The front door was unlocked; it opened with a hushed creak of hinges and Lia stepped inside, kicking off her sandals and closing the door behind her. She paused a moment, listening. The only sound was the slow breath of the air conditioning through the creaking ducts.

"Hello?" Lia said. There was no answer.

It was only the yellow glow of the back porch light, visible through the kitchen windows at the end of the hall, that kept Lia's heart from beating out of her chest in sudden panic. She had not been abandoned. Not again.

Lia found her aunt in the backyard, rocking slowly on a wide porch swing set in the middle of the lawn. Her head was down, bowed towards her lap with her short dark hair shadowing her eyes, her only movement the small pushes with her feet that kept the swing moving. Cradled in her hands was the portable phone.

"Aunt Jan?" Lia called softly, standing at the top of the concrete steps.

Her aunt looked up and tried to smile. "Hey," she said, her voice sounding worn, and Lia knew it was more than the dark shadows across her face that made her Aunt Jan look so tired and old.

"Has there been word?"

Her aunt shook her head and glanced away. "No," she said. "Nothing yet."

Of course not, Lia thought, shoving down the sudden hope and tears. What had she expected?

Lia walked down the steps and into the backyard. Situated on a lot shaped like a piece of pie, her aunt's house had a far bigger yard in the back than it did in the front. No fences separated it from the neighbours' yards, only a few carefully planted saplings, so it seemed that she and her aunt were all but lost in a great field of neatly trimmed grass.

At the far end of the yard there was a chain link fence along which ran a tall stand of poplar trees, their white-backed leaves fluttering in the night air. Behind that ran Highway 21, the two-laned artery that connected the town to everything else along the coast of Lake Huron. On the other side of the highway were a Sobeys—a local grocery store—and a Canadian Tire. For a long moment Lia just stood, staring through the trees to the stores' wide, empty parking lots, and the red and green glow from their signs.

"I made dinner," Aunt Jan said at last. "Hot dogs. I left yours on the barbeque to stay warm."

Lia nodded her thanks. Her dinner sat on the top rack; the hot dog, bubbled and slightly blackened at one end, and toasted bun had long since cooled to air temperature. Lia took both, slathered them with ketchup and started eating, barely pausing for breath. As she chewed, she realized she'd forgotten lunch. Again.

"I'm sorry I missed your call," she said after a few moments eating in silence. "I didn't grab my phone in time."

"That's all right." Her aunt tried and failed to sound cheerful. "You have a good day?" Lia watched as her aunt's fingers ran over the portable phone, lingering on the call button. She suspected that her aunt's day had been as wonderful as her own—which was to say, not at all.

"I went down to the pier," Lia said. "Watched the boats. Listened to the bagpipe player." Watched the ghosts. It all sounded so inane.

"Ah," Aunt Jan said.

A sudden breeze, rustling the poplars, and the passage of a large truck heading north on the highway was almost enough to fill the silence between them.

"You know," Aunt Jan said slowly, "your mother used to do that when she was pregnant."

At this, her aunt had Lia's complete and total attention.

"Oh?" Lia took another bite of her hot dog, nearly choking herself in the process.

Aunt Jan nodded. "In the summer, at least. She used to be gone for hours at a time. Sometimes it would go dark and we'd have to look for her, Mom and I—your grandfather was still too mad at her for getting 'knocked up,' as he used to say, to talk to her at that point—and there she'd be, just sitting at the end of the pier, staring at nothing.

"She said she had a lot to figure out. I guess she did, at that."

Lia felt like saying "Me too," but somehow the words wouldn't come out.

"I went with her a time or two," Aunt Jan continued after a moment, still staring at her lap. "We hardly spoke while we were out there, just sat and watched the sunset, then went home. I always felt like we were waiting for something that never came." She shook her head.

"You think she went to hear the Phantom Piper?" Lia asked.

"No, that's a more recent thing—only in the last ten years or so. Story's older than that, though, far older."

Lia nodded, thinking of the Phantom Piper's bronze plaque on display in front of the lighthouse keeper's museum. It told the story of Donald Sinclair and his family, new immigrants from Scotland, travelling to make their new home in the growing town of Penetangore. When they left the nearby port of Goderich, the weather was cloudy and cool, yet as the vessel sailed the sky grew dark and stormy, the waters heavy, and a thick fog began to obscure their view of land.

Donald Sinclair, afraid for his life and the lives of his family, got out his bagpipes and began to play a lament. In distant Penetangore, it was said, another piper heard his song and began to play in return. It was this song, and his own musical calling, that at last led the family to safe port and their new home.

Whether Sinclair ever knew who had played the song that had called them to safety, the story did not say. Yet for years afterwards, he had gone down to the shore and played his bagpipes as the sun set, calling wayward travellers home.

"Mom needs a song," Lia said softly, then shook her head. If only it was that easy. She could call for as long and as hard as she wanted, but there was no way of knowing what nature of darkness her mother had lost herself in, what stormy waters besieged her or what fog closed her in. What lament could Lia play but the slow song of her regret, the guilt and loss and helpless love that had all but immobilized her? And what kind of song was that?

"Come on," her Aunt Jan said at last, standing, wrapping her arm around Lia's chilled shoulders and leading her towards the door. "Let's get you inside."

Lia didn't think she could ever sleep, exhausted as she was, but had not the strength to protest. Eyes heavy and head bowed, she let her aunt take her into the house and lead her up to bed, the summer night silent and heavy around them.

—•—

When Lia woke hours later, curled beneath blankets just thick enough to keep the air conditioning from freezing her sunburned skin, she thought that the rain had woken her. Heavy rain beat down on the ground and against her closed bedroom window with the speed that only a summer storm could bring. As she shifted beneath the bedding, thunder rolled in the distance, once and again; the storm's heart was over the lake, but coming closer.

Turning onto her side, Lia opened one eye to look out the window, peering through a gap above the sill that the lowered blinds could not quite cover—and froze. Outside, the rain seemed to have turned the street into a river. The gutters were heavy with streams of rainwater, and as she watched more pounded down, patterning the dark road with reflected light from the streetlights. But it was not this that stilled Lia mid-movement or that stopped her breath within a mouth that still tasted of sleep. In that thin strip of window, Lia saw a reflection. A ghost.

Her mother.

Slowly, as if speed alone could force history to flee, Lia turned to face the vision.

For one deceptive moment, with the darkness of the room veiling her sight, she almost thought that it was not a ghost but her mother in truth—as if the woman, lost and afraid, could have made her way to this single room in her sister's house, the house they had both grown up in, to stand and watch her daughter sleep. But the light from years past fell upon her mother's face and hair, a face unlined and hair permed into wild curls, and Lia saw the ghost for what she was: an instant of the past played back, nothing more.

Lia sank back onto the pillows. She almost wished she could cry, but she was so very tired, and so tired of crying. Never had she so desperately wished her gift of past sight gone. How many times had she heard people say that they would do anything for a glimpse of a lost loved one. Faced with the reality Lia felt pain to the point of illness. Was this what her life was to be? Day after day on the pier, night after night of restless sleep, always searching for—always watching—that pregnant, teenaged ghost. The young ghost of a woman who had left her, abandoned her; the ghost of a mother who was never coming home.

Thunder crashed outside, the storm drawing closer, and against the window pane the rain rattled its urgent, staccato beat. Lia watched the ghost, counting the seconds until she too would inevitably be gone.

But instead of vanishing, the ghost began to pace. Back and forth across the bedroom floor she walked, her head down, hands pulling absently at her hair or rising to cover the slight swell of her pregnancy. There was a quick, erratic energy to the ghost's movements, a nervous tension that spoke of indecision.

"Go," Lia mouthed to the ghost, the quiet word catching in her throat. She wanted to hide her face; she wanted to scream. "I can't live like this," she whispered—a desperate plea. There was nothing that Lia could do to change the past, and no ghost could bring her mother back to her. Still, the words felt like betrayal.

It was only as the ghost paced into moonlight of a night more than sixteen years distant that Lia saw what the darkness had concealed: that the ghost wore jeans with a red patch on the knee, an oversized t-shirt, and wide hoop earrings. The exact same clothes that she wore in the glimpse Lia had seen that afternoon on the pier.

Slowly, Lia sat up, pulling the sheet to her chest.

The ghost paused, took a deep breath, and began pulling on a coat. She moved quicker now, her decision made, running her fingers through her tangled halo of curls and shoving a set of keys into the jacket's pocket. In the light of a moon that Lia could not see, Linda Weatherell's face looked much as it had that afternoon on the pier: drawn and afraid. But something else tempered the young woman's features now; determination, Lia thought, or courage just strong enough to override the fear.

With sudden certainty, Lia knew that the ghost was leaving—she knew not where—and that she had to follow.

Lia shook her head, denying the sudden impulse. This could not, would not, be her life. She would not be ruled by ghosts. Her mother was gone, and nothing that the ghost of her mother's younger self did or saw or said could possibly change that.

There is nothing you can do, Lia thought angrily, and stared after the ghost as she walked from the bedroom.

Surely, Lia thought, she'd vanish now. The ghost would disappear, the moment ended, and Lia would be alone. Again. Always. But she watched the ghost walk slowly down the hall, and straining over the sound of the rain, Lia thought she could hear the soft thump of her ghostly footsteps by the front door.

And she knew that if their positions were reversed, her mother would never have let her go.

Praying that her aunt would forgive her if she rose to find her gone, Lia shoved off the covers and hurried quietly after the ghost, pausing by the front door just long enough to shove her feet into her sandals. There was no time for jeans or jackets or goodbye notes; Lia eased the door open as quietly as its old hinges would allow, closed it behind her and rushed out into the darkness after the ghost of her mother.

The rain was a shock. Though a summer storm, the water was cold, stinging. In mere seconds, Lia's pajamas were stuck wetly to her body, her hair plastered to her head and cheeks. As she ran out into the flooded street, searching for the ghost, the wind lashed the rain into her face, almost blinding her.

Lia caught sight of her mother's ghost walking with her head down, her hands deep in her jacket pockets, her permed hair flying about her face, untouched by rain. Lia followed, wiping water from her eyes, thinking that any moment, surely, the ghost would vanish—but she didn't. Down and around the street on which her aunt lived, Lia trailed the ghost, turning with her back onto Durham Street and continuing towards the heart of town.

As they came closer to Queen Street, passing the river and climbing a hill steep enough to make Lia gasp for breath, the ghost began to increase her pace. No longer did she stare at the ground as she walked, but rather scanned the road, peering cautiously about as if searching for something that she didn't quite know how to find. Faster she walked, and faster still; within moments, the ghost of the pregnant Linda Weatherell was all but running. Hindered by rain, the wet fabric of her pajamas and the waterlogged leather of her sandals, Lia found it almost impossible to follow.

"Mom," she called, as if the ghost could hear her. But of course, even if she could hear the sound of Lia's voice, the ghost wouldn't have responded. She probably didn't even know that the small life that grew inside her was a daughter, never mind that she herself would age to become a woman known as "Mom."

So intent was she on following the ghost, Lia didn't see the branch that the storm's winds had cast onto the sidewalk—not until it was too late. Crying out, she fell to the ground, scraping her hands and knees against the wet concrete, her chin hitting the sidewalk with a skull-rattling crack.

For a moment, Lia could only lie on the ground, paralyzed by the sudden pain. Then, groaning, she rolled onto her side. One sandal lay in the gutter, a small dam for the runoff rushing down towards the river, and in a sudden flash of lightning she saw that the palms of her hands were dark with blood. She looked up. Her mother's teenaged ghost walked on, head down, oblivious to her daughter's struggles.

She was going to lose her, Lia realized as she tried and failed to sit up. Now, as in their home in Toronto, her mother was going to walk away from her—and there was nothing she could do to stop her. No, she thought. Not again.

"*Linda!*" she screamed, pouring into her mother's name all her rage and helplessness, the feelings of three weeks distilled into that single word.

Ahead, veiled by the rain and the darkness, the ghost stopped. Lia gaped, pain forgotten. Slowly, the ghost of Linda Weatherell turned, her expression one of shock.

Across a gap of sixteen years, their eyes met.

With all the ghosts that Lia had seen throughout her life, there had been some who had—however briefly—appeared to see her. Those fleeting moments had startled, even frightened her, if only for a moment. But on closer inspection, she had always seen the direction of their gazes for the mere coincidences that they were; the ghosts' attention like the moving eye contact of paintings, nothing more.

This was different. Certainty rested in the base of her stomach, cold and hard as fear.

As Lia pushed the branch away with bleeding hands and struggled to her feet, the ghost's eyes followed her. Those familiar and strange eyes, their deep blue all but lost to the darkness, darted from Lia's hands to her eyes and roved across her face, curious and afraid. She reached out with the fingers of one tentative hand and then drew away, as if it were Lia who were the ghost, the sudden illusion that did not vanish.

The future, Lia realized. Her mother saw the future. Just as Lia herself saw into the past.

The eyes still locked together, gazing at each other through the permeable barrier of time, the ghost began to walk towards the girl who was to be her daughter.

The ghost whispered something. Lia did not know if it was the sound of the rain that stole her mother's words from her, or the fickle nature of her gift that did not allow her to hear those softly spoken words, but she did not need to hear her. In the moonlight that was cast only on her mother's face, she could see the slow movement of her lips as she said, "You can see me."

They were the words that Lia herself had been about to say.

Lia had so many questions, she could barely bring them into words. "How—" she started, and then, "Why—"

But there was no time. Lightning struck, an electric streak that rent the sky above and left Lia squinting at the sudden blue afterimages branching across her vision. Thunder crashed seemingly at the same instant.

When Lia could see clearly again, the ghost was staring at her with a look akin to the one that had crossed her face in that brief instant Lia had seen just that afternoon on the pier: a look of shock and fear, and then, following it, urgency.

Linda reached out her hand towards her daughter as if mere arm's lengths of air separated them, as it seemed, rather than the insurmountable distance of sixteen years.

"Quickly," the ghost said, her voice so young and tinged with panic. "Run."

And Lia did what she had done so many times before: she followed. Leaving her sandals behind her, ignoring the pain and her uncertainty alike, Lia followed. What else could she do? This was her mother.

The lightning, Lia thought as they ran, breath heavy in the back of her throat—it was something to do with the lightning, the storm. Her mother must have seen its light on Lia just as Lia could see the ghost's features cast in moonlight, and that brief flash of light meant something. Something, she was sure, that had to do with what she'd seen on the pier, the thing that had frightened her so greatly. Something, as Aunt Jan had said, that had made Linda return to the pier time after time— like Lia, sixteen years later, had searched for Linda herself. Because

Lia was certain, as she rushed after the ghost through the deserted downtown streets, that the pier was where they were heading.

The waterfront, so familiar to Lia in the daytime's sunshine and summer heat, was transformed by the darkness and fury of the night's storm. White-capped waves rose up and crashed upon the beach, their roar a constant in her ears. Never had Lia thought that the waters of a lake, even a Great Lake, could reach so high. The lighthouse, its squat white tower standing like a sentinel, watched over the harbour, its bright beam flashing out, illuminating the downward pour of water and the distant walls of clouds.

Ghosts, too, plied these waters, oblivious to the lighthouse's bright promise of safety. In the distance, Lia watched the ghosts of emergency flares arc up into the sky, vivid and futile, and in the illumination of a bolt of lightning that hit the water sizzling mere kilometres offshore, Lia thought she saw the great dark shape of a ship listing into the lake.

The *Ann Maria* sailed again too, though it was no decaying wreck that Lia saw, no mere beached schooner, but rather a tall twin-masted vessel that fought a storm of its own and the inevitability of its destruction. Lia could see the distant shapes of sailors clambering over its deck, fighting with the sheeting of its sails as the schooner sheered sideways and crashed upon the sand bar. As she watched, heavy waves began swamping its deck, forcing the crew up into the rigging as the lake attempted to claim them. She felt a wave of pity for those men and the townspeople who would die trying to rescue them, though their deaths were more than a hundred years distant.

On nights like this, Lia couldn't help but think as the wind and rain lashed her face, death seemed that much closer, the world's grip on life revealed for the thin and tenuous thing that it was.

She turned to the ghost of her mother, wanting to ask why she had brought her here, what was so important for her to see. The ghost stood at the edge of where the north pier departed the land, reaching out into the dark waters of Lake Huron like a concrete arm. But no sooner had Lia opened her mouth to call out than the ghost turned to her, still so urgent, so afraid, her hand reaching out to point at something on the pier behind. Their eyes met—and the ghost vanished.

No, Lia thought. No. There was nothing, no one—

And then the passing beam of the Kincardine lighthouse illuminated what the darkness and rain had hidden from her: a lone figure standing at the end of the pier. Lia stared, and took a slow step forward. No ghost this, she realized as the lighthouse's beam passed again; the figure was as drenched as she was, and as disheveled.

As Lia watched, a huge wave crashed upon the pier's end, sending spray high above the figure's head and swamping the concrete with a heavy wash of water. The woman—for Lia was suddenly sure it was a woman—did not step back at this sudden onslaught, but rather forward, closer to the edge. The woman looked down, her head bowed and shoulders slumped as if weighted down with a burden she could no longer bear.

Lia realized two things in the same instant: that the woman was going to jump into the raging waters beyond the pier and surely drown, and that this was her mother.

Later, she would not remember deciding to run. She would not remember the moment of sudden panic and absolute clarity that gave flight to her feet and voice to the rush of fear that all but overwhelmed her. There was only the memory of that terrified run, the darkness of the lake and the night sky on either side of the pier, and the rain-slicked concrete beneath her bare feet. Never had the pier seemed so long or so dangerously narrow. As she ran, Lia had only one thought.

She would never make it in time.

Her mother took a step closer to the edge as a wave swamped the pier, dark lake water rushing around Linda's feet and ankles as if the lake itself was trying to push her back. And in vain.

There was no time. As she had with the teenaged ghost, Lia did the only thing that she could think of: against the howling of the storm wind, the crash of thunder and waves, Lia screamed her mother's name.

Slowly, as if caught in memory or dream, her mother turned to face her.

The ghost's look had been one of shock and confusion as she met Lia's eyes in the electric moment of peering across years; but now her mother, no ghost but a living, breathing woman, looked at her with eyes that seemed dead. Lia stumbled when she saw her mother's face framed in the harsh glow of the lighthouse's beam and the shadows that came with night. Her desperate run faltered to a halt. There was no recognition there, she thought. No life, no emotion, only dull confusion and a weariness that knew no end.

"Mom," Lia whispered, her voice lost beneath the sound of the waves. Spray, cold and heavy, splashed down around them with the rain.

She would give anything to save her mother. But though she had a chance to stop her from stepping from the edge of the pier, what power did she have to save her from that darkness? In the distance, another ghostly flare arched heavenward: a light-borne plea that would always go unseen, unrecognized, unanswered. In vision and memory, out upon the roiling surface of Lake Huron, a ghostly ship sank within sight of Kincardine's shores.

Yet at the sound of Lia's voice or the soft movement of her lips, a frown crossed her mother's face, creasing her forehead and tightening the lines about the edges of her eyes. Her lips, cracked and bleeding, parted.

"Lia?" she said, blinking the rain from her eyes. "Lia, is it—?"

"Mom." Lia reached out slowly, not wanting to startle her mother and send her over the edge so close to her feet. Her heart pounded in her ears. Her hand closed about her mother's wrist, and step by step Lia pulled her back, away from the waves and the spray and the relentless darkness of the empty lake at night and into her arms.

At her daughter's touch, Linda's body seemed to melt, the tension and heavy determination pouring away, leaving her shaking. She spoke into Lia's ear.

"It was you," Lia thought she heard her mother say. "It was you." She didn't need to look at her face to know that she was crying.

"It's me," Lia said, putting her wet arm around her mother's shoulders and taking one of her hands into her own. Her mother trembled with cold and fear, her skin like ice beneath Lia's touch. Lia spoke, not knowing if her mother could even hear the words. It didn't matter. None of it mattered. The only important thing was that she was there, her mother was there, alive, and that Lia would get her to safety.

"I'm here, I've got you," she said. "Everything's going to be okay now. It'll be okay."

Together they walked down the long arm of the pier, the rain pounding down, towards the beacon of the lighthouse and the glow of the town beyond. She gripped her mother's hand tighter and felt her mother squeeze back, the two of them holding on like they'd never let go.

Sometimes, Lia thought, there was no stopping disaster, the ships lost in storms, the lives driven upon a rocky shore or cast into the deep. Yet sometimes the fates granted safe passage: an elusive thread of bagpipe song. A ghost to guide her home.

III

Sighing, Lia lay back and ran her fingers through the sand, feeling the sun's trapped heat in the golden grains. The beach was still warm though day faded into evening; the lake, all but flat, lapped gently at the shore. Beside her, her mother stared out across the lake, long blonde hair drifting about her face, her expression almost serene. In the week since Lia had found her mother—a chaotic week filled with police reports and hospital visits—this was the first opportunity they'd had to be alone.

Silently, Lia looked at her mother's face, seeking in its familiar lines the shape of the girl she had been: the young woman with a wild perm and oversized clothes, whose every movement had spoken of determination and fear. That girl had conceived a child and kept the baby against the wishes of her parents, even though it meant she had to raise her daughter alone. She saw images of the future and kept it secret, letting people think her crazy rather than tell of a gift that could be abused or exploited. She'd seen a vision of her own future, her possible death, and she'd kept going. In hope and in fear, she had kept going.

Turning, her mother met her eyes without question. She knew what face it was that her daughter saw.

And in her daughter, what did she see? In but a single moment, the meeting of eyes across the distance of years, their secrets had been exposed. So much lay unspoken between them, the memories surrounding them like ghosts.

"When you were a little girl," Linda Weatherell said at last, speaking as if she were weighing each word, "I used to watch you asleep in your crib. You lay there, so small, so fragile." Slowly, she shook her head. "And I used to think how terrible it was that someday I'd abandon you. Because when I was still pregnant with you that was the only vision I'd see. Over and over again."

She turned away, looking past her daughter to the piers. At the end of the south pier, a man and his son sat casting fishing lines into the lake, silhouetted against the red of the deepening sunset. On the far horizon, the square buildings of the Bruce Nuclear Station were just visible, the bottoms of the buildings obscured by summer haze. At last, she sighed.

"Of everything I've ever seen, almost all of it changed, shifted—but never that. Always, over and over, I'd see myself standing on the edge of the pier and I knew I was about to die. Nothing I did ever changed it.

"And then I saw you."

Her mother reached up and stroked the side of Lia's face with one gentle fingertip.

"When I ran, I was trying to escape that vision and what it meant. But it was too much—everything was too much to handle. Do you understand, Lia? I didn't want to do this to you. But I …" Her voice trailed away.

"And when I was there," she continued at last, "on the pier—when the vision was true—I could only think that the girl I saw so many years ago, whoever she was, wasn't going to come. She wouldn't see me in time.

"Can you believe it? All those years that I remembered seeing that face, that one hope of salvation in the darkness and the rain, and I never knew it was you. Not until the very moment that you saved me."

Lia reached out and held her hand, squeezing. There were no words—and even had she known what to say, she would never have been able to speak around her own tears.

Linda Weatherell had walked across the province chasing a vision —a vision of herself. A ghost of what could be. And for all her fear and worry, her guilty mourning for a mother not yet dead, Lia felt that she was perhaps the only person who could understand. After all, hadn't she done the same thing? Chased a ghost beyond all thought and reason, driven by an image that she alone could see.

As she watched her mother, watched her eyes close as she relaxed in a single unguarded moment on the beach, her lashes coming to rest against the pale skin of her cheek, Lia felt she truly understood her mother's burden. Just as Lia had always peered into the past, seeing moments of days and years gone by, her mother looked forward. But the past was a different thing, a place of things known and done, while the future was a place of uncertainty and possibility, always shifting. She looked at her mother, the woman she'd so hatefully called crazy, and thought of all the nights that she had woken screaming, all the days that she'd been unable to function, hands pressed over her ears and eyes squeezed shut—blocking out the relentless knowledge of things that might be, that could be, that would be.

But, Lia thought, then she'd had to face that future alone. Her secret kept hidden even from the only person who had any chance of understanding what she was going through: her daughter.

Too quietly for her mother to hear, Lia whispered, "Not any more." The road before them was a strange and uncertain one, a path strewn with ghosts and possibilities, but it was one they would face together.

Which was why, when her mother and Aunt Jan had approached her with the idea of moving to Kincardine, Lia had agreed. Finally she admitted that her mother needed more daily help than she alone could provide. And it was peaceful here, she thought, and beautiful, and with the knowledge that her mother was safe, the town's ghosts no longer pressed at her. The place had—if she had to admit it—a kind of charm that was growing on her.

Still, staring out at the lighthouse and the twin piers that guarded the entrance to the harbour, she knew that there were already so many memories here, not all of them good. She wondered how long it would be until she could look at the north pier without that fluttering feeling in her stomach akin to fear, or look at the ghostly shape of the *Ann Maria* and not have her throat tighten with remembered tears. How long would it be before she could sleep without seeing her mother standing on the edge of the pier, about to jump?

Could she truly live here?

Her mother opened her eyes when Lia sniffed and rubbed at the prickle in her eyes as the tears threatened to overflow. Softly, she smiled.

"Ah, sweetie," her mother said. "I'm so sorry. It's been such a rough time for you."

Lia nodded, trying to smile in return.

"And you haven't seen much of this little town, have you? The place where your mom grew up. Why don't we go do something—get an ice cream cone—just you and me."

"But I thought," Lia said haltingly, "that we would wait for the Phantom Piper."

"No, the Piper won't be playing tonight, it's—" Her mother stopped, glancing over at Lia. "It's Saturday," she said. "You haven't had a chance to see downtown Kincardine on a Saturday night, have you?"

Lia shook her head, and at that her mother's face blossomed into a smile—a true smile. How long, Lia wondered, had it been since she'd last seen a smile that bright on her mother's face?

"Come on," she said, taking Lia's hand and pulling her up from the sand. "You're going to love this." Together they ran up the boardwalk and over the bridge, then hurried uphill past the lighthouse and the large stone on the corner with its bronze plaque in memorial of Donald Sinclair and the Phantom Piper, up towards the town.

As they passed a local pub, two small boys ran past, calling to their parents over their shoulders. "Hurry," they shouted. "It's almost started!"

Ahead on Queen Street, Lia could only see a solid wall of people standing shoulder to shoulder along the sidewalk. She turned to look at her mother, but before she could so much as open her mouth to frame the question, over the murmuring of the crowd she heard a sound.

Tap!

It was a snare drum, Lia realized; no, many snare drums as in unison they began to play a quick and rolling beat. Then there came a low drone that built slowly, slowly, until all at once a great wail filled the air as countless bagpipes began to play a quick and stirring tune. Lia grinned as she recognized it: "Scotland the Brave."

Running the last few steps, Lia and her mother joined the throng. Along both sides of the street people stood, three and four deep, children perched on their parents' shoulders and, closer to the road, older people sitting on stools and folding lawn chairs, watching. Waiting. There were no cars anywhere that she could see, only people, the stoplights in the intersections ignored as they cycled through their colours, green, yellow, red.

But it wasn't the crowd that made Lia stop and stare: it was the band.

Down the very centre of the street marched a pipe band dressed in full regalia, tartan kilts and white shirts, with tasseled socks pulled up to their knees. At the front of the band there was a tall man with a great silver-topped baton, which he let rise and fall in time with the music and each step of his feet. The bagpipe players came first, then row upon row of drummers, their drumsticks beating in perfect time. At the very back, the drummers twirled their huge drumsticks with glow wands tied to their handles, spinning them in complex loops over their shoulders and out to their sides, never once losing the song's throbbing beat.

The band marched down the centre of the street, their song echoing from the buildings, seeming to fill the entire town. And as the band passed, the spectators left their positions at the side of the road and began to follow. Like a great flood, the people of Kincardine fell in behind the Scottish Pipe Band and walked down the centre of the street in one great parade.

"Come on," Lia's mother said again, grinning as she tightened her hold on Lia's hand and pulled her into the crowd.

They truly were a parade, Lia thought as they walked. People still gathered on either side of the road to watch them walk by, waving and laughing. All around her were people, more people than she'd even known were hidden in the small lakefront town, families and seniors and young couples and children. Even from the windows and balconies above the shops, people watched.

But it was only Lia who saw the other spectators, the ghosts who lined the street and rooftops, memories of years gone by standing alongside the present. They, too, laughed, smiled, and pointed as the parade went by, seeing not this parade but ones from years past: year upon year of history and tradition playing out in a single moment in the heart of the town called Kincardine.

Peering upwards, Lia waved to a little girl in pajamas, and laughed as an old man and his friends saluted the pipe band with their bottles of beer. She didn't know if they were ghosts or people as real as her, flesh and blood, and it didn't matter. Moments like these tied them all together until there was no separating past from present, no way to differentiate what was from what had been.

When the pipers at last reached the end of the downtown strip, they slowly turned into a store parking lot and the sound died away. A police officer had parked her car across the road, smiling as she leaned against the cruiser's front fender and watched the parade slow to a stop.

"What happens now?" Lia asked, watching the milling crowd. In the small parking lot, drummers let little children try the drumsticks, the uneven booming noises punctuating conversations. A small line of people had formed outside the local ice cream shop, and ice cream dripped from more than one small child's face.

"Now?" her mother said. She almost giggled as she replied, "Now we go back!"

After a moment, the leader called the band to attention and they stepped back into their rows, the crowd again gathering on either side of the street.

"Kincardine Scottish!" he called. "Pipes ready." The low drone of chanters filled the air.

"And—*march*!"

The drums exploded into life as the bagpipes again sang out in one echoing voice, and the band marched back out onto the street in the direction from which they'd come. The glow wands on the drummers' sticks were whirls of colour and light in the gathering darkness, sketching out patterns in the sky in time to the bagpipes' song. And, as before, everyone turned to follow.

With one arm, her mother pulled Lia close as they walked.

"So we're heading back to the place where the band started marching?" Lia called to her over the music.

"You got it. Victoria Park."

"So the band and everyone else just march down the street, turn around, and go back again? This is the silliest thing I've ever heard of."

"I know," her mother said. "Isn't it great? Growing up, I always said we were crazy."

"You do this every summer?"

Her mother laughed. "Every summer?" she said. "Lia, we do this every week!"

And Lia couldn't help but laugh too as the great crowd of people swept them along. All around them bagpipes called out, the joined voices of the instruments clear and strong. In life and memory, theirs was a song that could defy fog and storm, a song of life and ghosts that filled the town, echoed through it.

No, Lia thought, she could not know what lay ahead; not even her mother knew for certain. But she was not alone. Smiling, Lia squeezed her mother's hand and followed, the bagpipes singing her forward.

Guiding her home.

When I was asked to contribute to this anthology I knew I was going to pick a musical reference, because music is such a large part of my life—either when I'm playing myself, or appreciating the music others make. So I thought of some of my favourite Canadian musicians.

There's Leonard Cohen—poet, author, singer-songwriter, and now Zen student—and Robbie Robertson—who was once a part of the Band—but I've already done stories inspired by their music. ("Scars" for Cohen and "Making a Noise in This World" for Robertson.) Then I thought of Fred Eaglesmith, but that didn't feel right, so I kept casting about. Lynn Miles. Ian Tamblyn. Jenny Whiteley.

After awhile I decided I was going about this all wrong, so I did what I'll often do when I want to get a story going. I just started to put down words to see where they'd take me. Half a page in and I knew where I was going and what the inspiration would be: "Universal Soldier" by Buffy St. Marie. It's an old song from the sixties that was a hit for the Scottish folk singer Donovan and, unfortunately, has as much relevance today as it did when it was written.

~ Charles de Lint
Ottawa, summer 2005

The Universal Soldier

by
Charles de Lint

*"They're gemmin," the janitor told me when I asked.
"Little mobile histories of a place. Kind of like fairies,
if you think of them as the spirits of some particular
area or space. They soak up stories and memories, and
then one day they're all full up and off they go."*

"Where do they go?" I said.

*"I don't know. I just know they go and they don't
come back. Not the same ones, anyway."*

– from "Sweet Forget-Me-Not" by Ahmad Nasrallah

"Excuse me," the soldier said. "If it's not too much trouble, could you tell me the best way for me to take to get to the Lakefront Pier?"

The two girls looked at one another and began to giggle.

"Did you ever—"

"Not me."

They spoke at the same time, stopped to let the other continue, then started to giggle again when neither did.

The dark-haired soldier waited patiently for them to finish before repeating his question.

"We're not supposed to talk to strangers," Belinda said.

Jane nodded in agreement. "That's what Charlotte says, and she should know. She's older than us."

"By three days."

"Which still makes her older."

"But we do, anyway."

"Speak to strangers, that is."

"But only if they have kind eyes."

"Which you have, by the way."

Belinda nodded. "Kind, but haunted."

Belinda was the blonde, taller and far more buxom than the petite Jane, with her boyish figure and short dark hair. Jane wore a top hat, a pair of tight faded blue jeans, and a black jacket that was cropped on the front and sides, but had tuxedo tails at the back. Belinda was in a vintage pink tulle dress with a lace bodice and a full skirt that cascaded to her knees in a froth of white and pink with accents of fine black netting. They were both barefoot and could have been going to a prom, except today being Halloween, he assumed they were either on their way to an early costume party, or they simply liked dressing up.

It was hard to tell their age because of their artfully applied make-up. The soldier put them at somewhere between fifteen and twenty. He had five sisters and knew that girlish giddiness wasn't attributable to any particular age.

"Perhaps if I introduced myself first," he tried. "Then you might discover that we're not so much strangers as simply old friends meeting for the first time. My name's Parker Paul. I know that's confusing, having a first name for a surname and vice versa, but I assure you, the choice was entirely out of my hands."

"Why do you talk so funny?" Belinda asked.

Parker raised his eyebrows. "Do you mean my accent?"

"That, too. It's just—"

"You talk like someone in a movie," Jane finished for her.

Belinda nodded. "Yes, you're very wordy."

"That comes from two years in an English boarding school, I'm afraid."

"Of what?" Belinda asked.

"I'm sorry?"

Jane cocked her head. "Why?"

Parker smiled. He was used to this, too. Two of his sisters were considerably younger than him and delighted in pretending to take everything he said literally and then pestering him with questions. Time spent with them had obviously been a training ground for just this sort of situation.

He looked from one girl to the other, his dark brown eyes solemn.

"I suppose it all depends," he said, "on the colour of the spoon."

The girls clapped their hands.

"Oh, very good," Jane told him. "You really must be a long-lost friend."

"Oh, yes," Belinda agreed. "Moon-wise and spinning very still."

"And since you're an old friend..."

"...we won't tell you how to get to the Pier..."

"...we'll take you there, our very own selves."

With that they slipped up on either side of him and hooked their arms in his.

"It's this way, Mr. Paul," Belinda said.

They led him off down the sidewalk, deftly steering him through the crowd so that while it seemed as though they were forever about to run into this oncoming pedestrian or that one, they always managed to find some way to walk three abreast without bumping into anyone.

"Are you of the Stanton Street Pauls?" Jane asked.

He looked in her direction and nodded.

"You know they don't live there anymore, don't you?" Belinda added.

She had her head cocked prettily, the question repeated in the arch of her eyebrows.

"No, I hadn't heard," he said. "It's been so long since I've been back and everything has changed."

"How long have you been away?"

"It feels like a very long time. I've been...overseas."

Belinda nodded. "Is that where it happened?"

"Where what happened?"

"Where you died," Jane said.

Parker stopped and disengaged their arms from his. He looked from one guileless face to the other.

"What a thing to say," he told them.

"I suppose it was rude," Jane said, "just coming out with it like that."

"Though that doesn't make it any less true," Belinda added. "Does it?"

"I…"

"You can't pretend you don't know," Jane said.

Belinda nodded. "Because if you didn't, how would your ghost know to be waiting for the moon to rise at the very place of its death, on today, the one day when the dead can walk around wearing skin and bones like the living?"

Parker studied her for a long moment, but all he said was, "You seem to know a lot about ghosts."

"Not really. Mostly they just drift around, all…"

She looked for the word.

"Ghostly," Jane said.

Belinda nodded. "Exactly. We can hardly see them and they certainly aren't able to have an actual conversation—at least not usually—never mind hold your hand or give you a kiss."

"I'm not giving you a kiss," Parker said.

"I know," Belinda said. "Because you already have a sweetheart. Or you did, before you died. And you hope to see her on the Pier."

"How do you know that?"

"We might not know a lot about ghosts," Jane told him, "but we do know about love."

"Is that so."

"Oh, don't go all huffy," Jane said. "We're bringing you to the Pier, aren't we? Or at least we were until you stopped in the middle of the sidewalk and became an immovable object." She gave him a little poke with a finger. "See? You can't be budged."

Belinda gave him a poke as well.

"He's like a lamppost," she said. "Rooted to the pavement."

"Stop that," Parker said as she went to poke him again.

Jane looked at her wrist, though she wasn't wearing a watch.

"Time's a-wasting," she told the soldier. "If you want to make your rendezvous, we should keep walking."

"Unless you have money for a bus?" Belinda asked, her voice hopeful.

"I don't have any money."

Jane nodded. "Neither do we. We keep telling Charlotte that we should have money, but she doesn't seem to think it's necessary."

"Because she doesn't have to walk all the way to the Pier," Belinda said.

"That's twice you've mentioned someone named Charlotte," the soldier said.

"Is it? I wasn't keeping count."

She looked at Belinda who shook her head.

"I wasn't either," Belinda said.

"It's a good thing someone was," Jane told the soldier.

Parker sighed. "I only meant that as a preamble to asking you who she was."

"Not dead, that's for sure," Belinda said.

"Who she *is* then."

"Ah." Jane took his arm again. "She's like our sister."

She slipped her arm in his and started to walk once more and the soldier let her lead him off. Belinda fell in step beside him and took his other arm.

"But she's not really your sister," Parker said.

"That depends," Jane said. "Let's say you have handful of seeds that all come from the same plant. When some of them sprout, are they siblings?"

"I can't even pretend to understand what that means," Parker told her.

"Well," Belinda said, "you know how, for a ghost to be born, someone has to die first? It's like that, except totally different."

"Totally," Jane agreed. "But otherwise, just like that."

Parker decided that to press for clarification would only make him more confused, but he still found himself asking, "And that would make Charlotte?"

"Definitely the oldest," Belinda said.

"Of the three of you."

"Five, actually," Jane said. "You can't forget Gina and Kathy."

Belinda nodded. "Well, you could, but it wouldn't be very polite."

"So there are five of you."

"Yes," Jane agreed. "There are five of us in our little pod."

Belinda shook her head. "Pod doesn't sound right. Maybe we should say flock."

"But we're not birds. How about gang?"

"Tribe."

"Clan."

"Posse."

"Which do you like best?" Belinda asked the soldier.

"I don't feel qualified to offer an opinion," he said.

"Oh, pooh. Everybody has opinions."

"I meant an informed opinion," he told her. Then for lack of anything better to say, he added, "I have five sisters."

"Sisters!" Jane said. "That's perfect. Sisters. As in 'sisters in crime,' or 'sisters of the heart.' I like it."

"It *is* perfect," Belinda agreed. "You're a clever soldier."

"Do you miss *your* sisters?" Jane asked the soldier.

Parker nodded. "I think of them often."

"Then how could you just leave them behind to go off and fight in some silly old war?"

"Not to mention your true love," Belinda added.

"It was my duty," he told them. "When I serve and protect my country, I serve and protect them as well."

"So you volunteered?"

He nodded. "My father didn't want me to go. He told me that soldiering was for poor people who didn't have any other options for their future, not for bright young men with the whole of the world waiting for them. But I disagreed. If our country was going to war, it was the duty of all of us to defend our freedoms and rights. We argued. A lot. But I signed up anyway."

"And then you died," Jane said.

Parker's brow furrowed. "It was a car bombing…this time…"

"What do you mean this time?" Belinda asked.

The soldier brought them all to a stop once more. He again

disengaged his arms from theirs and rubbed his brow. He looked up into the sky but his gaze was turned inwards.

"I...I seem to remember dying more than once..." he told them.

"You sound like us," Jane told him. "We sort of die all the time, but then we come back. Or some part of us comes back—enough so that it might as well be us."

"Except it's not," Belinda said.

Jane nodded. "No, not at all. But it all feels familiar because we know what to do and where to go and what stories to collect."

"I don't understand," the soldier said.

"Well, you know how everybody—"

"Every*thing*," Belinda interrupted.

"Everything," Jane agreed. "There's a story in everything and everybody. Lots of stories. There's the one that's inside them and then all the other ones that get born when they bang up against somebody else's story."

The solider gave a slow nod.

"Well, we're the ones who collect those stories," Belinda said.

Parker wasn't quite sure what they were telling him.

"What do you do with them?" he finally asked.

"They fill us up and then we go away and other girls come along to collect more stories."

"Go where?"

Belinda gave a breezy wave with her hand. "Oh, you know. Away. Back into the bigger story of the world."

"You mean you die?"

Jane giggled. "Oh, no no no. How can we die when we were never born?"

"Are you telling me you're not human?"

Jane looked at Belinda. "Says the ghost of a dead soldier."

"But I *was* human."

"Oh, like ever having been human's such a big deal."

The soldier shook his head. "What are you?"

The girls shrugged. "What are you?"

"Apparently, the ghost of a dead soldier. One who's died more than once. I…if I let myself think about it too much, I can't count all the battlefields…the times I've died…"

"It sounds like reincarnation," Jane said.

"I don't believe in reincarnation."

Belinda laughed. "If something exists, it doesn't matter if you believe in something or not. It still *is*."

"Is that what happens to you?"

"We're not sure," Jane said.

Belinda nodded. "And besides that, it's not important."

"Our stories aren't important."

"Just the ones we collect."

"I would think," the soldier said, "that every story is as important as another. Otherwise it means that hierarchies and caste systems and however else we divide ourselves are real."

Belinda cocked her head. "That's probably right." She turned to Jane. "After all, we're carrying around our own stories, too. We just don't have to collect them."

"Because we live them," Jane said.

Belinda nodded. "Which means they'll come with us whether we want them to or not."

"But they're not as interesting to us," Jane told the soldier. "We'd much rather hear other people's stories. And we especially want to hear your stories."

"Why would that be?" Parker asked.

"Because normally ghosts don't talk. Normally we can't even see them."

"And when we do," Belinda added, "they're all drifty and focused on what they can't have."

"Or what to set right."

"I don't feel either impulse," Parker said.

"Oh no? Then why are you going to meet your true love on the Pier?"

"Because I said I would."

"When did you make that promise?" Belinda asked.

"I…I don't remember."

"Well, I think it's terribly romantic," Jane said.

Belinda nodded. "And a bit sad."

"Bittersweet," Jane said.

"Bittersweet," Belinda agreed. "Exactly."

"You don't know that," the solider said. "What makes you think she won't come?"

"Well, if you're one of the Stanton Street Pauls," Jane said, "it has to turn out sad because they moved away ages ago. That means your going away and dying and all happened ages ago, too. So even if your true love is still alive, she'd be really old."

Parker smiled. "Old? As in her mid-thirties?"

"No, *really* old. Like in her fifties or something."

"She might be too old and decrepit to come," Belinda said. "No offense."

"None taken," Parker told her. "But she will come."

"How can you be so sure?"

"Because I promised her and she promised me."

The two girls exchanged a worried look, then Jane sighed.

"Well, come on then," she said, taking his arm once more. "We shouldn't keep her waiting, should we?"

The soldier let them lead him off again, one girl on either arm. He tried not to gawk at their surroundings as they walked, but it was hard to stop. Everything had changed—drastically. The buildings were impossibly tall, all metal and glass. There was so much traffic, the vehicles all so sleek. And the crowds of people, hurrying, chattering into their cell phones, dressed in an array of styles that bewildered the eye…

Except…except…

It was all familiar as well.

They were walking down the sidewalk of this busy street with traffic rushing by, the tall buildings on either side. But at the same time they were walking through an older version of the city. Many older versions that flitted in and out of his awareness. One moment a modern bus was pulled up at a stop. The next it was an old streetcar. Then there were only horse-drawn buggies slowly passing by, the horse hooves clopping on cobblestones. Then it was a dirt road. Then a field and they were following a narrow game trail.

Then, just as abruptly, the modern city was back.

"Which one are you now?" Jane asked.

He looked at where she walked on his right, arm linked with his.

"What do you mean?"

"You keep changing," she said. "Your hair goes from short to long and then back again."

"And your skin changes colour."

"And your uniform changes, too."

"Sometimes you're hardly wearing anything—"

"—and then you're smartly dressed again," Jane said.

"How do you do it?" Belinda asked.

"I don't know," the soldier said. "I'm just me. Parker Paul."

Except that didn't seem to be the right name. Parker had died in the trenches in France during the Second World War. While he...he'd died in the desert. He'd been part of a combat patrol, west of the city, when their attacker detonated explosives directly under their vehicle...

No, he'd died in a jungle, cut down by a sniper...

He'd died in a forest of pines and cedars, struck by an arrow that had come whistling from between the trees, the bowman unseen...

He'd died at sea, when a broadside struck down their mast and he'd come tumbling down from the crow's nest...

He'd died in a grey uniform, fighting his brother who wore the blue...

He'd died under the clubs of another tribe's warriors...

He'd died...he'd died...he'd died...

But he was still Parker. Or at least Parker was still a part of him.

He brought them all to a halt again.

"It's not so far now," Jane assured him.

Belinda nodded. "We really do know where we're going."

"It's not that," he told them. "It's...there's something wrong with me. I'm too many people, all at the same time."

"Maybe you're the unknown soldier," Jane said. "There was probably one in every war."

"More than one," Belinda added.

Jane nodded. "Sadly, that's true."

Parker shook his head. "No. If I concentrate, I know who every one of these people inside me are."

"Then maybe you're the well-known soldier," Belinda said, then added, "Sorry. I didn't mean to make that sound like a joke."

"She didn't," Jane said.

The soldier nodded. "I know."

They began to walk again. In the far distance, they could finally catch glimpses of the lake, a shimmer of water between the canyon of buildings on either side of the street.

"How did you know I was a ghost?" the soldier asked after they'd gone a few more blocks.

"We just *did*," Jane told him.

Belinda nodded. "It's what we know."

"Who's human and who's not."

"Do you meet a lot of people who aren't human?" Parker asked.

"You'd be surprised."

"Though maybe not," Jane said. "Do ghosts get surprised?"

"That's right," Belinda said. "You don't hear of ghosts hanging around because they're surprised. They're usually sad or angry or lost or something."

"You surprise me," the soldier said. "Every time you open your mouths."

They walked in silence for a few moments, the girls opening and closing their mouths with great exaggeration.

"How many times were you surprised?" Jane asked after a half block of that.

"You're very strange girls," he told them.

Belinda grinned. "Says the ghost."

"If you think we're strange," Jane said, "you should meet Gina. She collects bobby pins."

"But only ones she finds on the street," Belinda said.

"And then she arranges them in patterns on the tar of a roof that overhangs the alley where we born-ish."

"She says 'born-ish'," Belinda explained, "because that's the easiest way to describe how one day we were just there."

"When the day before we weren't."

"I still think you're stranger," Parker said.

"Is that a good thing or a bad thing?" Jane asked.

"It's neither," Belinda said before the soldier could reply. "It just is."

"You mean like there's no box to fit us in?"

"There could never be a box to fit you in," Parker said.

"I don't know," Jane told him. "I've seen some big boxes."

"I meant metaphorically."

"I knew that," Jane said, then stuck out her tongue at him.

Belinda suddenly stopped, bringing them all to a halt. She reached up and straightened the soldier's tie.

"We're almost there now," she said, "and you need to look your best."

Parker looked up and saw that they were only a couple of blocks from the street that ran parallel to the lake. The two girls industriously brushed dust—real and imagined—from his jacket while he stood and stared. He didn't recognize any of the stores on this street, but he knew the shapes of the older buildings. And he knew the old hotel he could see down by the shore front. The Pier would be to its right, hidden from sight at the moment by the buildings on the other side of the street.

"Are you nervous?" Jane asked.

He shook his head.

"Of course he's not nervous," Belinda said. "He's a soldier. They're brave and never get nervous."

"That's not true," he told them. "I'm always nervous in battle. Sometimes I get so scared I don't know if I'll be able to hold my rifle."

"But you do."

He nodded. "You have to. The men you're with are depending on you. At that moment, the reason you're there, the reason you're fighting, doesn't mean much at all. You just want to get the mission done and survive, protecting as many of your companions as you can."

"Hence the brave part," Belinda said.

"I suppose."

Parker felt uncomfortable. There was nothing glamorous about war. Time spent on the front lines was an even mixture of boredom, fear, and the horror of combat. You didn't remember to appreciate the boredom until the night was filled with mortar shells and bullets.

He wasn't sure how to convey that to his two young companions. Wasn't sure he even wanted them to carry the burden of the knowledge.

"You're not our first soldier," Jane said. "That's how we know you must be brave."

Belinda nodded. "You're not even our first ghost."

"Except the others never talked to us."

"Why not?" he asked.

"I guess we didn't meet them on Halloween."

"I need to go," he said.

Jane gave his sleeve a last brush with her fingers.

"Of course you do," she said.

"Do you mind if we follow?" Belinda asked.

"We won't come too close."

"And we won't interrupt or eavesdrop or anything."

"We're very good at not being seen."

"Or at least, people don't see us unless they need to."

"What does that mean?" the soldier asked.

Belinda shrugged. "I don't know. It's just that if a person's open enough, and seeing us can make a difference, then they often do."

"And for some reason," Jane added, "it makes them feel better."

"Well, I know that feeling," he told them.

"So can we tag along?" Belinda asked.

"We'll be ever so…" Jane looked at Belinda. "What's the word I'm looking for?"

"Inconspicuous."

Jane nodded. "Exactly. We'll be so totally inconspicuous that not even a super secret agent spy-type satellite could hope to conspicu' us."

Parker laughed. "Of course you can come. I'd like you to meet Angeline."

"That's a pretty name," Belinda said, linking her arm with his again.

Jane did the same on the opposite side and they continued down the last couple of blocks until they finally reached Lakeside Drive and there was only the wide street and lakefront hotels between themselves and the lake. Wolf Island was half-hidden in mists, but they could clearly see the Pier and the ferry that was just leaving port on the far side of the long wooden and concrete structure. The wind blowing in from the lake held a faint echoing scent of fish and weeds.

"At least that hasn't changed," Parker said.

"Do you mean the Pier?"

He nodded. "The Pier. The restaurant at its far end. The ferries. The island. It's all the way I remember it—or at least, more so than the walk we just took to get here."

They crossed Lakeside and walked in the shadow of the hotels until they reached the parking lot in front of the Pier.

"But they didn't charge to park your car back then," the soldier said as they walked by the booth where a man sat waiting for customers to be either entering or leaving his lot.

"Everything costs money now," Jane told him.

"It would have back then, too," Parker said. "If they'd only come up with the idea and thought they could get away with it."

"Do you see her?" Belinda asked.

They stepped from the sidewalk onto the Pier and Parker shaded his eyes to look down towards the restaurant. A radiant smile woke on his face.

"I'm guessing you do," Jane said.

She and Belinda disengaged their arms from his and let him go on ahead. They watched him approach an old woman in her sixties whose own face lit up as he reached her. They embraced.

"I knew it was going to be sad," Jane said.

Belinda nodded. "She's so old and…" She peered more closely. "Oh, my."

"Yes, she's a ghost, too," a voice said from behind them.

The two girls turned to look at the man standing behind them. He was tall and handsome and also dressed in a soldier's uniform, although his was more contemporary than Parker Paul's and his skin was a dark brown where Parker's was pale.

"Do we know you?" Jane asked.

"Only a piece of me," the soldier said.

Belinda looked back down the Pier to where Parker and Angeline walked towards the restaurant at the far end.

"The piece that was Parker Paul?" she asked.

The new soldier nodded.

"You're not a ghost," Jane said.

He nodded again.

"But you're not human either. Who are you?"

"Most recently, I was Tim Sanders," he said. "But I'm Parker Paul, too. I'm Nadiv Levy, Dasya Rao, Akio Yamamoto, Asgrim son of Bodvar, Zerind Nagy, Bobby Whitecloud, Emilio Sanchez, Tai Phan, Jason Smith…"

He changed as he spoke, becoming each man, showing a wide variety of races and uniforms. Occasionally, there wasn't even a uniform. Just a loincloth. Or a vest and leggings made of animal skins.

He let his voice trail off.

"You're all the soldiers Parker thought he was," Belinda said.

"I am."

"But if he's a part of you," Jane said, "how come he's walking down the Pier with his true love? How's that even possible?"

The soldier shrugged. "His duty's long done and love is stronger. So I let him go."

"So he does get a happy, romantic ending," Belinda said.

"He does."

"Except she's old and he's not."

"You don't see her through his eyes."

"But you do."

"Easily."

"Because he's still a part of you," Jane said.

The soldier nodded. "And so long as there are wars, I'll be other soldiers with other names. We fight and die and then we're born to fight again. It's been like this since the first time one tribe of early men fought with another and will go on for as long as men wage war against each other."

"And you're okay with that?"

The soldier gave her a sad smile. "It's not something I would chose. It's just the way of my world."

"So you never get a happy ending," Belinda said.

He shook his head.

"We're more alike than you think," he told them. "We both carry the stories of the world. The difference is, mine are born on the battle-field."

"And now your story's part of ours," Jane said.

"I hope it's not too dreary."

"Well, it's sad," Belinda said, "but that's the thing with stories. You don't get to choose what kind you find."

"And maybe, if they were all happy," Jane said, "a person wouldn't appreciate how good they had it when their story was good."

Belinda sighed. "That's a dumb reason to have a sad story."

"I know. It's just a theory."

"I don't know why there are sad stories," the soldier said, "or why there have to be wars. You'd think that eventually people would realize that we're all the same under our skin. That the enemy that we hurt is no different from our own brother or son."

"You'd think," Jane said.

"But I'm happy to have met you," the soldier told them. "Now I have the cheerful memory of the pair of you to sustain me the next time I'm viewing an enemy through the site of my rifle."

"I suppose," Belinda said, not particularly comforted by the idea.

Except why did he have to go to these wars in the first place? Couldn't he just refuse? And if he did, then who would fight the war? No one. So it seemed very much up to him.

She wondered what the polite way to tell him this was, but before she could say anything more, he faded away with a ghostly "farewell." She looked back down the Pier and saw that Parker and Angeline were gone as well.

"This," she told her companion, "has been a particularly weird day."

"It has," Jane agreed. "And we never did get to meet Angeline."

Belinda nodded. "But I suppose that doesn't matter, because at least Parker did."

Jane smiled. "He did, didn't he?"

"I liked him," Belinda said with a touch of wistfulness in her voice.

"What wasn't to like?"

"Well, he was dead, for one thing."

"That wasn't his fault."

"And he already had a true love."

"Maybe you'll find one, too."

Belinda's features brightened. "That's true. I should go look for one right now."

Jane took her hand.

"I'll help you," she said.

Hand in hand, they turned their backs on the Pier and the lake and walked back into the city, where the thousands and thousands of stories they hadn't met awaited them.

And maybe a true love, too.

Percé Rock, Photo by Jack Chiang, Summer 2002

The Lady of Land's End

by
Genevieve Kierans

Gaspé: easternmost peninsula in Quebec, Canada, where the Appalachian mountain chain ends precipitously in ocean. Best known for the unusual pierced rock formation that lies just off the coast. From the Mi'mag word Kespeq, *meaning "land's end."*

Maggie watched in fascinated horror as *La Dame en Blanc*—the Lady in White—floated across the scrubby summit of the giant rock that lay just off the sheer cliffs of the fishing village of Percé, Quebec. The rock emerged from the northern Atlantic like the petrified prow of a giant ship, a ruddy limestone monolith capped with a thin thatch of sea grasses, its seaward end drilled into a yawning archway by millennia of waves pounding against its mighty base.

The Lady trailed a veil of fine mist that spilled over the thin grass, spreading, thickening, and finally congealing into a cold fog that ate away the view. First the ocean...then the rock...then the town... The fitful flash of the lighthouse beacon splashed across its back as it rolled languorously up the beach towards her, dissolving the world as it came.

"There will be a wreck tonight, Marguerite," said Grandpère, making her jump. He joined her on the veranda. "The Lady in White walks the rock."

The wind, which had been quite brisk earlier that day, was dying, but Maggie shivered anyhow. The distant clatter-squawk of gannets and the rhythmic sh-shushing of the waves breaking on the beach below sounded eerie and incongruous in the invisible world

She clutched at the railing and grasped for normalcy. " It's Mar-ga-ret," she said, for about the thousandth time. "Not Marguerite. And that's no ghost, it's just a trick of the light." She almost believed herself. The flare from the lighthouse whipped white, then red, light through the fog, briefly casting the rock in crimson gauze.

"You see?" There was no one on the rock.

Are you sure about that you saw something.

"Margaret," said Grandpère, using the English pronunciation. "Right. I forgot."

The moisture had begun to condense on the ugly, black-rimmed glasses that made him look like one of those crazy seabirds that populated the craggy coastline. He took them off to wipe them on his heavy flannel shirt. Below the cedar railings, beaten by the weather to a textured grey, the fog continued to advance, swallowing the terrain in its path. The revolving lighthouse beacon sliced across the landscape, first white, bathing the fog in silver, then red, staining it with blood.

It's just a reflection of the goddamned light isn't it?

How many people had died on that rock?

My father Daddy no I can't think of that!

"It is said that when the Lady in White walks the rock, a soul is forfeit," said Grandpère, taking out his pipe.

The gannets chattered from the fog.

"Some even say that the seabirds are really the restless spirits of all who have met an untimely end."

As though agreeing, a disembodied foghorn began a melancholy warning.

Maggie shivered again, not entirely because of the cold.

What a crock now the bloody stupid old man's gonna tell me one of his stupid old legends goddamn mum for dumping me here all month while she's off having a good time with that guy I'm nearly sixteen old enough to be on my own.

But Grandpère did not pursue the story. Silence and tobacco smoke hung in the still air between them. Finally, he tapped out the bowl, pocketed the pipe, and turned back to the house. "Put on a jacket if you're going to stay outside. The fog can be chilly."

Well—duh—do I look *stupid or something?*

"I'm not cold."

Maggie clamped her teeth down hard to keep from shivering until the screen door banged shut.

—•—

The minute she woke up on the morning of her sixteenth birthday, Blanche de Beaumont knew that something wonderful was going to happen. Maryse had already drawn back the bed curtains, and the sunshine spilled across the polished floorboards and splashed across the embroidered *fleur-de-lys* on her silken covers.

Blanche bounded out of bed and danced over to the tall window. The spring air, as she threw open the doors and stepped onto the small balcony, was soft and warm.

"Mam'selle," protested her maidservant, entering with the *petit-déjeuner.* The rich aroma of that new delicacy, *chocolat,* imported from the Spanish colonies, mingled with the buttery scent of steaming croissants and made Blanche's stomach rumble. "You cannot go out on the balcony undressed—*en déshabille.* It is most improper. At least wear a wrap!"

Blanche laughed, and leaned further over the balcony railings. There was an unusual amount of activity in the courtyard. A rider wearing the household colours had just arrived.

"Maryse," she exclaimed in delight as she recognized her brother. "It's Richard! His ship must have come in early."

It had been almost a year since her brother had undertaken the perilous crossing to New France, lured, as were so many young adventurers, by the promise of the fur trade. Richard appeared to have brought home a companion, whose insignia she did not recognize. But he cut a most dashing figure as he swung down from his horse.

"The Chevalier Raymond de Nérac," said Maryse, who knew all the gossip. "They say he has a brilliant future."

Blanche's face was thoughtful as she allowed Maryse to lead her back inside.

—•—

During the night a small tourist craft had run onto the rocks off nearby Bonaventure Island, and its sole occupant, a holiday-er from East Lansing, Michigan, USA, had drowned in the frigid water.

The local old men, faces etched from decades of exposure to salty winds, congregated on the porch of the local *dépanneur*—convenience store *cum* gas station *cum* post-office. Above them gannets the size of small geese swarmed, swooped, and dove: screeching, crying, clattering. Always in motion. Never silent.

"*Eh, bien*," said *le père* Jean-Baptiste, whittling a piece of driftwood. Now he was too old to fish he carved figurines for the tourists. This one looked like a whale. "*Qu'est-ce-que tu veux?* What do you want? *Les touristes*."

"Always happens," commented another. "When you see *La Dame en Blanc*... it's curtains, for sure." He drew his hand across his neck in a slicing motion.

The others nodded sagely and puffed on their pipes or cigarettes.

Maggie paused a moment on the steps, loading the milk, bread, and mail into her knapsack. "Do you mean," she asked, "that every single time you think you see the Lady in White, there's a shipwreck?"

The most garrulous of the geezers took his pipe out of his mouth and jabbed the stem towards her.

"*La p'tite* Marguerite," he explained to his cronies. "Young Marguerite, Jean's grand-daughter from Toronto."

"Ah, *oui*. I remember. The daughter of Marie, is she? Or Bernard?"

"No, Bernard had no kids."

"I heard he went off West somewhere, and married a foreigner."

"I never heard that. I think you're loosin' it, *mon vieux*. Gettin' old."

"No, I am certain. I had this from my Nicole who heard it from a friend of hers over Bridgeville-way."

Le père Jean-Baptiste dismissed this. "I wouldn't put money on anything someone from Bridgeville says. Marguerite is Marie's child."

"Didn't she marry an *anglais*? English fellow?"

"*Oui*. It was *un scandale*. Ran off when she was sixteen."

"Ah."

"And Marguerite was the child."

"Didn't she just remarry?"

"Who? Marguerite?"

Exasperated, Maggie shouldered her pack and thumped down the wooden steps, startling a bird that had just settled there.

Old farts never answer questions goddamned hick town dumb ghost stories only two more weeks.

But curiosity nibbled at her imagination, and she wished her grandfather had told her more.

Grandpère was out when she arrived back at the house, and she poured herself a pop as she went through the mail. Most of it was for her grandfather, academic journals and the like, but there were several postcards from her mother, all postmarked the same day as though she had suddenly remembered to send them, and all full of what a wonderful honeymoon she was having on her cruise.

Like I give a shit what she does with that guy.

Maggie pushed them aside, and went in search of something to read.

When she had been little, and had visited Grandpère with her parents, she had loved the old shingled homestead perched against a wall of conifers high above the ocean. It was a house of wonder and endless diversion. From floor to ceiling, every single wall, even in the bathroom, was covered with books. And every bookshelf was covered with some artifact: African masks, Indonesian spears, European engravings. Even framed jewellery. One particular trinket stood out: an ancient-looking golden locket on faded white velvet backing...

Old fishing nets, colourful glass floats, lobster traps, and mobiles made out of shells dangled from the exposed pine beams. The old maple floorboards, twisted here and there by damp and age, were littered with statuary, drums, elaborately carved chests, and mismatched furniture. But most of all, she had loved the smell: a musty, mysterious blend of tobacco, dust, pine resin, ancient books, and old wood that whispered of love, and safety, and family.

But that had been when she was little. She hadn't come since her dad had died. Now she was too old to play hide-and-seek in the cluttered rooms, or dress-up with the exotic masks. And she was sure she was allergic to the smell, because she was hadn't stopped sneezing since she got there. The house was creepy and boring. No computer. No Internet. No TV. And the only radio station that came in seemed to only carry French-Canadian fiddle music.

She padded down a hallway made even narrower by bookshelves, and entered her grandfather's study, which had the most books and the best light for browsing. A near life-sized, vaguely humanoid statue of some dark wood stood sentinel at the door. She circumvented it distastefully, and tripped over a long tree trunk that had been left on the floor.

Bloody junk everywhere could have broken my ankle.

"It's a didgeridoo," said Grandpère from behind her, making her jump. He must've been in the house the whole time, because she hadn't heard the screen door slam. "It's made by termites."

"Ugh!"

Creep me out!

"Ghost stories are over there."

"Ghost stories are for little kids."

"Why don't you go out to the rock? Get some fresh air. It's a calm day."

"Been there. Done that."

Never going back there not without dad I don't want to think about this.

"Don't you just have, like, a decent book? A mystery?"

"A mystery, then," said Grandpère. He reached behind a vaguely Mexican-looking mask of someone with corn on his head, and pulled out a slender hardcover.

"Voilà! Un mystère."

"I wish you'd stop talking French all the time."

"You used to know it, once."

"I'll be outside. 'Kay?"

—•—

When Blanche laid eyes upon the handsome Chevalier de Nérac, destiny spoke. She knew in the deepest recesses of her heart that they were meant to be joined in love. The young couple spent many a happy day in each other's company, strolling through the *château's* stately gardens, hunting the forest deer, or dancing at the many *soirées* and *divertissements* held in their honor. At summer's end they were betrothed, with the wedding planned a year hence, on her seventeenth birthday.

Summer gave way to fall, and fall to winter. Then one day, as frost gilt the gracious lawns and neatly clipped topiaries, a rider galloped down the broad avenue to the *château*, bearing dispatches from the King.

Blanche watched his arrival from her balcony, and it seemed as though clouds had rolled across the sun and a pall fallen across her spirit. She knew, even before Raymond came to her, that they would be parted.

"The King has ordered me back to New France," said her Chevalier. "The Iroquois Indians are harrying the *habitants,* and I am commanded to the Fort at Québec to restore order."

Blanche tried hard not to let the tears that were drowning her soul reach her eyes. There was no question that Raymond must obey the King. But New France was so far away, and the trip so perilous, especially so late in the season.

"I will be back in spring," promised the Chevalier. "Before your birthday. And we shall be joined in wedlock. And never separated again. Be brave until then."

Blanche lifted her chin bravely and smiled. "This will keep you safe, my love. May it be a symbol of my own heart, which is forever in your keeping."

And she gave him the gold locket she always wore around her neck.

—•—

The deck chair outside was covered with guano.
Gross me out bird shit everywhere.

Maggie grabbed a nearby gardening tool and chipped the crusty white droppings off the chair. The autumn sun and the exertion made her warm, and she took off her windbreaker before curling up with her book: *The Legend of Percé Rock*.

Bloody old man gave me a ghost story after all.

She almost got up to return it when she caught sight of the byline. *By Jean Raymond.* She knew her grandfather was a published scholar. She hadn't known he wrote fiction. She decided to give it a go, after all.

—•—

All through the cold winter months, Blanche prepared her trousseau. Her father had ordered the sheerest Indian silk, the most intricate Breton lace, and yards of tiny seed pearls for her wedding gown. She and Maryse stitched and sewed and embroidered until their fingers were raw. And if Maryse noticed her mistress' waist thickening, she said nothing. Somehow, the next morning, the gown had been let out.

Come spring, Blanche had a wedding dress fit for a princess, and only her faithful Maryse knew her most deeply guarded secret.

But there came no word from her betrothed, no sign of him, and when her seventeenth birthday came and went, Blanche knew she could wait demurely at home no longer. When her brother next set sail for New France, she stood at his side, resolved to seek out her one true love. And father of her child-to-be.

—•—

With the gentler seas of early summer, the ship not only survived the crossing but made the voyage in record time. Beneath the voluminous folds of a thick woolen cloak, Blanche patted her swelling belly and whispered a prayer of thanks to Mary, the Mother of Perpetual Help, as the ship finally pulled into the wide Gulf of the St. Lawrence. The end of her journey was only days away and she had great hopes of finding Raymond.

—•—

No one saw the pirate vessel until they were almost upon it, and then it was too late.

After a brief exchange of fire, the slower, heavier merchant ship was boarded. Everyone on board, except for Blanche, her maidservant, and Father Jean, a Jesuit missionary (it being bad luck to kill a priest) was slain, thrown overboard into the icy black waters to die of exposure before the dawn of another day.

At first, sparing Blanche's life was an economic decision. She was clearly a valuable hostage who might be ransomed.

But it was not long before the pirate captain fell under the spell of her beauty. So enamoured was he that he decided he must keep her for himself. She was completely in his power, and he could easily have had his way with her, but he wanted her forever. He would have the priest marry them. So joined by God, they could never be parted by man. Whatever her feelings, a wife was bound to obey her husband. Divorce was unheard of in Catholic France, and considered a grave sin. She would be his for as long as they lived.

"I will marry no one but the Chevalier Raymond de Nérac," said Blanche proudly. This infuriated the pirate.

"And where is this paragon, this Chevalier."

"New France," said Blanche. "Obeying his King. But such as you wouldn't know about things as duty, or loyalty, or love."

The pirate captain was incensed at her words. "You will marry me," he told her. "But first I will show you New France. If you see your Chevalier, I will even let you go to him. But I do not think you will find your Chevalier so easily."

He ordered his crew to bring the boat about, closer to land. Blanche saw ochre-coloured cliffs, topped by thick forests of pine trees as far as the eye could see. The sky was filled with huge seabirds, swooping and chattering as they fished. The pirate captain seized her roughly by the arm.

"There is your New France! Do you see your Chevalier? Of course not. Foolish girl, this land is greater than all of Europe. You will never find him in it. And so you must marry me."

Blanche stared at the vast wilderness in dismay. The gannets called and plummeted like mad things from dizzying heights into the waves below.

"I will marry you," she said at last. "Tonight."

"I am glad you have come to your senses," said the pirate captain.

—•—

The sound of something heavy falling to the porch beside her startled Maggie out of the story. A large gannet had landed on the veranda, and now perched on the railing, a scant foot away, staring at her. It was much, much larger up close than she had imagined, and its beak looked very sharp. *Some even say that the seabirds are really the restless spirits of all who have met an untimely end.*

"Shoo!" she said.

The bird opened its beak, almost grinning, and hopped from one foot to the other. One leg seemed to be injured.

"Go away!"

The gannet bobbed its head.

"Ugh! Get lost! Horrible bird!"

Maggie flung the only weapon she had handy, her grandfather's book, and the bird launched itself into the air with a cry. She followed it with her eyes. It headed out towards the rock, and became lost in the drift of birds that congregated there.

"That's not a very nice way to treat my book," said Grandpère, behind her. She hadn't heard him come out.

"I'm sorry. I was scared." She peered over the railings. The book had fallen some distance, and had lodged on a rocky outcrop. "I'll get it."

"How long you been afraid of birds?"

"I'm not afraid of the goddamned bird. It just startled me."

"I see."

—•—

That night the ship drew near Percé Rock. At that time, it had two holes, and at high tide a ship could sail right through them. The night was still, but a fog was rising. The captain waited on the deck for his bride, and at the appointed hour, she was brought to him. She had dressed herself in the sumptuous white gown she had worked on so hard all winter, and strands of pearls were twined in her hair. Even the rough-and-ready crew of the ship exclaimed at her loveliness.

She smiled, and held out her hand to the captain. And he signalled her guard to remove her bonds and step away. But the instant she was free, before anyone could stop her, she dashed to the side of the boat, and threw herself into the welcoming waves.

The water was calm, but the fog was already curling around the hull. The crew lowered boats, and tried in vain to find her, but to no avail.

Then the lookout cried out in fear from the crow's nest. Out of the swirling mists they could just make out the vast fortress of the rock. On its summit stood a figure in white. It was Blanche's spirit. She raised her arms, as though muttering a malediction, and a terrible grinding began to convulse the pirate ship. It began to shudder, then shake, then groan, at length transforming from a ship of wood, to a vessel of stone.

And thus was Blanche avenged.

And to this day, the stone pirate ship is visible off the Cap des Rosiers, within view of Percé Rock.

And it is said that whenever the fog gathers around the rock, the Lady in White appears, making sure that the pirates have not escaped their dreadful fate.

—•—

The sound of the foghorn woke Maggie in the middle of the night. She had been dreaming she was being chased by a giant bird. The flare from the lighthouse bathed her room in light, sending white-red shadows cavorting across the bookshelves. She could see the rock clearly from her bedroom window. If she got up.

She lay there a few minutes, counting the blasts from the horn. It sounded every fifteen seconds. A thick fog, then.

Should she look? If the fog was so thick, she might not be able to see the rock at all. There was no point.

But her feet seemed to have other ideas. They had carried her across the room to the window before she knew it.

The Lady in White floated across the rock, trailing her veil of mist. When she reached the highest point, she raised her ghostly arms towards the sky.

Maggie stood and watched until the fog had enveloped the rock.

—•—

"Weather comin' in," said *le père* Jean-Baptiste. He was carving what looked like a gannet. "Wind veerin' to north."

"Looks to be a bad 'un."

"Bad as October '98?"

"The storm of '99 was worse."

"Ah, but that was in December."

"It will be bad enough," said Jean-Baptiste. He whittled in silence for a bit. "The Lady was out last night."

"When you see *La Dame en Blanc*…" affirmed *le père* Jean-Luc. "It's curtains, for sure." He drew his hand across his neck in a slicing motion. The others puffed and nodded in agreement.

Maggie stared in dismay at the telegram in her hand: coming home early.

How the hell do you come home early from a goddammed cruise?

Her mum missed her, it said. They had disembarked in St. John's and rented a cabin cruiser. They would be in Percé by tomorrow.

No there's still one more week I'm not ready for a new father.

"Eh! Marguerite! I hear your *maman* and new *papa* are coming tomorrow?" said Jean-Baptiste.

I don't want to talk about it mind your own effing business don't want to talk.

Maggie swallowed the lump in her throat, and it sat like lead in her belly. She managed a curt nod and escaped down the road to the path along the ridge.

The long grass had been well trampled into a sandy, red footpath that snaked its way along the cliff-edge. Here and there, the soil was scraped clear, revealing red-speckled slabs of smooth slate. On one side of the path, taller grasses, dotted with prickle bushes, bunches of purple daisy-like flowers, and tall feathery goldenrod stretched a short distance before becoming absorbed into fenced pastures or private yards. To the other side, the cliff fell away steeply, plummeting to a narrow rocky strip of beach which would be buried come high tide. Now it swept out in a narrow rocky causeway to the monolith that gave the town its name.

Maggie hadn't consciously planned on going down to the rock. But distracted by emotions, her feet found their own way to the steep path down the slope. There used to be a small cleft inside the archway, a small niche above the tide line where she had hidden as a child.

Need privacy no nosy old men need to cry.

She sprinted across the exposed ocean floor and inched around the leeward side of the rock, hugging the limestone walls for support. Crustaceans scattered away from her groping hands, scuttling over the petrified bodies of their distant ancestors preserved forever in the sedimentary stone. At length she reached the giant archway, and she clambered over its ragged lip into its shelter. There. Just as she remembered. The niche was easier to reach now she was bigger, and she pulled herself up easily, tucked her feet under her. And finally, she released the lump in her throat. And sobbed out the pain that had been so long churning in her heart.

—•—

It is said that the Chevalier de Nérac had nearly frozen during the bitter Québec winter, and then had been held prisoner by the Iroquois for many months. And when he finally escaped, and had learned the sad fate of his beloved Blanche, he had settled in the Gaspé, where, on foggy nights, he could sometimes spy the Lady in her beautiful white wedding gown keeping vigil on the rock.

—•—

It was much darker when Maggie awoke, and for a moment, she wondered if it was night already. The sky outside the archway was dark, purple clouds piling on top of the swelling ocean. A cold wind lashed the rock.

A storm.

You stupid imbecile falling asleep like a goddammed stupid tourist on the rock.

Angry water swirled beneath her, ankle-deep already. Shit. Shit! SHIT!

You can get your feet wet and make it back or stay here and till the tide goes back.

She shivered. She didn't relish the notion of clinging to the rock all night. Her grandfather would be worried. She lowered herself from the ledge carefully, cringing when she reached the cold waves.

Cold cold ignore it big stupid baby just water not deep.

She picked her way carefully over the loose stones. The waves tugged at her shins.

Hurry careful cold don't rush stupid stupid stupid.

She could no longer feel her feet.

Careful careful you'll get frostbite easy slow down you're doing ok it'll be ok.

The rain came just as she reached the mouth of the arch. All at once, with no prelude. It hit her like a waterfall, driving her back into the scant shelter of the archway. Her soaking jeans dragged at her legs.

You can't stay here tide coming go back go back go back.

A large swell rushed through the hole, slapping her thighs. She clutched the rock for support. From somewhere in the gloom, the foghorn blasted. Far away, a distant horn answered. A new fear seized her.

Oh no Mum mum's on boat there will be a wreck no oh no lady in white.

The flare from the lighthouse flashed across the water, scattering light across the wall of rain. Something shimmered between the raindrops.

What's that? Nothing go back.

Something glittered between the raindrops.

Another gust of wind. Another wave. Maggie's hands were numb. A loose stone rolled beneath her foot, throwing her off balance. She scrabbled at the wall of stone, but her frozen fingers slid off the wet rock. Her ankle snapped beneath her and she plunged headlong into the roiling water.

HURTS Oh hurts leg hurts hurts just like dad don't want to die oh no just like dad leg hurts.

Her other leg found some purchase and she tried to stand, but another swell seized her and pushed her clear of the rock and safety. She went under.

"Marguerite!"

Hurts hurts so cold I'm gonna die.

"Marguerite!" A ghostly voice rippled in her mind. "Marguerite. *Vite.* Quickly. Give me your hand."

Lady in white soul forfeit take me not mum not mum so cold.

Through the murky water, Maggie could just discern a female figure, no taller than herself. It hung suspended, unaffected by the storm that tossed the waters.

I'm dead seeing things this is the end mum I'm sorry for being a bitch.

But her hand reached out and clasped the ghost's, and it was real. As solid as her own.

With dizzying speed the spectre pulled her upwards and out of the water, up through the driving rain, past the rock to the shore, up the cliff well past the tideline, depositing her finally beneath a shallow ledge. Maggie winced as she jarred her broken foot.

"Th-thank you." said Maggie through chattering teeth.

"Drowning—*ce n'est pas agréable*—is not so… pleasant," said the ghost with a smile. She removed her cloak, and draped it over her. It may have looked ethereal, but it was warm.

Warm oh so warm doesn't hurt no more what do you say to a ghost?

"Did you really drown yourself on purpose?"

Warm so warm.

"I came to Nouvelle France to marry *mon* Chevalier. Certainly, no filthy, stinking pirate!"

She spat emphatically, a very strange gesture for a ghost.

"But look, I will show you a thing." She raised her arms, and out of the storm flew an enormous gannet, the largest Maggie had ever seen. It hovered above her for a moment, and then its shape shifted like the mists which so often wreathed the rock.

"You see?" said the Lady in White. "I am reunited with my Chevalier, after all."

It was a bird. And yet it wasn't. Maggie rubbed her eyes, but the double image remained. An enormous, human-sized sea bird… and a handsome young man in period dress.

The ghost and he gazed at each other rapturously.

"So it is true that the seabirds are spirits?" A delicious drowsiness was creeping up her limbs. Anything now seemed plausible. Even possible.

"Do you know about these birds, Marguerite? They often mate for life. Together, they choose their nesting site, build the nest, and nurture the nestling. But they are remarkably long-lived. If a bird's mate dies when they are both young, should it just continue, for the rest of its life, alone? Is it not better to love again, if it comes, than to forever mourn? And so, sometimes, they choose another mate."

"I suppose." She really was very tired.

"I must leave," said Blanche de Beaumont. She began to fade. "Those who care for you are coming."

Another bird flopped down on the ledge. Even by gannet standards it was awkward and ungainly on land. One leg seemed injured. It lurched towards her and cocked its pale blue eye.

"Oh. It's hurt its leg too," said Maggie.

Just like bird on balcony broke leg like me like Daddy.

"That's how my Dad dies. From a goddamned broken leg."

Goddamned blood clot never said goodbye.

"Adieu, little Marguerite," said the ghost of Blanche. She didn't so much fade as dissolve into the rain.

Maggie didn't feel cold any more. Just tired. Her eyes closed despite herself.

The gannet spread its wings, almost two metres across, and flapped them.

"Goodbye," she said sleepily, sinking into a delicious lethargy.

Then, at the edge of consciousness, a man's voice. Beloved. Familiar. Sorely missed.

"Sleep, little Maggie. Let go, it will be ok."

It is also said, though not by as many people, that the Chevalier befriended a poor young woman named Maryse, who had survived a shipwreck. Or pirates. No one was certain. What was certain was that Maryse brought with her a premature baby, which, but for the grace of God, would surely have died. And the Chevalier took it as his own.

"I have a present for you," said Grandpère. He had carried her outside for a late autumn BBQ. Her mum was buttering the hotdog buns while her new father tinkered with the coals. It had been he who had found her, and carried her back to her grandfather's home. He really wasn't too bad—even knew how to program Java. And there was no denying her mother's joy, manifest every time she met his eyes.

Is it not better to love again, than to forever mourn?

"Just between you and me," said Grandpère.

It will be ok ok OK.

Grandpère handed her a little picture frame which she recalled seeing in his study.

"It's been in the family for many years, Margaret. I thought that now you should have it. It will keep you safe."

Maggie looked at it. Resting against a velvet background gleamed a tiny, golden locket. She looked knowingly at her grandfather. She knew, now.

"Marguerite," she said. "It's Marguerite."

And above her a crook-legged gannet cawed agreement.

About the Contributors

DANIEL ARCHAMBAULT lives in Vancouver, but grew up just outside Manotick, Ontario, the town in which his story was set and where Watson's Mill actually exists. Dan hasn't seen the mill ghost, but he hopes he will one day. On the other hand, he has skated many times on the Rideau Canal, the longest skating rink the world, including many training sessions when he was a competitive speedskater from 1987-97. When he is not writing or reading weird stories or watching friends skate in the Olympics, he is pursuing a Ph.D. in Computer Science at the University of British Columbia. As a writer and reader of fiction, he has had the opportunity to chair Green College's Read/Write café, and has recently become a member of the West End Writers' Club, whose members he thanks for their insightful comments. "The Ghost of Watson's Mill Is Online" is Dan's second fiction sale.

ALISON BAIRD was born in Montreal, Quebec, and spent her early years in the neighbouring town of Pointe Claire. As a child she read everything she could get her hands on, including fiction and non-fiction, but enjoyed tales of magic and wonder most of all. Alison developed a passion for fairy tales, folk tales, and mythologies from all over the world, as well as more modern tales of the fantastic: her favourite childhood authors included Lewis Carroll, E. Nesbit, Kenneth Grahame, J.M. Barrie, Madeleine L'Engle, C.S. Lewis, and J.R.R. Tolkien. She noticed, however, that there seemed to be very few stories of this type set in her own country, and the idea of creating magical tales with Canadian settings soon occurred to her, later emerging as a theme in many of her own writings. After publishing some of her poems at the age of 12, Alison decided to pursue a career as a writer, and is today the author of some ten novels as well as numerous works of short fiction. Her books—most of which fall in the fantasy genre—include *The Dragon's Egg* (a Silver Birch Award regional winner), *White as the Waves* (a Violet Downey Book Award finalist), *The Hidden World* and its prequel *The Wolves of Woden*, the three Willowmere Chronicles, and the adult fantasy trilogy, The Dragon Throne. She now makes her home in Oakville, Ontario.

JULIE E. CZERNEDA has been a finalist for both the John W. Campbell (Best New Writer) and Philip K. Dick Awards, twice on the preliminary ballot for a Nebula, and has won three English language Prix Aurora Awards (Canada's Hugo), one for her standalone novel *In the Company of Others*, one for her short story, "Left Foot on a Blind Man," published in *Silicon Dreams*, edited by Martin H. Greenberg and Larry Segriff, DAW Books, and most recently, for editing *Space Inc.*, DAW Books.

A former biologist, in 1985 Julie became a full-time non-fiction author and editor, contributing to textbooks used in schools across North America. In 1997, she happily switched to fiction, since then publishing ten SF novels with DAW, several translated into Russian. Her latest is her Species Imperative trilogy, *Survival, Migration, & Regeneration.* Julie has five more novels under contract with DAW, including her first full-length fantasy, *Turn of Light.*

As editor, Julie's *Space Inc.* explored daily life off this planet and, with Dr. Isaac Szpindel, she co-edited the alternate science history anthology *ReVisions*, both from DAW. Currently, she is working with co-editor Jana Paniccia on *Under Cover of Darkness,* a look at covert societies and *Misspelled,* a look at magic gone awry. Julie also edits the original Y/A SF anthology series based on science curriculum topics, *Tales from the Wonder Zone*, winner of the 2002 Special Award for Science & Technology Education from the Golden Duck Committee, as well as the *Realms of Wonder* YA fantasy anthology series linked to language arts. She is a SF Consultant to *Science News for Kids* for *Science News* and a sought-after speaker, conducting presentations on science fiction, science, and writing in both Canada and the US. The future? Suffice to say, Julie is having too much fun to stop any time soon.

CHARLES DE LINT is a full-time writer and musician who presently makes his home in Ottawa, Canada, with his wife MaryAnn Harris, an artist and musician. Internationally renowned, his most recent novels are *Spirits in the Wires* and *The Blue Girl*. Other recent publications include the collections *Waifs & Strays*, *Tapping the Dream Tree*, and *The Hour Before Dawn*, and *A Circle of Cats*, a picture book illustrated by Charles Vess.

JAMES ALAN GARDNER lives in Kitchener, Ontario, with his wife, Linda Carson, and two rabbits who hate each other. He has published nine science fiction books, the most recent of which is *Gravity Wells* from Harper-Collins Eos. Gardner has won the Prix Aurora Award twice, and has been a finalist for both the Hugo and Nebula Awards. In his spare time, he practises and teaches kung fu.

ROBEN GOODFELLOW was born and raised in Orillia, Ontario, then moved to Toronto upon high school graduation to a) find a job and b) explore a city she'd fallen in love with during weekend raids as a teenager. It was here, while relaxing in a common room of the university that she first heard the ghost story expanded on here.

Her working life has had its low points (telephone sales of frozen meat being the worst); its high points (working for Penguin Books); some powerful moments (as a wedding officiant); and some bizarre moments (being hired away from a barista position to a highly successful turn as a foreign trade consultant). She has hitchhiked across the country, and has enjoyed several awards for community service and one for writing. Her previous writing credits include theatrical reviews, customized wedding ceremonies, and an advice column. She lives in Toronto's lower east side with her husband Ross (on whom the mannerisms and humour of her 'Reznikoff' are based), their cat, and an extensive hat collection.

TANYA HUFF lives and writes in rural Ontario with her partner Fiona Patton, six and a half cats, and an unintentional chihuahua. Her twenty-first book, *Smoke and Mirrors*, came out in hardcover from DAW Books Inc, July 2005. Her next book and the last in the series, *Smoke and Ashes*, will be out in hardcover in spring/summer of 2006. When she isn't writing, she gardens and complains about the weather.

LORNE KATES is currently earning his Bachelor of Applied Technology degree in Software Development from Seneca College in Toronto, Canada. Since this is Lorne's first story in print, you can't just plug his name into a search engine and learn all about him, so he's written this bio. He advises that if you are ever waiting for him at Point B, look for him to arrive from the direction of Point Q... because that's the way you have to go to get to anywhere worth arriving at. He'd also like to thank everyone on the Urban Explorer's Resource forum for their invaluable insight.

GENEVIEVE KIERANS is a scholarship graduate of Queen's University with a major in English Literature and Drama. Genevieve also studied advertising copy writing and magazine journalism, and is conversant in both French and Spanish. She is a past board member of the Toronto Drama Bench and Toronto Theatre Alliance, has served two terms on the Board of Women in Film and Television-Toronto, and is the former Chair of its Policy and Publications Committee. Following a time as a professional actor, she became a published journalist, then publicist for 18 years. With her own company, Genevieve's clients included the Hospital for Sick Children's first ever telethon, TV series such as *FX: The Series, Road to Avonlea*, and *Kids in the Hall*. All along, she has been a writer. Her story "Mirror, Mirror" took first place in the Science Fiction Writers of the Earth contest, making her the first Canadian to win this award. Her story "Lady of Land's End" took second prize the preceding year. She is currently at work on a fantasy novel. Genevieve suffers from ALS (Lou Gehrig's Disease). Although this has made it increasingly difficult for her to produce her work—she typed "Mirror, Mirror" with one finger—it has in no way dimmed her creativity and drive.

MARK LADOUCEUR has been writing since he was young, thanks to encouragement from his parents. His career aspirations have included firefighter, race car driver, starship captain, member of the fellowship, and Jedi knight. As a substitute he enjoys writing about worlds of his own making and seeing what kind of trouble he can get his characters into. When not writing,

Mark enjoys reading whatever he can, whenever he can. He finds it nice to say that his daydreaming in class has actually paid off now. Mark lives with his wife (a kick-butt copy editor) and adorable daughter (not that he's biased). This bio would be longer, but "Windigo" is Mark's first published story.

CLAUDE LALUMIÈRE lives and writes in Montreal, where he was born. Until 1998, he owned and managed Nebula, the genre bookshop he'd founded in 1989. Since then, he's published hundreds of reviews and essays in newspapers, magazines, websites, and critical reference books. As editor, he's assembled six anthologies, including two volumes of all-new Canadian speculative fiction: *Island Dreams: Montreal Writers of the Fantastic* and *Open Space: New Canadian Fantastic Fiction.* His own fiction has been appearing since 2002 in Canada, the USA, and the UK, most notably in *Tesseracts 9,* an anthology of Canadian speculative fiction edited by Nalo Hopkinson and Geoff Ryman; *On Spec,* Canada's leading SF journal; *Interzone,* the UK's top SF magazine; and *The Book of More Flesh,* an anthology of zombie fiction that features one of his most popular stories, "The Ethical Treatment of Meat." Claude's stories are often inspired by music. "This Is the Ice Age" finds its roots in the Martha and the Muffins' album of the same name. The title of his first published story, "Bestial Acts," comes from the lyrics to the Kurt Weill/Bertolt Brecht song "What Keeps Mankind Alive?" In 2006, he is teaching a workshop for the Québec Writers Federation, "Science Fiction, Fantasy, and Horror: Writing and Selling Short Stories."

KARIN LOWACHEE was born in Guyana, South America but grew up in Ontario. Her first novel *Warchild* won the 2001 Warner Aspect First Novel Contest, published in 2002, and was a finalist for the Philip K. Dick Award. Her second novel, *Burndive,* was published in 2003 and debuted at #7 on the Locus Bestseller List. It was also chosen as one of the best books for young adults by the American Library Association in 2004. Karin was twice nominated for the John W. Campbell Award for Best New Writer. Her third book, *Cagebird,* was released in April 2005. Her short story "The Forgotton Ones" appeared in the anthology *So Long Been Dreaming: Postcolonial Science Fiction & Fantasy* and was a finalist for the Prix Aurora Award Best Short-Form Work in English. Her stories so far explore the effects of war and trauma on young people.

DERRYL MURPHY'S first short story collection, *Wasps at the Speed of Sound,* was published to critical acclaim in 2005. He has had stories published in a variety of books and magazines, and is currently Art Director for *On Spec* magazine. "Over the Darkened Landscape" is intended to be the first in a series of stories involving the two main characters. His own dog refuses to talk to him, but that doesn't rule out the dog making sarcastic asides under its breath.

FIONA PATTON was born in Calgary, Alberta, and now lives on eighty acres of rural scrubland with her partner Tanya Huff, six cats of various sizes and eccentric personalities, and one tiny chihuahua that thinks he's a fierce farm dog. She has four heroic fantasy novels published by DAW Books, *The Stone Prince*, *The Painter Knight*, *The Granite Shield*, and *The Golden Sword*, as well as approximately two dozen short stories. Her most recent book *The Silver Lake,* also from DAW, was published in November, 2005.

KARINA SUMNER-SMITH has lived in southern Ontario for most of her life—including many summers spent just outside of Kincardine. A short fiction author and novelist-in-the-making, Karina has had her work published in anthologies *Summoned to Destiny* and *Children of Magic*, as well as in magazines including *Strange Horizons, Lady Churchill's Rosebud Wristlet*, and *Flytrap*. After getting the most generalized degree she could possibly find—an Arts degree in Humanities—Karina entered the dreaded world of the Day Job, and now balances the need for financial income with her writing and other creative pursuits including blogging, crochet, and a new side business in jewellery design.

LYNDA WILLIAMS' first novel, *Throne Price*, co-authored with Alison Sinclair, was released by Edge Science Fiction and Fantasy in 2003, and made the short list for the Benjamin Franklin Award for best popular fiction of the year from an independent press. *The Courtesan Prince*, set in the same fictional universe, came out in 2005. Lynda also serves as chair of a small university press and produces an online journal, "Reflections on Water." She works as Project Leader for the Centre for Teaching and Learning at the University of Northern British Columbia, in Prince George B.C.

Credits and Acknowledgements

The publisher wishes to thank the following sources for excerpts, illustrations, lyrics, and other materials used in this book. Care has been taken to determine and locate ownership of copyright material. We will gladly receive information enabling us to rectify any errors or omissions in these credits.

EDITORS' NOTE: You will notice variations in the spellings of certain words in this book, notably Windigo/Wendigo and others. We have elected to use the spelling presented by each author, as these words reflect regional differences.

In Order of Occurrence:

Mirror, Mirror by Genevieve Kierans
"Lies" (1981) by Stan Rogers, *Northwest Passage*, Copyright ©
1981 by Stan Rogers, Fogarty's Cove Music. (SOCAN)

Windigo by Mark Ladouceur
Windigo: An Anthology of Fact and Fantastic Fiction (1982) edited
by John Robert Colombo, Copyright © 1982 by John Robert
Columbo, Western Producer Prairie Books, Saskatoon.

All the Cool Monsters at Once by James Alan Gardner
Mysterious Canada (1988) by John Robert Columbo, Copyright ©
1988 by John Robert Columbo, excerpt reprinted by permission of
Knopf Canada/ Doubleday Canada/ Random House Canada.

Over Lunar White by Lorne Kates
"Toronto's Lost Subway Stations" (2005) by James Bow, Copyright
© 2005 by James Bow, Toronto Transit Website Archives.

Under Summons by Tanya Huff
The Legendary Guide to Prince Edward County (1994) by Janet
Kellough, Copyright © 1994 by Janet Kellough, Kellough
Productions, Picton, Ontario.

Walking with Wolves by Alison Baird
Folktales of French Canada (1979) edited by Edith Fowke,
Copyright © 1979 by Edith Fowke, NC Press Ltd., Toronto.

This Is the Ice Age by Claude Lalumière
This Is the Ice Age (1981) Martha and the Muffins, Copyright ©
(1981) by Martha and the Muffins, rereleased 2005 by EMI Music
Canada.